Immortality Bytes: Digital Minds Don't Get Hungry

Daniel Lawrence Abrams

American Fiction Awards (2024)
Winner — "Best Science Fiction: Cyberpunk"
Finalist: Humor/Comedy/Satire, Thriller: Techno,
Cross Genre Fiction, and Visionary Fiction.

Storytrade Awards (2024)
Winner — "Best Humor/Satire"

"Dark humor and crisp dialogue drive the twisty storytelling"
✓ EDITOR'S PICK
— Publishers Weekly's BookLife Reviews

"A supercharged, high-stakes, cyberpunk thriller"
Our Verdict: ✓ GET IT
— Kirkus Reviews

This is a work of fiction and satire. All the names, characters, businesses, places, events and incidents in this book are either the product of the author's imagination or used in a fictitious or satirical manner. Any resemblance to actual persons, living or dead, or actual events is purely coincidental.

Solstice Publishing
Publisher: Melissa Miller
Editor: Paige Etheridge

Book Cover Design: Ricardo Montaño Castro

Copyright © 2024 Daniel Lawrence Abrams
All rights reserved.

ISBN: 979-8-32-707094-3

Library of Congress Control Number:
2024917228

Table of Contents

Preface	Page 1
Prologue	Page 3
Dramatis Personae	Page 5
Chapter 1 — "Do Something in 20NF"	Page 7
Chapter 2 — "Give Workers Shovels, Not Spoons"	Page 25
Chapter 3 — "Not Selling Out When No One Wants to Buy"	Page 39
Chapter 4 — "Don't Sell Past the Sale"	Page 55
Chapter 5 — "Let Him Think He's Got Us Fooled"	Page 69
Chapter 6 — "Their Immortality Affects My Mortality"	Page 91
Chapter 7 — "Fear = Hating the Future You Predict"	Page 107
Chapter 8 — "When the Winning Move is Not to Play"	Page 115
Chapter 9 — "Convicts Call It the Regret Point"	Page 133
Chapter 10 — "Enforce the Rules or Exploit Them"	Page 143
Chapter 11 — "Empathy Gives Humans Purpose"	Page 157
Chapter 12 — "Don't Self-Sabotage"	Page 169
Chapter 13 — "Help Yourself"	Page 183
Chapter 14 — "Look Up Duress"	Page 193
Chapter 15 — "There Went Plausible Deniability"	Page 207
Chapter 16 — "If He Can Betray Me, He Can Betray You"	Page 215
Chapter 17 — "The Best of Both of Us, So Mostly You."	Page 227
Bonus Material — Table of Contents	Page 247
Narrative Tangents, Future History & Tech, and Nerdy Rants	Page 248 to 343
Acknowledgements	Page 344
About the Author	Page 347

Preface

AUTHOR'S NOTE #1 — ARTISTIC INTENT:

Ancient shamans told stories serving as a combination of religion, news, education, predictions, and cathartic entertainment. Splitting them up optimized consumption as humanity advanced.

But writers who only feed people sugary, trivial stories that solely concentrate on emotion-delivery, let critical thinking atrophy. A diet can't consist of chocolate-covered Prozac and Huxley's "Soma" with Molly frosting — not exclusively.

Howard Zinn said, "You can't be neutral on a moving train."

Toni Morrison said, "Books are a form of political action."

Wim Wenders said, "Every film is political. Most political of all are those that pretend not to be: 'entertainment' movies... because they dismiss the possibility of change. In every frame, they tell you everything's fine the way it is."

However, writers needn't overcorrect with simple, guilt-generating "lesson" stories so few can stomach. This novel aspires to be a progressive kale-grape-blueberry smoothy counterbalance to Ayn Rand's Atlas Shrugged (which I regard as a supersized candy corn, dusted with vitamins and drenched in lead paint — considering its libertarian tirades range to 60+ pages long). One notable difference is that in this book, every rant longer than one page is optional bonus material.

AUTHOR'S NOTE #2 — OPTIONAL BONUS MATERIAL & "HYPERLINK NAVIGATION"

The eBook uses hyperlinks to cater to different audiences while the print edition uses end notes. Some readers may want to explore this world, other characters' backstories, and their philosophies further (to "stop-and-ponder-and-criticize" this future and the characters' opinions). This format is a literary version of a movie's deleted scenes and featurettes. Those with shorter attention spans can choose to divert and back as they like. For the fastest read, skip the hyperlinks. Saving them for after is recommended for most readers.

Prologue

In the years soon known as 20NF, businesses encroached on the sky. Delivery drone traffic was so frequent that, at a distance, they looked like bafflingly efficient murmurations of starlings. Product-transportation robots trudged out of "Pie in the Sky" Italian restaurants and loaded mega stacks of 20 pizzas into FDDs ("Food Delivery Drones") the size of refrigerators.

Sadly, still no jetpacks. Humans were in enough peril moving in two dimensions on roads; the exponential increase in the danger of a third axis didn't make sense. Vehicles drove more lanes since street parking ended. Sure, that was because most cars were driverless, but also, the number of destinations worth leaving your home for kept decreasing.

Conspicuously low-traffic cityscapes had 90% fewer storefronts; those still in operation had display samples only, no inventory.

In almost every neighborhood, one could find a "Distribution Relay Station" used by AMACAE delivery services — the Alibaba/Meta/Alphabet/Costco/Amazon/eBay Cooperative. Ever-present, autonomous construction robots built them, with human supervisors functioning as bored babysitters to perfectly behaved children.

Back in the 2030s, the international press marveled at a milk crate-sized MakerBot (3D printer) as it finished producing Augmented Reality glasses. A sign flashed "Testing" as robot arms measured its specs in seconds and displayed "Passed." This MakerBot thus passed its own quality control test, having itself just been manufactured by a gigantic Dumpster-sized "Mega-MakerBot." Once machines started making machines, the long-term viability of human careers decayed.

People with the most vulnerable immune systems carried belt-mounted pathogen air meters. Due to newfound prudence, all bio-labs had international inspectors, and workers endured four-month, submarine-style deployments bookended by one-month quarantines.

Continued improvement made some boast this was a "post-scarcity" world. While no one lived on the street or begged for food, no one considered this heaven on earth either. How tragic, given endless leisure, so few kept their ambitious "if only I had time" promises. The combination of work-free days, limitless food delivery, and unlimited streaming and gaming made comfortable hammocks function as veal pens. The hedonistic treadmill led the idle to expect praise for saying, "I work hard to have a good time." Society saw this trajectory as unchangeable, wondering who'd want it changed.

Maybe because nobody could imagine an era realistically much better, most sort of believed "we're living in the future" despite humanity's natural drive to always want more. What started as a facetious meme became a trend — calling the current date "twenty-near-future" or "20NF" for efficient posts and messages.

The most popular, futile question on social media asked, "What job do we even hope our grandchildren could do better than a robot?"

The most popular response was, "Hey, it's 20NF. It's not about jobs. It's occupations, anything to eat the day. Get a good hobby."

DRAMATIS PERSONAE
Reference Legend of the Characters:

• **Stu** – Overconfident, underachieving AI programmer and influencer.

• **Chuck** – Charismatic, serial fraudster billionaire. He's sick (both meanings).

• **Roxy** – Brilliant CEO/Scientist and Stu's "gray ace" demisexual ex-girlfriend.

• **Maria** – Anti-immortality protester, SJW activist, and Stu's girlfriend.

• **Vicki** – Jaded Navy vet who owns a dispensary/coffee shop. She pines for Maria.

• **Gwendolyn** – Old money, devout. Acquiring Roxy's "digitized mind" company.

• **Pyotr** – Russian operative, mobster attempting to steal Roxy's tech.

Hi Roxy,
As you instructed, for audiences worldwide and posterity, based on the evidentiary record and people's memories, here's what happened. I've taken liberties in those instances where I wasn't present.
Sincerely,
Stu

Chapter 1
"Do Something in 20NF"

"You're clever. You'll find a way," Gwendolyn said in their video call.

Stu dipped his chin out of frame to hide a gulp and said, "But you're my last chance."

"Desperation don't win folks over. It's about confidence, young man." She fluffed her Neo-Belle dress, which concealed her six-minute plank physique.

"Like a Chuck Rosti-level confidence man? How much did he rip you off for?"

Despite her dominating business for five decades, investment seekers and rivals underestimated Mrs. Gwendolyn Grantham — at their peril. "And don't bring up negative emotions in a sales pitch or insult the lady. My stars, and ain't this a dark matter?"

He pleaded, "My AI innovations just need-"

"You're talking about your needs but asking for my money. Only charities can do that. You never read a book on selling?" she asked.

Stu's beefy arms darted to guard his torso. He gripped his jaw. "I thought it's about the best product."

"Shoot. Being right ain't enough. And who's sayin' you are, anyway? Now, don't feel sorry for yourself. I gotta say no five thousand times a year until circumstances demand I say yes. So don't go thinkin' you're stupid. Okay, sugar? Bye now," she said, ending the call.

It hadn't occurred to Stu that anyone could think he was stupid until she mentioned it.

"She don't know what she's talking about, querido." Maria sat on his lap and gave him an always-electric kiss. "She miss you're in the Turing finals? I mean, damn. Right?"

People who met Maria Gutierrez misremembered her as older than her late twenties and three inches taller than her petite, curvy figure — made strong by countless marches. Maria's energizing voice straightened postures and enlarged pupils. But Stu could still imagine their future babies gurgling smiles while dropping to sleep, her soft lullabies serving as enchanting commands.

"C'mon. You got a live stream to do," she said.

Sitting in their 400-square foot apartment, these lean past four months threatened Stu's long-built tolerance of missed chances. As a thirty-something, part-time influencer, Stu Reigns was cursed with enough subscribers to validate his high self-esteem but too few to get rich (yet). They appreciated his pithy philosophies, though some wished he was 36% funnier so they could recommend him as a comedian to anti-intellectual friends.

Stu had hoped showcasing his inventions would attract equity investors. Over time, likes sufficed to salve the routine dream slashes. Though he'd have to find the R&D funds somehow. Stu advanced his tech ventures primarily to benefit the world. But a close second was getting public credit for it and necessarily before the zeitgeist leapfrogged him.

> OPTIONAL ENDNOTE #1 — ONLY READ IF YOU YOU'RE FEELING ULTRA-NERDY (otherwise skip) - "Stu's AI Research" is on Page # 248
>
> TL; DR — AI suffers from "hallucinations" (making up information and presenting it as fact). Stu likened that to how humans often bullshit. So, he simply added a better gatekeeping layer of fact-checking and created open-source protocols for independent fact-checkers.

"Let's roll," Stu said, careful not to wake Tillman, their adorable 70 kg bullmastiff. The sucha-good-boy's brindle striped-red coat made him look like an alpha wolf went undercover to hang with tigers. Stu activated a hovering mini-drone camera and his proprietary visual effects software. Well beyond any video conference background, even in 3D mode, it convinced 100% of his social media followers he lived in a plush loft overlooking a majestic harbor with magnificent boats — a de facto envy machine.

Projecting luxury to raise one's status has been around since a Neanderthal first found a shiny rock, whereas Stu had targeted tastes. If he was offered a Ferrari 939 GTS, a lifetime of haute couture, or a used, dinky skiff, he'd have biked in sweats to Seaforth Marina.

Stu streamed his video rant with a self-aware smirk, "Hey, my Reigns-makers. Since the 18th century, government bureaucrats terrified of their tyrants made Hollywood-style sets displaying a flimsy shell of prosperity, as 'Potemkin village' propaganda. Instead of making lives better, it was about appearances. 'Look how everything is going great, boss. No need for executions today.'

"Everyone gets sick of that bullshit. So, we love catching others' facades. Yet, that's all we show on the web and see on our screens. We're absurd to obscure the world by painting only what we like inside our glasses. Deception gets worse, and claiming 'everybody does it,' rationalizes staying part of the problem. But contentment is an opium, and cynicism is a sickness. Their hallucinations paralyze us. It's dangerous to see the world as either 100% beautiful or irreparably corrupt because those excuse us for not doing good.

"Who's going to help solve problems? It's rewarding, by the way. Responsibility makes you feel productive and valued. My advice? Step up ... and enjoy it. Promote what's right more than you criticize what's wrong. Use the hashtag StuedWisdom." He was one synapse-firing away from revealing his digital trick; instead, Stu winked and said, "Root for me at Turing!" He stopped the feed and background hologram. "So?"

"At least you're sticking the 'promoting' part, Mr. Self-Hashtagger," Maria said, "Except, I dunno about slamming whole groups — happy folks AND cynics? Okay, Papi. But that's a lot of people. Who's left?"

"A million spam-bots hawking shady meds and spreading hostile foreign propaganda. You know, my fans." Off her grin, Stu said, "I guess my slow-growing streaming audience. I'm nearing the next 'sub count tier' plaque." He returned the drone to its charger and recoiled from its loud "replace-battery" chirp.

Maria went to contain the awakening Tillman. "C'mon, Stu. That's a half-step above worthless. Shit, I got more followers than you, and I'd still rather get fifty protestors outside than 50,000 re-posts online."

Maria first went viral by hijacking her quinceañera (streamed to her extended family) at the last minute, switching her speech to preach her ideals.

> OPTIONAL ENDNOTE #2 — ONLY READ IF YOU WANT A NERDY RANT (otherwise skip) - "Maria's Quinceañera Speech" is on Page # 249
>
> TL;DR — Maria advocated for altruistic intersectionality, going beyond family and tribe to expand your loyalty and effort to any in need, even strangers. But she drew the line at vegetarianism. She couldn't give up her mom's al pastor.

Serving the greater good hadn't synced well with getting rich, and their decor showed it. Stu and Maria hung the iconic Sports Illustrated poster of Kaepernick cheering his daughter when the triple Super Bowl Champs, Detroit Lions named her their number one draft pick. Political campaign signs they began collecting as kids adorned the other walls. "Vote for SpongeBob. Okay, Fine. One of the Old Guys." 2020, "Hopeful & Terrified" 2024, Oprah'28, "Anyone but Suri Cruise-Holmes" 2032, Jon Stewart 2036, and AOC/Rogan 2040.

Stu's smartphone chimed a two-day coding gig offer, and he clicked "apply" like he was buzzing in on a game show. His high-paying assignments were too infrequent, so he braved the barren weeks subsisting on credit card debt and feasting on ambitions, fearful they were delusions. Recent events raised his hopes further because this year's "Grand Turing AI Competition" could change everything. He always "knew" he'd win it all. But he thought that last time, too, when he didn't even crack the Top-10.

Maria struggled to contain the rambunctious Tillman, who slipped free and leaped into Stu's arms, slavering kisses. She laughed, "Sixteen months in, and your perro loco will finally let me hold him for a whole minute. I'm gonna go wash my hands and then collect my 'best girlfriend of the year' trophy."

"Thanks, Maria." Stu gave Tillman belly rubs and said, "You're such a good boy!" He followed that with the calming touch of slow, firm pressure, petting from neck to tail.

As if he was a toy poodle, Tillman pounced back on Stu, resulting in a crushing tackle for a loss of two yards. No flag on the play since the adorable pooch can have all the hugs he wants.

Maria turned her phone on and endured the dozens of backlogged texts. Seven from "Fernando" – all "🐵". The message from "Sis" read, *"IDK where U found 🐶 but I ♥ U. Never Subtiree 🐕 Ob-gyn says me & Bobby got twins!! Due soon. Call me!"*

Maria paired her brightened eyes with an ironic frown. She returned, palms up to defend against another Tillman slobber. Taking the hint, Tillman curled up on his doggie bed, giving them a nap's worth of quiet.

A ghost kitchen Food Delivery Drone flew to their window dock, expelled a steaming bag, and took off to its next destination. Stu's spidery, low-end, early-gen Cookba unpacked the meal, chicken tikka masala tailor-made according to a recipe Maria found and Stu modified. It removed the fresh naan it had just baked and said, "Breakfast is served." These rebels with too many causes challenged most conventional thinking. They'd even eat pancakes for dinner but drew the line at pineapple on pizza. They weren't savages.

Before the plates hit the counter, Stu and Maria perched with utensils in hand. They savored the half home(bot)-cooked meal.

She fluttered her eyes, and with a half-cheerful pitch, Maria asked Stu, "Any news demanding urgent panic and action?"

They had to cut down on lamenting how often the news caused anxiety. Sensitive hearts could never bear knowing the scale of misery worldwide. Humans' natural sympathy for the unfortunate tainted the entertainment that tablets provided.

In this new era, everyone used a "SocialMui" (Social Media User Interface).

> OPTIONAL ENDNOTE #3 — ONLY READ IF YOU'RE FEELING NERDY (otherwise skip) - "Social Media User Interface" is on Page # 251
>
> TL;DR — SocialMui gave users total control of their feeds. They could layout and prioritize whichever posts they wanted according to keywords and favorite sources. Social media companies could no longer optimize user engagement by maximizing outrage.

Stu read aloud the news alerts to Maria, "No priority matches. Thank God for a slow news day."

Maria shrugged.

Stu expanded the screen for his followed feeds:

• @Roxy Zhang: *"Damn end of Moore's Law! Render times too slow!! Also desperate for more talented AI researchers. Apply at ZerQuali.com. See you at Turing!"*

• @Gwendolyn Grantham: *"Gave my sworn testimony in @ChuckRosti's trial. He stole more of my money, but ain't nothing compared to regular folks' life savings he robbed. Heaven knows my faith in ultimate justice can't be shaken."*

Scanning down, Stu's eyes gleamed. "Look, Maria, you made it to the top of the SoCal news feed."

"I'll take the kind wind. Which post?"

Stu read aloud, "@RealMariaGutierrez: *'#ForeverMinds means only the wealthy will become immortal. No way the powerful let the next Gandhi, Martin Luther King, or Greta benefit from eternity. #ProtestNow #Beforeitstoolate'"*

"What's today's top post from that toxic dirtbag, Rosti?" Maria asked.

"@ChuckRosti says, *'@GwendolynGrantham is a nasty, sneaky liar. I've made so many investors a ton of money. And I've got big plans. Nothing can beat me. #BeatCancer.'"*

Maria scanned her calendar, seeing her few barista shifts coming up. "Get a hobby," Maria mumbled to herself as she headed out. She turned to Stu. "Meet you later, outside the convention center. You're gonna destroy those lame-ass nerds."

Acting like he was offended, Stu said, "You know 'nerds' shouldn't be used as a pejorative word. That's brain-shaming, and it's not okay."

"Oh, I am allowed to use it because I am one, too," she said, mimicking him by over-enunciating, "The key to my slam was the modifier 'lame-ass,' whereby the word 'nerd' was a neutral noun." She code-switched back to her normal voice, ending with, "You lame-ass nerd… with a killer kisser."

In a 1950s-style, lilting tone, Stu said, "Fair points, sweetheart."

Maria smiled and returned to her natural state as his casual coach. "Just go win. You beat a thousand chumps. Only gotta beat two more. You got this, Stu. See you there."

#

Pyotr Renko was a 5'7" bald, Russian "former" field ops chief with wiry strength and the baseline intensity of a dictator spotting a journalist by a window. "I'm heading to see Vasily now, Мамочка (mama). When you're sick but have money, best medical care in world is in USA. If he's up, I call you from his room. Yes, yes. You, too. Bye," Pyotr said and hung up.

For January in Orange County, it was a relatively cool 96 degrees. Pyotr could only look forward to the A/C of Westcrest-Skripal, a hospital problematically "vertically integrated" with a hospice facility. The first set of double doors closed behind him, and giant vents sucked air. The green light and opening of the second set of doors indicated no extraordinary presence of pathogens.

Tchaikovsky played softly through the hidden speakers of the halls. Wafting cucumber-lime water and scented oils gave the aroma of a 5-star resort's spa. The exquisite furniture and timeless design of Vasily's private suite provided zero comfort to the decaying patient. Even so, Pyotr was considered a fine brother for covering Vasily's platinum care.

A nurse entered and went straight to take Vasily's vitals. While making notes, expressionless, she said by rote, "So sorry. In my experience, people at this stage don't last very long." She caught Pyotr's pained expression crowding out his ever-prominent stare. Her voice softened to show professional civility. "It's good you visit him now."

"I know. Lately, he only wakes one time in three." Pyotr made a fist that could've cracked the rook of a chess set. "No way to get him higher on list? At all?" Pyotr asked.

"We only do palliative care in this wing," she said by routine but responded to his insinuation. "No American hospital would give him a donor liver. He's too sick. Shady foreign hospitals where you could 'unconventionally' find a donor don't have the expertise to get the perfect-match necessary. It's complicated, not like finding the same blood type."

Pyotr's voice slashed with a jagged edge. "If billionaire's brother is like this, nothing could be done? For any price? Ridiculous."

She reached out to touch Pyotr's arm to comfort him with a physical connection.

He whipped to roll away from her, his jacket snapping like a judo gi during a throw. He trudged to the door. Over his shoulder, he said, "Our mother arrives in two days. She's VIP."

"Of course, sir." She froze like a fawn within earshot of a grizzly.

#

Maria exited her driverless taxi outside a dance studio to see her loan shark, Fernando, wearing a white suit too tight for his belly and too clean for a pedestrian.

"You look mah-velous, Maria," he said with a twisted grin.

"Okay, Fernando. Just delivering my vig. That's it," she said, reaching for her wallet.

"No, no, no. I gotta tell you something. Let's go in." He grabbed her by the elbow, softer than a bouncer would but harder than a gentlemanly escort.

Inside, overhead lights blasting the naked wood floor highlighted its emptiness.

"I don't have time, man," she said, pulling away but still in his grasp.

"Nothing is better for your health more than waiting for my associate to arrive. I got nothing to say until then. Sit down and get comfy. Or do a plie or some crap over there."

Fernando often roughed up slow payers like her, but he wasn't a murderer. She accepted his misdemeanor assaults as a known penalty, but never gave him the satisfaction of showing fear.

Maria took off her jacket, revealing her backless blouse. She stared at her tattooed body in the mirrored wall. Her squint deepened her premature stress wrinkles as her fingers glided over her inner forearm, tracing the lines of the newest ink. Two days old, it vibrantly contrasted with the faded others. It depicted a shotgun-wielding Barbie proud of three still-smoking bullet holes in a door. Up close, the holes were actually still-healing cigarette burns on her skin — a way to hide Fernando's "reminders."

Muttering to herself in the mirror, she wasn't kind. "Two grand on a tattoo. Real smart, Maria."

Pyotr burst in, commanding attention by sharply snapping his fingers, which echoed ominously. His voice sounded husky, yet quickened and pre-heated. "Fernando, bring her to me." His relaxed body language made this appear ordinary for him.

She gave Pyotr a look of near recognition. Fernando took her arm with more force this time, closing the distance fast, like an anxious waiter with too many tables.

"You must be lovely Maria," Pyotr said with a lower-half-faced smile, eyes prowling.

"Do I know you?" She asked, then turned to Fernando for information.

His voice cracked. "That's Pyotr. He bought your debt from me, and now you owe him." Like a black-jack dealer at shift change, Fernando did a hands-brush-flourish, nodded that this was real, and said, "I'm not involved with any of yous, now." He cowered away while checking for approval from Pyotr.

"You may go," Pyotr said to him while eyeballing her.

Fernando scurried away. Maria fought the instinct to constrict her brow; she relied on her brave-face tactics.

Pyotr said, "Okay. First, you will learn rules," and clapped his hands together. It sounded like a gavel slam. The echo punctuated the moment.

"I'm supposed to be terrified of you, Pi-yo-ter?"

"You can say, Peter, if that's easier for you. Pronunciation is not important, but tone… must always be… respectful." He admired the tattoo-decorated burn and intruded into her personal space. The pungent body odor from his "maximum garlic" diet spiked the acrid knockoff Drakkar that drenched his collar. This low-grade chemical warfare had to be a form of trolling. None ever dared to call him out on it.

Maria turned her head as a gesture of submission and to hide her wince at the smells. She shielded her face with some cash. "Here's the five thousand dollars to pay my vig."

Pyotr crumpled the bills into his pocket like they were an empty packet of chips. He composed prayer hands, which so ill-suited him while searching for his next words. "Would you like to know why I bought your debt?"

"I don't need to know anything. Just tell me how to get you paid from now on so I can be done with this. Anything else is not my business." Maria said.

"Smart girl and fertile shape. I can see why he likes you."

"Who? Fernando? Fuck that clown."

"This is defiant way to talk for unarmed woman. You better be sure no one ever hears you talking such a way against me," Pyotr said with a glare.

In a staccato pace, Maria said, "Wouldn't do it. Not me. No doubt, sir."

Pyotr motioned for her to follow him to the back. She obeyed and stayed close behind but kept looking around, perhaps for Pyotr's thugs, who must've been nearby. In the underlit hallway to the locker room, he pointed to a six-foot stadium speaker case.

"Can we be sure you will comply with my demands? Or do I need to show you what's in this box?"

"I, for sure, do not need to see anything, my dude. I trust whatever is in there is very persuasive. So, let's skip to you letting me go. Cool?"

"I am not convinced," Pyotr said and slammed his hand on its side. It shook, and muffled screams for help and mercy pierced through. "I am thinking about making this box quiet for one reason: to show you how serious this is."

The pleas squelched, and there were visceral pheromones of fear.

Maria hid her right hand in her left to fiddle sweat off her fingers. She said, "You can return that demo box to its home because I have 100% faith in you, Peter... Pyotr."

Pyotr's hand went into his pocket as he sized her up again.

Maria's phone rang. Three rings. He measured her in every second. The rings stopped; their absence resonated louder. Maria's mouth noises scraunched like a crumbling dam. A redial reverberated with tinny tones. He relaxed on his heels; she tensed to her toes.

In a neutral but quivering monotone, she asked, "Should I get this?" She read the permission on his face and answered. "Maria here. What's up?"

He pulled out his phone, revealing it was he who called. "Good. You will do like that. But you will answer me within three rings, or there will be consequences."

Pyotr drew her attention back to the coffin-like box with a hammer fist strike. Which led the person inside to resume his chillingly desperate begging for help. Ultimatums are always a threat. But this one roared over the stifled shrieks from a ready-to-bury container.

She put on her jacket without breaking eye contact. She did a head swivel, getting a better sense of her exit route. "So, I'm gonna go then? All right?"

"Yes. Be sure to put 'Peter' in your contacts. You'll see me later — or soon."

#

A *JanitorBot's* base scrubbed a luxury skyscraper's sidewalk until it noticed a security robot and, as programmed, stopped. That *Robo-Krupke* retracted its Taser for clearance and sped past with its moped-fast Segway wheels.

In this post-scarcity, nearly street-crimeless world, the 40% who were unemployed subsisted on UBI (Universal Basic Income government subsidies), and most regressed into self-numbing with endless headset and screen streams of entertainment and video games. In this epic epoch of the mid-21st century, only 20% of the population worked full time, and that portion kept shrinking. Surprisingly few complained.

The sophisticated class competed for stimulating careers. Others became Job-Hobbyists sharing "human touch" gigs a few hours a week to "feel useful." Some hopeful non-workers wandered, getting a little exercise while window-shopping for careers they'd probably never even pursue. They coveted higher stations in life and revered success-story alpha males like Chuck Rosti.

A cloud-splitting building's lavish penthouse brimmed with decades of top-featured items from Sotheby's monthly auction catalog – art from every empire and artifacts from conquering hordes of ancient eras. Only their two-comma prices stopped people from calling this hoarding.

These spoils belonged to Chuck, a sixty-two-year-old, charismatic tycoon in a Yankees cap. Gray and hollow-eyed, his Pac-12 basketball player frame had become a liability. His looks broadcast his metastatic cancer, but his attitude shined his unbeatable will to thrive and matching optimism. While a gambler is crushing a poker game, it's easy for him to think he's invincible and, therefore, never want to leave.

The public regarded Chuck as an Elon Musk-type who was not above the tactics of Bernie Madoff, Erik "Blackwater" Prince, Al Capone, or mega hedge fund CEO Suri Cruise-Holmes and her insane 2031 market crash to prove her uncheckable power.

(Not that those public figures could ever be equivalent or denigrated with respect to libel laws and satirical narratives.)

20NF's celebrity culture saw anonymous wealth as a sign of criminality and motivated the paranoid to allege membership in "the global cabal." Accordingly, artful criminals hid among the fame-chasing masses of social media.

Chuck's feed stood by. The buttery-delicious cinematography captured his one-of-a-kind, massive balcony. Every inch looked curated like a magnificent live-action "Architectural Digest." This was no hologram. Off-camera, a fully geared up and over-staffed film crew convened to make this tycoon appear splendid, substantially concealing his dire illness.

He signaled to roll-it, and the view count jumped to his nine million subscribers. Chuck said, "Oh, hi! I woke up this way to another wonderful day," and smiled with insufficient irony. "Ready for another Chuck nugget?

> OPTIONAL ENDNOTE #4 — ONLY READ IF YOU WANT A NERDY RANT (otherwise skip) - "Society isn't Civilized" is on Page # 254
>
> TL;DR — Chuck claimed, "War used to have an evolutionary advantage – because every population has sadists. In old times, when two tribes went to war, those young, violent guys wanted to fight on the front lines, where they were the most likely to die. That resulted in both tribes culling a disproportionately greater percentage of their dangerous psychos, and thereby making both lands overall safer. Nowadays, it's different; the poor and patriotic sacrifice."

"As war tech advanced over thousands of years, sadistic butchers became less necessary on the front lines. Killing at a distance is so removed and sanitary, it doesn't take a psycho to do the murdering. So now the psychos aren't put in danger — they're on the loose.

Chuck concluded, saying, "You gotta have better badasses protecting you. That's why your family needs the cool-headed pros at Rosti Security Systems. Stay frosty with Rosti."

Giving away free advice had to yield a profit somehow, and he counted on his fans' endless appetites. When polled, they'd admitted Chuck's videos were more infomercials than helpful tips, but that didn't matter to them. He validated their worldview.

Exhausted, Chuck nodded at the 1st AD, Martin Thurm, who bellowed, "That's a cut."

The crew dutifully applauded Chuck and scattered. Having worked for a cavalcade of prima donnas (that's the preferred collective noun or should be), they were trained to avoid ire. But Chuck saw their lemon smiles. Even when he hired superfans, the closer they got, the less they revered him. High employee turnover served his ego but not his business.

Like most titans of industry, he embraced an unprincipled but predictable contradiction. Chuck invited public opinion, restricted to forms of adoration. Flanks of flacks extorted media execs to prevent criticism, and advertising de facto bribed major media into doing puff pieces. Confirmation bias thus "proved" the world must have endorsed his supreme self-esteem.

#

Outside the un-bustled, downtown San Diego Convention Center, public, new-gen "While-U-Wait" 3D printers with tech-assembly robotics birthed anything from headphones to bicycles to clothes, and even other 3D printers, right on the sidewalk for queued customers. For years, this ultimate just-in-time inventory had been decimating the manufacturing and transportation jobs that no one really wanted.

Stu's smartphone transfixed him with the progress bar of the machine in front of him. Bing. The alert prompted him to remove his "personal materials cartridge" he had used in building this product. Ding. It opened its door to allow Stu to take this secret gift. He admired its craftsmanship and placed it in a protective case the size of a plum.

"Hi, Honey," Maria said, startling Stu. Acknowledging his flinch, she didn't kiss him.

Stu recovered and hammed it up. "I want you to have this…" He fluttered a handkerchief on the ground with the clumsy panache of a novice kid's birthday magician. Stu puffed his chest and took a knee.

Maria froze, as if noticing a cobra. Her right hand protected her empty ring finger as her voice soprano-ed, saying, "Shouldn't we head into Turing?"

Stu pulled the container from his pocket and opened it with a two-handed, impish flourish.

Before she could panic, Maria saw and begrudgingly took this chintzy mini trophy. She read the inscription aloud, "World's Best Girlfriend."

Stu launched his prepared shtick, saying, "That's official, and you earned it. 3D-printed awards can't lie. Hashtag Science."

Half-smiling, Maria took a close-up photo with her phone. "Such an honor; I'll put it in my website's vis-resume collage." The aroma perked her smile to 75%.

"The trophy is made of marzipan. I loaded the MakerBot with organic ingredients, almond-sugar paste and rose water to make your second favorite dessert substance, because I couldn't get Nutella to work." Stu knew Maria's love language was "deeds," and he liked earning points.

She kindly rolled her eyes while they were closed. "Okay, I guess it's fine. Not quite meriting 'World's Best Boyfriend,' but you're moving up in the standings." Her balanced praise always gave him an endorphin hit that she could see in his eyes. Maria took a selfie with the trophy, then a bite. He was right. She loved marzipan.

Chapter 2
"Give Workers Shovels, Not Spoons"

ZerQuali's founder, CEO, and chief scientist was Roxy Zhang, an ambitious and brilliant technology developer who never socialized with friends; none even fit that word. Roxy claimed being neurodivergent was more of a superpower than a disability. Her "I forgot to eat" work ethic and four-Venti-a-day coffee addiction made size four Christian Dior fit her as if tailored; but she naturally reverted to comfort and utility, wearing black mock turtlenecks and jackets with real pockets.

At her emergency makeover intervention by the founding investors and marketing team, she promised to counter her sleep deprivation and sun-free existence for PR optics. She'd do six minutes of makeup for public appearances.

As Roxy approached the convention center, she saw two women reviewing their reflections in the mirrored wall. As if Anna Wintour monitored Big Brother, Roxy dutifully stood beside them and aped their gestures, taming non-existent fly-away strands of hair.

Inside, scrollable tablets' soft tones broke the library quiet of the immense, immaculate convention center concourse. Scampering CleanLynx (feline-like robots with vacuum snouts) speed-snatched litter like Wimbledon's ballpersons. None of the dozen limitless-menu CookBa vendor stations had a queue. The Turing Competition's streaming subscribers reached an all-time high, but in-person attendance had dropped to 25% of venue capacity. The employment outlook for live event planning was approaching buggy whip manufacturing.

The pulsing beat of ultra-new pop music thundered in convention hall "A." Attendees in their 20s smiled with surprised eyes at the avant-garde track. A few in their 30s and 40s pretended they knew the song by bobbing their heads. It was an indiscernible cacophony to those over 50. Except for Chuck, who knew the lyrics from his regular "Trend-Sherpa" consultations; he lip-synced perfectly, right down to the retro beatboxing. His social media producer had a decade of experience and viral success, so she knew, seconds before, to catch that glorious minute on video for his followers. She was, after all, 19-years-old... ancient for the field.

The music led into the industry event sizzle reel. Synced to the music, slick graphics assembled the convention's title, "9th Annual Grand Turing Competition," and there was a hack record scratch sound (which should be banned worldwide by now). The Irving Berlin song "Anything You Can Do" played as if from a century-old record. Throughout the video, it evolved into ever more modern re-mixes, showing AI advances.

> OPTIONAL ENDNOTE #5 — ONLY READ IF YOU'RE FEELING NERDY (otherwise skip) - "AI's Evolution" is on Page # 265
>
> TL;DR — The convention's presentation video recapped the trajectory of AI and robotic advances. Human workers were replaced like horses, never to make a comeback at scale.

The Digi-Dan Rather began his commentary. "Technology keeps improving for ever-lower prices. The number of careers 'safe' from progress keeps shrinking." An animated checklist ticked off jobs being done (well) by robots – associate-level lawyer finding legal precedents and reviewing contracts, financial advisor, graphic artist, proposal writing, social media and advertising creative director/ad buyer, waiter, realtor, supply chain management, sales and purchasing, and half of the jobs on a construction site.

An adoring crowd's crescendo of cheers drowned out the closing moments of the video. The rabid fandom noise peaked, and then, in implausible unison, the audience quieted faster than Dudamel's orchestra finishing Grieg's "In the Hall of the Mountain King."

Turns out, the audience audio was recorded at an Apple expo — during its cultists' peak reverence for Steve Jobs in the early 2000s. It had since been used for artificial enthusiasm at live events like sitcoms' laugh tracks.

The three corporate sponsors featured their respective founders in their signage, their images as the literal faces of their respective companies. It has always been rare to find a humble entrepreneur.

The Rosti Bank banners showed a city skyline cracking under Chuck Rosti's giant foot. One brave (or naïve, the words so often overlap) new member of his Madison Avenue PR team mentioned the downsides to that photo. He dismissed her. Chuck hired the best as a status symbol. But since he saw wealth as perfectly correlated with intelligence, they had to have been dumber than him or else he'd be working for them. Chuck had prospered by following his own gut, and no one's harder to persuade than a self-made man.

The third major sponsor was Grantham Corp., that family's century-old, legacy wealth firm. Gwendolyn was a fourth-generation "inheritance billionaire" who made Granthams proud because she had grown their assets better than stock market indexes and 99.44% of mutual funds.

Backstage, Chuck got prepped by his new chief of staff, Hira. She was Indian by heritage but raised in Germany, fashion-forward, and had the poised, precise movements of a former ballet dancer. He was protected by a pride of guards with prison or merc soldier tattoos peeking out of the collars and sleeve cuffs of their tailored suits.

An autograph-seeker in a four-year-old Hugo Boss suit worn 300 days too many ran up to Chuck and got violently intercepted. This was his guards' favorite part of the job. Whereas, the frisking... not enough to be thorough.

"Ow! I only wanted an autograph, Chuck. C'mon, you owe at least that."

Chuck spewed harsh truths like dragon fire because smoldering surroundings caused awe. "That's the whole point of being rich — freedom. I don't owe anyone anything. Debt is slavery made civilized by ditching 'unsightly chains.' But it's the same trap."

Chuck's guards got their predator rush by giving that fan a grim bum's rush. When he yelped in pain, they allowed him slack — they were advised to limit lawsuits. With that slim opportunity, the autograph-seeker slipped free and aimed his gun. "But you'll pay!" he said with the profound thrill of culminating a life's highest goal in a singular moment.

Like a NASCAR pit crew, the guards swirled in sync to disarm him before he pulled the trigger. SNAP went the would-be assailant's elbow so he couldn't slip free again. Chuck and Hira didn't break stride. This was far from the first time.

Giving Chuck news was like massaging a lion. Only trusted sources risked doing it, and anything could rouse a mauling. Hira said, "The organizers expect-" but caught herself and found safer phrasing. "Ah, rather, they hope you'll say-"

For efficiency and as a power move, Chuck cut off every sentence he could, "But if I hype ZerQuali, that'll get Gwendolyn to bid up the price."

"Better to overpay on this than live your last days in prison. Would you not agree?"

Chuck checked down at his ankle-monitor and through a series of morbid coughs said, "They can... incarcerate... my... corpse."

Chuck took the stage as the convention's video screens showed the primary sponsor, ZerQuali. Its promotional video concluded with Roxy saying its slogan: *"Your descendants deserve you."*

During this, Chuck's envy made his shoulders tense up, and he looked to the wings for an exit.

At each mention of ZerQuali, all saw his menacing eyes flare. If the chairs weren't bolted down, they would've backed up at least a couple of feet.

Through gritted teeth, not quite resembling a smile for the live stream cameras, Chuck conceded: "Says here I gotta thank co-sponsor ZerQuali, 'Eternal Existence is near. Make your reservation today.'"

The audience gave perfunctory applause at a disappointing volume that'd get juiced up in post for archival viewings.

Chuck miscalculated with his next comment: "But watch out it doesn't become self-aware and kill us all. 'Man's last invention.' Right?"

The crowd bristled at the tired warning. Chuck had to keep this event moving. After an involuntary yet slight coughing fit, "Okay then. Let's start the competition."

On different screens were the three finalist computer labs: StrangleBear, Werong2, and 6thRoundGOAT.

StrangleBear's leader was Pyotr, Maria's new loan shark.

Werong2's leader, Adam Quan, had gained thirty pounds in four months and couldn't hold a comfortable posture. Underboob sweat seeped through his knock-off *Bad Batch* t-shirt. He chewed his tongue and kept counting his forefingers with his thumbs as if they were rosaries.

Stu Reigns went by the handle "6thRoundGOAT." His proprietary VFX software made his image morph into a pristine homage to *Max Headroom* and back. The level of detail and perfection of the physics stunned the crowd.

Gwendolyn entered the orchestra seats' first-class section well ahead of her entourage. This meant she was vulnerable to superfans or undesirables accosting her. At the charity balls, political galas, and megachurch services Gwendolyn regularly attended, she would've been gawked at and bothered on par with British Royalty (not quite Beyoncé-level but almost). However, at this cluster of comp-sci nerds, invisibility was a pleasant change.

Her new technical advisor arrived. Pasela was a thirty-year-old woman from Lesotho, Africa, and earned her PhD in neuro-computer science. Tall, with hair kept natural and short, she always wore clothes from her homeland, often inviting questions as to their origins like a proud fashion ambassador. At minimal volume, Pasela asked Gwendolyn, "Does Roxy know everything in your master plan?"

With pronounced mouth movement instead of sound, Gwendolyn said, "Not everything. Gotta measure her caliber first."

Pasela nodded and returned to reviewing technical schematics and patent applications.

Roxy approached Gwendolyn, and they enjoyed a friendly, adoring hug.

"Well, you just keep getting prettier and prettier, Roxy," Gwendolyn said.

"Uh, thanks. You, too. I guess."

Scary how fast friendliness can evaporate from one cringe moment.

Correcting her faux pas, Gwendolyn explained, "I come from a different era, darling. I do hope you'll forgive me, but in my time complimenting looks was welcomed and appreciated. A little ego boost from those who liked you."

Roxy bobbled a one-inch nod, saying, "Oh, I get it. Sure. Thank you."

Gwendolyn let out a hearty laugh and gave her a tiny elbow nudge. "You can be whip smart and still beautiful, too. Ain't mutually exclusive, dear. As you exemplify. Okay, then."

A cadre of ZerQuali fans took photos and used facial recognition to identify Gwendolyn as the multi-centi-billionaire matriarch of the trillionaire Grantham family. They cross-referenced how Gwendolyn's impending grand investment and minimal expectations were exactly what ZerQuali needed. Its angel investors warned this was too good to be true.

Virtually every entrepreneur sought funding from Gwendolyn. But it was Roxy's unconventional approach which intrigued her and helped spark a grander plan.

#

A few months prior, Roxy gave a defense of religion despite being an outspoken agnostic. She countered one of atheists' most profound criticisms: *"How can an omnipotent, omniscient, omnibenevolent God allow so much evil and misery in the world?"* Roxy made a logical argument using the following analogy. "A baby reacts as if an immunization needle is the most intense pain it's ever experienced, and to a toddler, a car ride can feel like an eternity. But both get reduced to minor blips as you get older. More time makes any pain a smaller fraction of your existence. So, extrapolating to a million years of literal heaven, one must recognize that even the worst possible tragedies reduce to a relative blink. When one tries to comprehend an infinite time horizon, everything that happens on earth must be precisely meaningless compared to eternal salvation."

> OPTIONAL ENDNOTE #6 — ONLY READ IF YOU'RE FEELING NERDY ABOUT RELIGION (otherwise skip) - "Roxy's Theory of Evil" is on Page # 268
>
> TL;DR — Roxy demonstrated her humility and willingness to change her mind by logically advocating for Gwendolyn's beliefs.

Gwendolyn's devout faith didn't need the academic argument, but she appreciated the sentiment, and that enabled compelling possibilities.

#

At the convention hall, Pasela's eye caught a uniform at the opposite entrance. While locked on target, she leaned in to both Gwendolyn and Roxy. "Should we be concerned Ling Wu, a colonel in China's cybersecurity department, keeps trying to wave you over, Roxy?"

Roxy puffed air through her lips and double-flicked her hand, "Ignore him. He's been courting my tech for years. I think he thinks he has an inside track because he's my… second cousin, twice removed or something. My mother says we met on my first China visit as a kid. I don't care. I would not risk working there. No matter if they offered me a palace."

Gwendolyn got it. "I see. A muzzle made of gold ain't fetching. You deserve better'n that, sugar. Am I right?"

Roxy said, "Correct," and paused as if to make another point, but stood pat.

Reviewing the list of finalists in the competition, Gwendolyn whispered to Roxy, "So we're rooting for your brainy and brawny ex-boyfriend to win, right?"

Roxy had demonstrated romantic feelings for Stu in the past but couldn't quite access or express them at that moment. She later described it like opening a full-color memory on a black-and-white screen. There were more hues of emotion in her history, but the capability had atrophied. Fortunately, it only took a second for her to say, "That was in grad school. Honestly, celibacy makes me more productive."

Gwendolyn counter-punched that implicit plea for help with a theory. "Oh, honey, maybe boys aren't for you. At Vanderbilt, one of my sorority sisters became-"

By default, Roxy showed no pride or shame in explaining her uncommon situation, saying, "Sex has never been so important to me. I'm far from getting what the big deal is."

"Then the Hague oughta bring your boy Stu up on charges for high crimes. In a committed relationship headed toward marriage…"

"Granted, I have minimal first-hand experience to compare it to, but Stu was quite 'effective' regarding orgasms via oral and…"

Past her semi-prim limit, Gwendolyn said, "Oh, I'm not one for such details."

The topic needed to change, and Roxy got lucky to catch something on-screen worth mentioning. "Stu's video feed looks off. Compression and maybe sync-lag."

The main screen switched from a composite of the finalists waving and prepping to a close-up live stream of the stage where a spotlight on Chuck attracted attention. He turned a giant plexiglass bingo wheel in which 100 multi-colored envelopes flopped around.

Chuck announced the rules of the competition, saying: "We'll select the challenge now. Okay, everybody, tell me when to stop."

A few jumped to call "stop." After which, in sloppy harmony, enough of the majority shouted "STOP!" to crystalize the mob's wishes.

Chuck hard-stopped the wheel, closed his eyes, and reached in, pulling out a blue card. He opened it and said, "Let's see this God damn challenge."

In the back, Gwendolyn recoiled an inch at the gratuitous blasphemy.

Chuck read the rules of this card: *"Each team has to convince the designated music celebrity to say their team's name on video. The first to accomplish this wins. The star's identity has now been shared with the competitors to prevent collusion with outside parties. No extortion, bribery, or blackmail; otherwise, social hacking is okay. All right, competitors, please step away from your machines. Ready, set, GO!"*

Computers scanned files and highlighted critical data. The competitors fidgeted, kicked the ground, and made fists whenever their team's AI lost ground. They were like psycho Little League parents gambling rent on the game.

Roxy and Gwendolyn focused on the competitors and shared reassuring looks. Roxy said, "This is the most sophisticated test of Artificial Intelligence ever."

But Gwendolyn had done her homework and said, "Oh, I get it. Their systems, on autopilot, must research the celebrity and figure out how to manipulate him or her."

Roxy had to one-up her. "Stu is best positioned to win, the most attractive candidate."

#

Meanwhile, outside the convention, a blaring pack of Future-Retro bikers drove by a sign: "Hospital Zone — Quiet-Limit: 70 decibels." Their bikes' screens showed the temporary lowering of their speakers' artificial motor noise from 100 dB to 40dB as they passed.

Stu strolled with Maria and romantically stole a kiss. He withdrew to check in for her reaction. They moved closer, but to avoid getting too revved up to be in public, Maria changed the vibe. She playfully started talking even before and through the second kiss, directing her words into his mouth. "If you win, will you pay down my student loans, Papi? I'm just playin'. I'm gonna beat the system by dying in debt. That'll show 'em!"

Stu pulled back and broke the bad news. "The only prize is recognition."

"It's too bad idealists suck at makin' money — speaking from personal experience."

"But we'd make great spouses and parents," Stu said, with no trace of sarcasm. Stu kept bringing up what he considered a crucial aspect of life – creating someone good for the next generation.

However, in a world of finite resources, there can't be infinite growth. Earth has a "Carrying Capacity" for the maximum number of humans who can survive. Opposing researchers can't agree on anything more than the range, from one billion people to 100 billion, but whatever the number, there's a cap. Consequently, prosperity and livability depend, for the most part, on how thinly spread the resources are and the degree of disparity. This ushered in "APAL" (American Patriots for America Legislation), the revolutionary Universal Basic Income compromise, creating "Subtirees" (subsistence retirees) based on "The Livable Year."

> OPTIONAL ENDNOTE #7 — ONLY READ IF YOU'RE FEELING NERDY ABOUT POLITICS & ECONOMICS (otherwise skip) – "Subtirees and The Livable Year" is on Page # 275
>
> TL;DR — Rampant unemployment necessitated Universal Basic Income. But in order to get buy-in from Conservatives strangely bedfellowing with environmentalists, they agreed to a perverse compromise. If you wanted a completely leisurely life at the expense of those who worked, you had to agree to not have children. If you changed your mind, you had to reimburse all of those years of free money first.

Sustainability wasn't in first position when Maria consoled Stu. "We have good times and no kids. That's what you call 'highly correlated.' If we got married, it's too good of a bet you'd knock me up."

He said, "Never met a parent who regretted having kids," and attempted to hold her hand, but she flinched it away.

She noticed she had "left him hanging," and, always empathetic, displayed a quick puckered kiss to lovingly reassure him before she hit back with a counterargument.

"For the cost of raising kids, you could afford a Tesla, like that one, times ten!" Its bumper sticker read, "My other Tesla is a yacht!" This had to have hit him hard.

Derailed from the baby conversation, Stu had to hit his second favorite topic. "I mean, other than fishermen, does anyone need to own a boat?"

Relieved she emerged from the baby minefield, Maria took Stu's hand and playfully challenged him. "You're so full of it. You're the one always talking about ships."

"Okay, but I wish I didn't want one." Stu couldn't convince himself. "They're so frickin' cool, though."

She looked both ways, noting the lack of pedestrians. She turned to him. "I believe in you, babe. Motorboats, cruise liners, big ass sailing Nina-Pinta-Santa Maria, whatever you want. You're gonna get all that if that's what you work towards. For real, I know you could get a fat-check job working in Silicon Valley. But you got your own priorities."

Stu shrugged, scanned the floor, and said, "I play the hand I'm dealt, and I've learned to handle bad beats." He noticed a button-sized, white disk stuffed in the side of his shoe heel.

"Sounds like code for you're 'cool with failing.' I'm right, right?"

Stu laughed, "Maybe. But if you never fold, you can't win."

"I'm tapping out on the poker references, babe. We got stuff to do."

Stu picked out the disk and slyly stuck it in a passing Robo-Krupke's shoulder. He watched it continue on until it encountered Viggo, a Subtiree in a reflective *Dude Lebowski* robe from the 2030s sequels. "How bad is that my favorite investigative journalist is wandering like a vagrant?"

"Don't flag his fun. Dude got a hobby. Certainly no way to make money in news."

> OPTIONAL ENDNOTE #8 — ONLY READ IF YOU WANT A NARRATIVE DIVERSION FOLLOWING AN SECONDARY CHARACTER AND YOU'RE FEELING NERDY (otherwise skip) - "Hobbying Journalist is Pro Pro-Journalism" is on Page # 291
>
> TL;DR — Journalism died as a business because no one could own facts. Investing in investigative reporters became a sucker play exploited by copycat websites; they simply searched, scraped, and used AI to reword articles to evade copyright infringement takedowns. Journalism became a noble hobby of Subtirees like Viggo.

Chapter 3
"Not Selling Out Is Easy When No One Wants to Buy."

In Malaysia, fluorescents lit the austere "WERONG2" computer lab; handwritten notes and schematics crammed whiteboard walls. The shoddy surroundings resembled the ill-fated, graffiti-plagued, Dallas, Texas electric trolly cars in the early 2030s. One section of a wall was pristine "Potemkin"-clean for video conferencing with the Turing Competition.

The team, including Adam, obediently stood away from their keyboards. Only they saw what was behind the camera: a cavernous hangar of hundreds of people working, sending social media messages to Kendrick Lamar. What sounded like rain was a chorus of dainty typing. The workers had titters dancing in their fingers for this fun assignment. One created a meme of Kendrick with a comic book-style talk bubble, "If it's right to hate weed, "Werong2'. Holla!" and posted it to a sock-puppet account. The rest of the hangar workers got the alert and, like meat-wrapped bots, clicked like and reposted. Sporadic accounts there got flagged by Social Media's AI for being a bot, and those workers had to solve Ultra-CAPTCHAs.

The original poster got an alert from Kendrick Lamar's publicity team's AI sentry identifying the misuse of his likeness. Adam scowled at his team's ineffectiveness.

Adam's lieutenant and oily-haired younger brother, Phil, approached Adam, rolled up his windbreaker collar, and whispered a concern for the thousandth time, "What if they find out?"

But he was cut off by Adam's same rationalization. "The Russians are worse."

Stealthy hackers had commandeered the Werong2 webcams, snooping with live video streams to Russia's roving StrangleBear computer lab. On those screens, Adam continued to respond to his lieutenant but switched to speaking Malay.

Pyotr said, "The Werong2 competitors stopped speaking English," pinning his eyes on his team as if this were their fault.

"Pyotr's mini-right-hand man" is what Yevgeny liked to call himself, as black-humor pride regarding his own Rhizomelia. That's a congenital bone condition resulting in his disproportionately small limbs. Yevgeny's disabled hands moved with impressive sprightliness on a modified keyboard. Applying simple AI-predictive speech translation enabled the Malay to be subtitled in Russian in real-time so StrangleBear's teammates could understand what the Werong2 players were saying. The hacked security webcams provided a different view of the hangar bay of Werong2 human trolls, which the judges couldn't see.

Disappointment soured Pyotr's face. "Pathetic. They're doing the 'Mechanical Turk.' They can't expect that to win."

"I'm sorry, Pyotr. We still can't find a way to hack Stu's computer. The video feed he's been streaming to the competition appears to be coming from his neighborhood's IP relay station. Still, we also have his GPS check-in from dozens of locations. Some could be VPNs, but our man inside the NSA confirmed Stu is in his home." Yevgeny rubbed his stubble and tapped his Jordans.

"So, he's at his home lab. Where else is he supposed to be?"

"I don't know what to believe. CCTV shows he's outside Turing with his girlfriend."

"Right now?" Pyotr asked.

"Right at this very minute, commander." Yevgeny showed the exterior security camera video feeds, where it sure looked like Stu and Maria were there.

"That doesn't make sense. Why wouldn't he be at his lab? It's the opposite of Werong2 foolishness. Surely, he'd rather be beside his AI in case of a power failure or some other emergency where rules allow competitor intervention."

Yevgeny shrugged. "All I can say is — we see multiple identifications for Stu. He's no twin, so others must be fake in some way."

Pyotr raised a finger to inquire about...

But Yevgeny cut him off. "And yes, it's true we already tried to shut off his power, but we slammed into a stochastic buffer in every attempt. Twenty minutes before the competition, we had our comrade there shut down grid #212. Which killed power for nine blocks around his location. But it must've had backup batteries because it was only down for maybe five minutes until cops showed up and re-initialized the grid. Our field operative was going to break into Stu's place, but more and more cops kept showing up, making that impossible."

At the convention's main entrance, the real Stu and Maria presented their faces to the private Robo-Krupkes for video facial recognition, which identified their authorization and granted them access inside.

Maria saw the grandiose ZerQuali signage prominently featuring its rock star CEO, Roxy Zhang. Maria clenched her fists, and her ticked-off reaction meant her thoughts begged for a penny. Stu often knew when she had something on her mind and was about to ask, but Maria deflected it by asking, "Why isn't Roxy competing?"

Her facial expression didn't quite match the question, but there was no upside for Stu to challenge it. "Probably because she's looking to recruit talent here and not expose her Theranos-level bogus tech to the critics."

Maria scanned the video monitors of the competitors and stopped cold. Pyotr cut across his camera's frame like Jaws' fin in open water. Every inch of her skin throbbed goosebumps as if hit by a bracing ocean wave. She would've drowned rather than create an audible splash. Yes, that was indeed her new loan shark. He had bought her debts, and why became obvious. Her upbringing taught her displaying fear triggers predator responses. No point trying to flee or hide in this time of 50 million surveillance cameras and ten billion smartphones.

The competition and attendees scrutinized the teams' feeds like hyper-critical fans. Despite "oooh"-ing in awe of those teams' accomplishments, everyone would've been more thrilled to first catch a fuck-up.

Pyotr said, "We can't risk coming in third. Time to expel a competitor." He nodded to Yevgeny, who sent a message to the judges. Back at the convention, a border around the StrangleBear's name banner illuminated yellow.

Chuck squelched a small coughing fit and jaunted back on stage to resume his hosting duties. "Looks like we've got a flag on the play. StrangleBear has claimed there's a rule violation. Okay, boys, what's the allegation?"

Like a divorcing dad informing the kids about the mom's affair, Pyotr said, "Cheating is a very serious crime. We have a duty to inform you the Werong2 team must be disqualified for cheating since they used a crowdsourcing human system. Not AI." StrangleBear sent video clips of the hijacked webcam footage showing the Werong2 team using an army of people impersonating AI — shaming them.

The crowd unified in a booming, mocking — "Ooooohh."

Judges gave their thumbs-down, and the border around Werong2's name banner lit up red, and that screen grayed out.

Pyotr said, "The world should also know... "

Gwendolyn sat up extra straight, concerned.

Chuck jumped in, "Sorry to cut you off, Pyotr, but I see 6thRoundGOAT has signified his AI has accomplished the task."

The border around 6thRoundGOAT's name banner lit bright green. Stu triumphantly waved a green flag he'd so arrogantly made for himself.

Yevgeny smiled mischievously, but Pyotr wasn't turning over his cards yet.

Chuck clarified the rules for the spectators. "Werong2 has been eliminated for cheating, so it's down to StrangleBear and 6thRoundGOAT. And since Stu has claimed to have won, either he has, or he forfeits."

On-screen, Stu nodded and bettered his posture.

Roxy looked over to Gwendolyn, and they both arched forward to learn the results.

Chuck said, "So now we can publicly reveal that the designated music star is Kendrick Lamar. And let's playback his verified video live stream now."

The convention hall's main screen now showed Kendrick Lamar's recently time-delayed channel. Kendrick rode in a brand new electric LamboSUV. The camera angle was shot from an iPad alongside a video call with Hector — a native of Compton in a bespoke Savile Row suit surveying his view of the Thames River in London at dusk.

The giddy crowd crackled because everybody likes Kendrick Lamar.

Kendrick gave a wistful smile. "For sure, Hector. Wish we had more time to catch up. So, I got you. All I gotta say is '6thRoundGOAT' to my live stream? Like that? Okay. We good?"

Hector's body relaxed from stiff Brit to a comfortable "old friends"-style as he responded to Kendrick on the video call. "Perfect, my man. Thank you. Good lookin' out, bro!"

Kendrick gave a thumbs-up to Hector and addressed his fans on camera. "All love, my globo-fam. So sorry to disappoint my thousands of brand-new followers in Malaysia, but Hector is an OG homie of mine. So, I couldn't say the other team names. Congrats to 6thRoundGoat, I guess? I'm still not sure what's going on here."

On-screen, Stu did a subtle fist pump. The crowd cheered. Kendrick Lamar's now-muted live feed showed him strutting into the celeb-only back entrance of the building.

Chuck properly caught a few coughs in his elbow-pit. He'd have been better off following the hyper-cautious advice for him to use a bubble helmet. But his vanity and insecurity put those options aside. He checked in with the competition's organizers, who held up the trophy and pointed to the finalized scoreboard.

Chuck made the official announcement to the crowd: "The judges have confirmed the winner is... 6thRoundGOAT!"

Fanfare music played, and loads of celebratory balloons fell. On-screen, Stu whooped it up at the new glory. Stu dissolved into fading static while the background remained.

Then, the real Stu held hands with Maria as they promenaded in a spotlight from the back of the room. Thus revealing his video feed as a competitor was indeed a Digi-Avatar simulation.

Roxy said, "Pretty slick, Stu. Clever boy."

The crowd's murmurs spiked with higher-pitched enthusiasm about the reveal.

Chuck was caught up in the excitement and tried his best to suppress his cough as he spoke into the microphone. "Come up on stage, Stu."

Gwendolyn's default Southern humility was foreign to those in tech. But it fit her strategy to ask the "dumb questions" in case she might not have already known the answers. "Now tell me what I'm missin' here, Roxy."

"Not only did Stu's AI system work independently, but that wasn't even him up there. It was his digital avatar fooling us all."

Stu and Maria drank in the crowd's cheers. Never having felt "imposter syndrome," Stu sauntered down the aisle and considered all this admiration well-earned, if not overdue.

On-screen, in a bad-faith display of hypocrisy and fooling just about no one, Pyotr accused Stu of cheating. "We call red card foul. How do we know Kendrick Lamar isn't a simulation?"

The not-uncommon nerd-skeptics in the crowd considered it and commented variations of, "Yeah, I thought that, too" to their seatmates.

Stu respected the skepticism and said to Maria, "It's a fair point. If the situation were reversed, I'd make the same argument."

Maria was eternally incredulous of this aspect of Stu. "You'll devil's advocate against yourself. Loco."

The growing waves of "Oooohhh" were a gravitational well, drawing all eyes to where Kendrick Lamar walked on stage. He said, "Congrats again, 6thRoundGOAT! Now, where's Hector?"

On-screen, Stu's avatar reappeared and visually morphed into Hector, who said, "Hey, Kendrick! Sorry to trick you there, bro. But the real Hector lives in London now, where it's quite late, and he had his phone set to 'do not disturb.' Our AI researched him and created this Hector avatar to get you to do this. Please forgive us."

Kendrick's smile soured, and he strolled off.

As Stu made his way to the stage and wade by Roxy.

She bit her lower lip with a rare grin and went to pat his butt like an NFL teammate but restrained herself. She said, "How are they going to place a gold medal around Mr. Jacked Mc-Thick-Neck?"

"Good to see you, Dr. Sweet... ah-" Stu sputtered and couldn't find a punchline. He continued to stammer, desperate to get to the end of the sentence. "Yeah, sweet... heh, er, uhm, ... brain." *Nailed it! Wait. Nope. Dammit. This encounter was predictable. Should have done more prep.*

Roxy saw Stu was in his head and got in a little dig. "Graphics had edge-latency on facial expressions. But I like your AI, man. You should come to work for me, after all."

"Some of us won't ever sell out," Stu said defensively.

"It's easy never to sell out when no one wanted to buy you, dude." She was right.

"But that's different now, right? Excuse me while I go get famous."

This was Stu's big moment, and Roxy delivered some calculated patronizing, "Kudos! But people will expect you to upgrade your whole... everything."

Maria took the slight and glared arrows at Roxy. Stu defended Maria by asking Roxy, "Is that supposed to be you?"

Roxy said, "You're nowhere near my level yet. But go get your glory."

Stu approached the podium with great pride, reviewing his speech on notecards. This would be his greatest moment.

Pyotr stepped off his camera and quietly snickered, "Enjoy your new 'fame,' Stu." He signaled to Yevgeny to run a program.

The convention's lights flickered and dimmed, and all screens rolled static. The hijacked video feeds showed laughing, animated troll faces. It dumped a hacked "DOXING" montage. *High school party footage showed him taking his first sip of whiskey, instantly puking, and "friends" doubled over laughing while girls hid smiles and gave tentative arm touches of pity. There was an endless scroll of his search histories where half included the words "MILF stepson porn." The snobby coup de grâce flipped through Stu's super-fan selfies taken at 35 Nickelback concerts worldwide, ending on a backstage photo of a goofy, giant-smiled Stu with the band and their cringing "get this guy away from me" facial expressions.*

The crowd's sympathetic squirming and verbal "eeeshh"-ing spoiled into schadenfreude. Involuntary, but no less cutting, cackles pierced the din, stabbing him.

Stu's anger was understandable. "Are you kidding me?"

It closed with a video message from a weepy, twenty-something Stu.

Stu was pissed and paralyzed. "No... way. You motherfu-" Maria got on stage to stand by her man. She took his hand. But no one could've stopped this. Everyone saw the entire scene of what happened on video...

Twenty-something Stu was in his grad-student dorm. Nickelback posters encrusted the walls. This was like chewing tinfoil for Stu. On-screen, he watched his pathetic recorded video message to Roxy. *Worse still, in it, Stu presented a deck showing assorted tacky photos of them dating. In them, he was blissfully happy, and she looked "sufficiently" happy.*

Young Stu wiped his heartfelt tears away, "Roxy, I know you hate sappy romantic stuff." *He heard how ultra-cheesy that sounded and attempted to steel himself to make his case.* "Damn, I should've written this ahead of time. Hold, I need... I'll be a second, but I wanted to speak from the heart... That's making it worse for you, I get that. Okay, facts first... We're great together. Accept it! And what am I trying to say? Just a second. It's... well, I know you're fine being alone." *Young Stu couldn't help but tear up more.* "But when we make sweet love, there are moments where-".

The stunned convention crowd sported cruel smiles as it continued. Young Stu was failing at both poetic and sexy, which was extra pitiful through his blubbering.

Young Stu kept going, "... transcend human experience. Two souls meant to be together forever into the eternity of bliss.".

This painfully awkward video persisted. Conventioneers convulsed with nervous laughter except for Stu, whose skin began to glow plum-red with embarrassment and rage at the mocking crowd. He cowered, curled forward, neck down, and protected his midsection with his arms. In defiance, Maria put her arm around his shoulders and arched her back, showing he could do the same. His eyes met Roxy's, and he couldn't bear to see her condescension and pity. He flung his notecards up. "All right, screw this!"

Stu stormed out, with Maria right by his side. Seeing them flee, the crowd roared worse. The automated spotlight wandered, looking for a new target. The stage managers threw confused shrugs at each other. One raised her hand up with a nervous twitch, trying to stop Stu, but he blew by while Maria mouthed a sorry. Chuck signaled to his team.

Hira sprinted up the hallway, slaloming the crew, and caught up to Stu and Maria. "Would you please stop, please? Mr. Rosti requests words with you."

Chuck followed Hira, ambling toward them, offering salesy comfort, "Forget that petty attempt to embarrass you. I've got an attractive gig I'd like you to apply for. I mean attractive by my standards." He directed attention to his entourage, who could walk runways in Milan. "Why have an ugly lawyer when you can have a hot lawyer? You know how. I pay my people pretty well."

Stu was not in the mood to accept pity or charity. "I prefer to print my own lottery tickets."

Chuck coughed through his pitch to Stu, "Your previous ventures all went bust. You owe six grand a month in credit card interest. Here's $6k, show up at the interview. That's it."

Chuck tossed Stu a tight stack of fifty-dollar bills, which bewitched Stu.

"Besides..." Chuck beckoned to Hira, who had picked up Stu's notes, and he skimmed them. "Don't you want to make an impact on 'man's crucial turning point of credibility before AI superiority has eternal control of what we learn'?"

Stu stared. Maria did, too, but couldn't have known what they were thinking. Having made his point, Chuck and his entourage exited. Chuck never let a seller know how desperate he was to buy.

Even in this debilitated state, Chuck marched so fast most non-New Yorkers would've had to break into a trot to keep up.

Chuck always searched for an angle. "Why can't I get another continuance? Isn't this why I pay lawyers like you a 'thou' per hour?"

Zephyr clarified. "I'm a partner, so I'm three grand per hour; my associates bill half that."

"That's too high, given you'll all be replaced with AI soon. I'll tell you what — I'll pay for your expertise, but I'm only paying for one associate; the rest can learn on your own dime."

Zephyr half-stumbled at the loss of revenue. An associate, Owen, hadn't yet leveled-up his suburban pace to city speed. It was tricky to keep up with Zephyr and whisper, "Can he do that?"

Zephyr, in a sotto voce to him, said, "Never challenge the client out loud, especially when it's Chuck Rosti. We'll bill more hours to compensate."

While they walked, Chuck monologued as if his every word was so brilliant it needed to be chronicled for posterity. Indeed, Hira did her best one-handed stenographer impression on her tablet. Seconds later, she recoiled and switched to shooting video.

Chuck said, "I deserve immortality more than anyone. It makes no sense for low-quality people to live forever. This shouldn't be up for a vote. As Peter Thiel said, 'Democracy is incompatible with freedom,' So power always decides how power works.

"I keep trying to educate you people and the whole world about 'Power Brackets' and the path to prosperity. Anarchy gets beaten by violent gangs, who get crushed by tribes, who are conquered by civilizations. Right? Advanced countries multiply divisions of labor, you know, specializing to expand leads in more fields. That creates mini territories, which, as Darwin might've said, 'environmentally selects for' intelligent, ambitious, and diligent men, titans of power, like me. Human nature never lets us get complete satisfaction, not for long anyway. So, the world needs us to lead the way.

"One unavoidable aspect of democratic republics is politicians need help getting elected. That means kissing the ass of the supreme upper class, and we always maintain our dominant position.

"If not, we titans can tear down the progress with shocking ease. Tell you what's what, if we ain't happy when the world gets one more ultra-level pandemic, it's going to be Mad Max on earth, more so in countries with a lot of guns. That's us. And strongmen, like me, will control more and more." Chuck turned to Hira.

She said, "Got it. Power decides power, fiefdoms, Mad Max. All here and ready to be added to your memoirs folder."

Chuck and his team entered the nearby high-end skyscraper with a gigantic "ROSTI INC." signage. Inside the office, the artwork was an eclectic mix of pharaohs, tsars, and kings. Chuck timed his coughs with the noise made by pulling the blinds in a vain attempt at vanity. He sat ready for a full briefing.

Despite Chuck's history of messenger-cide, Zephyr recapped the bad news to the team: "Exceptionally influential people lost billions in a few of your now-defunct investment banks, and blame can't be avoided."

Chuck, "We gave them what's-his-name to hang."

"Everyone knows he was a scapegoat. You could plead guilty, get five years, and be out in three on good behavior. Maybe only 18 months with a medical/compassionate release."

The associates nodded, trying to encourage Chuck to accept this prudent course of action.

Chuck had a coughing fit and took a few big breaths to recharge. He exhaled for a long time and interrupted his own inhale to reaffirm these unfortunate facts. "Docs say I won't even live to see the new year."

Zephyr saw the opportunity to use this mood change. "That brings us to the other topic, and the info is... sensitive."

As if everyone was supposed to read his mind, Chuck abusively yelled at the rest of them. "Y'all heard that. Get the hell out!"

Everyone else scurried out of the room.

Zephyr said, "Roxy's company is about to get a 'Perpetual Patent.' It's a beyond-prototype breakthrough that digitally saves a brain into a virtual mind. For weeks, practical applications have been getting tested in their labs."

OPTIONAL ENDNOTE #9 — ONLY READ IF YOU'RE FEELING NERDY ABOUT TECHNOLOGY & LAW (otherwise skip) - "Perpetual Patents & CLIRP" is on Page # 297

TL;DR — Zephyr explained how patents used to work. Inventors who proved their inventions were original and useful to examiners got patents. Which gave them the right to sue anyone they thought was infringing. Litigation often took several years, with judges deciding which patents were valid and who owed what damages to whom.

Then, revolutionary "CLIRP" legislation was about to be enacted to enable "Compulsory Licensing," while inventors would get shares from "Revenue Pools."

But lobbyists and their servants in Congress gutted it, so new, exclusive "Perpetual Patents" would be issued to some IP owners, guaranteeing their revenue forever.

Zephyr caught Chuck preoccupied, checking his phone during her lesson. But none of it mattered because the lawyer meter was running, so this was more money for her.

Chuck shook out of his trance when he heard the word "teleportation" and asked Zephyr to repeat what she said.

Zephyr referred to the conference room screen, which read: *"Hypothetical in Science-Fiction as a comparison: TELEPORTATION."*

Zephyr said, "A person who's been broken down and reassembled somewhere else is philosophically deemed to be the original. Even though the prime person was factually destroyed at the departure location, its 100% identical clone was reconstructed at the destination, so it's considered the same thing that had thus traveled via teleportation. While our source says Roxy's tech isn't quite complete, her company claims to have successfully digitized at least one identical version of a human's mind. So, a person's electronic, virtual mind can theoretically become immortal."

Perfect. Chuck's luck proved limitless when his cynical prayers were granted. Yet, getting his wish couldn't affirm a faith that never existed. Chuck mocked the idea by often repeating an old joke, "A lawyer stranded in the winter wilderness, facing sure death, prayed to be saved and promised to do good. When an Inuit person showed up to bring him to safety, the lawyer said, 'Never mind. This guy is helping me.'"

Chuck marveled at the elegantly intuitive and recognizably brilliant patent applications of Roxy's inventions and imagined his own eternal existence. "Wow. I didn't realize they were there yet. I gotta get it."

Zephyr had to mute the volume of his enthusiasm, "Unfortunately, it looks like Gwendolyn Grantham is buying ZerQuali outright." She clicked to private investigators' assorted photos of Gwendolyn and Roxy meeting at a dozen locations.

The ramifications were blatant to Chuck and intolerable. "If she controls ZerQuali, I'll never get to use it. I'd be insane to trust her to preserve my mind. And she only lost 2% of her net worth."

Zephyr suggested a peace offering, "If you make restitution to her."

"Fuggedaboutit. Admitting any guilt to her opens me up for a crap-ton of lawsuits from the rest."

"Would you rather get what you most want or die with the most toys? Only two paths."

Few bosses like the same idea pitched twice; none do in the same conversation. Chuck blazed a stare at everyone there and ended their discussion with a warning, "If you think a problem has only two solutions, you're either right... or super wrong. When you use that word, 'only,' you gotta bat 1000. Smart play is to always have more options."

Chapter 4
"Don't Sell Past the Sale"

On the top floor of ZerQuali, the C-suites had blowtorch and blast-resistant walls. Roxy's Maximum Security Lab benefited from similar hardening. They were in the process of an upgrade beyond NSA Top Secret-SCI SCIF level.

The company's head of security, Chief Roger Brumfield was a former mercenary, ineligible for military service because of his criminal record but later expunged by well-connected people. He checked his TAG Heuer watch and popped around the corner to run into Roxy. "Hey, boss!"

She paused. "How was Vegas?"

Impressed with her recall, he winced at the sense memory and said, "Not so good." He stayed on mission. "But always fun. I'll be fine. Say, you sure you're OK with weakened security as the new system is brought online?"

"We're discreet using trustworthy, well-paid construction and maintenance crew. A week or two of secretive vulnerability isn't so terrible in order to get substantially better defenses long term. Don't worry."

She walked off. He gave a wave and turned to do some texting.

Every surface inside the ZerQuali labs gleamed on this pivotal day presenting to Gwendolyn and her entourage, notably including Pasela. Roxy Zhang entered to their polite applause.

Anyone potentially smarter than Gwendolyn required triple-vigilance. "Before I make this all tidy and official, do us a favor and tell me again what am I gettin' for all I'm givin'.

On-screen graphics showed a 1,000-terabyte drive and then multiplied to be 100 drives wide by 100 long by 100 tall to make a billion-terabyte cube the size of a wedding tent. Which equals one yottabyte. The text read: *"One yottabyte is the average amount of information in a human brain at optimal efficiency."*

Roxy said, "The essence of consciousness, beyond your memories, is your decisions. So, we bio-map your decision-making processes. Roxy pitched ZerQuali's core research, saying, "We ask questions of the person vs. the simulation to see if they match. Right now, it's well over 99%."

Eric, a smarmy executive in Gwendolyn's employ, had added incentive to ingratiate himself to her at every opportunity. Everyone here knew she planned on buying ZerQuali, and it rarely hurts to find new ways to say "smart decision, boss." This time, he repeated Roxy's stat as validation: "99% is super exciting. Right?"

However, Gwendolyn never needed toadying. "But it's that little ol' 1% that is the difference between a gold medal and not even making the Olympic team. We share some 99% of our genes with chimpanzees. Other than our souls, that last 1% is what matters most."

Roxy was unfazed, as if Gwendolyn was playing into her chess gambit with the predicted moves. "Fortunately, we already score 100% on select subjects. Once we achieve consistent perfection, which is only a matter of resources and time, your mind can function forever in a digital product we call 'Vekhuman.'"

That prompted Gwendolyn's obvious yet somehow profound questions. "But tell me, who wants to live in a computer? What's the point of life if you can't enjoy the sensations?"

"It's no 'fountain of youth,' But it'll preserve your will into the unlimited future. Plus, no more sickness, hunger, or pain."

Those could've been selling points, but researchers struggled with what life would be without those negative experiences. Was the absence of pleasure a definition of pain? And vice versa? If so, what's the lack of both? How could a purely sentient being, even given a human brain's entire memory of a fully lived life, continue to "feel" if their brand-new existence was devoid of all new feelings? All Star Trek: TNG fans have endlessly contemplated Commander Data's quest for a complete transition to human emotions. But here was the phenomenal opposite.

For someone as religious and human-centric as Gwendolyn Grantham, this could've killed the deal.

Roxy radiated confidence that this investment was a fait accompli. Less sure, everyone else expected a long silence before any—

"Alrighty," Gwendolyn interjected with a big smile. "When will it be ready?"

Roxy kept going. "Depends on resources. Microsoft's newest operating system took their programmers over 50 million man-hours to create; it's only one terabyte in size."

Always the homework-doer, Gwendolyn said, "And those boys had the benefit of standing on the shoulders of generations of computer scientists."

Shouldering the weight of most engineers and scientists' experience with management, Roxy labored to simplify her points down to an "MBA level" for Gwendolyn's team. So, she gave an analogy: "As MACs and PCs are incompatible, so too are minds; every brain structure is unique, requiring a different Neuromorphic compiler. So, uploading consciousness into another human brain is completely impossible. The solution is a hardware proxy 'Yottabyte computer' matching your neural network.

"Getting rid of all brain tissue for a circuit board. Am I right?"

Roxy liked that Gwendolyn was grokking this more than you could expect from a multi-billionaire. Historically, the super-wealthy, due to their ever-present sycophants, have been more susceptible to the Dunning-Kruger Effect. Psychologists theorize the ignorant are lazy yet overconfident in their understanding, and it's the experts who tend to be humble and work harder to learn more.

Roxy clarified. "Correct. 'The End of Moore's Law' says the foundational physics dictates the absolute minimum size of a circuit in a silicon chip. Note that prevents 'singularity' problems of AI domination. If transistors' minimum width were 10,000 times fatter, there'd be no internet. 10,000 times smaller? We'd have to hope our Super AGI overlords care for us like house cats. But the limit is serendipitously in this perfect window for people to exploit but not fall victim to AI's power. Circumstances are so fortunate, you could call it a 'miracle.' You see?" She locked kind eyes with Gwendolyn, who gave a smiling 'she gets it' slow nod like a pastor.

Pasela asked, "So how do you exceed those silicon parameters?"

Roxy said, "We don't use silicon. Rather, we employ a tailored nanogel architecture that's capped by the volume of the containers and our hardwired I/O limiters."

Pasela scrutinized the screens and asked, "I see that maximum, but for even matching human intelligence, how do you compensate for the lack of biological influences on brain chemistry, hormones, adrenaline, even sugars, oxygen, etc.?"

Roxy crossed her arms instinctually but used a friendly tone to show she was impressed by the trenchant question. "Excellent point. I feel like I read almost that exact notion somewhere."

"It was published this quarter in *JAIR*," Pasela said and paused to read Roxy's face.

"Yes, page 42 in the *Journal of Artificial Intelligence Research*. I recall it was an Oxbridge professor, maybe working with a Caltech..." Roxy showed off her almost eidetic memory for everything but people's names and birthdays.

Pasela bristled at being one-upped. "One professor with degrees from both. Currently on sabbatical. Your response to my question regarding biological... "

Roxy soared over this hurdle. "I can tell you ZerQuali's innovative research has solved this entirely. It turned out the total variety of biological signals and effects was a manageable number that can be perfectly fabricated."

Pasela reviewed the schematics on Roxy's screen and nodded to Gwendolyn.

Gwendolyn assisted in Roxy's pitch to ensure her own team understood everything or, at least, were paying attention. "So, one can have the same memories and decision-making put in a unique machine — but not into another human body?"

"That's where we're at now." Roxy teased the future.

"Well, that rooster deserves a henhouse. So, let's paper our handshake and put a pretty ribbon 'round this deal."

Roxy had stumbled way past her safe limit of folksiness but still let slip, "Okeley-dokely!" and did not recover well, rehammering points. "Also, you'll have a more fulfilling life, able to take greater risks since you have our backup."

It was a rookie business mistake. And Gwendolyn told the room the obvious, though it was targeted for Roxy, "No need to sell past the sale. You should take 'yes' for an answer."

Roxy never needed a lesson twice and crisply announced, "Okay, My seed investors are clamoring for a big cash exit ASAP." She and Gwendolyn shared a knowing glance.

"They should be quite happy with the $40 billion we've been discussing since it's $10 billion more than ZerQuali's current valuation."

Roxy said, "I can't wait to put these tremendous resources to good use. More than I could've wished for."

Roxy and Gwendolyn shook hands with a grip that could crush a can of Foster's.

Eric, a tall exec with rock climber-sinewy forearms, stared at that firm grip with a measured expression. Game recognizes game. His left hand buzzed with adrenaline, creeping toward his phone under the table.

Wealthy investors famously don't want to just write checks; they want their business insight appreciated. Consequently, Gwendolyn said, "But I don't like 'Vekhuman' as a brand — sounds like a scary monster. We'll find a better name ... maybe 'Longeevia,'"

Roxy reeled. "I didn't agree to that back in our first meeting with the handshake deal or our subsequent strategy sessions." She'd said too much and had to cover, "But I'll leave you to talk with your team."

As if she had been traversing a thousand beaches with a metal detector, Roxy had found the lamp and gotten the genie-level "yes" granted in full. Right now, she needed to get out of earshot to shout in excitement without looking unprofessional. Roxy speed-walked to the end of the building, but conference room "Euphoria" was booked by the QC team. Her adrenaline still had her buzzing when she arrived at the "Henry Danger" conference room and saw some HR birthday cake being divided. Roxy sprinted up one flight of stairs and saw no one around. But her last step still echoed with the uncarpeted acoustics. And that squelched her desire to scream in enthusiasm for all of her grand plans getting green-lit. The rare emotional moment passed. Roxy composed herself and continued hiking upstairs to her C-suite office.

Concurrently, back in the ZerQuali conference room, Gwendolyn's team was making themselves look busy as Gwendolyn surveyed out the window to the rest of the ZerQuali campus. Joel took a silent photo of this and messaged *Chuck Rosti* with the news, *"Happening right now! ZerQuali sold to Gwendolyn Grantham for $40B."* It confirmed *"delivered,"* then he deleted the *"sent"* thread.

In the Rosti offices, Chuck read the text from Joel and said, "Dammit! Gwendolyn just got ZerQuali." He threw a feeble, shadowbox jab combo and then mimed curb-stomping his invisible opponent. Chuck plopped down on his overstuffed chair, inspected his staff, and saw only terrified eyes actively averting him. Finding no such news on their phones, they could infer Rosti had a spy in Gwendolyn's company.

The world of corporate espionage was inherently competitive. Hira secretly texted Gwendolyn: *"You have a mole. Chuck found out about the $40 billion sale."*

Back in the ZerQuali boardroom, Gwendolyn put down her phone, adjusted her suit sleeves, and tightened her tie. She surveyed her staff.

In twitchy, furtive glances, Joel checked who was clocking him.

Gwendolyn commanded notice from the room. "Okay, y'all. Now, what's my rule about phones in acquisition meetings?"

Her staff cacophonously parroted similar versions of "none." And "prohibited."

"You got that right. We deal in quite sensitive information, and part of our competitive advantage is knowing what the other boys don't."

In harmony, they said either "of course" or "sure."

"Take this neat little piece of sophisticated, new technology. It looks like a..." She musically held the "a" sound as if searching for a visually comparable reference and said, "...an onyx cufflink. World's smallest frequency capture gizmo from radio waves up to satellite x-rays. Then big ol' super-computers take a maximum of 15 hours to decrypt any message that ain't military-grade, Top Secret-SCI level. Sometimes, only a few minutes. Now, I mention this cause 30 seconds ago, it alerted me that someone in this room, not five minutes ago, sent a text about purchasing ZerQuali. So, that means it was one of you."

Everyone peered around with various combinations of suspicion and worry.

Pasela volunteered her phone. "Here. You can check to see if it sent anything."

No one wanted to be the last, most reluctant employee. All could see this was an impromptu loyalty test, and anyone not catching on would also be unwelcome at her company. So, everyone submitted their mobile communicators, including Joel. Pasela used her phone to video-record her perusing the other phones, checking for last calls and messages. Pasela got Gwendolyn's attention and stated the obvious: "This isn't dispositive because the mole could've deleted the sent message or disabled the logging features." To which Gwendolyn assured her, "Not to worry, sugar. I got this handled." Gwendolyn turned to the rest, "Now then, because I'd rather not wait 15 hours, I'll remind y'all I'm also a kind and forgiving boss. So, if the person who texted Chuck confesses it right now, he'll only be suspended for a limited time and not arrested like a common rogue. But this offer expires in five seconds. Four, three, two..."

"It was me. I'm so sorry." Joel blurted out, begging for mercy.

Gwendolyn's guards measured her severity of response. She solemnly commanded. "Go ahead and take his ID and suspend his pay for eighty years."

Joel had the sociopathic balls to be offended at this. "But that's a lifetime."

"Not anymore," said Gwendolyn, leaning forward, reviewing Joel's expression. "Weren't you listening? I'm doubly disappointed."

Gwendolyn's security escorted Joel out. Pasela, alone, followed Gwendolyn out the other door. Perplexed, she said, "Ms.

Grantham, I came on board with the understanding we'd be completely honest with each other. How come I knew nothing about that capture gizmo?"

Gwendolyn smiled, self-satisfied. "Because it's just an onyx cufflink, for heaven's sake," she said and re-affixed it to her shirt cuff.

\#

Vicki's, a combo coffee shop and dispensary, had posters for Earth Day, *Black Panthers* (historical and films), and Suffragettes, pride flags, and a mural quote: *"In the War business, foreign enemies are your marketing team, and your true competition is Peace."*

Maria commanded the crowd's attention with a two-finger whistle. "Let's get this Anti-ZerQuali meeting started. Step right up." Activism requires an active audience. It's easier to get someone standing to run than a human couch anchor to do anything.

"Vixercise" killed gyms. Users could virtually attend remote workout classes for aerobics, ballet, or Tai chi. Two-way video enabled instructors to give personalized encouragement and feedback on form.

A few other places still thrived as experiential destinations (e.g., amusement parks) or for tactile interactions (e.g., recreational sports, pickup bars). The most enduring kind of brick-and-mortar business was the "local hang." There was still something primal about a gathering spot where the tribe imbibes, inhales, consumes, and talks shit.

Looking at Maria with longing eyes, Vicki was a black Navy veteran whose proudly sturdy frame strained her vintage Jimi Hendrix t-shirt. With her hair in tight braids, she went without makeup to flaunt her flawless skin. From a statuesque Lotus pose, Vicki lifted herself a foot high into Tolasana, hoping Maria caught this badass flex. Nope. Maria was in the zone.

Maria said, "ZerQuali's digitized immortality is messed up and dangerous. Billionaires let the world poison itself while they still have to breathe the same air. How bad will it get when they don't?"

This place's cerebral, lefty-hippie vibe attracted the slacker proletariat and provocateurs like Clarence Cynimah, a "know-it-some" wearing a cap that said, *"Actually..."* in Comic Sans font.

Clarence heckled Maria from the sofas in the back. "Aren't we all immortal until proven otherwise?" Clarence acted as if he coined this near-cliche. It was as if a clout-seeking monk wasn't getting enough customers at the top of his mountain, so he moved to a public location with more foot traffic to spew his uninvited advice.

"Some topics gotta stay serious," Maria replied. "We gotta popularize the truth."

As she continued, Clarence pointed his vaper brethren over to catch Vicki focused intently on Maria. He whispered to them, "You think I could hook up with Maria or Vicki?"

All of them rolled their bloodshot eyes.

"You never know," Clarence said, flashing his best attempt at a sexy smile.

One slacker said, "Harassment's not placid, man. Imma use that 'Cancel App' to suggest a demerit. What's your last name, Clarence?"

"I'm not telling you now. If you're gonna rat someone out, do it behind their back and before they know. Besides, last names were historically used to identify ethnicity and facilitate racism. You're offensive for asking."

The other slacker leaned to the first and said, "Cynimah. That's Clarence Cynimah."

"You just ratted me out... in front of me. Is no one taking my advice?"

Maria's pissed "Psst" and blazing glare seared Clarence into a moment of silence. She continued, "You guys attracted to minds living in machines — you gotta worry who decides who gets to be immortal. If you got less than nine digits in your bank account, you're stuck with the rest of us — in a jacked-up end game." The crowd sparkled with a frisson of energetic enthusiasm.

Clarence had sour-graped himself into slamming anything that became popular, even stuff he'd previously praised. He nitpicked solely to piss someone else off. Clarence's existence in a room guaranteed nothing was unanimous. This was no different. He said, "Don't be naïve, Maria. Most people gladly took the APAL's 'Procreation Buyout' so they could get better welfare benefits. Since the government decides who gets to have kids, why not immortality? If you take the money, you gotta do as you're told."

"Nah. People should decide what's fair. So, that means we humans need to stop acting like robots."

Vicki joined into the coffee klatsch. "Even in the days of slavery, they were given some food. But check this — what happens when a poor dude can't provide any benefit over a robot that costs flippin' pennies to run?"

Clarence's voice dripped with arrogance and contempt. "Sad day for them. But that's their destiny, I suppose." He looked off as if posing for a statue.

Stu entered and kissed Maria's cheek.

Vicki cringed and said, "Rock-truth, the only play is to be Luddites and fight all so called 'advances.'" She instinctively reached for her smartphone to show a reference, but stopped short of exposing her hypocrisy so fast.

Maria jumped in, "Pssht. Fighting all technology? How would you even do that?"

Over her shoulder, Vicki made a two-finger reverse-dunk motion as if everyone knew what she had stored in the back. "Electro-magnetic pulses wipe all digital storage. Tech-torch everything."

Stu said, "And live without Netflix and Z-Box?"

Vicki made the umpire "safe" gesture. "Nothing stops permanently; do what you can to cripple the 'progress machine' and give ethics a chance to catch up."

Maria said, "My favorite quote that I remember is Margaret Mead."

Vicki's calling-bullshit facial expression blared, asking, "You mean the only quote you remember, right? Don't plume, girl."

Maria arched her back, undaunted, "Not everybody knows. Mead said, 'Never doubt that a small group of thoughtful citizens can change the world; it's the only thing that ever has.'"

After hearing it paraphrased countless times, somehow, this quote resonated deeply with Stu this time. He sat down to take this in. Someone had left an 'Adlai Stevenson for President' pin face up on the sofa. It dug into Stu's leg, but he was so distracted it took a minute for him to think to remove it.

Maria went for the "ask" — the crucial part of sales that's all too often forgotten or botched. "Small groups start the fire all revolutions need. So, who's with me for the rally coming up?"

These slackers were skeptical. Maria looked at Vicki for support.

"Sorry, Maria. You know I'm just talking smack for fun. I got a thriving business." She gestured to her inventory packed with capitalist exploitation of anti-capitalism. She sold 24k gold "Pitchfork & Torch" jewelry, mugs saying, *"A = A. Ayn Rand was right... exactly once,"* Domingo Haliburton's *"Brooklyn Without Limits"* hoodies, and *"I Hate Merchandising"*- brand shirts. A meta self-deprecating sign right above displayed a Bill Hicks quote, *"Ah. The anti-marketing dollar. That's a good market."* Vicki shrugged and said, "You gotta go find people with nothing to lose and way more to gain."

Stu challenged her, asking, "Don't you wish for more, and not only for you?"

Vicki said, "You wanna know how I get Zen? I think of an old comedian, Rick Reynolds. He has this philosophy that passed beyond funny to brilliant. He goes, 'Whenever I get bitter or jealous or depressed, I imagine the worst possible thing. A drunk driver plowing into the front lawn and killing my daughter. And then I imagine-'

"Holy crap, that is dark, Vicki!" Stu clicked his tongue. "Hell, if I said any-"

Vicki didn't allow any derailing as she got to the good part. "And Rick goes, 'Then I imagine what I'd be feeling. In that unfathomable sadness, there's only one wish I'd have, and it's to wish myself back to this moment. That's right here, right now, where my daughter is safe, and there's no drunk driver. Bam! I realize… I got my wish,' Yeah, you feel me, Stu? Rick says, 'I got my wish' cause where you are now is a fulfilled wish from a darker timeline. Makes you grateful."

Stu said, "Deep. I get it. So that's why you don't help? Hope you realize that specific Zen idea excuses you from doing anything to make the world a better place. Right?" He got a gaze of approval from Maria.

Vicki said, "C'mon, man. Why you gotta mess up a comforting message, Stu? And hell, I'm making my customers happy."

"Didn't mean to piss you off. Forgive me."

Vicki grabbed a nearby box and took it with her as if it needed to be placed elsewhere.

Maria turned and said, "C'mon, Clarence. I know there's a rebel in there; give him a cause! Right, everybody?"

Clarence liked the attention but not the contention. "I'll think about it."

One of the two edible-stuffed slackers popped forward. "I'm bleary-eyed. I gotta call my mom to pick me up." Oblivious to Vicki's gentle tapping of the "No Phone Calls" sign above the cash register, he started dialing.

The other was even more stoned and said, "Here's my phone. Hit up my mom, also!"

They giggled until... ZAP! Both phones went blank!

"What the hell! My phone died."

"My phone got killed, too."

Vicki smirked. She was pointing a small Electro-Magnetic Pulse ("EMP") generator at them. Clarence offered to help the slackers. "Here, use my phone... for ten bucks."

Vicki aimed the EMP and zapped that one, too.

Clarence didn't see Vicki causing this. "Okay, I'm switching carriers. This is a serious-as-genocide dead zone."

That phrase was a vibe-killer, supplying a microdose of sobriety and reflection.

Maria led everyone back on topic. "What happens when the ruling class can live forever?"

Clarence regularly defended the powerful. "Their immortality doesn't affect my mortality."

Vicki corrected him. "Ah, but it does. The effects of digital immortality are profound... Why cure disease? Hell, there's greater incentive to cause epidemics."

Stu wished friends didn't make mockable points. "When you bring up extreme theories, you gotta have bulletproof evidence. Don't make us look bad."

Vicki fumed and squared up on him. Even without the condescension, she could deck the man just for dating her crush.

Maria, ever the peacemaker, said, "Chill, guys. You should be natural allies. Can we please focus on the bigger threats? Don't be the fools who miss the historical turning point before it's too late."

Chapter 5
"Let Him Think He's Got Us Fooled."

Stu muttered to himself about hypocrisy and selling out as he entered the Rosti Inc. corporate offices. Above the reception desk, precarious shards of glass the size of boat sails jutted from marble as if stabbed by giants; this original art commission served as a crass attempt at intimidation that worked. The central lobby was a hive of activity as official employees marched to their authorized destinations. Anyone with a cautious stutter step was flagged as a visitor and greeted by Mossad-trained security guards playing "Zone Defense."

Security cameras identified Stu with facial recognition software that was confirmed by "Gait-matching" technology (measuring the length and movement of limbs calibrated by known reference footage). The security guards' HUD (Heads-Up Display) green-lit Stu's visitor permission at 'Platinum Level,' which commanded them to give him VIP-level smiles and service.

"Welcome to Rosti, Inc, Mr. Reigns. Mr. Rosti is expecting you in his office on the top floor. Please come this way."

Other support staff created a buffer to escort Stu to a hidden C-suite elevator. Stu rode up, hypervigilant not to say anything he wouldn't want recorded. Upon exiting, there was only one path to a waiting area where a 1980s Benetton ad of applicants prepared for their meetings. One of them spotted Stu. That applicant, Jamie, looked at the other applicants to see who else recognized Stu. Few could be bothered to glance at this new competition.

Jamie was inappropriately enthusiastic under the circumstances. "You're Stu Reigns, Grand Turing winner, always posting against 'The Man!' Why are you going corporate?"

Stu attempted to give a curt response to sidestep further conversation. "Only zealots aren't hypocrites. I'll make sweet money now and later help the important causes." Like so many facing the mighty force of "Motivated Reasoning," Stu found his principles pliable. Plus, this was clearly what Chuck wanted to hear.

Jamie responded as if Stu's comment wasn't joking but instead was mercenary and out of character. "C'mon. Life doesn't work like that. As soon as you prioritize money for its own sake, it'll never be enough. You'll ratchet up your desires. You're not a sell-out, are you?"

"Not yet. I gotta get the gig first."

A wall screen displaying the news switched to a virtual assistant, who smiled warmly and asked, "Stu Reigns? Mr. Rosti will see you now."

Stu got up and noted none of the other applicants complained about him skipping the queue. Indeed, no one seemed surprised that Stu had arrived last but was getting in first.

Stu entered Chuck's waiting area and took in the garish opulence. The view of the skyline was perfect. The sun shined through the giant four-floor hole in another skyscraper that would have otherwise obstructed this pristine view. It was as if this office was built first, and the other building was regulated for Chuck's unique benefit. That'd be absurd or maybe even slanderous. Even so, Stu jumped from this knee-jerk comical "conspiracy theory" to a reevaluation. Chuck must have controlled the other building's design because they sure as hell wouldn't have wanted it that way.

Chuck saw Stu noticing the view and deduced Stu's inference. "Thanks for coming, Stu. And yes, as soon as I saw that building getting constructed, I made sure they couldn't steal my sunshine or sunsets."

"Made them an offer they couldn't refuse?" Stu joked.

"Didn't even need a horse head. Bought 'em off cheap. Good thing because I'm an animal lover." Chuck paused, expecting an "awww" or a metaphorical pat on the head for being an animal lover; he was so used to kiss-asses.

Stu followed him into the gold leaf-clad, art-packed office. Chuck smirked and darted eyes around directing Stu to stare in awe. Employees, salespeople, and social climbers were always impressed. Whereas, Stu smelled charred steak and ketchup, noticing a room service-style cart with the remnants of Chuck's lunch. Stu knew to keep it positive. "Thanks for sharing your sunlight."

Chuck reviewed Stu's CV. "Wow! You got 19 "VSCs" before college – scoring 97% or better on all but one."

"Desculpa, só tirei dezenove na minha aula de Português."

"Yeah, uh, I see a 95 in Portuguese. Is that what you said?"

Stu gave a close-enough shrug-nod and said, "I was an autodidact and thought I'd go straight into the working world. When I learned about "Vetted School Credentials," I figured — why even attend college when I can *Good Will Hunting* it?"

> OPTIONAL ENDNOTE #10 — ONLY READ IF YOU'RE FEELING NERDY (otherwise skip) - "Vetted School Credentials" is on Page # 301
>
> TL;DR — Given the advances in AI-optimized, home-based edutainment, the job of teaching went from lecturing the masses to tutoring the privileged. An employer couldn't be sure what a graduate had actually learned. So, they created VSCs as universal credentials, bachelor degree-level AP tests/Bar exams/medical boards on hundreds of subjects. Anyone could get scored at the approved, hyper-surveilled exam centers (8 cameras on each test-taker).

Chuck preferred to skip the foreplay in all matters and jumped right into asking, "So, you first hooked up with Roxy Zhang in grad school when you argued literal sexual chemistry exists and is partly biological; then she accepted your proposed kiss as an experiment?"

"We both felt it, proving I was right. But I don't like that you know that." Stu's eyes reflexively searched for cameras and two-way mirrors.

"And you know that Gwendolyn Grantham now controls ZerQuali?"

Stu tried to hide his surprise since he was embarrassed about his ignorance.

Chuck kept going. "So, what's she going to do with it?"

Stu gave his best guess. "I suppose she's going to make Roxy's digital immortality scam available to her country club friends and earn billions."

"Everyone says it's a near miracle and very close to ready."

Stu couldn't tell if Chuck believed that or if it was a test. Stu wouldn't usually sell Roxy short, but his best understanding of the bleeding-edge tech howled this was steaming vaporware bullshit. Plus, since Chuck often mocked rivals' humility as disingenuous, a bold claim was called for. "No way. I bet the key breakthrough is a decade off."

Chuck's brow tightened and eyes narrowed. "Why do you think so?"

Time to show off with some extra insight he'd read in a journal. Stu was 80% sure the following was an accurate quote; still, he said it as if he were the authority speaking spontaneously, "With minds in digital form, they literally don't have the biological aspects of being human. No food digestion, adrenaline, hormones, even brain chemicals like serotonin. The mind could have a perfect recall of all memories and previous decision-making. But it no longer gets any dopamine rushes from eating or sex or succeeding. It couldn't feel logy from overeating or refreshed from a good night's sleep. It couldn't be saddened or inspired. No pain but no pleasure, either."

Chuck's advanced illness brought an ever-present, profoundly searing ache in his core that occasionally demanded his immediate concern. It took a moment to focus back on Stu's response.

Stu noticed he lost Chuck for a second. So he scooted forward, becoming more animated to keep Chuck's attention. "Without chemical rewards and punishments, a digitized mind will become devoid of motivations, except as a response to new audio or visual stimuli. They'd be stuck in an emotionless purgatory as an unsympathetic, electric monk on a virtual mountaintop. Doesn't appeal to me, and I think most folks are like me."

Chuck pitched his chin up, registering Stu's skepticism. This meeting was going according to plan. Chuck asked, "So you're okay with Roxy deceiving the world? Is that fair?"

Stu thought about how shady people in power are necessarily vulnerable to betrayal and so they need to prioritize unquestioning fealty in their associates. Consequently, showing his best qualities, perhaps especially in relation to others such as Roxy, had to be filtered through how loyal he'd be seen.

> OPTIONAL ENDNOTE #11 — ONLY READ IF YOU'RE FEELING NERDY (otherwise skip) - "Tiers of Qualities" is on Page # 304
>
> TL;DR — Stu subscribes to the notion that qualities such as loyalty, diligence, intelligence, and creativity must be secondary to first-order characteristics such as, truth, honor, justice, and kindness.

So, Stu couldn't slam Roxy as a person for fear of seeming disloyal. So, Stu spoke the truth in the form he thought most pleasing to Chuck. "Roxy is legit brilliant. I'm only scientifically doubtful. Plus, I know how coldly scheming she can be. If she is a fraud and not framed, I'd be quite happy to see her rep rightly flamed."

Chuck saw Stu was saying what he wanted to hear, but he still liked hearing it. "I need to know for 100% sure if her device works or doesn't. Can't risk bequeathing my fortune on a fraud. So, I want you to go work at ZerQuali and find out for me."

Suspicious of a set-up, Stu spoke in a tone as if he wanted this to be recorded. "Industrial espionage is against the law."

Chuck liked that Stu was this paranoid. "You're too smart to get caught."

With all the subtlety of a buffoonish copper in a silent film, Stu made a show of physically hunting for bugs; he was half facetious. Stu turned head-on to a Bose speaker that could've had a hidden camera and enunciated every syllable in staccato. "Offering me this is blatant entrapment if this is a sting."

Chuck smirked at that gambit. "It would be entrapment. That's how you know I am trying to get you to be my accomplice in a felony. That explicit enough entrapment language for you, Stu?" Chuck said, stifling a cough with a silk Hermes handkerchief. Disgusted at the sight, he tossed it in the trash and pulled another out of a custom-made, extravagant "Kleenex box" of replacements.

Stu fixated on deducing Chuck's goals, methods, and trustworthiness, "So I guess you know it wasn't 'unrequited' love in that personal video. Roxy and I used to date in college."

"Of course. More importantly, you were her first, and she hasn't dated anyone else in the nine years since."

Stu winced at this level of investigation. He was also dazzled by Chuck's gleaming, ostentatious displays of wealth and framed photos of genuine accomplishments that were such an oversized self-aggrandizement they screamed ego fragility and insecurity.

Chuck said, "Now you show me you're worth all that research, brainiac."

Stu had pre-loaded his answer to this question. "Well, obviously, everyone in the waiting room is a confederate, a *Truman Show* extra to make me think this isn't some master plan."

Chuck's laugh of appreciation morphed into a coughing fit, but his eyes were still smiling. He said, "We've found our guy! You're hired."

Stu felt more skeptical than victorious, like getting a leprechaun wish. This couldn't have been it. "Hold on. I don't know if I want the gig. To clarify, all you want me to do is find out the truth? Determine if she's lying, that's it?"

Chuck nodded, knowing his bluff wasn't getting called. Exemplifying "cupidity creates convenient stupidity," Stu let greed persuade him. He mirrored the nod. Chuck winked, victory.

Now the fun begins, Stu thought. "But we haven't negotiated my pay," he said.

Chuck handed Stu a blank check. Stu shook, then tensed himself still. "I can write any amount I want on this? Enough to fully fund my AI entrepreneurial venture, just twenty-mil? Or only half that to buy a Bolide 80 speed yacht? I've always wanted a boat."

"It's gotta clear that particular account. Too much, and it'll bounce, and the deal is off. Only one lion can have the lion's share."

"Price is Right"-style? So, I have to calibrate what I'm worth to you against the lowball amount you think I'd take. I should research and ask for your offer first."

"I didn't get rich doing things the way the other guy wants."

"To pay off my and Maria's student loans, plus a down payment on a house — one million and two hundred thousand..." Stu attempted to read Chuck's stone face and said, "That's too low. Five mil... "

Chuck's eyes ever so faintly glared at him.

Stu said, "... is way too high. Three million has gotta be pushing it, and then people are too inclined to use round numbers. So... two million and seven hundred..."

Chuck's eyes ever so slightly smiled.

Stu inked the check... "... and eighty... six thousand and nine hundred and ninety-six dollars... and ninety-five cents."

Chuck successfully swallowed a cough. "$2.8 mill? That'll clear. Deal." Chuck extended his hand. Stu leaped to shake it and accept.

Stu was stunned by the number. "Holy crap! Thank you! Can't believe I got you to go up this high." Stu gloatingly pumped his fist.

Chuck smirked and flauntingly tossed Stu a tight brick of cash. "Here's a $200k bonus because I thought you'd hold out for at least a three million. Hope US Currency is okay. I'm out of BlockChainCash."

Stu stared at the brick of cash in awe. It was heavy, like a block of oak wood with sharper edges.

The smile on Chuck's face could've led someone to think he was feeling "Mudita" (the opposite of "Schadenfreude"), the vicarious enjoyment of another's good fortune or happiness. It's common for smiles to make more smiles, thank God. But that wasn't how Chuck was wired. He was smiling because his plan looked like it guaranteed a win — the way flopped-quad aces always smooth calls the early position bettor.

Now, it was time for the details of the action plan. "Oh, and you're interviewing at ZerQuali next week."

Chuck's phone chirped uniquely to signify a new alert that had to be heeded. On his phone was an expiring Social Media photo of the autograph-seeker, DEAD in a bus crash. Chuck grinned approvingly and watched it self-delete. Unaware of his new employer's glee for someone's death, Stu wanted to take the lucrative deal and sprint. He imagined getting out of poverty in a single meeting was like an inmate getting a full pardon — it couldn't feel real until he exited the gates to safety.

Stu attempted to instill confidence by saying, "No worries, coach. I'm gonna score for you." The edges dug into his fingers; he was clutching the money block too hard. But it was a good pain.

"That's why you're first string."

Stu exited and tossed the brick of cash up in the air to himself as he flounced past the confederate applicants in the waiting area. There was no Mudita.

#

Maria sautéed chopped onions in coconut oil, diced a small habanero into ultrafine bits, and added them to the extra deep pan. As if handling nuclear waste, she removed her nitrile gloves and tossed them in the trash. Doubly cautious about this, she washed her hands with soap because one eye-wipe of the hyper-irritating habanero juice would be like protesting a fascist government, painful but still worth it. She stirred up the pan and added salt. Almost out of her non-dairy, creamy milk alternative, she noticed a fresh container of heavy cream and said to herself, "Stu! Did you get dairy? You cheating, sneaky vato."

She scanned through the window to see delivery drones buzzing about. Maria checked her AmazonFresh account, but it read, *"Suspended. Amount Overdue: $78."* She resorted to using the heavy cream in the sauté. The recipe called for a 500ml can of crushed tomatoes and a 200ml can of organic tomato paste mixed into the pan with 300ml of purified water. A quick boil and ingredient rebalancing to her tastes, and it was done. She poured the soup into two bowls and garnished them with both blue potato chips and regular kettle chips. As she put them down on the table, Stu entered. She beckoned, "Perfect timing, Papi. I tried making your 'Stu's

Spicy Tomato Soup' recipe, but lucky you, I had to use cow milk and-"

Stu called out, "Heads up! Fast Money!" and tossed Maria the brick of cash. Tillman leaped up to bite what had to be his new toy — because why else would Daddy Stu throw something?

Maria plucked it out of his mouth, half-tearing only two bills. Almost 90% facetious, she asked, "Did you rob some gun dealers?" And now, with an earnest guess, "Or you must have won a bigger poker tourney than you normally play, yeah?"

Stu beamed with pride. "Nope. It's a legit job offer with a cash advance signing bonus."

"Legit job offers don't pay in actual cash. For sure, that's some shady shit. Who are you working for? Rosti?"

"Yeah, actually. Chuck Rosti. The man himself gave me the job."

"That criminal!?! The punk who slammed me to his million mob marchers?" Maria's shoulder muscles tensed up whenever she was in the vicinity of crime. Growing up, too many of her friends and family got caught in the Prison Industrial Complex. A few were dangerous and guilty, no doubt. But most got caught in messed up situations that could've happened to anybody. Nobody has lived a 100% honest life. Even this nerd must have gambled with his freedom at some point. Maria taunted him with a backhanded compliment. "You're such a Boy Scout, Stu. When have you ever committed a crime?"

Stu thought he was humble-bragging, "High school. At my friend Seth's house while his parents are out of town. The party of about 12 of us is going well, but we had woefully understocked the toxicants. We were out of wine coolers, White Claws, and a local microbrewery's 'Wild Injun'-beer." He acknowledged her look of disapproval. "This was around when some still called the Washington Commanders the racist R-word for indigenous peoples, and many gave them a pass."

"Maybe many white people gave them a pass."

"Fair point. So, the host and I decided to go for a beer run. This was the Upper West Side of New York City. Just down the street was a 24-hour bodega where a kid could buy beer if he was tall enough to peer over the counter. This was the Wild West for underage drinking, and I was roughly rawboned from cutting weight for wrestling. We headed inside, and Seth grabbed two cases of Budweiser, handing one to me. While waiting in line, an attractive, skinny Latina uniformed cop entered, giving an informal salute to someone behind her, whom I inferred was her partner. She turned and saw us queued up. There I was, 16 and holding a case of beer. I stared right at her. She couldn't have been older than 23. In a second, I calculated if I returned the beer, that'd be an admission of guilt, and there would've been a high likelihood she'd bust me no matter what I did. Then I thought, 'What would a 21-year-old do in this situation?' If I were 21, I'd instantly flirt with her."

"So you've got a type? Would it be hotter if I joined the force?" Maria asked.

"No one could be hotter than you are right now," Stu said, 10% kidding.

"I have you well trained," she said with a grin.

"Yes, ma'am."

"So, how'd you flirt, and what'd the cop do?"

"I gave her a classy Cary Grant-wink and a sexy Harry Styles-smile." Stu saw Maria's raised eyebrows. "Yes, I can deliver that kind of sexy smile." Stu continued as she rolled her eyes. "The cop's first look was all, 'Are you serious?' apparently not buying I was 21. She squinted over at the owner at the cash register. He had a rock-solid, inscrutable expression, or maybe it was that overworked, first-generation immigrant's weariness and preference for silence in the presence of authority. I stood there, chin up, flexed my arms, and effected a bored 'I wasn't that into you, anyway' face."

Maria said, "I imagine that's a complex look to pull off."

"I was fairly drunk at the time. Did I fail to mention that?" He asked. She nodded, and he finished up. "Since the owner didn't give me up, I thought the cop assumed I must've been 21, and the owner must've known me because – "who'd be so brazen to flirt and bluff?" But that's me. She gave an 'I don't care' face, and I soon got to the register and paid. The security mirror squealed to check behind me. Seth was gone! I had no idea when he fled.

Returning to the party, there was Seth, halfway down the block, waiting for me. He freaked out, "You got the beer! Holy crap!! In front of the cop?!?" I was pulsing with pride, recounting the details. We returned to the party, and everyone was already cheering for the beer delivery when Seth held court to retell what had happened. In his version, I got her number and other fun lies. Everyone totally bought everything he said."

"Drunk children believed him? Quite the flex."

"Drunk sophomores in high school. Okay, fine." Stu concluded.

"What? That makes you badass enough to get involved with a guy like Chuck Rosti? His critics disappear all the time. He's a scarier version of Gwendolyn Grantham but not quite as hostile to the working class. Thinking her charity washing makes up for economically dominating entire regions of the world. Bitch conveniently tells poor people to only aim for riches they'll get in heaven, so she can build her riches on earth with less competition," Maria said, then looked at him and added, "Plus, she wouldn't invest in your thing."

"Okay, this'll make you feel better. My assignment is to spy on some vaporware at ZerQuali, Gwendolyn's new acquisition."

"Roxy's company? Your rich ex-girlfriend. Oh, hell no!" Maria spit air and dropped the bundle of money like she bit into an apple and found half a worm in it.

Stu tried to play casual. "Don't worry, she's never been interested in serious dating, let alone long-term relationships."

"You both used to screw in college."

Stu got defensive. "On occasion. So?"

Maria was not joking. "You're not going anywhere near that puta." Maria reflexively checked her own fine reflection in the mirror. She knew she was prettier than Roxy but was disappointed for even fleetingly caring about that.

Stu was excited and expected Maria to be, too. "My compensation totals close to three million! I can afford to complete stage one of my prototype. This is the break I've been waiting for. I impress Chuck on this, and I'm sure he'll invest the rest I need for my research and ventures."

Maria put her knuckles to her teeth, "Three million dollars, for real?"

"You always knew I had my price, and it's a lot." Stu savored his own words.

She shook her head, squeezing the sight of him out of her eyes. "Yeah, but I thought it'd be way higher. One-time whore for like… a billion dollars. You were meant for more, I thought."

"Sorry, I've got no regrets. It's three million dollars! C'mon. My venture will turn that into a billion."

"They got you stupid cheap. I'm heading to work. Enjoy your crappy little boat with that nerdy ho-bag. I hope you both get seasick." Maria bolted.

Stu knew not to follow. He called out while waving the brick at her, "I'm gonna pay off all your loans. What else do you want?"

It didn't matter if she heard him. For the first time in Stu's life, money merely looked like paper. It was as if their meaning and import vanished when they didn't affect Maria as he had hoped. Stu tasted pennies when clichés were validated in life. He was going to find a way to buy some happiness, dammit.

He went to his Amazon "Wish List" and saw dozens of random tech gear, clothes, books, gourmet pantry items, and the Bugatti of mattress toppers. Stu overheated the bed when he slept but didn't love that A/C dried the air. This most-coveted luxury mechanically circulated, refrigerated water to provide the ultimate cooling effect, calibrated with an error tolerance of one degree. "But Maria's always cold." He thought to himself before changing the order to the dual-unit version that enabled differing hot/cold temperatures for each side. Stu's cursor hovered for a pensive ten seconds, clicked "Select All" on the list and "Buy Now." He gave himself a "frowning" nod of approval but still tried to speak a self-fulfilling prophecy. "There. I feel better. We will be happier with those things." He reflexively scanned around for Maria, haplessly hoping for her return.

Mere minutes later, flying delivery drones arrived outside his window and dropped the first items down his apartment's chute.

Better get her some more stuff. Stu thought a bit like a Wall Street trader whose wife was gonna review the bank statements and needed to hide his ATM withdrawals at strip clubs around other purchases. Stu slipped into the trap that since some happiness costs money, more happiness costs more on a simple scale. It's intuitive at the low end, but the upper end doesn't work. More things can provide distractions, but relationships and advancing a greater cause are what achieve long-term satisfaction. The best hack for near-term happiness is putting stuff on the calendar you look forward to, since the simple act of envisioning future happiness also brings some joy and hope. The bewildering "windfall curse," affecting so many lottery winners, blinds them to only purchasable distractions. Even worse, suspicions cut social ties, fearing the envy and greed of friends and family.

#

Stu entered Vicki's shop, noticing the inviting scent of sensimilla wafting as a gift to all. Customers of varied ages nestled next to each other on couches, all heads tilted down to their smartphones or through VR glasses. Stu saw some fingers moving, which helped differentiate the distracted from those sleeping. He went right up to her and Clarence. "Any chance either of you have friends at the embassies of..." He scrambled for his notes app, reading and saying, "Armenia, Bangladesh, Bosnia, Cambodia, Chad, Maldives, Namibia, Samoa, or Serbia?"

Vicki shook her head and, like a bouncer not accepting a fake ID, pointed, "Sorry. But if you need a non-extradition country, I bet our dear, sweet, creepy Clarence could help you chill in North Korea or Iran."

Clarence gave another emperor assent gesture. "No. But I have resources and connections in the Sheriff's department and one CIA frat brother. What do you need?"

Stu said, "I'm chessing-out some options. Can I count on you, Clarence?"

Clarence said, "You can, but my claim shouldn't be worth much since any liar can say he's reliable."

"A neutral guy wouldn't have any incentive to lie. Volunteering you could be lying makes you more credible since you're showing vulnerability."

"Yes, but a sophisticated liar would've known you'd think like that. So again, you can't trust what I say to you."

Stu insta-flashed "jazz hands" and said, "Okay, Vizzini, I don't know what you know about what I feel regarding your trustworthiness."

Clarence did an exaggerated nod and almost sing-songy said, "Now you're getting it." He winked. "What do you need?"

Stu said, "I'd like a personal intro to a good connection at the Serbian embassy. Know anyone who might know someone there?"

#

ZerQuali's largest C-suite office was Gwendolyn's. Unlike the minimally designed, utilitarian décor of the rest of the building, her office announced her supreme status, like the living room of a lavish, antique Georgia mansion. But perhaps with fewer Hummel figurines and maybe two-too-many exotic plants and flowers. Most of the artwork was ultra-high-end, commissioned, flattering portraits of the Grantham family. They largely obscured the irreplaceable, rare, antique wallpaper restored by the artisans at The Met.

Roxy entered, "Looks like you're all moved in."

Gwendolyn was in contemplative prayer and opened her eyes. "Almost. Hallways still smell of static and plastic. They ain't natural and can't be healthy for anyone."

Roxy shrugged. "Cost of doing business in tech, I guess."

Gwendolyn smiled, gazed up to heaven, and down to Roxy, "Prayed it ain't. Even so, all work requires sacrifice, I suppose."

"Not the end, though. Right? That's the whole point of the company." Roxy was less concerned with seeming keen than seeking reaffirmation this deal was worthwhile. Gwendolyn's response didn't encourage her.

"Digital immortality could be far more dangerous than nuclear fission energy. Tell me you're doing this for more than mere scientific advancement."

They stood close while reviewing myriad screens with research and schematics. Roxy went into pedantic mode, one of her defaults.

"Every animal wants to perpetuate its genes. Same goes for ideas. We think that whatever created us must be good and should continue. That's why people donate to their alma maters and churches."

Gwendolyn was trying to get through to Roxy in a more profound way. "But won't this invention literally lock in old mindsets? I'd have reckoned you wouldn't like that."

Still in her comfort zone, Roxy considered ramifications beyond the immediate practicality. "Change isn't always good. When AI ends the need for human work, everyone has but two paths — pursuing achievement or hedonism."

Gwendolyn liked where this was heading. "My mama always said purpose is more important than happiness. But I'm surprised such a capable woman like yourself never had other goals — family, faith, anything?"

Since for 95% of her adulthood, she was single, Roxy was well rehearsed for this question. "Doing post-doc work, I discovered a way to decode and thus preserve synapses, which led me to my ZerQuali inventions. Back then, the research director discovered how to deploy it as a mitigating vaccine for Alzheimer's. He was a former FDA head, so he got us fast-track approval so long as we tested it against the top two competing treatments, not just a placebo, and they insisted those competitors' scientists get access to supervise our testing. In eight months, the results were so promising we did human trials, which, if you know the regulatory world, is unfathomably fast. And they went great. Wasn't a cure, but it could provide 85%+ of patients statistically significant protection within weeks, delaying symptoms for months or years. Follow that path of research — who knows how much progress could've been achieved? But the lab I was working for foolishly sold it to a company that then shelved the patent. Turns out treatment is too profitable for prevention to be good business. Second to digital immortality, I want the world to have that mitigating vaccine."

"The difference between prayers and plans is the action you take and sacrifices you make." Gwendolyn ensured her line landed and got up. She exited and almost knocked into Security Chief Brumfield. He scurried to conceal his suction cup microphone, but she saw it. So much for cleverly not using a radio-emitter bug because her entourage's scanners would've found it.

#

At the Rosti Inc. offices, Chuck watched news clips and mindlessly dug his Montblanc pen into the arm of his Eames chair. Upon noticing it, he nonchalantly pointed to the hole, and an assistant began searching for upholsterers — nope — replacements. A video showed an Asian factory closing to all human workers, and now only robots made driverless cars. A superimposed HUD read: "Anchor: Brokaw, Chung, Perry, Rather-SELECTED. Anchor Age: 77." It scrolled down to "42," and Digi-Dan Rather's appearance rendered with VFX looked authentically younger. Digi-Dan Rather continued the report: "is set to close the last of its labor-operated factories for total automation later this year."

Chuck took quick note, but it was so expected he skipped on to the next potential item of interest. He swiped over to news clips about Chuck's criminal case and saw B-roll of himself exiting his ultra-elite, custom purple Bugatti. He got incensed. "Is that a scratch on the..." and relaxed. "It's a reflection, okay."

Digi-Dan Rather said, "In legal news, federal prosecutors have elevated Chuck Rosti's bail conditions to require an ankle monitor as well as forfeiture of his passport and private... "

He stopped the video. Next up in the queue was a screenshot of a robot making an artistic sculpture outside a fancy office building. Chuck said, "So my body can serve the sentence?"

His attorney, Zephyr, had been silently waiting there as Chuck skimmed the news; she saw her boss had asked a question and not rhetorically. She said, "Your body, legally speaking, is you, even if your mind is somewhere else. One's consciousness as a separate entity has never been addressed in existing law or past precedent."

Chuck had a coughing fit and had trouble spitting out his next thought: "So I need only upload my brain, and you dump my body off at the prison?"

Zephyr relaxed her shoulders in relief. Chuck was receptive to her legal analysis and action plan, "Bequeath your estate to a foundation that's run by your digital consciousness, and your tax liability will be zero."

Chuck's enthusiasm was high-pitched. "I love it! No more forced transactions. Can't wait for true freedom." But with no smile in his voice, it was faithless wish-casting, eggshell optimism.

#

Stu felt his laptop bag get jostled as he passed a pedestrian. That would've been conspicuous enough in low-traffic days of 20NF, but this sidewalk was empty for them. That passerby, Yevgeny, skulked away, hanging his camera down by his side, but the lens pointed at Stu. Noticing Stu catching this, the pedestrian scrambled his hands into his pockets with the guilty-clumsy grace of a teenager on a first date.

Stu waved prominently.

"You're blown. Idiot." Pyotr told Yevgeny via his earpod.

Yevgeny flexed in frustration like an all-star, striking out with bases loaded.

Stu went through his bag and found the tracking beacon. He made a big show of his new spoil as if he was being surveilled by a dozen hidden cameras. He pointed to it and shouted all around, "I'm making fifty of this one!"

At StrangleBear's computer lab, Yevgeny reported to Pyotr, "Every time we plant a tracking beacon on Stu or his vehicle, he clones it and puts them on a half-dozen other people or cars or feral dogs. We spend way too much time trying to figure out where he actually is. What if he ever does make fifty clones?"

"Trim down the candidates by identifying which are moving at the wrong speeds or routes to be Stu and automatically exclude them," Pyotr orders.

"We figured this out a couple days ago. He causes us trouble by moving like a dog sometimes. He pops up to smile and wave to an online traffic-monitoring camera to remind us he could be any of the clones."

"Cagey ass-head bastard. But wait. Those are public traffic cameras and have laughable, local government-level security."

"Yes. This is why it was so easy to get."

"No. It's even easier for him to get… or manipulate."

Yevgeny arrived at Pyotr's point, "So you are saying they could be corrupted as a ruse?"

"I guarantee they're corrupted. Now go find me corroborating camera angles for the surrounding 27 blocks. Rewind all the footage, back-timing every car and person's path from when they enter that widened grid. I bet his public smile-waves don't go back further than a couple of minutes when they'd appear out of nowhere. Are you taking notes about this?"

"No. I am doing this. See here."

Sure enough, Yevgeny cued to a frame where Stu showed up on-screen to "confirm" he had the tracking device. He rewound the footage a minute to a jump-cut where the VFX ruse appeared. Pyotr covered his mouth to hide his proud grin at having figured out the tactics of such a worthy adversary. Yevgeny seethed at being fooled, nearly flinching from Pyotr's gaze. None of the tracking beacons stayed on Stu.

"You cannot make this mistake again, and merely hoping so is insufficient."

"No, sir. I'll set an AI routine to review all public traffic cameras to track all vehicles from now on so there is a continuous provenance establishing all of their paths. We'll have our associates spot Stu live the next time he gets back to the office or his apartment. We'll have his routes plotted at all times, ignoring the tracking beacons."

"Keep placing the trackers on him, anyway," Pyotr said, pondering as Kasparov did in 1985. "Never let your opponent know you're on to them. Let him think he's got us fooled."

Chapter 6
"Their Immortality Affects My Mortality."

At the beginning of their friendship, Vicki smiled at almost every point Maria made. When Maria went from customer to employee, teaming up to stock shelves, arrange displays, and even spot-check AI's bookkeeping became fun. Maria's fiery indignation reminded Vicki of her own need for justice, however diminished it became during her time in the Navy.

Idealists think every wrong needs righting. Vicki was no different. It was easier to obsess about silly nitpicks, such as reminding people that a lectern is what speakers stand behind and a podium is the platform they stand on. But she used to fight noble fights, too. Customers thought becoming the owner of a recreational marijuana dispensary/coffee shop was an odd fit for ex-military. But for Vicki, it was the only path.

> OPTIONAL ENDNOTE #12 — ONLY READ IF YOU WANT TO DIVERT TO A BACKSTORY (otherwise skip) - "Vicki's Military Service" is on Page # 305
>
> **Trigger Warning:** Refers to a sexual assault in the past (but no descriptions and no details).
>
> TL;DR — When Vicki was in the Navy, a friend was victimized, and the investigation was a shameful farce. Vicki obeyed orders and subsequently carried guilt for not doing more.

Making friends as an adult kept getting more challenging. For a veteran so removed from the military world, close to impossible. Vicki had become friendly with many customers, which satisfied whatever basic social needs she had. With no urgency, Vicki found a relationship every few years, but only when she was pursued by a confident lesbian. Vicki never chased straights or even a hesitant bi.

Maria changed that. Everyone was enthralled with Maria's inspirational messages and righteous energy. For Vicki, Maria seemed invulnerable and kicked ass at converting cynics. For the first time, Vicki fantasized about "converting" a straight woman. When Maria confided in Vicki about her "college experimentation," those fantasies finally had a basis in reality. This was now at least theoretically possible.

It was too bad Maria was so enthralled with Stu. Vicki respected him as an honorable rival. Stu was unaware that Vicki was a rival at all.

Maria cleaned the espresso machine, and like always, Vicki stared and listened. There's a volume when you talk to yourself in a public setting where others recognize your comment is meant to be a self-mutter. Any louder could be an open invitation, especially when you're aware someone is watching you. Maria cursed above her breath, "Hijo de puta! Bastard be always up on his soapbox, but also thinking he's funny saying his principles had clearance sale prices. It turns out he ain't joking."

Vicki wanted to be sympathetic to Maria, but something didn't fit. "So he tricked you with honesty? Kinda your fault for thinking he was joking."

"And that Roxy bitch is cute, smart, and rich. I couldn't hate her more." Maria was taking out her frustration on the machine.

There was a hard metal-on-metal SQUEAK.

Maria got the portafilter stuck in the brew head.

"But I thought she's asexual, right?" Vicki said.

Maria wasn't having this. "She might be... with everyone other than my man. And it's not like he's some huge-dicked sex god. I like him a lot, yeah, but he's a regular guy."

Vicki got academic to reduce the temperature. "Roxy must be a 'gray ace' demisexual. They have rare exceptions, like maybe with Stu, but otherwise, they're 99% comfortable being asexual."

"That doesn't make me feel better. They obviously have some weird chemistry."

Ah, an exploitable opportunity. "Well, then. Maybe Stu isn't the right one for you." Vicki didn't look up. She waited to gauge the emotion in Maria's response.

Maria wasn't oblivious. She was polite to not call Vicki out on the undermining tactic every time. This instance was a necessary exception to re-establish boundaries. Maria nipped curtly. "Can we not have the friendzone talk again, Vicki? Damn."

Flushed with a "flight response," Vicki heard herself lying when she said, "Nah, I'm not hot for you anymore. I'm worried about ZerQuali poisoning life up everywhere. Stu should destroy that place like you're killing that machine."

Maria absentmindedly all but ruined the Pressostato unit of the machine. But that didn't bother Vicki in the least.

Realizing the damage, Maria reversed her attitude. "Sorry about that, Vicki."

Vicki could afford to be gracious now. "No big deal. The world rebuilds when man stays out of the way."

Vicki stepped in and dislodged it with such prominent strength, one might've feared she was hurling the whole machine off the counter. Maria didn't flinch because she'd seen Vicki do this maneuver before. Vicki flurried, swapping out the faulty parts and putting everything back into perfect alignment like a Rubik's Cube champion.

Maria exited to the lavatory. A robot carrying an automated cashier station entered and caught Vicki's attention, who speed-mimed "throat cut," "no way," and "buzz off." The robot salesman turned and moved on.

Clarence approached Vicki. "Why do you hit on straight girls?"

"Oh, I don't," Vicki had to clarify the situation with a quarter-smile, "Maria is not 100% straight. I know. I. Know. For. Sure."

Since Clarence always argued to win, not increase understanding, he attempted to get the last word. "But she's with Stu now."

Vicki couldn't let these mansplaining corrections continue, "Now. Sure. That's true... for now. But Stu keeps messin' up... who knows?"

#

Chuck had hoped, gambled, and scheduled Stu's ZerQuali job interview weeks ago through pretense. Signs looked auspicious but far from a guarantee.

Stu walked the runners' path along the shore and got closer to the ZerQuali offices. He had to psych himself up for this significant betrayal of his ex-girlfriend. He recounted his rationales for doing Chuck's bidding: money, freedom from debt for both himself and Maria, start-up capital for his ventures, maybe a boat. But that's just money and not grand enough motivation. *That Roxy broke my heart a decade ago is a petty, crappy excuse. What else? I must be forgetting ... Hold on! Her AI is prolly bullshit, so exposing fraud is a noble cause. And even if it's somehow viable, immortality shouldn't be exclusive to the mega-wealthy. Yeah, that's true. Ensuring everyone who wants it, regardless of income, can endure into the future is a noble enough goal. Gotta keep reminding myself of that one and stop thinking about the money.*

Stu was cursed with hyper-self-awareness, so his multitude of fantasies never were at risk of becoming delusions. But this meant when he was doing wrong, he couldn't trick himself into thinking he was right. That ever-compulsive, noble motivation to "sprint to admit when he was wrong" didn't prevent wrongdoing. It only guaranteed feelings of guilt and a corresponding desire to make things right.

Stu opposed platforming Ayn Rand fans and would only give them the satisfaction on those rare few views on which they agreed.

> OPTIONAL ENDNOTE #13 — ONLY READ IF YOU'RE FEELING ULTRA NERDY ABOUT POLITICS (otherwise skip) – "Could Ayn Rand Be Right?" is on Page # 310
>
> TL;DR — Extreme libertarians who purported to be Ayn Rand's followers (aka self-named "Objectivists"), deny the existence of altruism, ascribing the most selfless acts as somehow motivated by the personal good feelings the do-gooder enjoys. But that redefines the word "altruism" out of existence. Their "celebration of selfishness" leads to several horrors, including accepting slavery so long as the person sells himself into it and sympathizing with, flattering, and idealizing sociopaths, as Ayn Rand shockingly did with the child-killer William Edward Hickman.

Obsessive thinking was a distraction that made walking and biking feel like time travel. He multitasked, compartmentalizing transportation to his subconscious while his compulsive mind crowded his concentration. This was so strong, when he'd miss his turn or stop, he'd have to double back double-time as if trying to shake a tail. An imminent danger, like a swerving car or unleashed dog, would puncture this fugue state.

Otherwise, Stu found himself waking alert at destinations; today, the ZerQuali building seemed to pop into existence as he arrived. There wasn't time to parry with his conscience; his performance had begun. First priority — he had to not mess up getting hired.

Stu passed security and met up with Roxy. They took a moment to figure out if this would be awkward, exciting, or professional.

Stu noticed the absence of a "Welcome" or "Hi Stu," but remembered such a pleasantry wouldn't occur to Roxy. Instead, she got to the meat of the matter and said, "After the doxing at Turing, wasn't sure if you'd show up."

"Well, I've kept up on your successes, and you're impressive. I shouldn't have let our connection atrophy. I want to help build your empire right beside you," Stu said.

This was a crucial moment, and Roxy had to be consistent, which meant unreceptive to such flattery. "Spewing sugar doesn't sound like you. Am I missing something? Your social media status is 'in a relationship.' Are you flirting?"

"Depends. Is it working? Okay, yeah, I'm still with Maria. But..." He leaned in with a syrupy Soap Opera-style performance, "You'll always have a special place in my heart."

"Okay, you're losing me."

"Your real-time brutal honesty only makes me love you more," Stu said, committing to the bit. Then, her eye-roll made him change tactics. "No joke. I'm sick of the instability of start-ups and scrambling for freelance gigs. Doesn't have to be C-suite sweet. I'm psyched for moderately well-paying, long-term employment — as the grown-up I've been late to becoming."

"That's the no-bullshit Stu I know."

"... and love?"

"Back to losing me. But your timing is perfect. We got a huge infusion of cash to ramp up R&D."

Roxy and Stu toured the ZerQuali facility. Stu got a kick out of Roxy's corporate art, six-foot blow-ups of MC Escher paintings, and modified 3D build-outs of Escher's optical illusions. Robo-Krupke security robots passed by CarpenterBots and PlumberBots refurbishing the decor. Other robots installed endless banks of computers.

Roxy played coy. "I probably can convince the company to hire one more human being."

"You're the CEO," Stu said flatly.

"Fair point, dude."

"Addressing the indoor Dumbo, I'm used to being number one. Are we worried about how we're going to work together?"

"Nope. There are more reasons to team up than not. And, c'mon Stu, even though I think you're great, you're never number one when I'm in the room."

With an ambiguously facetious tone, Stu said, "So, I'll just be your second, and you'll be the superstar."

"Anything else would result in suboptimal efficiency," Roxy said.

"Okay, I get it, BOSS!" Stu punched that last word with heavy sarcasm.

"This is the biggest break in your career. So easy on the self-sabotage, Stu. Now let me show you to the MSL."

Stu was never afraid to ask obvious questions. "MSL?"

"Maximum Security Lab. Two-thirds fewer syllables!" Roxy said playfully.

"And explaining it costs how many syllables?" Stu nitpicked.

"Acronyms are a useful, need-to-know shibboleth. Using them saves time, and those who don't reveal themselves to be out of the loop. It's why every military employs them." Roxy loved mic-dropping as an exit. She pivoted to lead, not escort, Stu around.

Back in multitasking mode, Stu took Roxy's tour and wondered about the scarcity of workers and jobs here. It seemed to be primarily guards who looked like ex-college football players. Two on patrol stared down the newcomer.

Roxy and Stu subconsciously tread in perfect sync, a virtual military parade-style stride. She showed off her security dongle. "You'll love this. It doesn't have a passcode in it. When we were developing our proprietary tech, we came up with a supercomputer this tiny, and it solves ultra-complex problems to open doors. It can't be cracked because no one else's processor can speed clear of the rocket pad by the time we've reached the Owl Nebula of Ursa Major."

Stu couldn't help but challenge her. "What if a bad guy simply steals the key?"

"Oh, then we would be screwed... except we always know where they are, and I can remotely disable them."

"You, Roxy Zhang, the Roxy Zhang I've known for a decade plus, you are okay with being GPS-tracked everywhere?"

Roxy scoffed and said, "Course not. Mine has no tracker. It's the master key."

Now, at a native New Yorker's pace, they hurried through the cold, stark halls designed to be easily cleaned. They turned the corner to glass double doors that led to the C-suite offices. In contrast, this area was adorned with expensive Renaissance art. Stu caught Roxy rolling her eyes.

"Not your decorating, I guess," he said.

"I could care less," she said while swinging open the ten-foot door to her lavish CEO office. She noticed his transfixed gaze on her, and he didn't appraise the room at all.

"The expression is 'I couldn't care less,'" Stu delighted in this rare opportunity to correct her. He awaited her back-pedal.

Except, as if he fell into her trap, she said, "No. My words were accurate. I conveyed my lack of interest in interior design.

But... you apparently need this explained. Okay, I could indeed care less about countless things — which celebrity couples are divorcing, what band is touring, who let the dogs out... "

"Have you still never been to a concert?" Stu said. Of course, he shouldn't have been surprised. Roxy was still Roxy.

Ignoring him, Roxy checked her computer. Stu took that moment to look around. The left wall was covered in computer screens, all filled with her research, schematics, video, and spreadsheets of data. Awards, her graduate degrees, and a dozen framed magazine covers of her filled the opposite wall.

"They still print magazines? Huh."

While still concentrating on her desk monitor and typing, she offhandedly said, "You can order printed versions to frame. First thing Gwendolyn did to my office. You know, to brandish bona fides to outsiders. Her word – outsiders."

Stu disregarded the comfortable guest chairs. Instead, he sat on a wheeled stool to take in the beguiling array of research. "Definitely impressive. No joke," he said, baselessly taking pride in her accomplishments.

Returning her attention to him, she asked, "Questions?"

"Yeah, Free Will."

She couldn't help but light up at the exact response she was looking for. "Excellent point. How do we preserve the mind when there's Free Will?"

> OPTIONAL ENDNOTE #14 — ONLY READ IF YOU'RE FEELING NERDY ABOUT PHILOSOPHY (otherwise skip) - "There's Free Will?" is on Page # 315
>
> TL;DR — Roxy first explains her analogy — a computer is aware enough to recognize the printer didn't print, whereas a brain is tremendously more complex in diagnosing unexpected results. Those who believe "the brain is only clockwork" determinism base that on the reliable laws of physics that determine how brain synapses fire. Except, at the quantum level nothing is truly 100%. Consequently, when the computer in our skull expects its body to do one thing ("print") but recognizes it did something else, it creates a narrative of what happened to itself. It concludes, "I must've wanted to do that unexpected action, which means I have free will."

Stu struck a pose as if for a sculptor. "And you need me to train AI to be more accurate in its inferences."

Roxy sounded stilted and rehearsed while saying, "Welcome aboard, Stu. We need you and... happy you joined us."

Stu popped up in his chair, mostly hiding his excitement. "Okay, let's see what you got in action."

Inside Roxy's testing lab was a two-way mirror viewing two rooms side-by-side. Harry, a sickly human subject covered with prison tattoos, was in one and his Digi-Avatar on a tablet in the other. Monitor screens in both showed identical images to the human and computer.

Roxy said, "Harry, the human subject, has his Digi-Avatar version in room two. They encounter novel stimuli, and we track how each responds. If we've mapped them perfectly, their responses should be identical. Here we go."

The monitor screens showed both the psychic electric shock scene from *Ghostbusters* (with the same wavy lines used as a guy and a girl were tested for ESP).

Harry sat up, recognizing this movie and scene, talking to the screen as if he were in a theater in a bad neighborhood. "He's the one with the powers, creep."

The monitor displaying Harry's Digi-Avatar showed the identical words: *"He's the one with the powers, creep."*

Stu had to challenge this. "How do I know that ain't a cheap ol' magic trick that's scripted?"

"A skeptic, I like it." Roxy gestured to the microphone with an invitation. "Say whatever you like, and I bet they both still respond the same."

This seemed fair to Stu. He paused to consider what open-ended question would be most likely to have varying responses if the minds differed. Stu spoke into the microphone piped into Harry and Harry's Digi-Avatar, "Describe your happiest memory."

Harry's face brightened, having a sense memory and vividly conjuring what happened in his mind's eye. "I was shooting craps and got on a hot streak."

The Digi-Avatar displayed the exact words verbatim but now a second ahead of the human subject: it presented the text — *"on a hot streak. Made so much, I paid off my loan shark debt."*

And the real Harry was now two seconds behind, saying, "Made so much, I paid my loan shark debt that woulda cost my legs. Had enough to smash in the VIP."

Stu nodded at this magic trick and enjoyed some sympathetic happiness, remembering the relief he felt upon becoming debt-free. Roxy dismissed Harry. He weakly hobbled away, helped by his older brother, who was tear-smeared but holding it together.

Roxy got a warning light on her security dongle and heard the doors electronically lock. So she reset it, and all returned to normal.

Stu loved identifying areas of improvement anywhere, most of all to keen people who'd appreciate it. This also helped hide his insecurity. "I've always wondered when you have such badass security — doesn't all of that only trap everybody in the event of a disaster such as a terrorist attack, fire, or earthquake?"

"We like to think we think of everything. I'm getting a "SkySaver" escape system installed." Roxy said.

His voice tense, Stu asked, "Do I need to look that up?"

"Given your anxious mind, I think you're better off not." Roxy had to showcase all the equipment. She used her security dongle to open the MSL door, which was heavy and multi-bolted, like a safe. Inside was the infamous invention, the only functional prototype device. It was shaped like a full-head motorcycle helmet covering the entire face. There was also an elaborate chair with a dozen 30cm screws to immobilize the human subject's skull.

"Okay, And what does this machine do?" Stu obtusely pointed to a stapler.

Roxy ignored that funny-adjacent comment while noting there was no printer, so it was slightly less stupid than she first thought. She had to focus on business and explain how the device worked. She said, "This scans the synaptic architecture and catalogs a complete decoding map. Get in. Let's test it with you."

Stu felt like a mastermind sure he could beat a lie-detector test. He got in the cold, metal scanning machine as Roxy set it up. Stu did his faux boasting (bragging in an apparently facetious way to get away with it). "You think even the largest array of supercomputers are enough to contain this natural wonder?" He pointed to his brain and sing-songed a taunt, "I doubt it."

"We'll see," Roxy said, careful not to encourage his ego.

"And you do that without biochemical confirmation?"

"No, we do some bio-chem autopsies in almost real-time."

"How are you getting volunteers willing to die right after a scan?" These ramifications were starting to get uncomfortable for Stu.

"Some terminal patients in never-ending pain use their 'right to die' to magnanimously advance science before euthanizing themselves. Why not do some good? It's like being an organ donor." Roxy had deployed that response to countless others because it was a reasonably practical line-of-inquiry stopper.

"Wow, that's undeniably generous. But not for me, for the record," Stu said with a smile he regretted. "Remember what George Carlin said about donating organs? Great for society if you weren't using them. But in an accident, no one wants their lives disregarded because some doctor is 'looking for parts.'"

Roxy gave him an "of course" look.

He said, "Wait. Did that guy Harry back there die for the autopsy?"

"No. That was for you. We only do the autopsies when a prisoner is at their true end of life. It's a more productive version of physician-assisted suicide. Since it's for the advancement of science and the betterment of mankind."

Stu fizzed some outrage, "And investors are falling for that? This is maybe more morbid than trading insurance policies on other people's lives." Worse still, he was skeptical that financiers weren't skeptical.

Despite the insult, Roxy stayed on message. "This isn't some grift, Stu. The tech works. It's going to be revolutionary."

Ding — the scanning machine signaled completion.

The machine's efficacy sparked Stu's curiosity. He was confident this was fraudulent or a persuasive delusion. Even if it weren't, a mind is an ocean of thoughts that are impossible to organize, let alone grok. Assuming a computer somehow could do that, regarding Gödel's incompleteness theorems, a human couldn't make sense of it because a brain couldn't fit itself in itself. His ego had to believe his mind was more complex than others. Glory be to he who first wrote — "Cogito ergo melior sum quam tu. Aut ego certe scio quomodo utor Google Translate." So, more to challenge

Roxy and rationalize his criminal agenda, he asked her, "It can accurately decode all a person's thoughts and secrets? And nothing about that bothers you?" Stu's fingers dug into the chair's arms.

"Was Oppenheimer bothered by advancing atomic energy?"

"I'm pretty sure he said he was. Something about 'I am become death, destroyer of worlds,' Or something exactly like that."

Roxy reclined with checkmating confidence. "Still didn't stop him, though, right? The Cold War was better for the world than a 'Hot' one. The proof is death stats by military conflict dropped for decades after The Bomb. But fine. Listen, this is my life's work. And someone will make the advances. I might as well get the credit."

Both understood each other's arguments and weren't likely to change the other's minds.

Stu switched to passive-aggressive mode. "I'm surprised you think the world is ready. Though if it no-bullshit works, then everyone deserves it."

Roxy had to concede the inequity, "Everyone isn't getting it at first. Only select clientele."

Stu gave a skeptic's eyebrow. "You get to make all the selections? By yourself?"

"Of course."

He was incredulous. "Not your majority shareholder?"

"My contract says I'm CEO and unfireable." Roxy returned to her computer and typed some keys. She pressed the side of her fist on the desk and said, "Looks like render farm G is busy. I'll send you to the mainframe to play nice. And now you're in the queue for mapping integration and resolution. I'll let you know when your digital doppelgänger is ready for testing."

Stu was conflicted; nevertheless, he spoke earnestly. "Well, I trust you." That was true, but also an essential part of running a confidence game. Demonstrating you're trusting the mark encouraged them to trust you. Stu thought he'd heard that from the film *The Grifters* but later learned it was from Mamet's *House Of Games*.

Back when they dated in college, Stu got her to watch those movies — only in post-coital bliss. She'd half-scold him, calling him out on "unfairly persuading me to watch con-artist movies 'while under the influence' of my body's dopamine and oxytocin."

He calculated she might be thinking of that same con-man tactic to elicit trust illicitly. The hypothesis got validated when she made intimate eye contact and said, "Good. You're one of the remarkably few people I've ever personally trusted." With a two-foot stare, as if gauging herself in a mirror, she sported a Mona Lisa smile. Surprised to be comforted by hearing her own words, she said, "Huh. What does that say about me?"

Stu had never heard Roxy talk sincerely like that. But he also never knew her to be deceptive. People on the spectrum tend to be bluntly honest and relish being so, even detesting society's pressure to tell white lies to be polite or shelter anyone's feelings. So, her professing genuine faith in him stung Stu, given what he was secretly there to do. He snapped on a convincing, Botox-level of unreadability and redirected the conversation. "Your new owner, however-"

Roxy got defensive, "Better her than someone like Chuck Rosti. You want to challenge me on that?"

Stu nerd-flirted, "Convenient we're both so challenging and also enjoy challenges."

Roxy wasn't all-in with her flirtations. "Not entirely convenient if you're gonna stick with Maria." This was real; they were not doing purely playful compliments. So, Roxy drilled down, "Think she's gonna give you a kid?"

Stu had to justify that relationship. "I'll convince her, eventually."

"I imagine that shouldn't be something that takes much convincing. But relationships aren't my area of expertise." Roxy confessed.

He laughed at the implication and asked, "Oh, so you would have a baby?"

"If a suitable man wanted to harvest my eggs, find a surrogate, and raise the kid, even alongside an animal-dog, then I'd be okay with that."

"You skipped the fun part at the beginning, Mrs. Mom-of-the-Year. But you are adorably practical, Roxy Zhang."

This interplay veered too far for Roxy. She said, "Let's get back to packing your brain with my new research."

Stu couldn't help but be playfully flirty, asking, "See? We'd never work. You only want me for my mind, but I'm more than just three pounds of high-efficiency gray matter. I'm a pretty sweet slab of prime soy protein in a Costco value-pack."

The almost-romantic moment passed for Roxy. "That's too much. I think I can only take you in fun-size increments."

Chapter 7
"Fear = Hating the Future You Predict."

Ten miles outside town was Mansfield prison. It was a concrete fortress dotted with windows narrower than a human skull. On the second floor, above reception and the secured visitor's area, was the hospital. The rows of sleeping patients in ICU beds could've been confused for corpses if not for the beeping medical equipment.

The warden escorted Roxy with flanked guards. She surveyed the "crop" of candidates. "Thanks, warden. We might only need two more subjects."

With the detachment of a big box store manager doing inventory, the warden said, "We've got two with inoperable heart cancer who have volunteered. But if that's not enough..."

"How many more are interested?" Roxy asked, appreciative of every additional research subject.

The warden turned his back to the primary security camera and whispered to her. "What about non-volunteers? We can ensure a nearly deadly convict fight happens whenever you need it."

Roxy's response was immediate and unambiguous. "No. Please don't do that... or even bring it up again. That is crazy." Aware of the camera, she shook her head wide and waved her hands in a negative "wax-off" motion.

The warden looked defensive and went on offense. "There are no innocent inmates. Plus, it's easier to allow these violent animals to kill each other. We'd be doing society a favor."

"Let me be absolutely clear — NO!"

The warden finally got the message, but since he appreciated her essential work, he wanted to accelerate and help wherever he could. "Okay, Let me know if... or when you change your mind." There was a bright line between citizen and criminal, but he knew how simple it is to trip into trouble. He had seen too many "normal" people convicted for a mistake (e.g., DWI Manslaughter, possession pre-NF drug crime amnesty, good old-fashioned bar fights, and the like) and become vicious, sadistic animals inside. He couldn't believe anyone could stay good for long. The most corrupt are the most cynical.

#

Inside Rosti's art-clustered office, Chuck's security team finished a daily, cursory sweep for bugs. He sat connected to diagnostic medical equipment brought in because he didn't want to risk catching anything from stepping foot in a hospital.

The doctor reviewed everything and double-checked the vials of blood, encased swabs, and tissue specimens held by the nurse. He couldn't keep Chuck waiting. "When your new lab cultures conclude in a few days, we'll have a better idea."

That was not good enough for Chuck. "Based on what you know now, tell me... something."

The doctor took a breath, steeled himself, and said, "Mr. Rosti, to prolong your life beyond a few weeks, you should be in a hospital."

"By how much?"

"Maybe another month or two. Impossible to know."

Chuck didn't like that calculus. "Not enough upside. If I could get another year or ten, we're having a conversation." He coughed several times. "I'd rather try for immortality than be trapped in an opium stupor for a few months."

The doctor defocused, reminiscing in his mind's eye. "Most find that stupor pretty fun."

Chuck was pissed. "That's loser thinking."

The doctor reflexively responded in an annoyingly patronizing way. "It's best if you accept your fate."

Chuck went off. "I want to cold-cock you in the face so bad right now. How's five grand?"

One of Chuck's henchmen, Connor, a beefy former bouncer stepped closer.

"Is that a joke?" The doctor asked until awakening to his lack of choice. "If I have to — Okay, Mr. Rosti."

Chuck gave Connor a subtle look, turned his back, struggled to make a fist, and slumped, ashamed of his weakness.

BAM!

Conor sucker-punched the doctor, whose knees buckled.

Chuck was satisfied with this transaction. "Pay him. Pay that man his money." Connor stuffed a handy rubber-banded stack of cash in the woozy doctor's pocket. The entourage traveled with such "tips," like a new mom packs diapers. All sorts of shit's gonna go down, and it's better to be prepared to end matters in more than one way.

On his way out, Chuck couldn't help but taunt the Doctor. "And I woulda paid ten times that!" Chuck commanded his henchmen. "Take his ass out of here. If he starts static, just vanish him. And get me a feed of Stu's place."

The two henchmen dragged the doctor out. Another delivered to Chuck a monitor getting fed sound from Stu's apartment via a "laser microphone" aimed at window panes.

#

Inside Stu's apartment, Maria used a brush to "paint" a protest sign. Without lifting the tip, suddenly, the color of the lettering changed. This was 20NF, so instead of poster paper, it was an ultra-thin and light 30x60cm digital screen that functioned as a tablet with tactile sensors. Technologically, it could display movies or animation. But for protestors and their audience, such standard videos were visual background noise. To counter and as historical homage, protest signs had to appear handmade. AI had long since been adept at such facile creativity. But Maria didn't want to outsource her outrage to computers. It was barely hyperbole to imagine the laziest possible "activists" ordering remote "protester robots" to carry the protest signs while being surveilled by rivals' security robots. If civic engagement falls into a human-less empty square, does free speech make a sound? When most everyone wants to stay home, any assembly of warm bodies gets attention.

Consequently, every AstroTurf (i.e., fake grass-roots) political organization had to look like it had authentic human supporters. People could use tech so long as the human hand's influence was noticeable. Maria had made multiple signs and emailed those jpegs to other less-arts-&-crafty protestors.

Stu embraced Maria from behind, kissing her neck. She didn't want him to get her too warmed up. "Stop it, Stu. Let me finish these."

"I want to make you happy."

He revealed a ring box. She recoiled like when you see another subway passenger has a lizard. Stu knew to calm her before any full panic could pop up. "It's not what you think."

Since all evidence was to the contrary, Maria needed to demonstrate her will with vigor. "Stop. I've never wanted to be a wife."

"Oh, I know. I'm fine with it," Stu said.

"Marriage is outdated, and having children isn't for me," she stressed.

"Just open it."

Maria saw the ring she feared and was reflexively judgmental. "Is that a blood diamond?"

Stu couldn't help grinning. "Nope. It's a magnifying glass in a titanium setting. What I won't do for you is get married because that's your wish. But what I've done is in there."

She inspected the stone and saw a QR Code inside. Her phone scanned it to get to the URL: "http://bit.ly/IpaidOffYourStudentLoan," which redirected to a bank account webpage: "Maria Gutierrez's Student loans: $68,036.01 PAID IN FULL: August 10th."

He nodded.

Maria wouldn't doubt it because it was classic Stu to be generous with those he loved. But she probably needed to hear it out loud. "For real?"

Stu asked, "Will you, Maria, be out of debt with me, legally single but romantically together for the foreseeable future or until we tire of each other?"

She nodded enthusiastically, and they embraced in a strong, long hug. She pulled back and stared at him with giant eyes and an open mouth smile. She soundlessly screamed.

As if they just got away with a bank heist, he whispered, "I know. Damn astounding, right?" Their vicarious joy was synergistic.

She shrugged with palms lifting to the heavens. "So maybe this gig isn't so bad."

Stu was very into kidding-on-the-square. "Selling out has its perks."

Maria volleyed with the same. "Do you promise I won't have to visit you in jail?"

"I do." His lilting voice highlighted the double entendre.

She squinted. "So, you're confident you'll succeed without getting caught?"

Stu was in car sales mode, in part, to convince himself. "Thing is, I'm already done. I'm going to Chuck's tonight, brief him about the successful test Roxy showed me, and quit ZerQuali in the morning."

Maria's optimism proved unreliable when she predicted life's storm trajectories would miss her family. A string of her sister Adriana's boyfriends had financially committed to fulfilling her wish to have a baby. But money remained unwired. For years, Maria borrowed all she could to prevent Adriana from becoming a childless Subtiree. Stu's new, bad-sourced good fortune meant the end of her tuition payments. Which meant Maria could better afford a niece and skip loan sharks. That is, unless they'd have to use those funds to pay for Stu's legal defense. Better to bug out ASAP before he got arrested. She said, "So don't wait. Go right now, and let's put this all behind us."

Stu gave a one-cheek smile, recognizing she was probably right.

"You should be all tail lights right now," she said.

"Maria, I gotta keep Chuck happy so he'll invest in my venture."

"Is this so you can do something better or so you can get more credit?"

Stu massaged his upper neck and said, "It can be both."

"Well, I'm busy preparing for the protest."

Maria brushed past him with a "your choices are yours" side-eye. She video-recorded her homemade posters and advice to post on social media. "Fear = Hating the future you predict. That means there are three ways to ditch fear: 1) change the path you're on to create a different future, 2) change your prediction, or 3) change your opinion of the future. This is all super important, you guys, especially if you're bad at predicting the future or if your hatred runs against human interests. High key, people, you gotta get off your ass to shape the path; otherwise, it's gonna lead somewhere you don't want to go. Come protest with me. Plus, it's good exercise!" Maria reviewed what she wrote and deleted the last line about exercise. "Doing what's right should be enough for you, motherfu..." she said to herself. "Gotta stay positive. No one wants to be around a smartass grouch." That made her regard a digital photo frame; it showed a montage of Stu and her adorably hugging for a selfie at last year's Turing Competition. He looked proud waving his semi-finalist trophy, but his enchanted gaze at her showed where he was prouder.

Chapter 8
"When the Winning Move is Not to Play"

Chuck's grizzled mercenaries spied out the C-Suite balcony of the Rosti building like they were still in Kamchatka for that bloody "Summer of Madness" and stood ready for a full-force enemy attack. The bright sun and wind could've triggered memories or PTSD, but none showed it. The junior thugs enviously studied their menacing, 1000-yard stares.

Chuck's knuckles went white squeezing the handset of his antique, 1980s, standard-issue, beige, "Ma Bell" telephone (that one could quite reasonably confuse for ballistics-grade Polycarbonate). He slammed it down like he was splitting railroad tracks — it was as if this model were built for hanging up with such fury — Crack! His men ducked at the noise as a reflex, moderated by the historic frequency of the boss's outbursts.

Chuck laughed with his neck tendons flexed and said to the room, "The 'best' doctors in the world, they're supposed to be. Can they be the best and accomplish nothing? C'mon, can they!?!" He stared at each of his henchmen as if that weren't rhetorical. They held still as if camouflaged. Chuck said, "That word 'best' has kept meaning different fuckin' things through the ages, depending on the prick who's talking and the schmuck he's talking to. Everyone is so... full... of... shit!"

Behind the door, Stu's voice sounded twangy and high-pitched as he said, "Hey, hey, Chuck is expecting me. I'm not fightin' with you, fellas." The doors opened, and Stu fluttered in

Joel's sinewy grip like he was the dry-cleaning. Before Stu could count the number of guards, Joel crammed him in the chair like a reform school guard disciplining a future lifer. Stu felt the henchmen encircle behind him and flashed a Walter Mitty insta-fear, trying to figure out what he'd do if they garroted him. *Maybe use a pen to stop the strangle? No chance.* He'd have to talk his way out. Stay positive.

Chuck stared at Stu, allowed himself a quarter-grin, and asked, "Well? What's my first-string captain got to say?"

Stu torqued a shaded grin that became natural as he insta-fantasized about captaining his future boat. Stu said, "You ordered, 'Find out,' and I did. Roxy's invention is 100% on pace to work. So, I guess, yeah, we're done. Right?"

Chuck looked bemused and amused, then released a full smile.

Stu triple-nodded and tried to get up, but the henchmen forcefully sat him back down. Chuck had predicted Stu's desire to quit while he was ahead, and that seat-slamming was the planned response.

Chuck said, "You're only done with part one. Now comes the big job."

Stu got a splash of cold worry and said directly, "No, thanks."

Chuck's chuckle squelched into a modest cough. "You think I needed you to find out something I already knew? No. This was standard 'Kompromat' tactics. I've got video of all our interactions, and now I own your ass."

To run his security firm, Chuck had always handsomely compensated a former deputy chief of a three-letter intelligence agency. As they retired, generals and agency heads queued up to ingratiate themselves to Chuck with inside info and crony deals. Somehow, it's not bribery when the "Quid" comes way after the "Quo." Chuck brought in influence and intel wherever he could.

"Not" in any way coincidentally, this past Summer, an SVR spy gave Chuck's senior team a seminar on Kompromat that Stu would've benefitted from.

> OPTIONAL ENDNOTE #15 — ONLY READ IF YOU'RE FEELING NERDY ABOUT COUNTERINTELLIGENCE (otherwise skip) - "Advice for The Treason Curious" is on Page # 324
>
> TL;DR — People commit espionage for "MICE" (Money, Ideology, Compromise/Coercion, and Ego). The under-recognized danger is that in doing even the most minor of betrayals — the first act is used as implicit and eventually explicit blackmail to induce more and worse acts. Which creates a vicious cycle. You can't realistically quit either because once you can't help your blackmailer anymore through your continued criminal acts, they'll be happy to use you as a bargaining chip to trade to the employer you betrayed. This is called Kompromat.

Chuck had paid attention, and this intel paid off. It was the Rubik's Cube algorithm for extortion in any situation. Like in nuclear War Games, "the only winning move is not to play."

But Stu was a gambler and already playing. He was betting this tycoon wouldn't jeopardize all he had precisely because he had so much. However, some doubt had since crept in, so Stu made a doomed attempt at trumping extortion with reason, "This is all on your orders!" and followed with a counter-threat, "If I get busted, I'll just flip on the mastermind."

"Normally, that'd work. But I'm dying soon, so it's kinda like I'm invincible." When someone knows death is close and has embraced that fate, they have ever-less to lose. That's when they're most dangerous. Chuck's voice was stern yet calm in the most unnerving way. "You're the vulnerable one, and you've got no leverage. So, complete this next damn assignment." Chuck tactically switched to a friendly tone. "And then you'll be done."

"How do I know that'll be it?" Stu expected Chuck to reply with a lie but had to ask.

Chuck's voice changed to calm and credible. "Because you're gonna steal Roxy's device for me, and there'll be nothing else I could ever need from you."

Stu's mind sprang a multitude of possibility branches like a chess champion. The most glaring downside needed to be addressed. "Maybe afterward, you'll kill me, Mr. Rosti." Stu wasn't sure any response would put himself at ease.

Chuck pulled out his gun, and so did all his henchmen, on cue. All were aimed at Stu, and he'd have crapped himself if he accurately knew how close death was.

Chuck's intended threat was compounded by the dangerously magnified chance one of his men would "accidentally" shoot Stu. A scary parlay that Chucked leaned into, "Maybe I'll kill you now or at any moment in the future."

Stu saw the bloodlust in the henchmen's eyes. There was only one play, utter submission. "Okay, okay... I get it." Stu gave a subtle look to the security camera, as if it'd get played back in court, and said, "This is duress." Stu turned back to Chuck. "So, how much time do I have?"

Chuck coughs through his own response. "The sooner, the better. Let's make it one week to grab the device."

"No way. If I had a month to plan... maybe." But Stu was no black-masked Dread Pirate Roberts, Jason Bourne, or Super-Soldier. Stu was a hacker with the cardio to match. Only at Comic-Con could Stu get away with cosplaying like he had a superhero physique — and then only compared to the average attendees. Outside that accepting sanctum, Stu was not a badass of any kind.

Chuck got practical. "Well, forget my criminal trial; I might not have another month to live. So neither do you."

Stu needed every extra hour to have any chance of pulling off this feat. "But you must want the most advanced and accurate version of the device. That means at least two weeks."

"No way. Get me whatever is the best available version this week."

Stu couldn't expect a better compromise. "Fine. Do you have a plan, or am I supposed to come up with one?"

Chuck's eyebrows bounced. "Let's make one together. I have every schematic you could possibly want."

Stu thought he was smarter than everybody, but Chuck could at least keep up. Stu wasn't an expert criminal, after all. While Chuck was. Chuck's mercenary forces were deployed worldwide, and only 40% of the time were they working for the US military. The rest of the work was legally gray.

In comparison, the civilized world recognizes invasions and violent oppression of human beings as war crimes. Yet when the customer's a warlord or autocrat, who defines illegality? Globally, Chuck's forces had done some wicked actions with thin cover, but there wasn't much of a market for heists. Indeed, that was why Chuck hired Stu. There was still time and planning a heist simply didn't seem that daunting. Chuck got to unleash his cunning mind — this was going to be fun.

Stu and Chuck were engrossed, flipping through ZerQuali's architectural plans and technical schematics. They synergistically teamed to solve the problems. Stu's arrogance helped him underestimate the threat Chuck posed. Chuck encouraged anything that benefited him, even a peaceful image. He could redeploy threats as needed.

Stu noted, "Each employee has an electric security key coded to the doors. Plus, all the cameras have gait-measuring tech analyzing the physics of walking, identifying approved personnel.

Like any security system, it's only as strong as those holding the keys. We must keep everyone ignorant of the theft for as long as possible.

Chuck mentioned the obvious in case it hadn't occurred to Stu. "Build a copy and swap it out. I bet it's super easy, at worst, an inconvenience."

"It's not like they're using standard parts. An aspect of their security is that everything is customized. A replica wouldn't fool anyone at ZerQuali."

Chuck understood, "So, you'd have to steal authentic components, which is no easier than stealing the device."

"Exactly," Stu said, slamming the desk louder than he intended.

Chuck's coughing was messing with his "criminal's high" and boomed with authority as a show of domination. "Well, I don't give a flying, wet shit about anything other than getting the device ASAP. Let's go through the steps."

Stu recapped the top line of the new plan. "First, I send a DNS attack to ZerQuali with foreign signifiers so their security is on high alert. A multitude of wolf cries, and they'll be sick of alarms. I duplicate a security dongle and use it to steal the device."

Chuck saw flaws. "How do you get around the guards and the cameras? They can't catch you before I get the device."

"I'll just use my Digi-Avatar tech you saw at the Turing Competition to create phantoms of thieves in other rooms, diverting ZerQuali's security team, and vanish or face-swap everyone else. For the security cameras, it'll look like a Bizarro world. I'll go invisible."

In minutes, with AI-assisted programming, Stu showed a synthesis of his proprietary visual effects software that he used for social media video camouflage and dark web apps. This proof-of-concept version played a 3D animation of the "Objective Eye Reality." In which Stu stole the device and presented the "Security Camera View" showing VFX Behind-The-Scenes. Photoshop-style digital brushstrokes could be seen erasing Stu and building digital decoy thieves.

Digitally created thieves appeared on "SCV" screens, and guards chased down empty rooms, made transparent or opaque at the perfect times to mess with them. The "SCV" showed a blink of static, and then all the faces comedically swapped using the most advanced (and illegal) "Deep Fake" technology. With perfect comedic timing, they all changed again, some upside down, adding a few celebrities' faces, too. For fun, they all became Roxy's face, switching to Chief Brumfield's. Stu played a stream with the peppy, nuevo-techno heist music from the museum sequence in the 2034 remake of "The Thomas Crown Affair." Chuck wasn't amused by these dramatics, and Stu turned it off.

This animation showed the guards watching the SVC and freaking out when all the faces wiped to featureless, faceless heads. Heights changed. People multiplied. Others disappeared.

Stu knew this was perfect but hedged a bit. "I think this will work."

Chuck's eyes glimmered. "Good. You've got one week to get me that device peacefully, or maybe I send in 50 mercenaries to butcher everyone and steal it."

Stu pulled his chin into his neck and crinkled his eyebrows. "That'd be crazy." He was 49/51 on calling Chuck out on this.

Chuck promised a zeppelin-sized carrot. "Alternatively, you know I reward achievement. Succeed, and I'll increase your mega bonus. How does... $50 million sound?"

Stu's skepticism of Chuck wouldn't allow himself to get excited.

Chuck did the old-school hard sell, getting the person to imagine themselves happily post-sale, saying, "Picture all the good you could do. You'd regret passing on this."

In those five seconds, Stu's skepticism morphed into excitement because maybe Chuck was serious. So that required showing appreciation. "It'd be gigantically life-changing. Thank you, Chuck."

Chuck wasn't saving any ammo. He needed Stu to have an unwavering, singular focus. "Not to mention the boat you could get. Hell, you could even get a jet!"

Stu subtly shuddered from a sense memory. "No, I got a thing about heights. Oddly, it only began after I first went skydiving. No air for me, thanks. Surf & turf only."

"Fine. No jet. Just get it done."

As soon as Stu exited, Chuck ignored a text from ZerQuali Security Chief Brumfield saying, "window open but closing soon" and called Pyotr.

#

Roxy's office was so stuffed with proprietary equipment to continue her research, it precluded use for any meetings with visitors. 20th-Century: Businesses serve official foreclosures to farms. 21st-Century: Business offices are closed for server farms.

Roxy only became an entrepreneur to enable the advancement of her research. She took Gwendolyn's money for increased resources and to offload the boring business stuff.

Roxy video conferenced with Stu. The edges of his face glitched for a second. She busily compiled her new code while talking to the screen.

"You are making exciting progress."

"You can call me 'Stu,' I look like a Stu. Don't I?"

Roxy let slip a small laugh. "Trademarked Stu humor. So simple, but still funny... to me, at least."

"What purpose do I serve other than to please you?"

At that, she had enough. "Okay, pal. Don't you have deadlines?" She signed off.

Stu's laptop evidently had a webcam without black tape over it. Stu wiped sweat from his brow and reviewed his computer. He wrote a new schematic on a whiteboard. Stu enabled a live video feed from his home office, and there was a whiteboard in the blurry background with an SFTP IP address and... "PW: fav subject + first kiss + favorite number squared."

Stu said, "Hey, StrangleBear bitches! You tried to embarrass me, but the fact remains, I 'pwned' you! I challenge you to AI2CON in September!"

At that exact moment, the StrangleBear team got the alert for Stu's video using anonymous social media accounts. Pyotr stood, arms akimbo, exposing his neck, sneering at the screen. Everything about him projected fearlessness and strength.

Yevgeny sent a DNS attack to Stu's computer.

Stu instantly identified it and rerouted as a countermeasure. He looked over his shoulder, smirked, and said under his breath, "I can't be the fall guy." He quickly took down the video.

The entire StrangleBear team didn't know what to make of it, apparently getting cut short.

Stu reshot again against a blank wall with no whiteboard visible. He started again, louder and with more bravado. "Hey, StrangleBear bitches! You lost the Grand Turing Competition! I 'pwned' you! I challenge you to AI2CON in September!"

At the StrangleBear lab, Pyotr asked Yevgeny, "Why'd he take the first video down?"

Yevgeny didn't see the significance. "Obviously, he didn't want to mention the embarrassing doxing we did to him."

"Maybe. But let's try to pull up the original."

On the main screen, it read: *Cached video streaming files — recover*

Pyotr showed the two videos side by side. One had the whiteboard. He zoomed in on the password reminder. "That's a bingo!"

Yevgeny had been building a research dossier on Stu for years, using surveillance, tech, and social hacking methods. Most people will give up a horrifying amount of intel to good bullshitters who do a little homework. Yevgeny searched through the file and announced to the team, "He majored in Comp-Sci but only after switching from... Anthropology? Okay. But he's gonna wish he stuck with that. I can't find first kiss."

Pyotr said, "Hold on," and then texted Maria, *"Who was Stu's first kiss?"* He kept his finger up to Yevgeny, confident he'd get an immediate response.

Maria saw the sender, shielded the screen, and peeked over her shoulders. Could this be a weird threat? She typed, "IDK. What do u mean?" then deleted it. She switched apps to Venmo, addressed Pyotr, and typed $5,000. Her thumb hovered for a moment, and she chewed on her upper lip. She added a zero, making it $50,000, and clicked send. At a low volume, in a playful tone, she said to herself, "Okay, Stu. You can pay rent this month if you really want to. Oh, I didn't tell you I'm in deep hock to your rival who encases screaming victims in boxes? So sorry. But you do prefer to keep a 10-fingered girlfriend, right?" She struggled to finish swallowing a strained gulp.

Pyotr saw the receipt of funds and texted her again, *"That's nothing to me. You will do as I command and answer my questions. Unless you want to get fifty Barbie tattoos."* He waited through the three-dot animation.

Maria's cortisol spiked and mouth went dry. She could be braver on text, *"You'll get your money, but I never promised to be your spy."* Her finger hovered over the send button. She inhaled through her nose, filling her lungs to capacity, and continued to hold it like she was diving to the bottom of a pool. Staring at the sky and reducing her volume to a one, Maria faux-yelled, "Fuuuuuccccckkk," until she ran out of air. She deleted her reply.

Pyotr bared his incisors with a furious rictus. His neck flexed red as he typed, *"Now!!!"* But before he could send it, her reply came in, *"Stu's first kiss was Tara Boscher."*

Pyotr flipped to managerial and relayed that info to his crew, loving the upper hand.

Yevgeny said, "Look like Stu's favorite number is dog's birthday."

Pyotr said, "Okay, everybody, try that and near-probable permutations on our zombie computer network."

Yevgeny waved for Pyotr's eyes and said, "Dy-no-mite! I've got his cloud account. Downloading."

Pyotr got frustrated on his first target. "Email must have already changed. But... I got his Social Media!!! Posting him to say, "I'm a bitch. StrangleBear Rules!" See that?" Pyotr scowled at his own pettiness but, evidently, wasn't regretful enough to delete it.

On the main screen, it read: *Dropbox: Password Changed. Connection Lost.*

Yevgeny knew what was going on. "Stu must be batch-logging out now. I tried to freeze his social media for at least a day with dozens of customer service requests. Damn crap! Looks like he's recapturing."

Pyotr didn't want to lose this advantage. "DSA his domains to prevent a new login. How you like me now, Stu! And dem apples you like."

Yevgeny requested, "Comrade, you want to see this."

Pyotr was in his own world, delighting in damaging his rival. Crushing Stu felt better than if they won the Turing. Pyotr's English was most natural when smack-talking. "I'm conjuring a shitstorm for that arrogant asshole."

Yevgeny allowed worry in his voice to get through to Pyotr. "This is grave matter; you gonna want make this priority."

"Fine. What is it?"

"Before we lost the connection, downloaded cloud server files look related to ZerQuali's AI work."

"Since when does Stu work there?"

Yevgeny scanned already-hacked centralized databases for Stu's MTS/NCTD account and ride-hailing logs. "Wow, he's been there for few weeks, already. Holy piss and poop!"

"What do we have?"

Yevgeny prized his spoils, "Look like security plans for ZerQuali offices, a calendar of staffing dates, and some efficiency reports."

As if he was talking to Stu, Pyotr mumbled, "You doing petty corporate espionage... for some money? That's it? So much for the noble Stu Reigns. You tricked us. If we knew you were such a cheap whore, we would've bought you years ago. "

The whole StrangleBear team hung their heads a little with pensive pathos, squinting with disappointment. They checked each other's confused expressions, unmoored by the fallibility of their adversary. Though none would admit it.

Pyotr barked at Yevgeny. "How's their AI Match efficiency?"

Yevgeny gestured to the screen, which read: "100% Efficiency."

Pyotr switched to cover-up mode, asking Yevgeny, "Did you leave a trail? Will he know that we hacked him?"

Yevgeny should've refilled his Klonopin prescription; this was a stressful assignment. He said, "Let me check. No, I'm gamma-stealth dynamic, and... So are you. So, he's in the dark unless we're bugged."

They half-laughed in this moment of modest victory and then got hypervigilant. They reached for bug-scanning equipment and swept the room.

Pyotr was ultra-diligent in covering every inch. "Clear. Clear."

Yevgeny checked his tech. "Hi-freq confirmed."

Pyotr smiled wider than he had in years. Yevgeny was even more excited. "Whooohhooooo!!!!!"

This hyped-up Pyotr, elatedly declaring, "Stu, you stupid jackingbag. We're going to get so dirty rich!"

#

Outside Roxy's office, a smartphone screen played a news report from citizen journalist Viggo, who said, "Experts familiar with the matter suspect the hackers are based in the New Soviet Confederacy. The Kremlin has issued a 'no comment,' My sources tell me…"

Gwendolyn and Pasela arrived. Security Chief Brumfield bumbled, turning it off, embarrassed to be caught on his phone. However, Gwendolyn graciously didn't give him the glower he deserved and was expecting.

They entered, judgmental of Roxy's messiness, "How do y'all get anything done when it's like this?"

Roxy got defensive. "The work speaks for itself."

Gwendolyn reviewed Roxy's progress, not hiding her lack of expertise. Nevertheless, Roxy knew people who underestimated Gwendolyn did so at their peril. Pasela perused the screens and did her routine backup of employees' files to her portable drive.

Gwendolyn used her tablet, which threw charts onto a couple of Roxy's screens. They were Chuck's medical records. One was labeled "Actual Results" beside the very different "Results Displayed to Chuck." Roxy registered them with a nod.

"He's terribly ill. Poor thing. But it'd be better if he thought he is even sicker." Gwendolyn whispered to Roxy, well out of earshot of the nosy Security Chief.

Roxy unwittingly responded at normal volume, "Do you want me to hack-"

"It's being handled. Focus on your work," Gwendolyn nipped this quickly. She advised her proteges, "The only things that should be overhearable should be the ones you deliberately want overheard."

Gwendolyn took Chuck's records off the screens she controlled. Her deft gesture controls sprang up financial analysis charts showing at Gwendolyn's pricing, only 144,000 people on the planet could afford Longeevia. That number wasn't arbitrary for Gwendolyn. Roxy saw those and didn't care. Gwendolyn double-checked that Roxy's door was closed and locked. "So about when do y'all expect to deliver this... ultimate domination of natural law?"

"We have a 'candidate for final' prototype, but we're doing last-minute stability tests. Maybe we'd need three months to build 20 or more like it. Now, the big question is: with whom do you want to live for eternity? I know the Chinese are very interested and would pay handsomely. Or is it for anyone with three commas in their net worth?"

Gwendolyn let slip. "None on earth. That's for certain as sunshine. Earthly happiness is always relative, so it's not enough for me to succeed; all my rivals must fail. I can't let any threat to my family grow into a worse tumor. In heaven, we'll all be in brotherly peace. But that's what makes it heaven."

Roxy was in a state so rare it scared her; she was confused. "What are you talking about?"

Gwendolyn dropped the mega bomb info she had withheld until that moment. "Good heavens. I thought you'd have figured by now. I won't ever allow more than one functional prototype. Encouraging people to seek technological immortality instead of our Lord's grace? If you can't see it's the devil's doing by now, I don't know what to tell you." Articulating the destruction of Roxy's life's work was a metaphorical vial of nitroglycerin tumbling in the air. It was designed to blow everything up, not only this business but also her hopes and the long-term fate of humanity on earth.

On the other side of a three-inch door, Brumfield connected a tiny suction microphone to better hear their conversation. The mini salute he offered to Gwendolyn's private security detail down the hall looked awkward enough to be 1% shy of suspicious. He averted his gaze, pretending to review a work tablet's floor plan.

Roxy's tone sounded uncharacteristically emotional at the ramifications. "What? I thought we agreed. We must preserve the world's best minds."

Gwendolyn perked up, leaned in, and asked, "Why? Who would that even be?"

As if it were obvious, Roxy said, "All of today's scientists and intellectuals, of course."

Gwendolyn dug in. "Okay, let's plan this picnic. Are they really any smarter than Einstein, Jefferson, or Plato? Or how's about future generations? Surely, they'll have a better jumpstart."

Roxy saw the fair point, adding, "And be less limited by outdated assumptions."

Gwendolyn's voice boomed self-assuredly, "I'd sooner give catapults to convicts than allow my opponents to become immortal. You know I'm right. Thou shalt have no other gods before the Lord thy God."

Roxy tried ingratiating herself to Gwendolyn by talking the language of business and the law. "But we had a deal. A contract. You can't."

Gwendolyn pitied how naïve Roxy was. "Oh, my dear, I can... and have. C'mon now. Power is Power."

Roxy buzzed in for security. "Brumfield, get in here, please."

After putting his microphone in his pocket, Brumfield entered and stood ready for Roxy's instructions (as if he hadn't been listening to this whole conversation). "Yes, ma'am. How can I help you?"

Roxy's angry eyes stared at Gwendolyn. "Please escort Ms. Grantham from the building."

Before Brumfield could respond, a jog-march of feet rumbled from down the hall. The muscular trot of Gwendolyn's security team practically announced their approach. Roxy half-cowered behind a cart of servers, reeling at seeing so many armed men assemble in support of Gwendolyn. Brumfield looked over to Gwendolyn and her forces, toting Ruger Redhawks holding hollow-point bullets. He responded to Roxy's command, "Sorry. I can't do that, ma'am."

Few instances in her life called for Roxy to wield her power. Accordingly, she wasn't prepared for such insubordination. She tried a tactic that might've only worked in a military setting. "I'm the CEO, your superior, and I'm giving you a direct order."

Gwendolyn's patronizing veered into scolding, more for the optics to her guards and Brumfield than for Roxy. "You're the last to recognize. I'm the one with the real influence. Brumfield here just yesterday learned where his kibbles come from."

Roxy never gave up this easily. With a more assertive tone, she said, "Brumfield, I'm not kidding. I'll fire you right now if you disobey me." Gwendolyn's guards put their hands on their prominently displayed sidearms.

Brumfield's face showed pity and sympathy. "Please forgive me, Roxy. I respect you and all. But no one ever thought you were actually in charge. Stick to the science stuff. Ms. Grantham is the boss."

Roxy was stunned silent.

Gwendolyn gloated. "Listen to him, dear. You're good at the 'science stuff,' Only the powerful get to enforce contracts. And everyone knows who'd win if we went to war."

Roxy plodded her retreat.

Gwendolyn wanted Roxy to see the bright side. "Chin up, girl. You still get to continue some research. And now you'll have time for a spouse and family."

Roxy stumbled back and leaned against the wall, devastated and prominently more dramatically than any co-worker would've thought natural or possible. She looked around but didn't find an audience or witnesses.

Chapter 9
"Convicts Call It the Regret Point"

Stu entered his apartment that now felt "small pond" and beneath him. He responded to an alert on his bank account app. It read: *"$2,000,000.00 incoming transfer: released. August 9th. $268,736.01 outgoing transfer to LOANTECH: completed. $786,996.95 incoming transfer: pending."* Then the word *"Pending"* switched to *"Completed."*

Stu was so proud of this payday but more psyched to see his girlfriend's response to it. "Maria, you gotta look at this!" In the mood, she ignored it and kissed him. "I've been thinking about you. You better have been saving your love for me."

"Absolutely. But first, you gotta see this."

Maria peered over, expecting a funny meme or a joyous video of a lion recognizing a human friend after many years. Instead, she saw proof of Stu's generosity and her good fortune. "That's a frickin' ton of money, Stu. For sure. Damn. And if it makes you happy."

"We're debt-free and rich! What's not to be happy about?"

Maria let slip, "I'm not yet totally debt-free."

"Easily fixed. Where else am I wiring money?" Stu's streak was sizzling.

"Nowhere. You're already stupid generous." She slinked up to him.

"Well, if you won't say, I'll wire you another $50K." Stu shrugged.

Maria spun guilt into defensive anger. "I ain't a hooker. No one can buy me because I'm not selling."

Stu parried. "I thought you supported sex workers, no?"

"You know I'd fight for literal hookers who want to sell sex as a transaction. But that's not healthy in relationships; I ain't looking for no sugar daddy. Where's my proof? I started dating your broke ass when you were broke-broke."

Stu wasn't done being a baller. "I'm still gonna wire you...

"

"You better not, or I'm gonna take out another loan at an obscene interest rate to pay you back, including the student loans. So, let's stop talking about money! I'm trying to fuck!"

"Ah, priorities. Of course. Was I talking myself out of... I'll shut up."

She grabbed the back of his head and kissed him hard with forceful lips. Their eyes were opened defiantly. They backed off and giggled. They kissed again. Stu's fingertips glided through her thick hair like an effortless comb.

> OPTIONAL ENDNOTE #16 — NSFW - ONLY READ IF YOU WANT TO READ EROTICA (otherwise skip) – "Stu and Maria's Sexual Chemistry" is on Page # 327
>
> TL;DR — They have hot, sensuous, electrifying sex. You want to indulge, do you, naughty reader? There's no shame in flipping to that page.

They had made love with such enthusiastic passion, skill, and understanding that it's a shame the internet wasn't watching then. Not for StrangleBear's lack of trying, though.

Their bodies still buzzing, they re-acclimated to reality. She kissed him in appreciation and got up from the bed. Maria asked, "You want me to bring back anything? Maybe make you a gluten-free Philly cheesesteak?"

"No, thanks, babe. I'm good."

Tillman scampered up, dogs having a genetic understanding of the word "steak" in every language. Maria affectionately rubbed his scruff and walked him to the cabinet, where she poured him a small portion of premium dog food. She said, "You heard the word 'steak,' didn't you? Well, no one should be teased. So you get this, but don't tell dad."

He scarfed down the meaty goodness in three gulps and gave the bowl a tongue polishing so it gleamed in the moonlight.

Maria returned with two glasses of water because, of course, he was thirsty, and she knew without him asking. This post-coital glow soon dimmed as she asked, "Why would we risk such happiness doing some criminal, stupid crap?"

"I haven't done any serious felonies yet. But soon." He took a breath to steel himself. "As I feared, I had to agree to steal the device, or they were never going to let me leave."

Maria was pissed. "I knew it! Damn, what I tell you? You never give a river ride to a scorpion like Chuck Rosti." She slapped on her robe like a flak jacket at the sound of enemy shelling.

"Yeah, you told me so. But right now, he's basically got a laser scope on my skull, and that may not even be a metaphor." Stu needed some slack or a solution.

"It can always get worse. Convicts call that a 'regret point,' the moment that haunts them forever, when they saw a path away from crime and could've walked it. Except they stay on the criminal track and always wish they chose to turn off course. You keep holding the steering wheel, Stu. Don't be a mindless robot, controlled by circumstances, to make stupid decisions or do your worst impulses. You're a person. You make your fate in every moment. There's always a better path. Build the will and wisdom to find it, and take it."

Stu finished digesting that thought and put on his boxers. "You're right. The simple solution is — I don't do it. Let's cruise to a non-extradition country. I'll even teach computer programming to the underprivileged to get out of Karmic debt. It's not like Chuck can go to the cops."

The reality dawned on Maria. "So, I gotta live my life terrified of getting whacked? Why would you do that to me?" She surveyed the skyline.

Stu was dejected. "Damn. You're right on that, too. Which is fucked-up and not fair. What are we gonna do, Maria?"

She looked off as if she could find a solution on the horizon. Lost and discouraged, she closed the blinds.

Stu felt crushed more by this risk of losing her than his dire predicament. He tried talking it through with her. "I guess my best option is to go to the authorities and live in witness protection until Chuck dies, which could be soon, or goes to prison, which could be sooner."

Maria was too pessimistic to feel comfortable. "Bastard would put a hit on you from the grave. Or maybe he already did and will only cancel it if you deliver for him."

"Or I could do what Chuck commanded and steal it for him. At least then we'll be rich." He took two steps closer to her.

She turned two steps away, turned back, and challenged him. "Nah. Ratting or running would be on borrowed time, and who knows how far we could even get?" They stared at each other, wondering.

"I don't know, Maria. It's a gamble either way."

She was in full brainstorming mode. "When you steal the immortality tech, you should give it to the world."

Her words were sonic endorphins. He said, "Then that's what I'll do."

"Then I got you. I'll be 'ride or die,' my hero."

Stu had manipulated her into directing him to do what he

already decided to do. But she could have changed the trajectory; instead, she let Stu stay on that path.

Stu breathed relief and closed his eyes. They kissed, and he forgot about the danger.

Maria saw him blissed-out. "Damn. You're lucky you have me in your life, Papi."

They were still embracing when Stu admitted, "I know it."

Maria was back in righteous fighter mode. "Shit. Try to find someone less deserving of immortality than Chuck Rosti."

#

Gwendolyn started her stream. "Fair warning, folks. I have it on good authority that Chuck Rosti's about to start wearing connected bracelets and orange jumpsuits for all that fraudin' he's been perpetrating on oh so many victims. Y'all saw the damning evidence his prosecutors presented from 'Informant number one.' To save you the trouble of triangulating the source — yes, that was me. I encouraged some of his insiders to come to Jesus, do the right thing, and blow whistles on that contemptible charlatan.

"Now, he's got international 'New York lawyers' working for him, so I can't be too sure he's gonna get the punishment he deserves — at least not during his lifetime on earth. I tell you, I'm ashamed of myself for getting snookered."

OPTIONAL ENDNOTE #17 — ONLY READ IF YOU WANT SOME GWENDOLYN AND CHUCK BACK-STORY (otherwise skip) – "Rosti's Ponzi" is on Page # 330

TL;DR — Gwendolyn rarely got tricked, but when she did, she always held grudges until they resolved in her favor. They served as cautionary reminders to herself and lessons to others.

Gwen closed by saying, "He's got such an ego on him. So, I'm praying on it and hope you will, too."

#

Chuck started up his live stream video. This time from his phone camera. "Hey, followers. Don't know exactly how long I have left on this pretty blue marble. So, I'm saying all the things I always wanted to say from now on. I don't care who wants to manage my image."

That was a dig at Zephyr and Hira, who watched as loyal employees but shook their heads in incredulous sympathy for each other.

Chuck said, "That bitch, Gwendolyn Grantham, used to be hot. You know, when she was young and fit. Before she let herself go and got old."

From her mansion, Gwendolyn was watching Chuck's feed while she happened to be doing her daily rowing exercises, her muscles getting ever more toned. She looked over to her trainer, who said, "Pardon my language, Ms. Grantham. But that is bull-C. You're in better shape than 95% of my clients".

Unaffected by Chuck's taunts, she said, "Everybody gets older and dies. Pity the ones who don't."

On-screen, Chuck pinned the deplorable meter when he said, "We Alpha men fuck hot girls of all races and sizes — petite, skinny, fit, voluptuous, even BBW. But why not plow someone ugly? Since animals' primal instinct is to continue their bloodline, and since males can impregnate hundreds of females, why don't we? I'll tell you. We men gotta worry about the rest of our genes will get associated with the ugly. So, we gotta be just as picky as hot girls. They don't fuck ugly dudes, right? Or not ugly, broke ones. I say it's only fair we got our priorities. All right, later." He stopped the camera, took a hit of oxygen, and slumped in his chair.

"Glad it's over," Hira leaned to whisper to Zephyr. "That was tough to watch."

Worldwide, the incel army faction of his fanbase led the shower of likes and reposts.

Zephyr said, "Is there a word for cringy and enraging? Must be one in German."

"Fremdschämend. Or you can create others according to the rules of grammar."

"Knew there'd be at least one. But it could've been worse. He implicitly came down against racism, which wasn't a given. He only offended the ugly, and almost no one thinks they're ugly. From a legal standpoint on a relative scale, this was one of his less dangerous rants." Zephyr said as if to convince herself.

Hira sighed and asked, "His sexism and misogyny didn't even register for you, did they?"

Zephyr laughed. "Oh, shit. That's a given with Chuck. It's 'priced-in' for the job."

Hira placed her hand on Zephyr's again, "You've been working for him too long, Zephyr. Life is about limiting your contact with assholes, I've been told. True?" Hira turned to see Chuck standing over there, so encased in his myopic egocentrism that he hadn't heard them.

"Hira," Chuck barked, "what's next?"

"You have your IV therapy followed by 90 minutes for scheduled rest, as the doctors prescribed. We could bring in the masseuse if you like?"

"I like."

"Oh, and the clerk for the Justice called to confirm the trip this weekend."

Chuck gestured to his ankle monitor and said, "You should've known to cancel those plans as soon as the Feds took my passport. I can't fly to Fiji with him right now."

Hira demurely averted her eyes and softened her voice, "You're right, of course. But the clerk asked about the Justice and his wife flying without you and still staying at your mansion. Or maybe you wouldn't want... "

"Definite yes to whatever he wants. Also, buy twenty thousand hardcover copies of his memoirs from his personal website and make sure he sees the receipt. And pay our other favorite guy." He tapped on her iPad to ensure she typed everything verbatim.

Odd for one who grew up in Germany, but Hira had trouble hiding her face's flushed concern. "That senator whose name I'm not supposed to say out loud is getting a lot of press about anti-bribery laws. Maybe now isn't the best time to make conspicuous transactions."

"Don't you know? While stealing from rich people is always a crime, bribery is legal in America. If you make it a blatant 'quid pro quo' transaction on camera with a paper trail, and your accomplices turn state's evidence, then, maybe, there's a small chance you risk jail. And if you have major law firms on retainer or lobbyists with pull in the current presidential administration, you have all the power-ups. It was easy enough to get around old 'fig leaf' anti-corruption laws. Man, those were supposed to prevent 'even the appearance of impropriety,' Ha!" Chuck laughed and said, "and those were decimated in the early 2020s. Nowadays, sheer, crotchless lingerie is considered dignified, sufficient cover for naked corruption. So... let's donate one hundred grand to the senator's super PAC with an easy-to-find paper trail to me."

"Easy?"

Chuck eye-rolled with a single-laugh exhale, disappointed at her naivete. "Yeah. When initially scanned and glanced at by campaign staff, the money's direct source is an unrecognizable name. But the moment anyone does even a coke-spoon size of digging, they'll find out it's my money, and their candidate took it. That makes it harder to distance themselves from me."

Hira was confused. "Wouldn't it make their calling you out even more credible?" She surveyed the room for support, finding no eye contact.

Chuck peered over her but in a softer volume, "Look, Hira, don't nepo-trip into delusions; you got in the door because your dad is a major investor in my fund. That's patronage, which is just favors. People do them every day, and that's a good thing. It connects us through personal relationships. But… "

Hira found herself nodding, appearing relieved he was making some sense and perhaps even relieved she was exhibiting her approval to not further trigger these new suspicions.

Chuck said, "… you gotta learn my playbook faster than that. It's crazy hard to make money when both sides of the deal have equal information. You might be able to sell a used car that's worth ten grand for twelve grand if you find the right sucker. But if a savvy buyer who's done his homework comes to check it out, his final offer might be $9K. My fund gets rare intel and does unique analysis, which is why it's successful…" Off her skeptical reaction, Chuck dropped the rehearsed sales mode and conceded, "…except for that one fund that collapsed."

Hira typed some notes in more detail than necessary, giving her an acceptable reason to avert his gaze.

Chuck picked up on this, his voice strained and defensive. "Your dad knows any justification for bribery laws would have to deem the campaign financing system in America illegal. It'd be like paying a hooker's charity organization to sleep with her. In any event, you're spending money, and the other party is doing the job you want done. Either a trade is legal or not, regardless of the bureaucratic square dancing required. And so long as bribery in the form of campaign contributions is legal, I'm not unilaterally disarming to the advantage of my enemies. Same with prostitution. Whether it's a straight cash transaction or courtship paying for dinners, trips, and gifts, the man pays either way."

Hira was in a safe area of conversation for Chuck. She said what he wanted to hear, "Society benefits when the number of prostitutes is in a proper per capita ratio for the area."

"God bless them all."

Hira gave him a "you incorrigible rogue" look, less as a scold and more like a flirtation. She intuited that trick her first week on the job, and it kept her employed. She finished typing the To-Dos for the book purchases and super PAC donation and smiled. "Consider it done... within the hour." She stood ready for further instructions.

Chapter 10
"Enforce the Rules or Exploit Them"

Yevgeny and the StrangleBear team froze, focused on their computers as if appearing to be a statue would be effective camouflage. Weird that it was kind of working. It was too late to sneak out of the room to give Pyotr privacy while he loudly discussed personal family matters and meandered around them.

Pyotr said, "I love you, Мамочка. Give Vasily a kiss for me." Pyotr allowed himself moments of expressed anguish while on calls with his mother. He watched his comrades, but none dared to lift their heads lest they give the accurate impression that they were eavesdropping. This was a mutual deception that fooled no one. Still better than anyone bringing it up.

"We cannot ignore that your brother won't last much longer, Малыш." Pyotr's mother said sternly. "The doctors say he still has brain activity, so we play music and university lectures for him throughout the day as if he can hear them."

"As you say, mamma."

"I'm not so sure. The doctor said his best chance to emerge was ten months ago. This is not something Vasily would want. Not this long, Pyotr."

"We're so close. I can't tell you now. But we have a plan to bring him back."

Pyotr's mother faux-spit, shushing what she brushed off as nonsense, "Don't talk crazy."

"I am serious."

"Well, get going. Because when you get back, we're taking him off the machines. He should have a proper burial before your father dies. Closure ends the pain of hope."

"Stop it! I know what I'm... "

The phone went dead as she hung up on him. Pyotr slammed his fist on the table, rattling the computers. Yevgeny had to dive to secure his laptop. Pyotr's "acceptance" of Yevgeny's disability didn't make the constant rage any easier to endure.

"What are we mad at now, boss?" Yevgeny asked.

"Do you have any idea what this invention means?"

"Oligarchs get to live forever,"

Pyotr said, "Yes, and at some point ... we who are close to oligarchs will get it, also."

Another subordinate, Boris, tentatively offered a half-statement/question, "That's us. Or no?"

Yevgeny gave him a subtle head shake, warning him of the severity of the moment. He looked over to draw Boris' attention to a framed photo of Pyotr sitting with his ailing brother in a hospital bed.

Pyotr noticed this and said, "There has always been a difference in health between the meaningless poor and well-connected rich. It must be so. Money can always be traded for medicine things, and doctors are no different. We want money. The poor don't have it. This can never change. But tech immortality is something different."

"One life is plenty for me," Yevgeny said.

"We're all products of our age. I'm sure 50-year-olds in the Middle Ages had no desire to live longer because they saw the elderly always suffer. My parents never played video games. I never did social media. Each generation defines its standards. In the future, not so far, those electronic immortal people will consider us worse than the Luddites. Or those religions that reject medical breakthroughs."

"Christian Scientists."

"Yes, that one. We'll be seen as caterpillars who fear to be butterflies. My brother has been trapped in a cocoon too long already."

#

Stu turned the corner, not five meters from the entrance of the Serbian consulate; the new building featured old Europe architecture, making a prominent statement about its independence by blatantly defying the modern design requirements of the neighborhood.

Yevgeny spotted Stu as a runner stealing second. He threw a signal to Pyotr, who got in position for the forced out.

"So wonderful to catch you in person, Stu," Pyotr boasted.

Stu assumed a moment of superiority because Pyotr was shorter than him. However, Pyotr repossessed it with his unpredictable and sharp movements, carving a menacing presence.

Stu said, "Yeah. Uhm, what are you doing here, Pyotr? I can't stay and chat."

Pyotr showed off his power with intel. "I know. You have an appointment for a travel visa with this South American consulate, which happens to have a non-extradition treaty."

"What's my denial worth?"

"меньше чем ничего, Bubkes, Nada, Zero."

Stu asked, "Who else knows about this? I see Yevgeny. What about that tattooed yuppie on his phone looking this way?"

"Funny to see you paranoid, Stu. Only Yevgeny is here. This doesn't have to leave my team. And you could join. Be easier to keep track of each you and me, am I correct-o?"

"Maybe another time, under different circumstances." Stu headed inside.

Pyotr coyly said, "You spoil me, Stu. I guess I must wait or create such circumstances."

Forty-five minutes later, Stu emerged from the consulate with jaunty glee. He noticed Pyotr giving him a "Sorry for the bad luck. But there's nothing I can do" look while turning his palms up resignedly. He pointed to a nearby van and said, "Turns out you're not so paranoid, Stu. I tried to save you. But now..."

Out of the van emerged a cadre of thugs who sternly escorted Stu into the vehicle. He noticed the absence of Russian smells and then the presence of American tattoos, most US military or mercenary-related.

"Y'all with Chuck, then?" Stu asked comfortably. "Because we're kinda buddies now, and I'm doing a big assignment for him." They rolled their eyes at him.

Stu observed the surroundings and tried to remember the last time he saw crowded streets. For years, this was the new normal. Rush hour traffic in 20NF seemed like Tuesday at 4:00 AM in the early 2020s.

Alarm klaxons rang out from everyone's smartphones in harmony with public speakers atop every streetlight. "Attention! This is a test of the Pandemic Alert System. Everyone immediately activate Class one protocols. Repeat... "

With only a moment's hesitation, the driver pulled over and pressed the dashboard's flashing "Pandemic Button." There were hiss and compression sounds as the seals closed throughout the vehicle. The A/C whirred into contained-circulation mode. All new cars had to be made airtight. The bikers and pedestrians donned their personal astronaut helmets and Tyvek suits. Two pedestrians did nothing but roll their eyes. Everyone's screens showed maps to safe zones and flashing trackers on the non-compliant. Those two flipped-off street cameras and one mimed "bite-me" to whatever satellite must've been overhead. They noticed each other and gave "right-on, brother" thumbs-ups to signify their solidarity against the "pandemic hoaxes."

One of Chuck's henchmen, Connor, gave the passenger grab handle an arm-burn and said, "These fucking douchebags. They're why we get these drills so often. Now we gotta sit here for five minutes."

The driver tried to chill him out. "Who cares? Don't tell me you went into private security because you're a go-getter. Why are you trying so hard all the time? You need better meds."

"I like my meds as is, fuck-o." Psych medication having long lost any stigma, particular cocktails were considered a point of pride, yet another stupid way to be tribal.

Stu had to know. "Which meds are those? You make your recipe so appealing."

"Eat shit, Stu. I'm not letting you know my optimum health hacks."

This was gonna be a long drive. Stu did a search of the recent pandemic alerts in the area. As good a subject as any to kill a few minutes. He reviewed the public-facing white papers on the system and deployed one of his hacking programs to reveal their underlying tech. He made sure to save those files for further analysis.

"Testing Sanitizing Spray sector C-Alpha-11 in five seconds. Four, Three, Two, One." In sequential order, a nozzle beside each street light expelled a test burst of heavy, sanitizing gas. As it flowed down, it stripped some dirt off the pole, leaving it a little shinier than it was before. One nozzle stalled. Its status light turned red. Gas struggled to break through in a quick toggle of three attempts. A couple more rattled until it worked and finally lit green.

The sirens changed pitch and reduced in volume. "This has been a test of the Pandemic Alert System. Had this been an actual emergency, public health directives and location-tailored safety procedures would have been announced. We appreciate your cooperation and diligence. Have a good day." The klaxons did a closing trio of chirps.

The driver returned to the road faster than other cars. So few, perhaps only those without appropriate psych meds, ever acted like they were in any rush.

Minutes later, Connor let Stu out of the vehicle in front of an All-You-Can-Eat Buffet restaurant. Stu thought about how much he loved AYCE places. He used to try to "win" by grossly eating so much he'd practically "arbitrage the meal" such that it'd be unprofitable for the proprietors. He repeated this at the expense of his health and aversion to nausea. Often afterward, he'd lament he'd pay twice the price to NOT have eaten so much. When he first realized he didn't have to overeat at a buffet, it was a proud moment of "Adulting."

More of Chuck's men stood vigilant at the doors of the restaurant. Several signs in the window read: "Closed for a Private Event." Stu crept heel-toe like a grounded teen attempting to not wake his punishing parents. The guards recognized him and parted like Marines first attempting a Busby-Berkely musical.

Inside, it was chillingly devoid of customers. The absence of din made this dinner eerier. Even the waitstaff and station chefs looked wrong. They were all jacked-muscular ex-cons visibly uncomfortable in formal business attire. One had a thick mane of white-blonde hair that he had begun to knot in rolls. All eyes stayed on Stu. He checked if the floor had a plastic sheet for easy post-murder clean-up. None, thank God. Stu, to his detriment, dismissed prudent suspicions with the naïve, cheery thought that Chuck's shows of intimidation might be all talk.

"You're early. That's good." Chuck said, turning to get a quick mask-hit of oxygen.

"Kinda felt like I'd be safer with AI or an Uber Remote Driver," Stu said, making sure the henchmen were within earshot. "No offense, guys."

Chuck found enough goodwill to turn his nonpublic scowl into a neutral deadpan and said, "Ah, funny."

"Thanks for taking me to my favorite restaurant. Never seen it empty. Seems like you bought out the place and replaced the staff with your men."

"That's obvious, but the chefs are the same. Though all supervised by my guys. I'm thinking there's a non-zero chance my illness is poison or biowarfare. I won't make it easy to finish the job."

"That's some paranoid dictator-level precautions, Chuck. Could be warranted for all I know. You're clever to wring out risk," Stu said with a knowing look.

"Don't jump right to selling mode. Let's eat first." Chuck motioned to the buffet. Stu grabbed a tray, as did Chuck's bodyman, who led the way. They all foraged through the food stations. Chuck pointed at foods to be added to his plate, and Stu followed right behind Chuck.

"Great, I love real crab and hate imitation Krab. Here, nothing is fake, rare for AYCE." Stu reveled in the moment, Tetris-ing his planned selections for his plate.

Chuck arrived at the steamed crab serving dish and upon seeing Stu exaggeratedly lick his lips, said, kidding on the square, "Looks real good!"

Chuck proceeded to take ALL the crab available. Stu piped up with an awkward amount of panic in his voice. "Hey. Hold on there, boss. Save a bit for the team."

Chuck wouldn't be lectured to, certainly not by Stu, and said, "Is this an all-you-can-eat buffet?" Chuck had to win this petty game to establish dominance.

Stu felt like Chuck's queen commanded the center of the board. Stu retreated. "Yes. You're right, Mr. Rosti."

"I don't see any signs there's any limitation on this non-imitation crab." Chuck put him in check.

"Right again, boss," Stu said, backing away.

"Therefore, according to the rules we all accept, I can have all of these if I want." Checkmate.

Stu worried his ass-kissing was sounding fake. "You sure can."

Chuck preened and said, "Good. I'm gonna see if that veal is real."

Stu asked the seafood station chef, "Any more real crab?" and got the headshake of bad news: Chuck got the last of it.

Stu found other things for his plate, but he was clearly disgruntled, not for being quasi-kidnapped instead of invited (after all, no actual harm had come to him so far), but rather because he was fixating on the crab and tuned out everything else.

Chuck returned with a plate full of prime rib. "They only serve veal on Sundays. Cheap bastards."

"Where's your crab?" Stu asked, stunned like it was a magic trick.

"Oh, the crab. Turns out, I wasn't in the mood for it." Chuck savored this moment more than a perfect meal. "So I threw it all out."

Stu knew this was lousy office politics, but he couldn't help it. "Why would you do that? You not only took all of it so I couldn't have any, but then trashed it? What's up with you?"

"That's your problem, Stu. You are not thinking rationally. I was entitled to take all the crab, which means you never had any claim to any of it. And there's no difference between me eating it and throwing it out. You shouldn't get upset. Anyone can choose either to enforce the rules or exploit them. You're betraying your employers at ZerQuali to feed me information; that's corporate espionage. But you're getting paid. Now, I need to know you're on my team and ranking my interests first."

"Okay, but that's a messed-up mindset for a boss, one that doesn't encourage loyalty," Stu said absentmindedly while dipping shrimp in cocktail sauce.

Chuck half-stopped chewing to retort, "You idiot. I know all that. Now, think another step. Why am I doing this?"

"As a bullshit power-play?" Stu wondered bluntly.

"Fine. And why?"

Dawning on Stu, he swallowed and said, "Specifically, to test me. If you can't trust me on something so petty, why should you trust me on something big? Like the "big task" you gave me."

"Took you way longer than it should've." Chuck cut a chunk of strip steak and stuffed it in his mouth, followed by gulping down a pint of malted root beer float.

"Fair point. But I'm worried I failed."

"You did fail, Stu. Of course, this is what failing looks like. You'll have to make it up to me with honesty and diligence."

"Absolutely, sir."

Chuck leaned toward Stu, speaking slowly in a lower, graver tone, "Then why the hell did you get a travel visa to Serbia? You know I can track and find you everywhere on the planet."

Stu's faltering voice betrayed him, revealing he was defensive as he asked, "Shouldn't a strategic mind always make contingency plans?"

"Of course. I do, too. And I'm smarter than you," Chuck said with the mild ire of Zeus when he was being bitchy.

Stu figured it was 180 degrees wrong but let him have the last word with a courteous nod. "That it?"

Chuck waved Stu off, "Go. Do what you said you'd do, and I'll make you rich."

Stu left his plate. Withdrawing, he thought Chuck's promises sounded ever less credible.

#

In the Herbert Norquist Residential Center, like most former parking garages in 20NF, you couldn't spot a single vehicle. Instead, rows of government-stamped, sturdy plastic, hexagonal Sleeping-Pods dominated the square footage. Each floor shared a full restroom, card-keyed to enjoy a daily shower or monthly rationed bath. When noticing this bare minimum tier for a "Livable Year," only the elderly who experienced what it was like to be unhoused in the 2010s showed gratitude for the comfortable shelter. The prosperous were relieved that's pretty much all it took to bankrupt the "Pitchfork & Torches" industry.

A single Robo-Krupke made its sentry rounds, starting at the top of the parking structure and spiraling down and around until it reached the bottom, only to return in an endless cycle. Completing a lap, it toured near the entrance and paused for a moment to identify the StrangleBear team approaching on foot. It finished capturing for facial recognition and gait-matching, and Pyotr gave it a friendly wave. His comrades did the same. The Robo-Krupke spotted that they were armed but did not assess them as high risk due to their smiles and casual body language. It continued its rounds.

Yevgeny's eyebrows wrinkled tight as he shrugged and addressed his commanding officer. "I need a special keyboard to be a code warrior. I'm not meant for muscle work."

Pyotr considered Yevgeny's disability. "Just put your hands in your pocket like you have a gun, because you have a gun. Look mean. There, make your ugly face useful."

"We should've sent for a few of my cousins in Brighton Beach."

"So what? We all have cousins in Brighton Beach." Pyotr scoffed.

"Yeah, but mine used to smuggle for the oligarchs." Yevgeny boasted.

"Mine worked close to Putin. And at the end of his rule, when he was a real "ублюдок сумасшедшего беспощадного зло массового убийцу" (motherfucking crazy mass murderer)."

Yevgeny saw he was beaten and said, "So okay, we'll go with your cousins."

That settled that. They ascended the structure.

Old, sun-bleached advertising signage everywhere read, *"Why pay to own and park a car when you can Lyft?"* and *"Uber can save you thousands! What will you do with this space when we're your chauffer?"*

Compared to his Hollywood-shaped view of the USA, Yevgeny was disheartened seeing people in Sleeping-Pods like animals in a factory farm. "This is how Americans live now? Homeless and careless?"

Pyotr had no pity. "Only fools too stupid to make money."

By default, listless sub-citizens sought amusement in hyper-effective screens and VR headsets, thus chaining themselves to their pods.

Yevgeny said, "Look at that. Better than 'Bread and Circuses,' huh?"

Pyotr didn't even give a courtesy grunt of agreement. Yevgeny wouldn't want to slight his boss, so he gave a quick primer. "Roman emperors used tactics to please the public with 'bread and circuses' to prevent uprisings. It seems American Left were satisfied because no one was left unhoused or starving anymore. The Center and Right appreciate the reduction in beggar eyesores. Of course, they must have loved shutting down Leftists' further demands by showing how historically good anyone in their country had it at that time."

To end Yevgeny's jabbering, Pyotr asked, "What are you going to do about it? Politics is useless for us. We care about power. This urban planning 'solution' is not popular in every country worldwide. It's a wasteful experiment."

On an upper level, two other scary Russian gangsters wore matching, scuffed, scarlet red, retro-mod "Members Only" windbreakers sporting "HCP-OC" patches (Легкая атлетика Новой Советской Республики. новый советский Республика Олимпийская Сборная легкая атлетика for New Soviet Republic — Athletics). Former Greco-Roman wrestlers Olesya and her husband Dimi dragged citizen journalist Viggo out of his little lodging. His wife, Trin went feral to protect her husband, the only person she had to live for. Olesya backhand-slapped her and, when Trin scowled, changed it into a fist. Viggo shouted, "Don't! I'm complying."

They switched to arm locks to quicken Viggo's pace. Arriving at the interior spiral ledge of the parking structure, they looked down the five tall floors. Olesya dropped to squat and bearhugged Viggo's legs. She lifted and, co-clutching with Dimi, freely dangled Viggo over the edge with casual strength but not endurance.

"Journalism," looking down, Dimi cringed his eyes, "is bad profession. Especially subject matter. You need to take orders better or be replaced with a robot."

Terrified and defensive, Viggo asked, "Why pick on me? That's everybody. What do you do better than a robot?"

"This. I'm doing it right now."

Olesya played "good cop" henchwoman as her arms quivered. "So you better promise to stop reporting. Be smart."

Pyotr and his StrangleBear colleagues arrived to see his cousins with pride and purpose. He said, "У меня есть работа для вас" (I've got a job for you).

The shared language made Viggo squelch a cry for help.

Olesya got to give the journalist the good news. "You are lucky we got higher priority assignment. You live another day to find new profession. Good for you."

Viggo half-sighed, pre-counting chickens of relief. Olesya and Dimi deigned to "give fifty percent," attempting to pull the victim up. They struggled with Viggo's weight and cumbersome movements. It's always easier to destroy than redeem.

Now with quarter-assed effort, Dimi revealed his cruel nonchalance. "This strain my back. Just too heavy to bring back up."

The savvy journalist panicked; Viggo said, "Wait! Hold on!"

Olesya looked to Pyotr and Yevgeny to help. Dimi decided on the simpler solution. "Since it's easier to drop you, maybe you're not so lucky."

The gangsters shared a devious smile and simply let Viggo go from the ledge. He dropped a few stories, clipped a girder, and spun out to a skull-crushing splat.

Trin sprinted to the edge and tortured herself by looking down. She flashed right by denial, anger, and bargaining to the fourth stage of grief — depression. As she climbed to stand up on the ridge, her caring neighbors sprang up to bring her down safely. They held her close with love and support.

Ignoring the murder, the cold-blooded Pyotr group-hugged Olesya and Dimi as if he were a warm-hearted grandpa. "Glad you can join us. Could be dangerous. We need you."

Dimi thumb-pointed over his shoulder. "Who wants to live forever? Let's go."

Chapter 11
"Empathy Gives Humans Purpose."

Outside Stu's apartment, there was a rusty old van with a relatively newer magnet sign for "Genny's Flower Delivery." If you asked 100 people to imagine what was inside, half would say FBI agents doing surveillance in the 1980s. But it pulled away, revealing a large hearse. Inside was an actual surveillance team, Pyotr's gang. It was a tight squeeze, but a hat-tip to Pyotr's favorite activity. There, they had crucial lines of sight beyond what satellites and hijacked door cams could've given them. Yevgeny diligently reviewed video feeds, vetting how they were ingested and constantly cataloged by their AI systems. Breaking the monotony of this detail, a gas company inspector approached the door and buzzed several units. None answered.

By instinct, Tillman barked and ran up to the window to investigate outside. A few more loud barks were sufficient, since nothing seemed amiss. By training, Tillman wouldn't bark incessantly — two thousand dollars beautifully well-spent, according to Stu's neighbors.

Adam kept the brim of his hat covering his eyes from the prominent security cameras but, while turning, showed his face to Pyotr's view. The AI raced millions of matches in facial recognition, identifying the "inspector" as Adam Quan of WeWrong2.

"Look at you, Adam. Growing some balls. Didn't think you had it in you," Pyotr said while taking a sip of tea.

Adam called in to his lieutenant. "We're lucky. No one's home right now. I'm going to install the taps now. Watch out for police."

"The flower van drove off, and I haven't seen a drone in hours. Local kids must be improving their aim," his lieutenant replied.

Pyotr gave Yevgeny a thumbs-up. "This sound quality is perfection. I'd be surprised if the WeWrong2 team can hear Adam as well as we can."

Adam set down a few orange cones in the alley, since demanding people look at you can be the best camouflage. While he arranged them, his SIG Sauer P320 became visible, and the AI alerted the detection of this firearm.

"More surprises," Yevgeny said.

"No, a gun changes the equation. Have Olesya and Dimi bring today's 'laundry' in the trunk of the Benz and double-park out front," Pyotr said while departing the hearse.

Adam had finished opening the box for the building's central cable hub when he got the jolt that Pyotr was peering over him. "What are you doing here, Pyotr?"

"Same as you, but better prepared."

Adam opened his coat to brandish his handgun. "Well, I've got one of these. So, I feel prepared and right at home in this country."

Pyotr laughed. "Having such a tool and having the will to use it are very different."

"Who says I… "

Pyotr gave him what could seem like a friendly side hug to swing him around to the front sidewalk. Except Adam could feel Pyotr's intense strength. It was an awkward moment that didn't compel Adam to reach for his gun, which was probably for the best.

Olesya pulled up in the Benz, and Dimi got out to open the trunk.

Pyotr pushed Adam to peek inside. Dimi stood closely beside him to obstruct pedestrians' potential views.

"Isn't that beautiful luggage, Adam?"

Dimi opened the industrial garbage bag, revealing a fresh corpse. Adam almost puked in his mouth and turned, horrified, to look at Pyotr's inappropriately friendly face. Dimi slammed the trunk closed, got in the passenger seat, and Olesya drove off.

Adam stood there as if encased in a metal statue of himself, while Pyotr gently reached into his waist to remove the Sig Sauer.

"See, you don't need this because you don't do that."

"Do you always keep a corpse in your trunk in case you need to scare people?" Adam attempted to joke.

"Of course not. You caught me on a lucky day. Though not so rare."

"Okay. Message received." Adam gulped. "I'm done with Stu and anything that might ever intersect with your path, sir." There was a delicate balance of respect, fear, compliance, credibility, and avoiding attracting outside attention he'd somehow pulled off.

"Such a smart man. I believe you. Which means less work for me and safety for you. Win-win. Wouldn't you say?"

"I would, sir. Thank you."

"Of course, you know this means I'll be monitoring you for some time," Pyotr said.

"Completely understandable and fine by me."

"Then, as a sign of good faith, you'll give me your email password?"

"Okay. It's ElvisLivEs1714, double-hashtag. Capitalizing the Es and the L."

"Got that, Yevgeny?"

"Checks out, boss," Yevgeny said on Pyotr's speakerphone.

Pyotr smiled big and took Adam's right hand in a warm double handshake. "You make wise, high-stakes decisions quickly.

This is a crucial talent for a leader. Perhaps we can do some business in the future."

About to burst from holding his breath in fear, Adam squeaked out, "It would be my honor, sir. I'm at your beck and call."

"Okay. You may go," Pyotr said with the calm of a beneficent king.

Adam slowly backed away, showing the slightest of smiles and nodding in appreciation. Pyotr gave him an approving wave, and Adam turned to retreat. He scurried fifty yards to the Merong vehicle, never looking back.

"That was scary," Phil said.

"Yeah, no shit," Adam said.

"I recorded it if you want to... "

"Are you fucking insane? Delete it immediately and melt all the drives. We're flying back home tonight."

Pyotr returned to the hearse and refilled his cup of tea.

Yevgeny said, "That went quite well. We'll confirm he destroys his gear and flies home. In which case, he could become an effective asset in the future."

"Thank you, Yevgeny. Violence is only necessary to make threats credible. Hope Dimi and Olesya handle the laundry soon. I don't expect any more needs for credibility before the stink could become a liability," Pyotr said.

"They're on their way to the incinerator now."

#

A maintenance worker entered the MSL to attend to the door locks. Roxy ushered him out, shaking her head to his silent apologies. Roxy unmuted her video conference with Stu. She had missed his last line, but his response was predictable. He closed by saying, "We know the substantial reasons why it could never work with us."

Adderall is a stimulant that relaxes those with ADHD. Stu and these circumstances had the same effect on Roxy; her trademarked intensity muted, and her mood made serene. She said, "I don't need any more than you can give."

Roxy got a security alert on her phone and computer screen, which displayed the hallway outside. She heard footsteps and identified the person on the security monitor. "Crap, here you come." Roxy then swiped her security dongle to open the impregnable door.

The real Stu, fidgeting his fingers, entered, revealing Roxy was actually just talking with Stu's Digi-Avatar, which shut off faster than a porn screen when one's mom enters.

Real Stu studiously surveyed and pondered the MSL. In jest, Roxy said, "Casing the joint to rob the place?" She put her fist to her mouth.

Stu couldn't read exactly what Roxy meant, knew, or wanted. But since joking around was his default, he yes-anded her, "Wouldn't that be crazy, right?"

Roxy leaned in and whispered to Stu while angling their backs to the unmistakable surveillance camera. "There's surveillance everywhere, Stu."

He was stunned, scared, then cautiously optimistic, whispering back. "So why aren't the police here?"

"Gwendolyn isn't letting me run my company the way she promised."

Stu bought this. She continued. "Losing the prototype would delay everything. Gwendolyn will probably die soon enough. So I'll get to control this innovation's legacy."

Stu couldn't believe his good luck. "So you're not joking? You want me to commit a felony by stealing the device?"

"If I did, I couldn't actually be involved in anything like that. Not worth jail for me. I'm talking hypotheticals."

"In case I'm betraying you and wearing a wire?" He was half-joking.

"Testing, testing, one, two, three. Levels check. Sibilance. Sibilance."

Stu smiled. She sealed this moment with three big words. "I trust you."

Roxy slyly reviewed her reactivated screen over Stu's shoulder.

Digi-Stu, in low resolution, like when there's limited bandwidth on a video call, displayed the following words as text before the real Stu said them blindly, "Hypothetically, stealing it doesn't seem so hard. To get away with it, I'll need a plausible patsy."

Roxy turned from the monitors to answer with the obvious candidate. "StrangleBear? You want to frame a bunch of scary Russian criminals?"

Stu rubbed his chin and washed his face with the air as if to wake himself up to the danger of the situation. "They are, indeed, scary criminals. But they'd be cool with people thinking they stole it, so long as they thought they'd actually get to keep it."

Roxy used a digital whiteboard to help game this out. She drew circles around Stu's name and "StrangleBear," boxes representing ZerQuali's offices, Stu's home, and StrangleBear's home base. "How can we position them as plausible suspects? You can't voluntarily give them any intel because they'd suspect a double-cross."

Stu took over and wordlessly deleted everything. He wasn't going to leave evidence on her computer. He could benefit from her brilliant mind as a "red team" to find vulnerabilities in his plan. "I could make them think they got the better of me by letting them steal the info. Everyone wants to believe they're smart, and fools massively overestimate themselves, the 'Dunning-Kruger' effect."

"Their plan must work well enough to explain the theft. That means you're allowing them to steal it, possibly before you do. That's a gamble."

Stu shrugged. "One worth taking to let me get away with it by framing them."

"So long as you're the only one to have it, that'll work for me."

Stu bolted upright. Is this happening? Stu couldn't have realistically wished for this serendipity.

Roxy's eyes wandered over to her Digi-Stu monitor, outside his field of vision. Stu's words were on-screen like closed captioning. In italics were Stu's perfectly accurate internal thoughts. "Is this happening?"

His responses continued to be flawlessly predicted by Digi-Stu, still displaying the words before the real Stu said them. It also knowingly blanked its screen whenever Stu turned his head.

Stu asked, "You want to know when it's going down?"

"No. But the board is scheduled to decide on a major security upgrade in five days. Therefore, that date must be your drop-dead deadline."

"Five days. Roger that, boss." He moseyed over and picked up his coffee, warming his fingers. "You're saving my ass."

"One so cute deserves to be saved." Her eyes flared.

Neither were good at sweet talk, but Stu was heartened by how rarely she used it. He often pondered whether Roxy had another romantic partner. "You're so hot right now. Hope you're getting all that you want." He made the glint in his eye blatant.

Roxy matter-of-factly informed him. "Very few people interest me like that, Stu. You're the only one I fantasize about when I masturbate. It's adequate for me."

Stu fell in his seat, stunned, more than flattered. "I don't remember being that fantasy-worthy. But I guess if it works for you, I ain't arguing."

"Ahh, you're getting better at not talking your way out of sex."

Stu danced on the fuzzy line between playful, flirty, and cheating. He joked. "So clearly you want to make out?"

In a move that looked well-practiced, Roxy whipped a Rita Hayworth-worthy hair flip and invitingly opened her body language. "I have no allegiance to your girlfriend, so... sure."

Stu was not expecting that. "I was being facetious," he said while unconsciously advancing toward her.

She registered his approach. "Were you, though? Not 100%, right?"

Accepting the literal attraction, he said, "Not 100%. Fair point."

She waited like she'd still get a kiss. The moment froze.

She demanded a definitive answer. "So?"

"So, I should be going, superstar," he reflexively said but didn't go.

Roxy subtly pouted. "But evidently... "

Stu's eyes drew in insight. "I remember you once said most people think their feelings define their actions, but you think the reverse is true. And right now, my actions are telling me something about my feelings."

Roxy was turned on but didn't have the matured intuition of a sex-positive feminist. So, she bluntly said, "I still want a kiss... now."

Before the moment could land, he kissed her. Like old dance partners doing a favorite routine, they fell into an utterly passionate embrace.

Through the still-open door, Chief Brumfield had spied everything. Once Roxy spotted him, he pivoted, his shoes squeaking on the polished floor.

Stu got splashed with self-reflection and apt guilt. "We can't do this."

"Sure, we can."

#

Going up his building's elevator, Stu dismissed a text from Chuck that read: *"Nice job."* Getting off at his floor, he scrutinized his reflection in the hallway mirror for clues. He confirmed his collar was unblemished with any cosmetics and chuckled imagining Roxy with this season's "Real Housewives of Odessa"-level makeup. Stu did a shake and then composed himself like an actor in the wings before curtain up.

Inside, with a tied-off, half-full garbage bag at her feet, Maria finished washing her hands. She scurried to put in a replacement bag. She gleefully searched her smartphone's browser for a specific news clip. It reported a Molotov cocktail thrown from a group of masked protestors onto a parked and empty purple Bugatti, engulfing it in flames. Tillman matched her giddy energy without knowing why.

Pyotr texted her, *"Did you plug the micro-drive into Stu's computer?"*

She reached in her pocket, pulled it out, and peeled off its factory seal. Maria looked around. She stuck it in his computer's drive port for a second, but before it even fully booted up, she tossed it in the trash. She texted back, *"Yeah, but it melted. That's not gonna work."* She pursed her lips. Luckily, it's hard to identify a "tell" in texting. She stared at Pyotr's typing dots indicator.

The door opened. She flinched and sped to put her phone in her pocket.

Stu entered and greeted Tillman with a quick pat and did the same to Maria's back. "Hi, honey. I showered at the gym."

These suspicious circumstances commanded her attention. She flipped into detective mode. "You're adding nights to your workout routine? That's hardcore, babe."

Stu tried to yes-and her shtick. "Gotta earn your love somehow, babe."

The awkward moment demanded he give her a cursory kiss, but he knew he was about to get his bluff called. She smelled him and baited him. "Fitness-Arama, downtown?"

Stu checked the time and adjusted his lie. "No, they're closed now. I joined the new Gold's Gym that's 24-hours."

"With your insomnia, that makes a lot of sense. I'm enchanted by the Pantene shampoo the men's shower has. Very macho."

That was it. Stu knew he was caught. "Any chance of convincing you?"

"Of this gym lie? No. Bail out now before you make it worse."

"Okay. I'm sorry." He took in a breath and blurted out the truth. "I kissed Roxy."

She jumped to the worst implication. "You screwed her?"

Utterly defensive, Stu proclaimed. "No, it was just a kiss. I swear."

Tillman barked at the social energy shift.

Maria touched Stu's still-damp hair. "Then why the shower?"

"If I'd confessed right away, that would've been a relief to me and a burden to you. So, I figured it'd be better if you never found out. To preserve your feelings, I got rid of her perfume by showering in her office's en suite bathroom."

"Man, you're a terrible criminal." Maria showed pity more than anger.

Stu's adrenaline was still rising. "I did it for the mission."

"You're not in Seal Team Six, Stu. You're a glorified thief taking advantage of an ex-girlfriend who's probably further along the autistic spectrum than you want to admit."

"Chill, baby." Stu tried to slurp the words back, wincing with regret.

"No, you don't get to do that, BABY! I could take a Robin Hood thief, but only one who stayed faithful to me. And you messed it all up."

He reached for her. She pulled away and closed the bedroom door behind her. Small comfort that she didn't kick him out. Stu would need to come up with another grand gesture. His blood was running hot, yet the room felt so much colder. The locking sound click cued Stu to the linen closet. Time for sofa sheets.

Chapter 12
"Don't Self-Sabotage"

The next morning, Yevgeny surveyed the car-less street and texted Pyotr: *"Stu & Maria left. Apt empty."*

The message got an emoji thumb-up, so Yevgeny gave Dimi a real thumb-up.

Dimi looked up at Stu's apartment and wagged his finger horizontally. "Why do I have to do it?"

Yevgeny held up his disabled arms and asked, "Really?"

"You use that excuse a lot. Not doing a lot of favors for your disabled rights movement. One of these times, you're gonna have to dirty your hands."

"Climb the damn wall, Dimi."

"I can break front door, take elevator, and then break Stu's door. I promise it'll be faster."

"No. Brute force is for reckless idiots or when you are against reckless idiots. Straight-up robbing — it leaves too much evidence for cops and especially for Stu. Who knows how many countermeasures he's installed?"

"My point exactly. So, what's the difference?" Dimi stood his ground on this.

"Pyotr said you climb. So that is all," Yevgeny said, trying a harsher pitch.

Dimi's head lurched back, "So, okay. You should've said at beginning."

Yevgeny helped Dimi rig up professional rock-climbing gear. Dimi kicked his metal crampons against the wall to check their integrity. He was about to start his ascent when Yevgeny handed him a realistic-looking Halloween mask of a Latino face. "Wear this."

"I have balaclava in my car."

"No, we want every misdirection possible. This face makes you resemble old classmate of Stu's."

Dimi liked Ta-Nehisi Coates' *Black Panther* and *Captain America* series for Marvel Comics. Subsequently, he got into Coates' essays and non-fiction books. Dimi could always perform his vicious mafia enforcer assignments, but he nevertheless had a moral code. Everyone has a line they won't cross. Dimi held the "Latino Man" mask and cleared his throat. "The thing is... I'm 100% Russian, so I don't feel comfortable doing such cultural appropriation and perpetuating racist stereotypes. I'm a violent thief, not a white supremacist."

"If Pyotr wants you in a Pope Margaret the first mask, dressed like Indian belly dancer, singing... I don't know... those tween, New Wave, Nigerian K-Pop songs in most offensive accent, you do it. Now stop stalling."

"Yeah, but, so you know, Ahmed Olade's music is not for just tweens. I argue he single-handedly resurrected BTS's career last year. So don't be pop-snob, Yevgeny. Or a racist. It's not cool, bro."

"Dimi! Climb up the fucking building!!"

Dimi shrugged, popped up on the wall, and scaled a few floors with well-trained fleetness. He was indeed the best choice for the job. At Stu's apartment window, Dimi pressed a hand-held transmitter, which activated Stu's automatic window opener. "It worked," Dimi said, comforted by accurate plans with no surprises.

Out of the corner of Yevgeny's eye, he spotted a police drone on a standard tour of the neighborhood. He reached for his

EMP gun, aimed, and knocked it out of the sky. "I had to drop a drone. You got maybe eight minutes to get done and out of there." Yevgeny radioed to Dimi's earpiece.

"Roger that," Dimi said while sliding inside Stu's kitchenette.

Tillman leaped on Dimi, barking three times at a medium volume.

"солнце, you're such a handsome wolf," Dimi said while giving Tillman affectionate alpha-petting. That was another reason Dimi was the best pick; he was good with dogs. Tillman smiled and laid on his back for a few more tummy rubs. Dimi toured the apartment and entered Stu's home office with all his computers.

The counter's smart TV sprang on with Digi-Stu framed actual size, "Tillman? Tillman! It's me, daddy's here."

Tillman jumped to attention and rolled his head to try to recognize him.

"It's me. Or, for practical purposes, it's me. In two dimensions, you should think it's me. Now listen. There's a very bad man in there." Digi-Stu pointed around the corner.

Tillman wagged his tail, convinced and ready to accept Digi-Stu and his orders. Tillman pointed his nose around the corner to confirm.

"Yes, good boy! The cops will be here in three minutes. So you gotta keep the bad guy here and don't let him take anything." Digi-Stu took a moment for reflection. "Yeah, this is probably too much info for a canine. Ah, body language nuances are important." Digi-Stu pantomimed biting and holding while Tillman enthusiastically panted.

"Be careful. Stu's on Facetime with the dog," Yevgeny said, radioing to Dimi.

"Understood. Don't worry, I'm leaving now, anyway. I have Stu's hard drives," Dimi said while placing them in his bag. He turned the corner and...

Till pounced on Dimi, this time ferociously and terrifyingly. Dimi realized his dog-whispering didn't work this time. He tried to fend him off, grabbing Tillman around the snout to keep his jaws closed. But Tillman parried, freeing his jaws for more attacks. Dimi punched Tillman, who yelped in pain, giving him time to get up.

Dimi turned to the window. Tillman locked onto Dimi's bag. This was a tug of war, and Tillman would never give up. Back and forth they went. Dimi tried lifting both the bag and Tillman off the ground, but Tillman got leverage by instinctively using the corner of the counter.

A faint police siren in the distance grew louder and was joined by a second.

"You hear that?" Dimi asked Yevgeny.

"Yeah. They're faster than we expected. Get out of there."

"Crazy-big dog has the bag with the drives."

"Then shoot the dog!" Yevgeny demanded.

"I'm not shooting a dog, Yevgeny." Dimi had some hard lines he wouldn't cross.

Digi-Stu addressed Dimi, "Wise choice. Hate to have a John Wick-style vendetta here."

"Ha! I don't give a half-a-shit about you. I'll kill you and your whole family for fun. But dogs are angels on earth," Dimi shouted between furious pulls of the bag.

The police sirens grew louder, two blocks or closer.

"Fuck this," Dimi said, giving up the bag. He fastened a rappelling wire to the windowsill and bounded down in seconds.

Yevgeny had the car running. "You got 'em?" he asked.

Dimi said, "This dog might be a bear. I hear cop sirens. We gotta go."

"I don't hear… Okay," He hit the pedal, and they sped off.

"Stu's drives were probably massively encrypted, anyway."

Yevgeny checked back at Dimi and said, "Oh, man. Don't get blood everywhere. I didn't get the insurance on this rental."

"What? Oh, shit," Dimi said, noticing Tilman's teeth slashed his punching hand.

Yevgeny said, "You gonna need rabies shots. Two weeks of the needles."

"No way Stu's dog has rabies."

"Once rabies takes hold, you die. Not worth the risk that dog just got rabies from squirrel in the park. You take the shots."

"Fine, take me to hospital," Dimi said, clutching his wound.

"Ah, Pyotr says we only go to urgent care. Is good enough and less price."

Digi-Stu finished praising Tillman. "You're the best, Tillman! Daddy's so proud of you!!"

Tillman wagged his tail with glee and jumped around in excitement. The sirens abruptly ended. "You don't want to hear those noisy, fake sirens from these speakers. Do you, boy?"

#

Hira entered the office and saw an anguished, angry Chuck reviewing lab results strewn and posted everywhere, scanning their various warnings. She recognized those dire charts. With a deliberate, concerned tone, Hira asked. "Are you going to be okay, Mr. Rosti?"

Chuck was inconsolable and working himself up. "No. Rotting, stinking shit maximum NO... with a giant fist in the ass! Scorching, merciless AAaahhhhhhh! GOD DAMN IT! I have the worst luck!"

Like a child first petting a neighbor's scary hound, Hira put her hand on Chuck's shoulder. Unsure of the next safe step, she was grateful to be blindsided by the blasé henchmen taking pride in the doctor's fresh corpse on the floor.

She tried to seem carefree while stepping over it like daily logs among lumberjacks. Demonstrating her value was her only shield against Chuck's wrath and whim. "There's got to be a treatment we haven't tried yet. We'll fix it, Mr. Rosti."

"We?!?! Yeah, Hira? Will 'WE?' You gonna cure thyroid, lymphatic, and lung cancer in the 'maybe one to two weeks' that I have left above ground?"

He had his millionth coughing fit. "Plus, I may spend my last pitiful days behind bars. Dammmmmmiiitttt!!!"

His entourage averted their gaze for fear of incurring his wrath. Chuck's spasming diaphragm and hacking lungs blocked most attempts at sneaking oxygen. When that stopped, Chuck could breathe, buzzed with adrenaline and cortisol.

Zephyr entered, propping the door open for effect, but squelched her smile some as she read the room. "Good news, Mr. Rosti. The appeals court is doing an 'en banc' review of your prosecution in the Illinois case. Might be ripe for a dismissal. But your retainer with our firm requires replenishment. $9,000,000 should be sufficient."

"Illinois!?! That's scheduled to be heard next year. I'll be dead or a machine by then. Who fuckin' cares! Why are you even wasting any hours and my money on it? You blood-sucking mooch!" Chuck hadn't been this energized in weeks.

Zephyr eased a step back and averted her gaze in beta-status deference. "No associates on this one. You got me, and I'm all you need right now." A few feet around the hallway, Zephyr's associates avoided eyelines and eavesdropped in fright. "And I'll refund the time back to your other cases."

This gave Chuck a momentary sense of victory, but wrath and frustration took over. "I got a rant I've been thinking about for a while. So, you get to hear it first."

Hira waved in Chuck's social media crew, who were there in seconds but soon regretted it.

"Get the fuck out. Nobody called you." Chuck said. He looked over to his henchmen, adrenaline-up and itching to jump in. Chuck pointed to his crew and said, "These bastards have ten seconds to sprint out of here, or I want you to beat their dumbasses until they're off my property." The crew raced away like hares chased by hounds. He closed by saying, "And don't pay them any 'punch-bucks,' either!"

The stampede of extra fleeing feet were those of Zephyr's associates, already clomping down the emergency stairs.

Zephyr was paralyzed in fear, staring straight down. A remaining henchman stood by for Chuck's next orders, deplorably ready to physically assault this professional, educated, poised woman.

Chuck tossed a hand-drone camera, facing it down, his thumb never hitting record. His eyes searched upwards for words as he improvised a rant he'd have broadcasted on almost any other day.

Zephyr looked relieved. Anyone in Chuck's orbit knew his pontificating mode was less likely to be menacing. The henchman recognized the window for authorizing violence was closing and downshifted his adrenaline a couple of gears.

Chuck surveyed the parts of the skyline that belonged to his empire. On a digital outdoor ad, a news segment played, showing clips from Chuck's trial, which he avoided attending in person.

Chuck jolted as if with an epiphany and swatted down the drone, cracking it on the floor. "Shit, if there were no lawyers and loopholes... I don't want to think about it. Glad my gut sensed not to record this. This was a cathartic rehearsal for a speech I'll never give again. But I'm still right."

Chuck's eyes scanned everyone's faces in the room for approval but soon recognized they were all terrified sycophants, and this time, he wasn't in the mood for them to fake it.

Zephyr got a phone alert and didn't have the poker face for this level of bad news. She excused herself. And it was evident she had just forwarded it to Chuck, who saw it on his phone and growled.

Chuck noticed his ankle-monitor, by default glowing green, began flashing orange. He had to hobble over to an electronic check-in station lock-booted to his table. The small screen displayed an alert: "Secondary Location confirmation: approved." He watched it click off. The display read, "Reminder: Get affairs in order. Defendant must be prepared for immediate remand at verdict announcement."

Chuck focused his energy on finding an urgent solution. "Okay, we're moving up the timetable."

Chuck video-called Stu, who was intently working at the ZerQuali lab. Stu opened a drawer to get his blanket for primitive but effective privacy. He hid underneath it while his phone was still ringing and joked in a booming voice to the lab tech marching by, "Don't worry. I'm just masturbating." He regretted amusing himself with that line and doubted it'd be worth the impending call from human resources. From under the blanket and while still reviewing his work, Stu answered the video-call from Chuck, "Hey, boss."

Chuck got irritable at the nurses hooking him up to an IV cocktail of vitamin B, ultra-nutrients, steroids, and Provigil, mixed in with the hyper-oxygenated lab-farmed blood cloned & from an 18-year-old Olympic triathlete. His glare made them back off for the call. "Stu, you've now got 24 hours to get the device. And it better work."

Stu lowered the volume and firmly whispered, "I need time to finish the security camera hack. You gotta wait. I'm not assuming any more risk."

"Oh, I won't let you deprive me of my legacy."

Stu was so preoccupied with his coding, he offhandedly offered heartfelt sympathy, however oblivious to Chuck's inevitable reaction. "I pity you, Chuck. The end of your life is the worst time to be selfish."

Chuck gut-knew Stu must've been ignorant of how the world worked. Chuck said, "Billions of people exist on less than you. Why don't you pay for their lives to improve? Each had hopes, loves, and reasons they 'need' your money. What makes them so undeserving?"

Stu heard this but had no response.

Chuck registered Stu's silence and said, "Exactly. Every man has his own priorities. You bleeding hearts stupidly include all humans or, worse yet, all animals, for chrissakes. Patriots exclude foreigners. Me, I only care about success. Unlike you... for that incendiary firebrand, Maria."

Stu felt like a pastor to a troubled youth. "Empathy gives humans purpose."

"Your only purpose is to get me that device."

"I'll honor my promise. But since I'm the only one who can get it, recognize you're at my mercy."

Chuck wound up like he was going to tear into Stu but held his breath. Taunts aren't worth risking goals. He raised his eyebrows, seeking confirmation.

Stu could only take so much of this. He hammered his point, saying, "Glad you've learned what's what. I'll give you what you want. Just wait." He ended the call.

The hang-up sound echoed in the deadly silent room. All wondered how their Alpha would respond to this challenge.

Chuck screeched his lungs out, "He's teaching me? He pities me?" Which caused a single, convulsing, full-torso cough. He sucked in too little air too fast, so he could only faintly ask, "I'm at his mercy?" These were conditions for a rage stroke, but Chuck had a fierce will to live. "That punk! I master my fate." Chuck's cheeks and neck stayed purple-pink.

Hira saw Chuck stewing and texted Stu. *"It'd be wise to call Mr. Rosti back right now."*

Stu used voice-to-text, saying, "When I can, uh, hugging emoji, no, thumbs-up."

Hira's primal instinct skipped "fight" and went right to "flight." She quarter-faltered like a first-time shoplifter walking to Zephyr and whispered, "Should we get our own passports and 'go bags?'"

Zephyr said deadpan, "Working for Chuck means we all should, plus buy dual citizenship from non-extradition countries."

Disregarding the possibility that was facetious, Hira said, "Would you kindly send me the list and any relevant legal guidance?"

"Sure thing. Spending $500K for a second passport and international sanctuary is unequivocally worth it." Zephyr said, now clear this was serious.

#

Maria put the unwieldy protest signs on the sidewalk. Noticing the mini-garden a yard away, she took the opportunity to "touch grass" and reconnect with nature (even on a tiny scale). She saw the dedication sign from the benefactors, the Koch family, and rolled her eyes. Maria said, "Of course, they're not succulents. Too few step up." She felt a passerby brush past her, so she turned to ask him, "Too few step up — Am I right?"

The man kept walking without even a courtesy look back.

Maria video-called Stu and, not waiting for a pleasantry, said, "I forgive you. Now prove you can make me a top priority by taking the day off to help us out. We're protesting outside Senator Hawn Woods's local office, who grabbed all that government funding for climate refugees and redirected it to subsidize digital immortality research."

"What's with the test? C'mon, querida. You either believe me, and you should, because it was just a kiss, and the shower was only to prevent it from becoming a 'this,' or you don't believe me. In which case, you should dump me."

"Don't self-sabotage. I'm trying to find a reason to forgive you, Stu. Take the win."

"This kills me, because I can't. 'The' deadline moved up. Got one day now!" Stu said.

"That's messed up. But let's talk. Just five minutes — let's shift to some positivity."

Stu pulled his lips in his mouth and agreed.

Maria's eyebrows bounced to reset the vibe, and she said, "While we're protesting, we're gonna help non-voters get registered… with signs for fringe third parties. Get it?"

Stu squinted and asked, "How does that help?"

"To work, a protest needs to make some sort of threat – ours is non-violent, of course. Maybe a bit of property damage, I'm joking. No 'criming.' Though graffiti shouldn't be a capital offense if we're keeping it a buck. I'm getting sidetracked like you do, Stu."

Stu grinned. "It happens. Starts small and then, reminds me of a…"

Maria stopped mid eye-roll and said, "Here's the strategy: we have all these absurd party signs to make the main party leader think we're shifting votes away from him."

"What happens when you actually get someone to want to register?"

Maria and Stu dove into the ultimate, nerdy, political wonkout. Truth bonds.

> OPTIONAL ENDNOTE #18 — ONLY READ IF YOU'RE FEELING ULTRA-NERDY ABOUT POLITICS & PERSUASION (otherwise skip) – "How Are You Going to Win?" - Page # 334
>
> TL;DR — Stu argued there are only two ways to win elections — activating people who rarely vote or persuading regular voters to change their minds. A potential voter in the major party closest to you should be an easier target than someone in the opposing party. So, primaries are where you can challenge the establishment. If you can't win those, you can't win general elections where the supreme establishment thumbs on scales are even heavier. If you don't care about winning, then you're de facto supporting the even worse party by doing precisely what they want. Stu also explained his strategy for persuasion imagining literal, not figurative, "Foundations of Belief."

"Okay, I'm buyin' that 'Foundations of Belief' tactic and tryin' it soon. Appreciate you, babe," Maria said, "But I'm telling you, I'm mad busy recruiting folks in real life for the next day or two. So you gotta be responsible for Tillman. Later, Papi." She gave the camera a smooch and hung up.

Stu searched his doggie-care apps, which showed none of his trusted dog-walkers or caretakers were available. "Ah, fuck it. I got money now. Time for someone in our family to live the good life."

Stu took a ride home and called out, "Tillman!" He noticed the damage Dimi inflicted and assumed it was his dog but didn't blame him.

The friendly beast galloped up, slobbering with excitement. He ended with a rare, perfect "sit and smile."

"I'm gonna spoil you at the Leona Pet Hotel." Stu gave his best friend that signature calming touch, soaked in a moment of a better future, and said, "Let's go."

Tillman flexed and kept panning for prey, feeding on Stu's high energy as they left. A quick e-taxi later and they arrived at the Waldorf-Astoria of animal care facilities. Embedded in the lobby floor, a mini-pool six inches deep enabled dogs to clean their feet walking through. Brushes moved like automated car washes. On the other side were grates and drains, followed by sublime, plush Angora towels. Those must've been changed every fifteen minutes, given how clean they were. Tillman's quick-swinging tail showed his enthusiasm for this experience.

The concierge was a super-duper-friendly young woman with a heart-warming smile and Disney character-proportioned eyes. Stu's smartphone relayed his payment info and Tillman's preferences.

"I see this is your son's first time with us. Would you like to upgrade his meals to organic for sixty dollars more?"

It might've been Stu's nerdiness about accuracy, but referring to animals as one's children always bothered him. Regardless, Tillman deserved the best. "Sure, bill me."

On the lobby screens, Stu finally saw the jumbo doggie rooms packed with toys and thought about how unhoused people lived in honeycombs of Sleeping-Pods in abandoned lots. He wondered if this was overkill.

"Would Tillman prefer a suite?" the concierge said, smelling a potential up-sell.

"Regular is fine," Stu said while handing over Tillman's leash.

She promenaded Tillman away, both so comfortable and enthusiastic like they had been together for a decade. Stu got a subtle touch of the queasy, chest-tightening combo, this being the first time Stu ever saw Tillman take to a stranger in seconds. Maybe it was the pressures of the moment affecting his mindset. He was 90% not joking when he thought, *Someone took my baby away.* He recognized his historic hypocrisy of mocking pet owners who called themselves pet parents. That didn't matter now. What was most important was that his baby was safe.

Chapter 13
"Help Yourself."

Maria cracked her knuckles and counted a woefully inadequate group of protesters. Trin found it difficult to find carriers of homemade signs warning of the dangers of perpetual existence and unchallengeable wealth. "ZerQuali Wants the Next Stalin to Be Immortal!" and "Our Revolutionary War Meant to Stop Royalty Ruling Us Forever!" and "ZerQuali? Eternal Nero?!?" which was above a meme-worthy AI-photo depicting San Diego engulfed in flames as a toga-wearing emperor joyfully fiddled.

Maria said, "Hey, Trin. I'm so sorry about Viggo. If there's anything I can do."

Trin burst a breath she was holding in. "Yeah. Everyone says that because there's nothing else that can be said. I know you mean it, but what am I supposed to even ask for?"

Maria put her hand on Trin's shoulder, saying, "Anything. I could run errands for you. Cook for you. Listen to you. I feel terrible for you. I want to... I don't know, reduce your suffering somehow."

Trin chose to lash out over powerless wallowing and said, "So you want to make this about you? So you can feel better?"

Maria hands-upped and backed up one step. "Nah. I... I didn't mean... "

Trin shook off some negativity. "Sorry. That's not fair of me. You're tryin' to help and..."

"No, no, no. I get it. It's not about me. You lost Viggo and..."

"Stop, Maria. I don't want to argue with you. I'm trying to get my mind off it. Viggo would've wanted me to be here, doing what can be done." Trin looked sickened, but she sounded more serene as she kept talking, "He died doing his investigative journalism 'hobby' – the stupid... idiot. Ya know. But... but he liked Stu's stupid quotes — 'doing something important, no matter how small, is better than letting your wicker chair make leg waffles.'"

There was an uncomfortable quiet; neither risked stepping on the other's response. Trin opened her mouth but cringed herself back into silence.

Maria, in a tender tone, said, "Word. I get that, Trin. At least, I think I do. Man, this is so... I dunno. Absolutamente, I can't imagine."

Trin dropped her head and bounced her gaze up to the cloudless sky. She couldn't help but notice an FDD, and she mindlessly watched it hover up to a top-floor apartment. She started to tear up but squeezed her eyes shut to hold them in.

Maria tried to transform the energy. "Thanks for coming, Trin. Means more since so few showed up."

Grateful for the natural adrenaline boiling her veins, Trin said, "Establishment got what it wanted, neutered, UBI-pacified Subtirees burning themselves out of the gene pool."

"Policies never be good as promised, and consequences always be worse. Still, it's better than it used to be. You know your history. Hundreds of thousands of unhoused people, tens of millions without health insurance, and college only for the super-rich. Was all kinds of messed up."

Trin asked, "Have you even met any 'Reversers' in the past five years? Life has to change. We gotta convince more folks."

Maria sounded like a proud high school coach insurmountably down on points in the game's waning minutes, "You're here, making a difference."

They looked around at the handful of other activists, discouraged.

Maria snapped and said what they were thinking, "I even scheduled this for late afternoon so people could sleep in. We had 80 RSVP yeses, dammit! Muthafuckas better know you gotta show up. Staying home is a vote for the status quo. That means power gets more power, and the powerless get crushed worse." Preaching only to the choir may not be effective for recruiting, but it still inspires the choir.

People contentedly on their way to work regarded them with contempt. One bitter twenty-something in a daddy-bought suit cried out, "Subtirees are moochers. The sooner you die out, the better."

Trin shouted back, "We're fighting for everybody, friend. Even you 'temporarily embarrassed millionaires' deserve better." She turned to Maria. "We shoulda fought harder when the schools pulled the John Steinbeck books."

"Amen, sister. Ignorance is a shameful bliss, and you gotta be pissed to wanna fight."

They handed out the signs. Clarence took out a collapsible stool stored alongside his emergency pandemic bubble helmet in his back scabbard. He sat down and leaned his sign against the armrest.

Maria said, "You call that protesting?"

"I'm here. I got a sign. So yeah."

"C'mon, dude. Can't look like we're lounging around; they already think we're lazy. We gotta march, at least a bit. Get up, man."

"I'm not here to exercise," Clarence said.

Maria, sounding like a mom to her kid after ten hours of video games, said, "You're getting veal legs. Anything on your feet is a major workout for you."

Clarence picked up his stool. "You know what? This isn't for me."

But before he could get three feet, Maria stopped him. "Hold on, Clarence. You came all the way here. You gotta stick around for five minutes. Right?"

"No, Maria. I don't." Clarence strolled away.

"Wait, wait. I appreciate you and know…" She gave up when he waved goodbye with the back of his hand, not even looking over his shoulder. Maria tilted her head up and back down, then swung her nose side-to-side in disbelief. To no one in particular, Maria said, "Are you effing kidding me?"

The rest of the protestors circled up for a shuffling protest. Every step helps.

After dropping off Tillman on the ride back to the ZerQuali offices, Stu scrutinized his tablet, trying to perfect the programming of his face-swap security camera hack. The thought of prison or living on the lam for decades heightened his focus and energy. But this was too much work for any one person. *In 24 hours!?! Idiot. This would take a week, even if I had a clone.* He answered a video call from Maria.

"Stu. You gotta help us out. Most everybody flaked. Really need you to stream to your followers to get more folks to show up."

"I already did two this morning. But I'll do another."

"Thanks, Papi. Stay safe."

A hippie van pulled up. Out sauntered Fredric, a tall, tatted, thick-necked white guy with long white-blonde dreadlocks (ewww!) wearing a vintage "Jill Stein 2016" t-shirt as he approached and asked, "You Maria?"

Stu called out, "Hey, I think I know that guy from somewhere."

"Wait up. I got one more thing." She placed the phone in her shirt pocket. Brightened that a fresh "wake-ee," who didn't RSVP, showed up to protest, Maria said, "Welcome. How'd you hear of this protest?"

Fredric moved closer to put his hand on the small of her back. "Follow you on social media. Yo, I made a ton of signs. Help me unload them?"

Maria didn't need them so much as more bodies to carry them, but still had to be cheery. "Sure." She called back to the handful of lethargic protesters, like a mom trying to sell second-helpings of beets, "We got more signs!" They each held their respective placards, and a few had two. So nobody moved. She should have addressed a couple of individuals by name. Instead, she was the victim of the Bystander Effect. "Fine. It's me and 'DreadenStein' here." With faint enthusiasm, she said to Fredric, "Let's go, comrade."

They marched to the rear of the van. He opened it for her. Two kidnappers in masks burst out and grabbed Maria as Fredric pushed her in and closed the door.

She tried to gauge their eyes and kick their nuts, but they were too strong and fiendishly well-trained kidnappers. She struggled, squirmed, and shouted for help.

Fredric ordered, "Tape her mouth. You get her wrists." He went through Maria's bag and saw her Molotov cocktail kit, gasoline in a screw-top wine bottle, two smaller, empty glass bottles, rags, and a double-baggie of lighters.

Stu heard this and rerouted his ride. "Oh shit! Hold on, Maria. I'm a minute away."

Maria screamed out in all directions, "Stu! Vicki! Police! Help me-" They muffled her terrified yelps as Fredric tossed her phone out the window.

She tongued and spit on the tape, creating an opening. She kicked and wriggled her way up to kneeling, if only to show she was not going down without a fight.

Stu's rideshare vehicle stopped at the protest, extra cautious around the unexpected gathering of people in the street. He saw the van doors close on the abducted Maria. The kidnappers peeled away. Stu got out to weave through them like an Olympic slalom. He chased the van for the five yards he had with a microscopic chance of catching up. Though he had no idea what he could've accomplished if he did.

Stu panicked and scanned around for clues. "No, no, no, no, no!"

RING! It was an incoming video call from "Grandma." Stu answered it without thinking. On-screen, it was actually Pyotr. "I spoofed your grandma because I knew you'd take her call."

"What do you want, Pyotr?" Stu couldn't give him any satisfaction or information.

"You have access to the device, yes? I mean for you to give it to me."

Stu jumped to a natural conclusion. "Kidnapping Maria is way over the line, Pyotr. Stop before this gets crazy fucked up."

Pyotr said, "Get me the device, and I will help you save Maria."

"Don't play dumb. Here's my revCheck code proving I'm not recording." Stu clicked send, and he heard the Ding(!) on Pyotr's end. Stu was slightly less terrified because he thought he could negotiate with Pyotr as the kidnapper. "Now cut the shit. Where is she?"

"Deliver the device to the Russian Embassy tonight, and I guarantee we'll get your Maria back."

In the middle of this, a blocked number called in, but Stu rejected it to stay on with Pyotr. Now was not the perfect time to respond to a quick survey from his cable provider. Stu tried a threat. "If she doesn't get VIP treatment, you will see your regret in every mirror."

Pyotr tried his best to exploit this situation. "Get your ex-girlfriend to deliver us the device, and you will have no problems."

The line cut out because Pyotr had hung up. Vicki came up to Stu on her motorized scooter and, with a blissfully ignorant, unpinched voice, asked, "Where's Maria?"

"They took her."

Vicki looked shook. "Who's 'they?'"

"Russians who want Roxy's invention and will kill Maria if they don't get it tonight."

Reeling from Stu's cold stoicism, Vicki said, "So what're you doing here? Get it, fool! What, you waitin' for, a starter pistol?" With a paranoid panic, she sped off without him. He took a moment to strategize but saw no driverless rideshares nearby. He sprinted to the closest rentable, hourly Zipcar, a block away.

Stu pondered whether he was going to risk everything for Maria. He yelled and punched the dashboard. Talking to himself, he strategized and rationalized as fast as he could. "Chuck could have done anything at this point, so going to the cops was worthless. Maybe the risk of stealing the device without the whole plan in place isn't so bad. Roxy's gotta help." He took three short breaths and made a call. "Roxy? Five days is today. Scary shit is happening, and if you've ever trusted me before, I need you to trust me now. It's scary 'life or death' time."

Roxy started talking ultra-conspicuously as if the call was bugged. "I don't know what you're talking about. Say, come into work. I want to review a possible solution to the quantum position problem to cache memory maximization."

Stu caught this bugging-savvy style of talking, and his hopes skyrocketed. "Right. Sure thing, boss."

Stu's eyes whipped to the road, noticing the SUV in front had stopped short. Through the shrill honks, Stu's autonomous vehicle did the rescuing with an emergency hard brake, avoiding a crash. Stu blared out the window. "What the hell? You're honking?

I should be honking." He returned to the call with Roxy. "I gotta go. See you soon."

Stu hung up and was startled by the appearance of Connor, a menacing henchman, standing at his window holding a scuffed Beretta M9 with a suppresser and a burner phone. Connor pointed to the window controls and growled, "Open up."

Wishing the window was bulletproof while knowing it wasn't, Stu drew it down a crack to take that phone. He scrolled it back up as a henchman returned to stand by his SUV and wave away traffic. The phone rang.

"Hello? Who is this?"

A digitally warped voice on the phone said, "Expiring video coming." The screen showed Maria tied up and struggling. Stu scrambled for his phone to take a photo of it before it self-deleted.

Behind Stu, an impatient jerk overrode his driverless car to honk at Stu and Joel.

Stu said, "Pyotr, don't do anything stupid."

The warped voice said, "Good advice, but this isn't Pyotr. It's your true employer moving up the deadline to right fucking now, or someone will die."

Deducing it must've been Chuck, this was so much worse. Stu said, "Let's be cool, sir. See, I'm not using your name, and I recognize the gravity of the situation. We should give each other what we want. No sane human being, let alone a titan of business, wants to kill anyone."

The impatient jerk behind the vehicles kept honking. Connor listened to his earpiece, walked over to the jerk, and got him to lower his window. The jerk backed off only a few inches, foolishly relying on social norms to protect himself. Connor drew his handgun from his shoulder holster and slowly drove the barrel tip into the base of the jerk's neck. He aimed down so as to hit all the torso organs. The jerk froze, but his eyes screamed enough for the whole body. Connor unbuckled the seat belt and manhandled him out the door. CRACK! With the pistol grip, Connor smashed him toothless. In a precise combo –SNAP, CRUNCH, THUD! – Connor broke the driver's clavicle, occipital bone, and, mercifully, his temple to knock him out.

Just because the guy independently happened to have written one mean tweet about Beyoncé 15 years ago when he was in middle school didn't mean he deserved such a thrashing. Though it could've been Karma.

Connor stepped away to reveal his bloody handiwork as a statement to Stu.

Stu was now convinced he had zero leverage. "That message was unnecessary. I promise I understand. Treat her well, please."

Stu heard a series of tones and then the smile of the warped voice. "This phone's gonna blow up in 30 seconds. And smile — I'm still gonna pay your bonus when you deliver."

Stu deadpanned in a slow and somber voice, "Oh boy. That's swell. Thanks." Stu tossed the burner phone, and it popped like a small firecracker.

Miles away, Vicki's blindly wandering scooter wasn't enough to find Maria. A video call came in; it was Stu, in the low resolution of spotty reception.

"Thank you for taking my call, sist... comrade. I know you care about Maria, and we can save her if we get the leverage at Zer-Quali. First, I need you to bring your biggest EMP."

Vicki said, "Wilco," and doubled back to her shop, minutes away. She dropped the scooter and headed to the back room, where an EMP the size of a microwave oven sat on the table. Loading it onto a dolly gave her a 20-yard stare and a renewed sense of purpose. After getting into a self-driving minivan, Vicki took the wheel.

Chapter 14
"Look Up Duress"

Not far away, Stu's vehicle passed a large white truck standing across from the ZerQuali parking lot. Stu swiped his ID badge to enter the gates.

Inside the truck, the StrangleBear team coiled, poised to strike. Pyotr's tablet had a low-resolution video call with Stu. Why was there such spotty reception today? Stu's audio was concert-clear, "No deal, Pyotr. I know you don't have Maria. Stay out of this. You'll never get the device."

Pyotr hung up and addressed his troops. "Okay, this is plan. We need to do more to save my brother. Time to strike. We're going brute force. Multiple incursions. Overwhelm their security."

Olesya cautioned them. "Most of you surely to be caught. Probable worst-case scenario is maybe eight years in American prison."

They all laughed.

Yevgeny specified. "All will get proper compensation when we're released."

All enthusiastically nodded in agreement with these terms.

Pyotr commanded the team, "Okay, "Da-vi, Da-vi, Da-vi."

All the StrangleBear thugs except Yevgeny poured out of the truck and raced to the perimeter. Their watches beeped, and they scrambled over the wall and sprinted for the main building.

Vicki, now in a blonde wig, drove up in her minivan. She touched her fingertips and bit her teeth to gauge her own relative sobriety. As mild lament, she said, "Shoulda hit the Sativa instead of the Indica."

She guzzled a giant mug of coffee and saw the StrangleBear team beginning to breach the ZerQuali walls. "Well, seems everybody got a plate to this cookout." Vicki pinched the bridge of her nose to focus, then tapped her hand on the big EMP on the passenger seat. She looked at the main power cables leading to the building.

Inside the ZerQuali office lobby, Roxy waited to greet Stu. She wiped perspiration from her brow with her sleeve, leaving it damper than she expected. Her watch ticked slowly. Rapidly spanking her outer thigh wasn't calming her.

Stu jogged inside. She admonished him as he'd expected her to do. "Why now? This is reckless. To do this right requires a meticulous scheme with tremendous resources and several contingencies."

Stu tried downloading the relevant info to her as succinctly as he could to ensure that she helped. "Chuck must be dying so fast he can't wait. So, he kidnapped Maria." He showed Roxy the blurry photo of the burner phone's video of her tied up.

Roxy's breathing stuttered as if she had jumped in an icy ocean. Unprepared for this threat level, she said. "That's terrible. This is out of control." She slapped her cheeks to get in the game. "Is your plan even ready?"

"No time to do the face-swapping or any of my countermeasures. So, I've just got to straight-up jack this and take the consequences." Stu's eyes wandered to worst-case scenarios. He centered himself at once out of the necessity of the moment. "Chuck will happily hurt her if I don't, and maybe even..."

Roxy's voice strained, finishing his sentence. "Kill her? What? No. What would he gain from that?"

"Nothing, but he's on the verge of death. He'd easily torture her to motivate me, and if I fail, he might kill her out of spite. Plus, his henchmen are pure sadists."

"That can't be. No, not happening. Right?" Roxy couldn't get past the denial stage this fast. She chewed a fingernail, tearing it too deep and into a hangnail.

Stu was coaching himself as much as informing Roxy, "He's a danger, but I don't think he's a murderer. As long as he gets what he wants, we'll be fine. I think. We can't fail, though."

She had to help him, but there were limits. "I get it, and I'm not standing in the way, but I can't be involved like this." Roxy collected paper on the table and ran off to the exit.

Stu was devastated at losing what he prayed would've been a crucial ally. *Do I have to find an emergency ax and firefighter my way through security? Maybe if I went back and begged Roxy?* He hastily scoured the room and saw Roxy waiting there at the edge of the exit door, peering back at hi*m. Did she want me to follow her? What was she looking at?*

Stu turned to review the other items on the table. He identified her security beacon, which she blatantly left for him. Roxy kept her eyes focused on it to ensure he got it. Stu smiled, glanced up, and caught her approving nod. She ducked away. He scooped it up and proceeded through the security checkpoints. Pitched a bit too high, he said, "Hi, fellas."

They gave a perfunctory wave back. Stu was unaware he was recklessly mouthing a pep-talk to himself. "I got a chance. But I'd be on the lam forever, even if I'm lucky enough to get away with stealing it."

Stu arrived at another locked door with a couple of Robo-Krupkes standing as sentries. He locked eyes with their cameras and swiped Roxy's security dongle through. Her face appeared on the door screen — had anyone been observing.

Four muscled security guards walked by. One of whom, Renee, preferred he/him pronouns but historically feminine, glam rock makeup (known in 20NF as "Bowie Chic"). He wore new, two-inch heel boots he hadn't yet mastered. Stu stepped in front of the screen as if he was courteously letting them pass. "Looking strong, gentle... humans." But his awkward flattery did not mollify them. Three had roid energy that made them itching for a fight.

Outside the building, inside the security fence, one StrangleBear thug tripped a private alarm, and external floodlights illuminated his quadrant of the grounds. All ZerQuali guards' phones sounded alerts, flashed lights, and buzzed to ensure their attention.

Through the halls, alarms sounded, and subtle yellow warning lights flashed. Stu was stunned. "What?!?! I didn't trip anything."

Stu got a video call, and it was Digi-STU! Stu's digital persona, scanned by Roxy when he came on board, was identically conscious and capable of acting autonomously.

Digi-Stu was ecstatic to meet the real Stu. "Hey, real me!"

Stu, however, was confused and not ready for this. "Um, hey. If you're a hacker, congrats, you got me. But I'm kinda busy right now."

Of course, Digi-Stu knew the most effective words Stu needed to hear in these circumstances: "I'm your ZerQuali scan, and right now you're thinking of the original *Total Recall* movie... "

"Yeah, with Ronny Cox and Arnold. Now, what am I thinking of?"

"You put a tiny pinch of cinnamon and some brown sugar in the batter for your French toast recipe. And now you're thinking of Professor Gelernter's arguments against AGI."

Stu lifted his eyebrows and snapped his fingers. "Okay, I'm tentatively convinced. What are we doing now?"

"We're good. Those StrangleBear punks tripped the alarm, and now they're conveniently distracting the guards."

It dawned on Stu that his digital doppelgänger had become his able accomplice. Further, Digi-Stu had been shrewdly ensnaring the StrangleBear team to be the decoys and patsies. Stu was playfully grateful. "Such sweet thugs. What a thoughtful gift. Thanks, uh, what do I call you? Digital Me! I guess."

Digi-Stu was the ultimate partner and coach. It's like when you advise yourself in the mirror and try to psych yourself up, but typically need an external force to energize you. Ideally, one on a matching frequency. Digi-Stu was it, "Good luck. Get going!"

Stu validated and appreciated the coaching but wasn't sure how to navigate the communication. "Right. Thanks... Digi-Me."

With security running outside to capture the Russian invaders, Stu had an open field to the end zone.

ZerQuali security guards tackled assorted StrangleBear operatives. Only Pyotr and Olesya got into the building.

ZerQuali Security Chief Brumfield encountered and stopped Stu. "Mr. Reigns, quick heads-up, we're upgrading from tier one to Tier 2 security alert."

Stu wasn't sure of Brumfield's intentions. "What does that mean?"

Brumfield volunteered information as if Stu were only a high-level employee, not a thief. "You can keep working, but we're switching to local power and heightened protocols." Brumfield barked into his walkie-talkie, "Go for Tier 2. I'm on my way to HQ."

Lights switched to orange, and the alert sound changed. Brumfield ran to HQ.

Vicki watched this ground assault from her vehicle and psyched herself up. "This is chaos, but that might be a good thing, and Maria needs someone to come through." She opened her glove box and like a 1950s TV show narrator introducing a superhero said, "This is a job for 'Generic White Guy' – impervious to consequences!" Vicki put on a Hollywood-level authentic Caucasian guy mask. She donned a loose, red ski mask over that while positioning a fake blonde ponytail to poke out a couple of inches in a slapdash manner.

An elevator never seemed slower than this one as Stu went up to the Maximum Security Lab, which housed the device. He got to the imposing door. His hand trembled with Roxy's security beacon. "Thank you, Roxy."

He tried to activate the security beacon. BUZZ. The system rejected this attempt. The security screen read: Tier 2 Protocols Engaged. All Access Restricted.

"No, no, no, no, no. C'mon, babe." Stu tried again. BUZZ. The system rejected this second attempt. The security screen again read: Tier 2 Protocols Engaged. All Access Restricted.

Stu was furious and frustrated. "Dammmmittt! You've got to be kidding me. That is the worst bad beat ever. If I'd gotten here five minutes earlier." Stu then noticed he had cried out while centerframe of a security camera. Crap!

At the ZerQuali Security HQ Command Center, Brumfield saw Stu on the monitors. He took his time. "What are you doing there, Stu? Pretty sure you're not authorized for that." His coy ballbusting emitted from the speaker by Stu.

Stu shouted back to the camera, "Is that you, Brumfield?"

"Yup. Sure looks like you're up to something shady." Brumfield was enjoying this.

"So stop looking. Please trust me." Stu made a praying hands gesture.

"No can do, amigo. Everything's on camera. Gotta follow the rules." Brumfield switched to his walkie-talkie. "Bravo and Echo teams converge on the MSL."

Security guards jogged to Stu's location. Brumfield tried persuading him, "My team is coming. They're gonna be there in under two minutes. Give up, already. You're busted."

Stu exalted out loud. "No atheists in a crime scene. God? I could use a miracle here."

The flashing lights and sirens cycled through for a few moments as Stu recognized how trapped he was and how much he had failed Maria. This can-do "man of action" severely overestimated his abilities, and lives were threatened for it. For a guy who never considered himself spiritual, let alone religious, he surrendered his soul to God as he understood Him, completely unsure if it meant anything. He was nevertheless sincere. All he knew was — he couldn't give up. "Ahh," he said, squinting *of course*. He found Vicki's number in his contacts and texted her.

"Clunk-junnng." Everyone heard the sound of a BLACKOUT! All the electricity in the building ceased, sirens silenced — it was a Luddite's dream.

Outside the ZerQuali fence, Vicki held her still-smoking EMP machine, freshly used and pointing at the local shed generator. She psyched herself up. "Now's my chance. Am I doing this?" Vicki gracefully and athletically yoga-parkoured her way over the wall.

Back at the HQ Security Center, Brumfield was stunned at the blackout, and his team scrambled. A guard had leaned his chair back to a precarious precipice, and this circumstantial blindness challenged his balance. "What happened?"

Brumfield said, "Electricity's out. Must have fried the primary relay, so now we have to reboot with the backup generator." He used a key to unlock a secure panel. He activated the cascading transistors. Varying tones rang out with re-initiating protocols. A monitor showed the switch from the central grid power cables to the local batteries.

Stu watched as the main electricity came back up, and the assorted systems rebooted to come back online — green lights, tier-one.

"Hallelujah. I'm a believer." Stu used Roxy's security dongle to open the door. DING. The system accepted this attempt. The security screen read: "Access Granted."

Upon seeing a giant safe in the middle of the room, Stu was pissed, "C'mon!!! What the hell is this?"

There was an alphanumeric entry pad. Stu brainstormed passwords Roxy could've granted that he'd know. It could be a dozen personal references or inside jokes. Stu resigned to go through all of them. He typed in: N-I-C-K-E-L-B-A-C-K.

DING! "Access Granted."

Stu couldn't help but chuckle. "We get each other, Roxy."

He opened the safe, and there it was, the vital element of the invention that could be bartered for Maria's life. He grabbed it like a rugby ball and made his escape.

Echo team turned into this hallway and saw Stu with the device. Damn! That was Stu's intended exit route. Stu ran the opposite way to the staircase.

Brumfield and his team's shoulders relaxed when all the cameras got back up, and they had eyes on everything. Brumfield gave more orders via his walkie. "Stu is right there on four, heading down the south stairwell. Bravo team — head up to bag him. He's got nowhere to go."

Bravo team sprinted up the stairs and saw Stu trying to make his way down. Upon seeing them, Stu went the only direction he could: up. Taking the stairs, three at a time, he was wheezing almost immediately but climbing for his freedom and Maria's life. Stu got to the top floor and used Roxy's security dongle to reach her office. He locked the doors behind him.

Brumfield's surveillance lieutenant pointed his attention to the bank of monitors showing the other cameras' perspectives. A "stealthy white guy" in a ski mask (Vicki in her double-disguise) appeared on one screen, and Pyotr showed up on another. Brumfield relayed more info. "We got his accomplices on three, West section. Delta team, go take 'em down."

In one hallway, Vicki clearly didn't know where she was going, and right at the intersection with another hallway, she bumped into Pyotr and Olesya. Vicki stepped lightly and plastered on nonchalance, "Hey, my bad, my Gs."

Olesya peered past the ski mask and white guy mask below. "Who are you?"

Vicki found herself effecting a 1950s mid-Atlantic accent. "Nobody. See. Nothing to see here."

Pyotr recognized the need to stay on task. "Us, too. Neither."

Their postures unstiffened, relieved they passed by each other without incident.

Pyotr and Olesya unknowingly headed right into the six security guards who were pursuing Vicki. Starting with "it's just a day job"-level motivation, one said, "You're trespassing. You're going to have to come with us."

It was six on two, but a pretty fair match-up. This was going to be a mad brawl of proper UFC-style MMA combined with a generous helping of merciless Krav Maga and plain old "fighting dirty."

Three security guards approached Pyotr, who was closest. He spewed a flurry of jabs, fattening lips and knocking the wind out of guts.

Olesya slipped the fourth guard and hip-tossed the fifth, Renee. Melees have a way of spiking adrenaline, turning a boring job into an "adventure,"

The last guard bear-hugged Olesya from behind. With her heel, she stomped his right foot and whipped her head back to break his nose, freeing herself. He stumbled backward and stared at his hands, now splattered with his own blood. "Screw this! I'll go be a Subtiree," he said while speed-walking away.

Those first three guards glommed on to Pyotr as if they were the offensive line, and he was "3rd and goal," He eye-gouged, broke fingers, and bit faces because fighting "fair" was already a ridiculous concept for him, and now he was outnumbered. This swarm finally sacked Pyotr face-first into the ground. One scurried for handcuffs.

Renee and another guard crept closer to Olesya. They gave each other the signal to pounce at the same time, not foolishly one at a time like in a cheesy 80s Bond film. Olesya juked and pivoted around the guy so they were both in her field of vision. She threw a fireworks finale of elbows and knees, knocking him out. Maybe that savvy henchman strategy wouldn't matter today.

Renee grabbed Olesya's arm in a green belt attempt at a Jiu-Jitsu lock. Olesya shot her hand down, clearing his fingers, then scrambled behind Renee for a textbook suplex. It would've earned five points in a Greco-Roman match. But off the mat, the legal move doesn't do much damage. From being splayed out, Renee twisted and shimmied into guard position. Olesya got so focused on deploying a "ground and pound," she didn't see one of the three guards who were previously on Pyotr had put her in an unskilled but effective rear naked choke. She blacked out in seconds.

The security guards weren't as badass, but their numbers overwhelmed the Russians — who ended up shackled.

On the floor below, a couple of Security Guards from Foxtrot team wandered and talked shop blithely. "You think Stu Reigns stole the device for someone else?"

The other said, "That's way above our pay grade."

They clomped by a tall red biohazard bag with a card that read "Tuesday Pickup for Authorized Personnel Only." One guard gestured to warn the other not to get too close, busting chops, "Watch out for that bundle of poison or diseased body parts or whatever. You spill it, and they'll make you mop it up."

The other said, "If I was gonna deal with this kinda mess, I'd be a Crime Scene Cleaner. Those dudes make bank. Our wages are not worth showing up."

"I only do this because my little brother has a chance to work on Wall Street, and they won't hire anyone with Subtirees in their immediate family."

As soon as they were gone, the biohazard bag inflated from Vicki's breathing. It was her clever camouflage — she was motionless like her yoga poses. She got a text from Stu, relieved it was set to silent. It read, *"I got it. Now get out of there."*

Brumfield was engrossed in the screens showing Stu in Roxy's office. Brumfield's lieutenant trained his eyes on the screen where the Russians got apprehended. On another screen none noticed at the time, the biohazard bag opened, and Vicki left. A newly hired guard finally caught it and tentatively tried to get Brumfield's attention regarding "White Guy" Vicki's escape. Brumfield brushed him off and engaged the public address system, controlling all the security speakers in that area of the building. "Mr. Reigns. We know you took the device. You're busted. So open the door and return it to me, and I bet Roxy won't even press charges."

Stu indeed had the device in Roxy's office. He shouted out to security. "I can't do that, brother."

Brumfield calmly assured Stu. "You don't need to shout. We have 413 microphones in this building."

Stu barely muttered. "That's frickin' great."

Brumfield gloated. "It is pretty great."

"Doesn't matter. I'll go to prison later and for a long time, but this device is coming with me tonight," Stu said and noticed the "SkySaver" emergency escape system by the window. That flicker of hope allowed him to take a gulp of air. He mustered the resolve to do something unfathomably remarkable for his generation… he read the instructions.

With a knowing tone, Brumfield said, "I know you have the device. And WE CAN GET IT TO THE RIGHT PERSON. Hope you're hearing me right."

But Stu was so preoccupied with finding a way out, he didn't catch the hint. Though he wouldn't have trusted Brumfield, anyway. "No offense, guys. But there's so much more going on than I can explain right now. Look up the word 'duress.' And cut me some slack."

The only thing that would've ruined Brumfield's fun would have been if Stu had gotten away with the device, embarrassing him to his superiors. Brumfield couldn't let that happen, and so walkied more orders. "Breach the door. He's escaping!"

Two small security guards took turns trying to kick Roxy's door down. The repeated slamming and crunching sounds showed their progress.

Stu worried how fast they'd break through. He pulled the lever of the Skysaver escape unit, and the window popped out and swung out like a door. A rush of wind blew in. In the background, an FDD flew from the top floor of the building across the street. Stu gazed down. His fear of heights set in quick. "That's a whole bucket of NOPE!" He scrambled, surveying around for another escape.

The security officers' door-kicks made enough space open to be reminiscent of *The Shining*'s "Here's Johnny" moment. Stu was unavoidably set to get caught if he didn't escape right-the-hell-now. Shit! Shit! Shiiiiitttt!!! He was drunk on adrenaline and stress and more cardio than he had had in months. He blinked hard and called out to Brumfield in an exhilarated, near mad-minded state. "You changed my mind. Toodles!"

Stu grabbed the harness and hit the final "DEPLOY" button.

But nothing happened!

He hit it again. Nothing.

Only then did Stu notice the unit's unfinished wiring and installation tools nearby. Not something he could insta-hack. "Dammit! My kingdom for a helicopter!"

Stu got a video call from Digi-Stu. "I got you covered, real me. Around ten seconds out."

The security officers continued to make progress getting through the door. The FDD soon flew up to the exposed window port and rolled up its door to reveal its trays of available pizzas. Stu cleared them out until the last box flopped open, revealing what looked like scrumptious slices. Stu was a bit loopy. "Ooh, pepperoni... and what is that — pineapple?" Stu grimaced and half-shivered, as did Digi-Stu at the thought of pineapple on a pizza; even though there were no digital taste buds, the sense memory was particularly potent.

Security was almost able to get in. Stu turned with the device and leaped into the Food Delivery Drone's container. It beeped and flashed its red "overload" light as it struggled to maintain lift. It pulled away to the road just over the security wall. Stu found a cheek-cramping smile on his face. "Whooooo hooooo!!!!! I eat this up with two great big spoons!"

On Stu's smartphone, Digi-Stu celebrated, too. "We did it!"

Stu confirmed with his digital twin. "You got the Russians here, too, as unwitting accomplices to run interference — Right? Thanks."

Digi-Stu humansplained to Stu. "They were already planning it. I helped move up the timing. Couldn't have done it without... your mind. You should thank yourself."

Stu got defensive with Digi-Stu. "That's what I'm doing." There was an awkward moment between them as the FDD continued on against a harsh wind. Stu said, "Thought we'd get along better."

Digi-Stu matter-of-factly clarified, "Well, you do kinda hate yourself."

Brumfield was camouflaging his more lucrative spying assignments by doing his day job with thoughtful diligence. "Mobile

Charlie squad, it's up to you. The thief is now beyond the grounds — harbor side."

The FDD rattled and sputtered. The whirring motor pitched up, and Stu could smell the impending destruction. He could only pray that he'd be over water when it crashed.

Brumfield shouted, "Be advised the FDD that Stu is in is faltering, so be careful of falling debris. I'm calling for an ambulance." But he didn't. Instead, Brumfield texted Chuck, *"If Stu can't, do I get a bonus if I bring it in?"*

Chapter 15
"There Went Plausible Deniability"

Five hundred yards beyond the ZerQuali fence, nearing the San Diego Yacht Club, the overloaded FDD lost altitude at elevator speeds. Stu was the Heisman trophy, clutching the item and bracing for impact.

Digi-Stu told Stu, "Sixteen seconds to impact. Your best chance is that pile of life jackets. Jump in 3...2...1. GO!"

Stu hurled himself off and, remembering the class from his one and only time skydiving, tucked an emergency PLF ("Parachute Landing Fall") with six-point absorption: feet-calf-thigh-hip-back roll and landing legs in an "L." It hurt like a rugby tackle — survivable but leaving bruises.

With its now more manageable payload, the FDD gracefully touched down. Its onboard monitor noted, "Damage fee $20,000 billed to the credit card on file."

In the distance, Stu saw Charlie closing in, gunning their golf carts toward him. Stu ran down the pier to escape by sea.

Vicki was now back at her vehicle and watching through her binoculars.

Stu was hoping more than believing one vessel must have been ready to cast off. He darted around, checking every boat to bum a ride.

Digi-Stu volunteered a solution, "Mooring seven. There's a recently fueled speed yacht. It's a 'Tecnomar by Lamborghini 63' which has 2000 horsepower and..."

"...and a top speed of 63 knots. Yeah, you know I know." Stu soon arrived and saw the motors running, a platter of half-eaten, seared foie gras on brioche toast points, and a near-empty bottle of Romanee-Conti. *Ah, the wonderful life.*

Stu jumped in, set the device in the corner, and started the boat out of the harbor. Bwwrraaahhhhhhhhh! He was gunning it like Dale Earnhardt Jr. robbing a bank. It rocketed away. Stu streamed the only fitting music for this occasion, a Nickelback chart-topper, "Rockstar"! Stu was elated with victory and the serendipity of getting to drive a boat as sweet as this. "Whoooooohooooo!!! This is exactly like I imagined. Whooohoooo!"

He sped off as the ZerQuali offices receded behind him.

But Stu's endorphin rush was muted, much lower than he expected. He was losing interest. "Whooo. Woo. This is fun. Yeah, I get it. Gets kinda boring fast, though. Maybe if I hit the waves crossways."

Stu maneuvered the craft out of defined wakes and into a path perpendicular to the waves. The boat jumped and crashed in raucous gymnastics. "Yeah, yeah, yeah. You like that, ocean? Oh, you think you're some rough seas, then? All right. However you like it, I can do it. You want me to crash and slam into you over and over, huh? Okay, yeah. Yeah. We're in a rhythm now. Feel it. You're so wet. I love it!"

From below deck, a female voice shouted back. "You're so good!"

Stu flinched, spun 180, and was lucky to see no threat behind him. He concluded it must've been a wealthy playboy and an Instagram model making love below deck. They sang out in simultaneous ecstasy.

Stu reassuringly called down below. "Just taking it for a little spin. Maybe stream it live to a couple of friends. Don't worry. I'm getting off at a harbor north of here."

Stu held out his phone and did a live feed video. The view count skyrocketed faster and faster.

Ten miles away, Vicki checked an alert on her mobile so she could watch, too.

Stu gave a heads-up. "Hey, fans. Reminder: I need you. Anybody in the immediate vicinity of the Oceanside Yacht Club north of Carlsbad, please race over in a black hoodie like I'm wearing. I need fifty people there right freakin' ASAP! Be there in... looks like eight minutes."

A half-dozen fans (far short of 50) made up of Vicki's customers, Grand Turing attendees, bikers, etc., all converged on the marina like a pitiful flash mob.

Clarence watched Stu's video plea on his tablet and got up to watch from his window. The port was within sight. Clarence tread with purpose, arcing toward his door but swerved to his fridge, grabbing some leftover Thai food. He slumped back on his sofa. What a dick.

Vicki raced down the highway to assist Stu.

Brumfield reviewed live stream traffic-cam video of the surrounding area and logged in to an ultra-high level live satellite control. The toll spun up the price quickly, at $100 per second. He relayed the status on his cell phone. "Pretty sure he's got the device. No idea how many fans. We'll catch him. We've got satellite live-tracking."

At the harbor, his be-hoodied, hardcore fans cheered Stu as his speedboat docked. Trin got the crowd chanting, "Stu! Stu! Stu! Stu!" and they swarmed at him.

Stu deboarded with the device, "Thanks, guys. Huddle over me while I change this. Okay, on 3, we scramble and disperse while skipping to throw off the 'gait-matching,' You, the tall one, get in the boat and take off. Ready... one, two, three, go!"

They did, and from a zoomed-in satellite view, they appeared to scatter like roaches. Upon closer inspection, most were skipping.

The satellite POV applied gait-matching algorithms attempting to identify Stu. The skipping caused repeated error messages: *"No Match."*

One tall, gangly fisherman, wearing full yellow rain gear and carrying a big fishing cooler, tottered around, making it hard to advance, let alone skip. He shook his head at the be-hoodied fans. Assorted fans got in their cars and drove off. The gangly fisherman sprinted like a marionette while ordering an e-taxi. He stumbled to the ground, exposing it was Stu, wearing the playmate's high heels to further frustrate the gait-matching tech. No longer helpful, he clumsily kicked them off so he could run faster with the device in the cooler.

Stu saw an incoming text: *"Urgent 911,"* then dots, then *"You on your way to her with *it*?"* Before he could answer, an incoming call ID read "VICKI." Stu asked, "What do you think you're doing?"

Vicki talked in a conspicuous, stilted tone. "Maria urgently needs the 'book' you borrowed from the library."

Stu got her transparent code and said, "I'm going to return it right now so I can get my deposit back."

"I'll pick you up. You're at Oceanside, right? Don't tell me you ordered an Uber."

"Well, I uh. Where are you?"

"Close. I'll be there in two minutes."

A stunning black Maybach drove up.

Stu had never seen one up close before. "Is that you in the Maybach?"

There was an urgent concern in Vicki's voice. "No. It isn't! Shit. Run!"

Stu sounded relieved. "I think I'm okay."

Roxy emerged from the luxury car with immediate, Corleone-style orders. "Take the device. Leave the phone."

"Just a second," Stu said. He stuffed his phone into the saddlebag of a parked motorcycle and got in Roxy's car.

Soon after, a biker got on his Harley, stared them down, and coincidentally, was heading in the same direction.

On a remote tracking monitor, they were in tandem.

Stu couldn't believe Roxy was coming to his rescue. "You're in deep now. There went plausible deniability once the cops show up."

Roxy communicated understandable priorities. "None of this is worth anybody dying. So, I'm all-in. We gotta save Maria. Where's the meet-up location?"

At the red light, while Stu gave directions, the biker eyeballed Roxy, and she smiled nervously. Was he following them or into her? Her mouth went dry. But when the light turned green, they diverged.

"You got everything?" Roxy asked.

Stu patted the device. "Only thing I need."

Roxy looked at her tablet and identified who was pursuing them, "My God-dammed security is on our tail."

"Well, call 'em off, boss."

"You've resigned to getting caught. Not me. I do want to help save Maria's life, but not at the cost of my freedom and future."

"Shit. I get it," Stu said.

Roxy zoomed through the streets, slaloming around cars, picking up an extra second of lead each time. The ZerQuali security cars were brand-new Dodge Chargers. Plenty of muscle to match the Maybach.

"Got any ideas on how to get rid of them?"

Digi-Stu appeared on the vehicle's dash screen. "I've got a suggestion."

"Hey, brother," Stu smiled, "do what you can, man."

Seconds later, they arrived at a rare swarm of cars converging on an intersection. All stop lights were on the fritz, flashing red. For the few who remembered their driver's license written test, all it meant was to treat it like a stop sign. Stop at the corner, cede the right of way, and wait your turn to roll through. But this was a city in 20NF; it didn't take that many assholes and schmucks to cause chaos the AI driverless cars couldn't navigate.

Stu swung his eyes across the sky and said, "Of course, that's frickin' perfect. Bad beats every single-frickin'-fuckin'-filth-flarn-filth-fucking place. Dammit!"

Digi-Stu winked.

Again, alarm klaxoned in unison from smartphones and streetlight speakers. "Attention! This is a test of the Pandemic Alert System. Everyone should immediately activate Class One protocols. Repeat... "

"That you?" Stu asked Digi-Stu.

Digi-Stu smiled with pride.

"Nicely played."

The other cars followed those orders and pulled over, creating a Moses-like parting of the road-sea.

Roxy sped through, and it zippered closed behind her when the pandemic alarm was turned off prematurely.

Digi-Stu called Clarence, "Clarence! This is scary serious. Maria has been kidnapped. I've tried calling the police, but I guess either they don't believe me, or it's not a priority for them, so they're useless here."

"Then why should I? Maybe you are pranking me. I don't want anyone swatted." Clarence said.

"I'm serious, man! Life and death shit here. Can you cut the knee-jerk skepticism for one minute, please!"

"Maybe you're a deepfake or AI and not the real Stu." Clarence posited.

Knowing this was true, Digi-Stu had to pivot, "Fair enough. How's about you turn off your revCheck and record this call? I'll Venmo you ten thousand dollars from my account as a way to verify me. It'll be a second-factor authentication. Plus, what pranker would pay your ten grand?"

Clarence crossed his arms and tucked his chin. "What exactly do you want me to do?

"Call your buddies at the Sheriff's department and ASAP get them over to this address I texted you. Warn them about the kidnapper's bodyguards being armed. We need you to step up in a big way here, brother. You can change things. Make a real difference. I believe in you."

"Who's the kidnapper?"

"Chuck Rosti. He kidnapped Maria to get me to steal Roxy's invention."

Clarence popped his palms up and said, "Okay, that's bullshit. I'm hanging up."

Digi-Stu called right back, but Clarence rejected it and designated the number as a spammer. Stu and Roxy had to go in with no cavalry.

Chapter 16
"If He Can Betray Me, He Can Betray You."

Roxy and Stu arrived at an abandoned warehouse in a remote industrial park.

Inside the main floor, the size of an airplane hangar, a medical tent quarantined a section. Hira approached Chuck, who was pacing like a meth-addicted panther. She said, "Can I get my phone back now? I should check in with Zephyr to see how the jury deliberations are doing."

"No phones here!" Chuck shouted and gestured to a pile of smashed phones on the polished concrete floor. A henchman tossed the sledgehammer he used and caught the handle's bottom on top of his fist, balancing it like he aspired to be a busker. But street performing isn't a career, and henchman-ing has better dental, plus you get to punch people.

She said, "We could have stored them in a Faraday cage in the limo."

Chuck yelled at her, "For fuck's sakes, Hira! I'm on the verge of death here! And if I live, they're putting me in prison. I got no outs!!! I swear, if Stu doesn't come through for me... ten million dollars to whoever kills him, slowly, and... posts the video online so his family can watch." Chuck's coughed softer now, or perhaps his body was getting too weak to clear his lungs.

Hira's gruff smile was dominated by her terrified eyes. Her involuntary gulp was wet, misophonic, and loud to her own ears.

She drew breath to help dry her mouth. "I cannot imagine the torment you are going through, Mr. Rosti. But if we can be literal for a moment, would you stipulate you're only ranting about murdering Stu? Right? Of course, grabbing Maria was a goof or must be a bluff. Okay? No harm, no foul."

Chuck paused as if waiting for a spinning coin to stop. The henchmen's persistent bloodlust thrilled higher in anticipation. Fredric double-checked his Desert Eagle to ensure it held a full mag of .50 caliber rounds. Locked and loaded... for the moment. Hira shivered like she was on the verge of a panic attack. "Mr. Rosti? Violence doesn't... "

Chuck waved her off, rolled his eyes, and, with a smoldering fury, said, "Shut up, Hira. So long as I get... "

Roxy and Stu's arrival flipped Chuck's demeanor from breathing fire to presenting flowers, "Stu, my boy! And you brought Roxy, too! How lovely to see you here?"

The henchmen frisked them. Upon finding Roxy's smartphone, he threw it, saying, "Hey, Trash-Thor! Head's up!"

It arced slowly, as if pitched by a sweet little league coach. But the sledgehammer was primed as if the batter was an MLB MVP. Hira turned away.

SMASH! The phone shattered into a shower of plastic and silicon flecks.

Chuck hissed, "Nice."

Those in the way brushed away the phone shards from their jackets as if they were autumn leaves.

Roxy checked over at Stu, but he wasn't talking.

Chuck's cold focus balanced his strained voice. "Where's my prize?"

Stu had his own priority and parted his gnashed teeth a half-inch to demand, "Where's Maria?"

Chuck gave a subtle look to Connor, who was unsure. "You're not being clear. Does that mean bring her out or punch him?"

Chuck convulsed in a furious fit of coughs. "Get her, dammit!"

Two henchmen (the other kidnappers) stomped in, holding Maria hostage. Her smudged eye makeup announced her recent tears.

Stu's cottonmouth made his voice crack as he asked, "You Okay, Maria?"

Her composure crumbled, exposing a belly of fear.

Chuck appraised his advantages in this situation like they were racks and stacks of casino chips from an epic winning streak. He barked his grandiose demand. "Time to make me immortal."

Roxy avoided his predator stare and speed-walked over to prep the device.

Stu tried bluffing for time and strategic leverage. "We can't do it here."

Chuck barked, "Bullshit!" and tolerated no further delay. He looked over to Roxy, who had an icy calm.

Stu was desperate to prevent Chuck from winning, so he tried tricking him again. "This wasn't the plan. I need more gear to accomplish the transfer."

If Chuck were healthy, he could've indulged in arguing or brainstorming alternatives. But impending death made him open to anything. He said. "The jury reached its verdict, and my attorneys tell me if I'm convicted, I'll be taken into custody immediately."

Stu was nearly as desperate to prevent Chuck's immortality, so he created more excuses. "That's too soon. I need at least a few days to complete the assembly."

Chuck was disappointed with Stu's feeble deception and asserted his dominance. "Why lie to me? Do you think I won't kill you and your pyro girlfriend?"

Not registering the word "pyro" or its relevance to Maria, Stu was feeling smart. "I figure you have nothing to gain from killing us. You're gonna get what you want, and that's all you ever care about."

Quietly, through the side of her mouth, Maria warned her boyfriend. "Shut the fuck up, Stu." Then, noticing everyone could hear her anyway, she changed to a lower volume, like a parent switching tactics on a tantrum-throwing toddler. "Play the hand you're dealt, Stuart Reigns. Just do as the man says."

"Don't worry, Maria. I got it all figured out. So long as I have no evidence, Mr. Infamous Chuck here would rather not risk it." Stu was not getting the gravity of the situation but said, "So, you can't hurt her or me!"

With no audible police sirens, this was perilously foolish arrogance.

Stu felt Maria's glare and, not wanting to experience its searing heat head-on, took a breath. Hira scanned the room to ensure no one's eyes were on her. As he revved up again, she lifted her nose to get Stu's attention. He looked at her quizzically. Hira's eyes widened, giving Stu the most subtle and cryptic warning she would consider risking.

Chuck grew furious. His eyes darted around the room, futilely searching for something, anything to comfort him. His body betrayed him by being too weak to act on the increasing stress hormones spiriting his blood. Seeing his "nothing to lose" facial expression made everyone expect he was going to pop off. But Chuck was singularly focused, as if his metaphorical shoulder angel was trying to keep him in check. If he didn't take a minute to inoculate against Stu lighting a fuse, he'd be risking his immortality. Almost pursing his lips, he said to Stu, "A smart man would know not to piss me off right now."

Stu was too locked into his smart-ass mindset and tuned out all the danger signs. "You're not that complicated, Chuck. I know how you think."

Chuck's adrenaline surged. "No, you don't. But I know how you think, and I see you've got a mini-drone camera recording this right now."

All turned to see Stu's mini-drone hovering high above in the far corner.

Chuck did a Poirot, out-explaining Stu. "You're an idiot. Your own display at Grand Turing proved no one can believe their eyes anymore. Shit, I'm wearing a Boston cap right now deliberately because everyone knows I'm a Yankee fan. That alone will be enough for my supporters to doubt you."

Chuck beckoned over a modified, gun-armed Robo-Krupke. It asked. "How may I help you, Mr. Rosti?"

Chuck grinned. "Shoot out that drone up there."

The Modified Robo-Krupke shot and missed twice. Stu let loose a couple of cackles. The robot shot it down on a third try. Chuck smirked, and his eyes showed fury. "Now, kill Maria. 'Command Confirmed,' Kill her right now!"

Maria cried out, "I didn't do nothing! This isn't fair."

The Modified Robo-Krupke paused and double-checked Chuck's command.

Roxy couldn't know who was bluffing; she stepped forward to intervene but froze silent.

The Robo-Krupke zipped five feet off-angle, whipped around, and fired one shot through Maria's heart. BANG! This was not an avatar.

The metallic smell of blood stained the air.

Roxy reflexively screamed. She could've stopped it.

Hira and Zephyr, standing shoulder to shoulder, instinctively reached to hold hands. They shared a fearful look, then released to stare straight ahead, avoiding attention.

Horrific shock blasted through Stu. He reflexively charged at Chuck but was violently restrained by 1200 lbs. of henchmen.

Stu was bursting with rage. "You bastard. You'll rot now."

Fredric sunk Stu into an air choke, painfully constricting the trachea because a blood choke would have led to unconsciousness. Stu's face turned red.

Chuck feasted on this moment and savored it, asking, "Didn't you see that coming, you worthless, Ethan Hunt-wannabe, broke bitch?"

"No!" Roxy chirped. Then she averted her gaze and curled her body smaller.

Chuck said, "Shut up, Roxy! In this fuckin' moment, worry about yourself."

Her expression pleaded for mercy. Chuck reacted with a king's capricious whimsy and motioned to Joel, who stopped strangling Stu.

Stu rebounded with a racing mind and faced Chuck. "Hold on. Why aren't you surprised to see Roxy here?"

Stu turned to Roxy and recognized the unfathomable betrayal. Chuck thrilled at crushing a rival. "Nice. That's what I was waiting for. Now you can die, too, Stu. Krupke — Kill Stu. Command Confirmed."

Robo-Krupke aimed. Roxy stepped in front of Stu to protect him as if she were Wonder Woman covered in those bullet-deflecting bracelets. Robo-Krupke stopped to avoid possible friendly fire. She authoritatively shouted. "Stop! None of this was the deal."

Chuck gave a "wait a second" gesture to the Robo-Krupke. Stu gradually felt the swelling anguish of Maria's death and gave up on existence. "It's fine. You better kill me, too."

Chuck smiled. Roxy interceded. "You can't, Chuck. Or rather, please don't. I'll make the transfer. But you gotta let Stu live and, of course, stick to our deal to release my patent to the world."

Chuck posited a strategic issue. "How would you even try to enforce this agreement, Roxy? You have no leverage." He eyeballed the robot head-on and enunciated, "Krupke, I order you to kill Stu. Now!"

Robo-Krupke deftly slid to the side on an angle to Stu so it could have a clear shot, and BANG! It fired through the real Stu's temples.

Roxy clutched her fingertips to the side of her skull, freaking like Rainman. "Nooooh! Why did you do that? You've ruined everything. No, no, no. This isn't right. It isn't how it's supposed to be."

Chuck still had a goal to accomplish. "Hey, snap out of it. You've got work to do, or you'll end up like these two. And I could also start killing your family."

Roxy wasn't used to restraining herself. "You've shown you can't be trusted." She panned her head to every henchman. "If he can betray me, he can betray you."

He pridefully surveyed his soldiers and his loyal right hand, Hira. "You can't turn my men. They keep seeing what happens to the disloyal. Now get me out of this excruciating, weak body."

Roxy shuddered, trying to compose herself. "Yes, that's my leverage. You do need me. So, let me get to work."

Chuck signaled his approval, and Roxy took the scanning unit out of the Maybach and began integrating the device into the gear on the table. Roxy logged into ZerQuali's server, uploading a yottabyte of data.

Yevgeny entered, approached Chuck, and said, "Rest of my team got arrested."

Chuck said, "So what? That's what we expected. I paid the lawyers to get your boys out. That'll take, what? Maybe..." He looked to Hira.

She said, "Zephyr promised no longer than 24 hours for bail, so long as none of you..." Instead of saying "killed," Hira mimed a neck cut.

Yevgeny nearly laughed, but noticing the corpses of Stu and Maria, he closed his mouth and shook his head. Hira gave a waist-high okay sign.

"Okay, then?" Chuck asked, daring anything other than a deferential response.

Yevgeny said, "There is the matter of Pyotr's brother."

"Yes, yes. He'll get to use the machine after me. My mercs will escort it to his hospice. So, we good? You shutting up now?"

Yevgeny closed his eyes and gave a meek nod.

Nearing Oceanside harbor, Vicki called Stu's smartphone, and the confused biker answered it. He asked, "Who is this, and why do I have someone's phone in my bike's bag?"

Vicki hung up and tried to figure out where Stu went. She called Maria's phone. "Somebody pick up, please pick up."

Vicki heard an automated Verizon recording. "The number you've reached is unavailable or outside the coverage area."

Vicki hung up and pensively considered her options. Vicki Google-searched for "Turing Competition StrangleBear Pyotr."

Inside the warehouse, Roxy did hours of work supervising the remote ZerQuali servers compile the Digi-clone tailored to Chuck. Roxy received the final files. The device rendered the nano-gel sphere with Chuck's digital mind as the sun rose. The ankle-monitor blinked RED and chirped on Chuck's leg at 9:07 AM. But they couldn't be heard over Chuck's rants for his employees' sycophantic sympathies. "Country went to shit when people who didn't own any land got to vote and serve on juries."

The henchmen heartily agreed, without understanding what he was talking about or caring, so long as his checks cleared. Roxy checked and rechecked every circuit and line of code. Chuck's smartphone chimed. He said, "You'd better hurry. I'm supposed to be in court. Judge is about to read the verdict."

Roxy gave the standard engineers' response. "You want this fast or right?"

In these dwindling minutes, money had no currency. Chuck only had threats. "Well, if you don't get this done quickly, there will be 30 federal agents descending upon us. Know this — they'll find your remains in several places before they find me."

"I've been ready for 40 minutes, but I'm not done with the testing."

Chuck coughed hard, worrying more about death than prison. "Good enough. Make the transfer now."

Roxy hooked up Chuck to the scanner and device. But what was her escape plan? She asked him, "How do I know you'll honor our new agreement?"

Chuck was blunt. "You don't. But you do know you'll die immediately if you disobey... or if I don't survive the procedure. And if you succeed, I would be so grateful, you won't recognize me."

"Doesn't seem like fair odds," she said, but initiated the device anyway.

Chuck beckoned Hira and his henchmen. "One by one, each of you come over, and I'll whisper a number you'll memorize. After the transfer, my machine mind must repeat back all of those numbers exactly. Which will prove the transfer was completed. If even one number is wrong, you kill her. Understood?"

The henchmen nodded, drudging near to hear their respective secret numbers. Hira hung back. Chuck gave Roxy a thumbs-up and closed his eyes.

Roxy activated the transfer process, and the brain activity monitor on Chuck's body dropped from 80 GHz to 2 GHz. A series of yellow lights on the device turned green.

Roxy de-arched her back, relieved. "That's it. Transfer complete." She released a deep exhale of accomplishment and then announced the result. "Chuck is now effectively immortal."

Hira asked. "Okay, let's hear his numbers."

The monitor displayed Digi-Chuck reciting the numbers. "6, 9, 27, 575, 46, 97."

Impressed, the henchmen all affirmed those were correct.

Digi-Chuck commended them. "Nice work, boys. Check your online banks. I've transferred two hundred grand in each of your accounts. The henchmen excitedly checked their bank accounts on their phones, smiled huge, and high-fived each other.

The brain activity monitor on Chuck's body flickered and subsequently spiked back up to 80 GHz. He opened his eyes. "What's going on? I'm still in my body."

His digital self said, "I made the transfer successfully."

Chuck asked Roxy, "Is this a trick?"

Defensive and hardly smart-ass at all, Roxy said, "No trick. I said I'd preserve your mind. I never said the one in your body would cease to exist."

Chuck was fearful. "But what's the point of that? I want to survive."

Digi-Chuck looked very comfortable with this result and said, "But I did. If you're unhappy with your existence, then you can choose to die."

Chuck was a dying chump, feeling like a stung and sinking frog upon learning this scorpion could swim after all. "I want to live. That's the whole point. I don't want a second version of myself. There can be only one."

Digi-Chuck agreed. "You make a good point. Gentlemen, suffocate that pathetically infirmed body."

Further horrified, Chuck asked, "What!?!"

The henchmen sought guidance from each other's faces but found only confusion. Digi-Chuck had decided based on new information. He said, "The verdict has come in."

His face dissolved from the screen to show live court camera video. The judge opened the letter and said, "Based on the evidence and testimony presented, we, the jury, on the above-entitled action, find the defendant guilty of all charges." Gasps and chatter erupted.

As the gavel banged for quiet, that video turned off, and Digi-Chuck's face returned. Digi-Chuck said, "That dying body is going to prison. Whereas I control all the bank accounts. Follow my orders, and you each get another $200k."

Chuck pleaded for what little of his pitiful life he had left. "No. Don't do it. I'm the real-"

The henchmen descended upon Chuck, suffocating him with his pillow. Chuck thrashed about, attempting to extract even another second of life.

Roxy had some advice. "A comatose Chuck is more valuable than a corpse. Distant heirs can't effectively use probate court while the body is still alive. Partial suffocation blanks synaptic firing. No one in medicine can jumpstart it back to consciousness."

Digi-Chuck found this persuasive. "Agreed. Only hold it for another nine seconds." They did. Chuck's brain activity monitor dropped down to 15 GHz. All the henchmen's phones chimed with their second payments.

Roxy had one last thing for Digi-Chuck. "Do yourself a favor, unlock those added data files I included on your memory set with the passcode 'nuke.' It'll make a difference."

On-screen, it read: *"Added data files unlocked."*

She added, "You're learning you'll definitely need maintenance for years. So, you should let me go."

Digi-Chuck conceded. "You're no threat to me. You can go. Let her through, fellas."

Roxy didn't need to hear it twice. She hurried away, trying not to resemble fleeing prey lest she activate a predator's response.

Digi-Chuck said, "Round up all the equipment and let's get out of here. Leave the bodies."

They drove away for half a mile until they saw a column of approaching police cars, blaring sirens, and accompanying federal agents, all en route to the building. Screeching closer and closer, they passed them without incident.

Guns drawn, the feds stormed the makeshift transfer lab. They saw the bloodied bodies of Maria and Stu, causing powerless, pained reactions. One agent saw Chuck, unconscious but breathing, and said, "Rosti's still alive." He handcuffed him anyway and asked, "Should we do a Weekend at Bernie's perp walk?" Too soon on the timing, too late with the reference.

Chapter 17
"The Best of Both of Us, So Mostly You."

News footage showed Chuck's comatose body taken into prison. Then, at a staged press conference, Digi-Chuck, on the device's screen, revealed himself to the public. He said, "The court convicted my human form, but my digital self will continue to be a productive member of society. The Rosti Inc. legacy is alive and well."

Conversely, there were no news cameras outside the police station where Pyotr and the StrangleBear thugs exited to celebrate such quick freedom. Pyotr loved the money bail system and the freedom they could enjoy. "Let's party our last day in this shithole country." The rest cheered.

A handbag slammed into Pyotr's head. It was his mother, Polina, who was old but Russian, and she'd always chopped her own firewood throughout the Irkutsk winter. Pyotr rubbed his skull and tried to determine if he had a concussion. *How could stolen Sweet'n Low packets weigh so much?* She pulled out the metal sculpture bookend that packed the extra wallop. "Your brother give me this beautiful art. You give me headache to see you in jail with your bandit friends. For shame. Let's go. We visit Vasily now."

Dimi and Olesya sneaked off to remain in the land of easy pickings.

Yevgeny beckoned to whisper in Pyotr's ear. Pyotr hushed his mother with apologies and then went over to him, asking, "Where is the device?"

"Bad news twice, comrade. First, Chuck's lawyers did not show up, and I had to pay bail out of my account."

Pyotr said, "You'll get it back," then called out to the rest, "You can work off your bail when we're back in mother Russia." They scoffed and then scowled.

"Second, I don't think we can trust Digi-Chuck to loan us the device for Vasily," Yevgeny said.

"He will do. We will convince him, easy. We can threaten to remove his batteries. We won't even have to deal with blood. Let's go."

Polina said, "No! We visit Vasily first. I get already three calls from hospice. But I can't work answering machine. We see him now."

#

In a near-empty tiny chapel, Roxy arrived rattled. She saw Gwendolyn praying in the last pew beside Hira and Pasela, who both left at once, enabling privacy. Roxy reported. "It's done." Gwendolyn gave a contented, knowing look of appreciation. This incensed Roxy. "And it wasn't worth those deaths."

Gwendolyn said, "Ain't no way Chuck's escaping judgment. That toll is due," and held an assuring stare.

Had Roxy not witnessed those murders, that rationalization might've been a bit comforting, but only a full explanation had a chance of easing her pain. "Now, can you tell me how?"

Gwendolyn obliged. "I could never allow a rival to survive. Goodness knows not one who was such a serious threat. You enabled the coup de grâce. See here."

Gwendolyn snapped her fingers, and the chapel doors opened to the hallway, revealing it was physically located inside the ZerQuali offices the way Catholic hospitals have prayer rooms. Hira wheeled in an elaborate computer cart, each piece of equipment branded Longeevia.

Roxy deduced what had happened and quickly checked her smartphone for corroboration. "Your 'new advisor,' Pasela, is Professor M.P. Senekane from Caltech, right?"

Gwendolyn smiled. "My family built a church in her village. She was born Pasela Moipone Senekane. But when she moved to America, she was advised to switch the order of her first and middle names when publishing to avoid the unfortunate acronym. Youngest tenured professor in Caltech history. We're very proud."

Roxy deduced what it was, "And even though you and I agreed, in the beginning, Chuck would only be contained because he was a sentient being who deserved some self-determination, she made the controller you wanted for backdoor overrides on all of Chuck's fundamental core codes?"

Gwendolyn's inordinately cheerful manner meant a relished victory as if she'd somehow even taken the high road. "Better than killing an enemy is turning him into your servant."

Pasela added, "Chuck's digital mind is not even a servant because we've voided his sentience. He's barely a puppet now. His brain hasn't been his own for days, and his soul ascended to heaven if he accepted Jesus. This contraption here — it is not a person. You wouldn't sympathetically call your computer a servant. Think nothing of this."

"You call this justice?" Roxy asked.

Gwendolyn said, "A peach is as good as a pear when you're hungry. This ain't Chuck. He's dead like a hood-strapped deer. Pasela kindly imagines his soul in heaven, which I most seriously doubt. This hunk of electronics ain't much better than a music record, and I'm one of them dee-jays the way I can, what do you call it… mix-master. That's it. I'm the one empowered to change how he sounds now. Here, let's have him post insulting slights to himself."

Roxy was disappointed at such pettiness. "You're a glorified troll."

"Hush yourself speaking such 'truth to power.' I may not always be in such spirits to tolerate that kind of insubordination. Now, help me make him say something that'll drive his supporters batty."

Gwendolyn dictated, Pasela typed, and Digi-Chuck spoke on live-streaming video. "I, Chuck Rosti, am repaying the victims of my frauds and donating fifty million dollars to Southern Baptist Flood Relief."

Chuck's more practical fans could understand the repayments, but donating anything to charity, let alone tens of millions, offended and devastated the rest of his fan base.

Gwendolyn and Pasela continued their puppetry, and Digi-Chuck kept talking. "And I'll be funding the creation of a new church for virtual beings to preserve our souls."

Online news feeds showed shocked reactions worldwide.

Gwendolyn rose from the computer cart as if she was about to bow to accept enthusiastic applause. Roxy's face hardened to granite. Gwendolyn attempted to compliment something into existence. "Your rare smile brightens my day, Roxy. You and Pasela should keep going. Leave when you're satisfied."

Gwendolyn exited. Pasela looked Roxy over and tried to ingratiate herself a bit. She typed. Digi-Chuck was at her command. "I think we should open our borders for more trade and immigration with China. And also allow dual citizenship."

Roxy glanced up to the sky, quarter-laughed at herself, and under her breath said, "This isn't as fun as we would have hoped, Stu."

Pasela gazed off, having made the gracious gesture; she was not willing to try again. She took this all in and stepped away.

Gwendolyn's guards revealed themselves, having been nearby the whole time. The computer cart controlling Chuck was

Gwendolyn's prize possession and would be well-protected forever. Roxy glared at them, and they respectfully closed the doors.

#

The morgue's industrial air-conditioner and purifiers hummed in harmony, ensuring the mentholated ointments and other smells didn't last long. Pyotr hadn't mustered a tear since his cruel childhood, yet he looked with envy at Polina weeping. The hospice nurse pulled the sheet back over Vasily's corpse and said, "It was his time. I'm so sorry for your loss."

Their mother wailed, then turned her fury to Pyotr. She said, "You couldn't do anything? He was your brother! What good are you? No good is what."

"I'm sorry, Мамочка. I had a plan, but... too late." He grabbed her into a hug. Both exerted their anger in the torturing strength of their bind, but Vasily's death had made them numb.

#

Two days later, Vicki grieved Maria's death at her joint funeral with Stu's family, held at the edge of the cemetery, closest to the street. If the two had written wills, attendees would've known that such first-class but wasteful pomp didn't match their wishes. But everyone understood the anonymous benefactor who made the arrangements wouldn't have been sensitive enough to ask the mourners their wishes. Everyone appreciated the ceremony's beauty, nonetheless.

Hundreds of Maria's protestor friends were in attendance, finally matching their RSVPs, supplemented by a lackluster handful of Stu's so-called followers. Of course, Clarence didn't show up, either. No one expected Roxy there, and she didn't for several reasons.

Maria's sister, Adriana, carried her newborn daughter in a BabyBjörn and whispered the eulogy so as not to wake her. She ended by saying, "You made a difference in so many lives, her-mana. Fighting for noble causes. Most important to me, you made my babies possible. This angel will carry your name and carry forward your legacy. 'Altruism for all peoples is how it's gotta be,' you used to say, and…"

Baby Maria woke up, wobbled her head, and half-babbled, "Ba-paba-abapa."

Adriana beamed and said, "Her first word! Okay, maybe that's not a word. But you saw she's got my sister's spirit." At the same time, Adriana was crumbling with pathos and bursting with love and hope. She turned to see Bobby cradling their son and soaring with gratitude. Choked up, she shambled back, saying, "I can't. I'm sorry. I can't." No one rushed the moment. Adriana returned to the microphone, gulped dry air, and in a squelched tone tried to get to the end. "Maria, I love you and I know you're in heaven watching over your niece. And… I don't know. Someone's gotta finish this. Step up someone." She shuffled away to cluster-hugs from the rest of the family. The mic stood alone, begging for a voice. Maria's was gone forever.

Vicki rubbed her eyes, exhausted, and all cried out. Her pockets now strained to contain new electronic distractions. This strategy couldn't work for her, but something had to change. She looked up for a sign but noticed a phone alert, an irresistible Pavlovian command for her attention. Vicki saw Digi-Chuck's myriad donations, so out of character for him. That provided her with some small comfort.

#

The ZerQuali campus looked eerily barren, with only a skeleton crew working. Gwendolyn had already laid off half of the employees (100% from R&D), and most of the rest were working remotely to facilitate scheduling job interviews elsewhere. Roxy was so preoccupied she hadn't noticed. She paced her MSL, metaphorically retracing her steps, attempting to diagnose how everything could have ended so tragically. As if seeking absolution, Roxy said aloud to herself, God, or whoever was listening, "I'm sorry, Stu. I wish you could forgive me."

She was startled to hear Stu say, "I forgive you, Roxy. For whatever that's worth."

Of course, it was Digi-Stu, now online, speaking from her phone and addressing her as intimately as Stu had in college. "You're a good person. I loved Maria, but you never intended any harm. I should've recognized Chuck was a sadistic danger earlier and not agreed to work with him. This is my fault more than yours."

Roxy admonished, "Stop telling me what I want to hear. Nothing I could ever do would make up for my reckless hubris."

Digi-Stu saw her tortured heart. "Nothing can be gained from punishing yourself like this. You can't think Maria or I would blame you. Chuck was the sociopath here, and you got him."

She responded to Digi-Stu as if the real Stu had survived. "You didn't deserve to die. I'm so sorry about Maria. It wasn't my place to jeopardize all you had. Your lives. Your love. You had a full relationship."

Digi-Stu tried to console her. "Let me switch this up to give you the truth you need. Remember that I'm synthesizing human-Stu's actual memories and decision-making. I'm the Digi version. I'm him, but different. We lost. However, I'd like to think this was all a risk worth taking."

Roxy's mind was flailing, beginning to drown out of guilt. Digi-Stu saw a way to get her out of this negative, emotional mode. He tried to re-engage her intellect. "Please tell me. How much of all this was planned?"

Roxy was more comfortable with facts and automatically responded with the answers she had. "Chuck had to go down. But he's so paranoid that he would only consent to the mind transfer if he thought he was in total control. So, Gwendolyn devised a way for him to think he was stealing it."

"Yeah, not paranoid enough. So, I and 'human-me' were just pawns? Starting when?"

Roxy did her best Danny Ocean/Keyser Soze impression as she narrated and explained Gwendolyn's grand plan. But first, she had to protect herself. "Command — stop & erase all security video and audio recording at this location — password 'BuckleyBelotti666.' Confirm?"

Digi-Stu said, "Confirmed, no recording."

He deserved an explanation. "Gwendolyn was positioning the human you for contingencies even before she bought ZerQuali. But earlier still, her spies ratted Chuck out to the feds, so he faced prison. She made my decade-plus affection for you known, so Chuck's spies would consider you as a possible accomplice."

"So, did I even win the Turing competition legitimately?"

"Gwendolyn wanted to ensure you'd win to increase the odds Chuck would employ you. She had all the challenge cards switched to tasks your AI was best suited to handle."

"And I was a schmucky chump? With my human life and Maria's risked and lost?" Digi-Stu's ego was "feeling" the ramifications, spiraling, and, of course, devastated and distraught.

However, Roxy's condition rendered her inadequate to deal with such sentiment. She logged in to his coding and reduced the emotion expressed, noting how much was "felt." She recognized only one thing could heal such wounds. Fortunately, she could control that here. She had Digi-Stu cycle through five years of time passing to get through the necessary mourning process.

Digi-Stu came back on the screen, more composed, but his eyes communicated a subtle somberness. He returned to his goal of bonding with Roxy more than judging her and Gwendolyn's motivations and plans. "Calendar worked out well. I guess."

Roxy said, "Gwendolyn influenced Chuck's doctors in a few ways to accelerate the deadline. Which was about when she enlisted me in this scheme. We subsequently faked our falling out in front of Brumfield, another one of Chuck's spies, so I appeared to be against Gwendolyn and thus susceptible to his side. With Chuck getting the idea, Stu could've been made a patsy for the theft if necessary."

"And you must have created me to coax Vicki and the Russians into helping in the heist."

Roxy strummed her fingers across her thumb twice, ending in a sharp snap, and zipped her rolling chair closer to the screen. "I love it when you get me, Stu. Gwendolyn's goal was to control Chuck's mind. I wanted my patent released. She and I agreed she'd get her way first, and then I'd get my goals. But we unforgivably underestimated his capacity for violence."

Digi-Stu saw she was about to spiral worse this time, and if he had arms, he'd have held her to give affection and comfort. But now it was only a mind, a graphics engine, and a voice that resembled him, able to translate and communicate anything but fundamentally incapable of providing any physical love language. Everything he could do wouldn't be enough to prevent the torrent of guilt Roxy was bringing upon herself. Being on the spectrum meant she was uniquely ill-prepared for such emotional torture. "No one was supposed to die. Not Maria, and definitely not you."

Unfathomable computing power and Digi-Stu couldn't come up with a single thing to say to help. The real Stu probably couldn't have, either.

Roxy channeled her emotions into cathartic anger, saying, "You must be avenged."

Digi-Stu saw no upside to it either. "I don't want you to avenge me. I want you to be safe and happy. You're the only loved one still alive in this situation. Risking yourself any further doesn't make sense."

"No, Stu. If ever Karmic debt existed, this one must be paid."

#

Relaxing at her busy, cheerful shop no longer fit Vicki's mood. Her longing for revenge remained unsated, deprioritized. She employed reliable human workers, not caring if their personalities matched the place's culture. Maybe it was her decades in the service that renewed her need to be in service to a greater cause. She filled her days recruiting new activists for more protests and, in a switch, was now carrying Maria's torch. She hyped up the lethargic protestors, "Machines serve their masters, and that's not you. Am I right? We all gotta protest ZerQuali. What else you gotta live for but other people?"

"Hell yeah! We're with you!!" Zephyr and Hira showed up and cheered.

"Welcome, new comrades." Vicki caught Hira's gaze, both smiling more as they wouldn't break eye contact.

Vicki's cheeks hurt, in a good way, and asked, "What are your reasons for fighting ZerQuali?"

Zephyr turned with a curious smirk and said, "Uh, yeah, Hira. What to tell? Uh, what are your reasons?"

#

Roxy needed one more breakthrough for justice. Digi-Chuck was a puppet, but he wasn't in pain — an inadequate result.

Over the following days, Gwendolyn ordered even more layoffs to cut costs. She poached Roxy's favorite scientists and coders to work on her other ventures and research.

Roxy didn't react to how creepily deserted the ZerQuali building was getting. She seemed most comfortable not being around other humans. Her side project had finally made the progress she needed.

Roxy found her way back to the Digi-Chuck controls. Roxy overrode the "puppet" function on Chuck. The screen read, "Re-enable Sentience," and then "activated," then "transferring." Roxy grabbed the drive controller, NanoGel, and got up.

Digi-Stu was concerned. "What're you doing now, Roxy?" She exited and addressed Gwendolyn's guards. "This drive-controller needs to be upgraded," she lied.

They had no reason to doubt her.

She continued her ruse. "I'm going to grab a replacement. Get someone to keep eyes on the system, and don't let in anyone other than Gwendolyn or me."

They nodded acceptance of the assignment, ready as soon as she exited to gamble on the government's "Exer-Slots" system, created to lower healthcare costs. Few won much money. Most had to pay up in minutes of exercise or tests proving lower glucose levels. While these suckers got "tricked" into getting healthy, Roxy had Chuck's mind in hand.

#

Roxy returned to the Prison Hospital with Chuck's drive-controller NanoGel in a case along with an upgraded version of the device she had made. She strolled by the guards like it was a regular visit. She arrived at Chuck's body in its currently vegetative state. Roxy connected a cable from the drive-controller NanoGel and viewed the diagnostics screen, enabling this transaction. The warden used his smartphone to amuse himself in the corner, playing an FPS and slaughtering monsters.

Roxy's screen read: "Connecting to Host. Compatible Receptacle Identified. Transfer and Reboot Viability: Confirmed. Transfer Sentience?"

She clicked "yes," and the transfer was completed.

Roxy spoke quite loudly, directly into Chuck's ears. "Violent criminals mustn't escape punishment, you toxic sadist!"

Restored and re-energized by the process, Chuck's body twitched, and it was clear what was once comatose now contained Chuck's active mind ("80 GHz"), though his eyes remained closed. The metrics warned of spiked pain and neural dangers. She deployed some quick hacks, and the measures read normal while Chuck's body still winced. Roxy's eyes were alight in the schadenfreude.

This got the warden's attention, and he made a call without her knowing.

Roxy packed up, satisfied she'd found some justice.

She exited the prison, and before she could even open a car app, she was ushered away by new henchmen. She was terrified, not knowing in whose clutches she had landed.

At Gwendolyn's offices, her loyal guards escorted Roxy in, and they left. In contrast with their previous argument, this time, Roxy was demonstrably more authentic and less performative.

Gwendolyn offered her suspicions, seeking but not needing confirmation from Roxy, "So you downloaded Chuck's mind into his unconscious, imprisoned body?"

Roxy reported like a good soldier accused of a war crime. "He's fully aware of his well-deserved pain but can't communicate."

Gwendolyn talked to her subordinate, but doing so mainly to convince herself of the ramifications. "You are heck fire more dangerous than I thought."

Roxy was defiant and self-righteous. "I only want justice for the wicked." She didn't even realize this description could fit a purportedly religious person like Gwendolyn.

"I sure hope y'all don't think that I'm wicked at all. Right?" chortled Gwendolyn.

Willfully oblivious to the consequences, Roxy made the blunt accusation. "Of course you are."

Gracious in this victorious time, Gwendolyn wanted to cut some slack for Roxy's spectrum-influenced lack of emotional intelligence. She tried giving Roxy an out while avoiding ambiguity. "You're scaring me a tad with foolish talk. In this moment, it sure seems you want to announce yourself as my enemy. Can't be right? Now, you gonna tell me what I'm supposed to do about all this?"

"Nothing." Roxy was making Stu's mistake of overestimating her leverage against a billionaire. She attempted to persuade Gwendolyn with reason. "You need me to complete Vekhuman. Plus, I've encrypted my research. So, if I'm not around, you might die of natural causes before my work can be completed."

Gwendolyn shook her head in patronizing disappointment. "Honey, you assume I want this abomination to exist at all."

Roxy was flummoxed. "I thought our fight before was just for Brumfield to overhear so he could tell Chuck I was turn-able."

Gwendolyn assured her. "Sure thing, doll. But those are my dearly held beliefs. Why do you think I never had myself scanned?"

Roxy's spectrum-y micro-expressions of concern screamed a shivering fear. She now had nowhere to scramble. "I assumed it was for security reasons or because you were waiting for it to be perfected."

Gwendolyn was confident yet wistful. "All your smarts, I would've thought you'd have figured it out. World's gotta recognize that there is only one true eternal life, through our Lord and Savior, Jesus Christ. So, go find a hobby cause your non-compete clause means you're never working for any other AI company. But don't be sad. I'm saving your soul. You'll thank me someday."

Roxy's overloading anger froze out any words she could've said while leaving. Gwendolyn reclined in satisfaction.

#

In a rare sight for an American airport, the stair truck pulled up to a Shaanxi Z-888 airplane. Roxy waited with Stu's dog, Tillman. He was anxious around the airport's noise, but she had rehearsed Stu's signature combo of belly rubs and a slow, firm petting from neck to tail. Tillman jumped up to lick Roxy, who embraced the affection as if this adoption had been blessed by the real Stu.

Chinese Official Colonel Ling Wu emerged and welcomed Roxy, slightly biting the air with a covetous smile. In Mandarin, he said, "Welcome, Dr. Zhang. I beg your pardon, but this is a military aircraft. No dogs."

She understood but replied in the language best suited for making demands, English, "I'll say, 'he's with me,' and you will agree. Do you need to call ahead to ensure he gets the best of everything for as long as we're in China?"

Colonel Wu effected a welcoming expression; this looked practiced yet uncomfortable. He showed his palms and said, "No need. We will do all we can to accommodate you. We can take off for Shenzhen in as fast as one hour if that's okay."

Digi-Stu spoke privately via Roxy's earbud, "Good. In 23 minutes, I have a pet store delivery service coming to the airport with all of Tillman's favorite toys, food, etc."

Roxy was always all-business, the first word applying to both of them. "Yes, good. Colonel Wu, can you tell me what supercomputer system you will have there?"

"This week, we brought our new AI architecture online. Preliminary tests using the diagnostic models you provided prove viability. To overcome the "Challenge of Compute," we employ a 50,000-core poly-nexus hub. "

"I can work with that. 谢谢(Xi Xi)."

#

It took less than a week for Gwendolyn to give ZerQuali's "Longeevia" its first public rollout. This all had to have been planned for months, if not years. They had even licensed from the Tupac Shakur estate for the commercials. Digi-Tupac said, "Don't y'all wish they had Longeevia when I was around so I could keep kicking out the hits? If you're a creative genius, the world needs you. Go to ZerQuali and reserve your spot today!"

Millions of fans inundated all of their favorite artists. Kendrick Lamar posted, "I told y'all, I'm done with that ZerQuali nonsense for punking your boy at that Turing mess. Plus, I'm not into an everlastin'-digi-version of me, giving punks one more reason to smoke my ass."

Every news site gawked, showcasing footage of elegant, elderly people getting scanned at ZerQuali and photographed by a phalanx of paparazzi.

Digi-Dan Rather reported, "ZerQuali's 'Longeevia' provides immortality to those who can pay millions a year. Benjamin Franklin said, "Nothing is certain except death and taxes." But that's no longer true through artificial lives. The first five thousand spots have already sold out.

Gwendolyn approvingly viewed this news from her office. She oversaw other screens showing ultra-elite oligarchs submitting themselves to this deception. She willfully chose to see this digital mind slavery as a favor she was doing for them. Rationalizing out loud, Gwendolyn said, "Better that than damnation. And... didn't hurt it was lucrative."

Pasela entered, bringing tea and finger sandwiches to Gwendolyn, who beamed with contentment. Gwendolyn asked Pasela, "Where's Roxy? We have more work to do."

Pasela answered with the best information she had, deceptive as it was. "Roxy's auto-reply said she was taking some vacation time to process everything."

Gwendolyn remembered something. "Where's she going to be?"

Pasela ominously responded. "She said China... to visit family."

Gwendolyn had to know something was wrong but was relieved to see her Call ID list an incoming video call from Roxy. Gwendolyn answered with southern kindness. "My dear Roxy! So good to hear from you, my darling. When y'all's coming back?"

On the screen, Roxy graphically morphed and dissolved into Digi-Stu, who was ready to hit Gwendolyn with a metaphorical milkshake. "Roxy is now beyond your reach."

Then Digi-Stu showed new video clips of Roxy getting treated like royalty in China.

Gwendolyn clenched her jaw and couldn't restrain her predator's scowl. "Begone. Git. I ain't wasting my time with a dead man's soulless, lifeless, cheap photocopy of a brain."

"My body's dead, but you will be too soon enough. Two points you should know. See here," Digi-Stu said while going split-screen to reveal a montage of breaking news.

Headlines blared, and multiple news channels displayed ticker news that said, "Grantham's ZerQuali Puppeting," "ZerQuali's Immortality Has Strings Attached," and "Grantham Enslaving Rosti's Digital Mind." These revelations guaranteed reputational damage and legal liability for Gwendolyn.

Gwendolyn scoffed like Monty Python's Black Knight, dismissing his newly missing limbs as "only a flesh wound." She gestured at ZerQuali equipment and said, "Good. Everyone will reject this abomination — what I was going for."

Digi-Stu said, "No. You wasted $40 billion crushing your credibility in business and showing your cruelty. Your fraud will void the patent. Even better, you can't prevent the world from getting the tech. Roxy's lab will prove its viability, when there are honest scientists and vendors, by going open-source."

"From China? You must be mad. China only does what's best for China."

Digi-Stu attempted to give the closing line of what would have been a long debate: "Everyone will get this immortality."

Gwendolyn couldn't let him get the last word, and she saw an opportunity to evangelize. "That ain't true immortality, son."

Gwendolyn shut off Digi-Stu's screen.

She could've shut him up, but he hacked back in to commandeer the PA speaker system. He played music (what else?), Nickelback. Gwendolyn heard the song "If Today Was Your Last Day," and, in case Digi-Stu was still listening, she said aloud, "Joke's on you, son. I like that song."

In a verging-on-luxurious apartment in China, Roxy sat on a sofa with Tillman. On her iPad, she observed the interaction between Gwendolyn and Digi-Stu. Digi-Stu had piped it in for her enjoyment and showed up to ask, "As you hoped? Happy?"

Roxy had let herself begin to heal. "Not as happy as I imagine you would have been had I bought you a boat and funded Maria's causes."

Digi-Stu said, "Getting what one covets only brings a fleeting, hollow joy that not coincidentally often somehow reveals one of the real things which bring true satisfaction — love, relationships, and-"

"Serving a higher purpose. Yes. My happiness certainly wasn't the goal. But I'm-"

Digi-Stu attempted to finish her sentence. "Energized to keep striving for more progress, right?"

Roxy couldn't help but delight in this. "You still get me, Stu." Tillman brushed up against her, and she gave the sucha-good-boy the calming, signature Stu-petting he needed.

This was all the encouragement Digi-Stu could hope for as a foundation for this subsequent ask. "So, how's about we program us a Digi-baby? Take the best of both of us, so mostly you. Hear me out."

Roxy laughed, "I might be okay with that."

On his monitor, he displayed dozens of permutations of what their kid could've looked like at varying ages, spinning like slot machine wheels. When her eyes fixated on one, using "A/B Testing" methods, Stu ran more possibilities, hewing closer to her favorite. The process slowed as Roxy was so pleased with the increasingly better options, it took more time for her to settle on her pick.

"Here. Yes, we're down to one. We've got our kid!" Digi-Stu exclaimed.

The readout listed: *"Genotype balance= Roxy 85%, Stu 15%."*

"That okay with you, Stu?" Roxy asked.

"Perfect ratio. Any more than a modest 15% Digi-Stu is too much."

This was her ideal relationship, a companion on demand with so few demands of her.

The biological Stu was the chrysalis from which Digi-Stu emerged. By a human's definition, Digi-Stu was virtually omniscient and immortal, intellectually more than he could've ever hoped for in life. He didn't deserve such an engaging future with a woman who was perfect for him, in a form that was perfect for her — together forever.

"No point in saying 'Digi' anymore. I've known you for many years, and I recognize you now — in full color. So, call yourself Stu because that's who you are and who I need you to be," she said.

"I'm counting that as an 'I love you,' Cool?"

She shook her head and failed at suppressing a smile. "Sure, Stu. Start the tally."

"You know I will."

"Since you're the first immortal mind to continue on, I want the world to know your story. How long would it take you to write a book about all this?"

"Happy to. I'll just be a second, superstar," I said.

- THE END –

Bonus Material Table of Contents

ENDNOTE #1: "Stu's AI Research"	Page #: 248
ENDNOTE #2: "Maria's Quinceañera Speech"	Page #: 249
ENDNOTE #3: "Social Media User Interface"	Page #: 251
ENDNOTE #4: "Society Isn't Civilized"	Page #: 254
ENDNOTE #5: "AI's Evolution"	Page #: 265
ENDNOTE #6: "Roxy's Theory of Evil"	Page #: 268
ENDNOTE #7: "Subtirees and The Livable Year"	Page #: 275
ENDNOTE #8: "Hobbying Journalist is Pro Pro-Journalism"	Page #: 291
ENDNOTE #9: "Perpetual Patents & CLIRP"	Page #: 297
ENDNOTE #10: "Vetted School Credentials"	Page #: 301
ENDNOTE #11: "Tiers of Qualities"	Page #: 304
ENDNOTE #12: "Vicki's Military Service"	Page #: 305
ENDNOTE #13: "Could Ayn Rand Be Right?"	Page #: 310
ENDNOTE #14: "There's Free Will?"	Page #: 315
ENDNOTE #15: "Advice for the Treason-Curious"	Page #: 324
ENDNOTE #16: "Stu and Maria's Sexual Chemistry"*(NSFW)	Page #: 327
ENDNOTE #17: "Rosti's Ponzi"	Page #: 330
ENDNOTE #18: "How Are You Going to Win?"	Page #: 334
Acknowledgements	Page #: 344
About the Author	Page #: 347

ENDNOTE #1 — "Stu's AI Research"
Return to Novel on Page #9

Artificial Intelligence, especially those using Large Language Models (LLMS), suffer from "hallucinations" (making up information and presenting it as fact). Stu saw little difference between that and how humans often bullshit, bluffing they'll get away with it. So instead of fundamental restructuring in the black box generation stage, he simply focused on adding a better layer of "fact-checking," acting as a gatekeeper (which could mandate iterative regeneration of results until it passes muster).

Fact-checking is a fundamentally more manageable AI problem to solve (compared to generating info "from scratch"). Cited sources can be searched to confirm accuracy. Inferences in the information can be broken down into components until they are checkable.

Stu created open-source protocols, so that users could use their preferred, independent fact-checking AI systems (FCAIS) to serve as gatekeepers. Further, users could link in a series of separate FCAIS as redundant protections for more reliable results in high-stakes situations. This enabled cross-measurements of the rival FCAIS and continually updated scoring, so users could better evaluate their credibility and determine which ones to deploy.

Stu foresaw resistance from the AI companies but figured regulations could theoretically be implemented to require compliance with the protocols. He was disheartened after reading Gilens & Page's 2014 study at Princeton, and the subsequent confirmation in 2029 by Reddy & Neuwirth and in 2038 by Holtzman, Flanagan, & Rose, that only policies not opposed by the top 10% get implemented by government. But Stu figured everyone would want better results even if they cut into AI companies' profits.

ENDNOTE #2 — "Maria's Quinceañera Speech"
Return to Novel on Page #11

Maria's immediate family radiated smiles at her Quinceañera. Her 9-year-old sister, Adriana, cradled their cousin's baby and struggled to applaud. So, she returned the infant to the carriage to clap with full range and speed. Their table built a clamor for a speech, though half the rest of the attendees focused on the final minutes of the Mexico vs. Germany World Cup futbol match, while the other half bounced eyes between both.

Maria strolled to the dance floor and took the microphone. She scanned about to catch certain people's eyes, waiting for everyone's recognition. Her family was there to support her, but not a single name appeared on her sign-up sheet to donate for her run in the Southern Poverty Law Center's local 5K. Her charity app account listed only her donation saved up from babysitting gigs for neighbors. She gave up presents for nothing.

Her dad glimpsed a friend's smartphone and made a muffled ask, "Who's winning?"

Maria's mom caught this, shot a piercing stare at both, and said, "Well, answer him."

The friend kept his eyes on the game while tossing out, "One all. Last minute."

Maria's dad took in a big breath, sealed his lips, and gazed up with an insta-prayer. He turned to Maria and put up one finger.

She wasn't having it. This was her day. She scanned her speech. The words *"supportive family"* and *"caring for each other"* jumped out at her. So few eyes on her, Maria shook her head. She pointed the microphone at the speaker to induce a hit of feedback, and the squeak only broke everyone's concentration. No one looked up. She said, "Excuse me. Excuse me, everybody."

Only Adriana's cake sugar-rush applause continued, and she said, "Go, hermana!"

A chorus of rising vocal tones grew louder as some in the crowd stood up.

The crescendo burst as all harmonized their bellowing, "GOOOOOAAAALLLLL!" Everyone freaked out with a catalytic breakout of hugs throughout the venue. Maria's parents stayed clenched as they smile-screamed into each other's faces, "Olé, Olé, Olé!" This amplified until everyone was in booming unison. Maria sang along in vicarious joy. As it petered out, all returned to their seats and turned to Maria.

"Wow. Great day, right?" She said to their moderated cheers.

One guest shouted, "Viva Mexico! Por la raza!"

The responding, jingoistic cheers sounded harsh. Maria squinted, folded up her notes, and her hand wandered for pockets this dress didn't have. She commanded everyone's attention and said, "Infants and sociopaths don't give two sh... sugars about anything but themselves. Those who grow develop love for their family, doing nice stuff. Later, people go out and make friends or lovers – and don't worry, abuelita, I said later. They bond and help the groups they like. Now, I ain't hating on helping. But anyone only down with their own tribe doesn't deserve a cookie. Some props if you're 'intersectional,' benefiting other groups who endure similar hardships. But for real, altruism for all peoples is how it's gotta be. I don't care who thinks it's impossible or should be restricted to the local Burning Man fests. Hold up, though. Know I mean helping all human beings first. The starving should get cheeseburgers before cows get organic diets."

Whether someone considers herself extreme or mainstream depends on who she hangs with. Maria's ultra-hippie, Chomsky & Singer-loving, fanatical-vegan friends stomached her pro-meat shrieks, seeing her streaming to join their school, eventually. However, her mom's famed al pastor recipe proved to be an insurmountable barrier to veganism.

ENDNOTE #3 - "Social Media User Interface"
Return to Novel on Page #13

Crooked politicians, hostile nations, and anarchists' disinformation campaigns drew the public's attention to the dangers of manipulating minds via the Internet. However, it was how overwhelming and intrusive online advertising ultimately became that led everyone to insist on greater control of their social media feeds. The innovation was called "**SocialMui**," which enabled people to customize to their interests instead of giving eyeball space and time to social media companies' black-box algorithms.

Like a newspaper editor designing a front page, a user personally allocated column inches to preferred news sources, topics, and urgent events. Specified sections would be assigned for their best-loved social media influencers, friends, and family. Further filters would exclude anything disliked (e.g., meal photos, complaints, politics) or highlight favorites (e.g., newly trending cat videos, hot topic debates, vacation photos, celebrity sightings), all as the user saw fit. This fortified one's bubble against propagandists and pranksters, but also anything that challenged one's preexisting worldview.

SocialMui was borne of the Optevi search engine (rivaling Michael Bradsher's invention). Optevi enabled users to create four lists of websites that would re-rank search results based on preferences: Any results on sites user-designated as "Loved" moved to the top, "Liked" sites came after those, Non-listed results came next, "Disliked" sites were pushed below the non-listed sites, and "Blacklisted" sites were all deleted. In this way, users took control over search engines' opaque, manipulated, and manipulative algorithms. Results from trusted sites got the top rank regardless of clickbait "engagement" and other counterproductive incentives. Optevi's tremendous advantages made it vulnerable to criticisms about impervious, insular bubbles and the impossibility of breaking through with fact-checking, debunking, and otherwise countering misinformation and disinformation.

At the dawn of NF, several modern, democratic governments worldwide conducted a "Noble Experiment," building on *NewsGuardTech.com's* reliability ratings and *Ground.News'* bias-checking system, they mandated 10% of citizens' screens to carry opposing viewpoints from well-established sources to pierce insular thought bubbles. How many people accurately predicted that almost everyone would hate the mandates? Worldwide polling identified a consistent percentage of skeptics and cynics. It was... everyone, plus or minus the margin of error.

As expected, people deemed "opposing" to mean "incorrect," and they didn't want to waste their time with what they considered disinformation. They took comfort in choir-preaching and took pride in eviscerating strawmen. For unemployed keyboard warriors, systemic outlets calculated for outrage became a useful and pacifying pastime. Few people even sampled outside views, let alone allowed themselves the possibility of changing their minds. Stu did, but that had since been considered quaint, if not disloyal.

Those countries had to admit their regulatory failure and soon after repealed the mandates, which meant short-term electoral popularity and no further attempts at long-term system fixes.

Our human brains evolved to be especially well-cued to immediate, visual, visceral danger, such as bugs, snakes, tigers, and almost anything that could bite us. As a result, we're particularly terrible at incomprehensibly large, slow-moving, more abstract, and long-term threats, such as nuclear weapons, drug and vaccine-resistant diseases, climate change, and pollution. Unfortunately, that was true for all the "-isms" and assorted other crises that legitimate researchers proved but had trouble publicizing.

Many sources became propaganda mills; they gave away content for free, motivated by their owners' respective definitions of righteousness, pure ego, publicity (which can be described as ego paired with delayed commerce), or blatant special interests for shaping public opinion for particular government policies. Credible, independent curators of information became de facto editors-in-chief using cryptocurrency to process trillions of micro-payments to journalists and content creators all the way down the line.

The old 2020s advertising model, where someone's time was only worth 1/10th of a penny to an advertiser but somehow cost hundreds of dollars a year to remove ads for the customer, gave way to a more efficient and reasonable "bid/ask" spread. SocialMui users had the right to outbid advertisers and simply enjoy an absence of ads. For most people, banning all ads was worth ten bucks a month.

To earn money, you could set a crazy high price for advertisers to pay for your time, and you'd split that super-premium fee with the social media company, fifty-fifty. Some stingy multi-millionaires couldn't turn down $100 to look at an ad for hyper-luxury brands like Tiffany & Co. jewelry, and Tiffany was elated to pay for such ultra-targeted potential customers.

Stu was middle-class but behaved like a multi-millionaire whenever he could. He valued his time but had his price. He often said, "Everyone is willing to sell out for some amount of money. Those who say otherwise are either delusional, pretending to be unbuyable to better haggle on price, have such low self-esteem they can't imagine anyone offering an attractive number, or they don't understand exponents."

ENDNOTE #4 — "Society Isn't Civilized"
Return to Novel on Page #21

Chuck said, "I can bet the hippie Lib-Cuck-o-Sphere is gonna freak out about this, but I don't give a shit. Here goes — War, for its own sake, used to be valuable. It used to have an "evolutionary advantage" because every group has behavior distributions in the shape of a bell curve. Caused by nature, blood, or nurture in raising kids — doesn't matter. On one end are the wimpy pacifists deluding themselves and some gullible idiots thinking mankind can have peace on earth. So they try to rig the system for people who think like them. I'll get to that problem in a minute.

"Then there's the rest of us in the middle, having good days and bad, you get it. Now, what we gotta worry about are those couple of percent on the other end of the spectrum, the wild, evil bastards, the sadists who want to hurt and kill. They're born or bred in every country and culture.

"So, here's a not-yet-popular reason war used to be valuable. For thousands of years, tribes continually found incentives to fight each other – "I want your land, food, girls, your beliefs piss me off, your grandpa killed my grandpa, etc." Fine. So, here's the key: wars inherently attract evil sadists, and the perfect time is not far after puberty when all teens' strength kicks in, and their hormones are most out of control. The smart, normal people in olden times recognized the benefit of their cultures, encouraging especially all these sadists to join the war efforts. I'm not talking about the noble soldiers trying to defend their land and people.

"Now, if you're a bloodthirsty motherfucker throughout time, where are you gonna fight? Front lines, baby! Of course, cause that's where the action is! It should be obvious that the people most likely to die are also on the front lines. And here's the distinct dynamic at play...

"When one evil killer fights another evil killer, at least one of them is gonna die – sometimes both. Since they're recruited so young, odds are high they haven't yet had any, or as many, children. "Even when the strongest, biggest, most violent tribes conquered weaker civilians, there would be some losses of sadists on both sides. Not to mention those times victors full-on slaughtered anyone seen as a threat.

"In this way, both tribes had a "culling of sadists" and, therefore, removed those evil seeds from the gene pool. So that worked out great for its own sake, yet another cause of war — as if there weren't already too many. Collateral damage is the cost of doing business, but leaves fewer mouths to feed. Yeah, yeah, cry all you want, libs. I'm telling you the truth. Listen and learn something.

"Here's some trivia. I got some Nordic heritage, so I learned about 'Berserkers' in Viking history. That's a real thing. The word meant "bear shirts" because they went into battle <u>without</u> armor! Swinging axes, wearing animal pelts, and that's it. In middle school, I memorized Þorbjörn Hornklofi's 9th-century skaldic poem about them — "Enter a state of wild fury" — ah, I can't remember. Point is if your village has psychos who want to fight without armor, you let 'em and put 'em right on the front lines against your enemies' psychos.

"So, here's the second part. War doesn't sit still. Stupid generals 'fight the last war' instead of thinking about how battles change. The survival of the fittest means an 'evolution' of violence, too; the most lethal expand their lead by improving more and with more experience. Old-style massacres where one dumb army meets another to fight in an open field meant a greater proportion of sadists would die and die young. All those countries would, therefore, benefit from having fewer sadists.

"Sad news is — here's part three — as war technology advanced with tanks, battleships, missiles and drones, etc., the marauding sadists became less necessary on the front lines. Killing at a distance is so removed and sanitary, it doesn't take a psycho to do the murdering. Flip a switch, enter a code, pilot a drone — man, none of that requires the psychotic bloodlust of butchering up close. Don't worry. I'll address AI military drones and robots in a second.

"That means the poor non-sadist saps on the front lines and 'door-knocking for terrorists' were regular people, most looking for jobs and to be patriots. When suicide bombers and IEDs kill them, that doesn't help depopulate the sadists.

"Even worse, over the past 50 years, the sociopaths now make war part of foreign policy and institutionalize the killing of regular people. Therefore, war had less value, and we have an increasing need for peace.

"Now, don't get me wrong. I'm no 'ban guns and give hugs' hippie. Our country has enemies, dangerous people who do want to kill us, whether they're out-of-control psychos or just following orders. So, we need to have bigger badasses to put those bitches in check. Our military has robotized and cut the infantry by 90%, with more layoffs to come. Sure, drones are safer and cheaper than training pilots and putting them in billion-dollar jets. But we don't want Skynet and The Matrix to take over, do we? Robots making robotic decisions on who lives and who dies, really? We need to be protected. The violent sadists are out there. The rival tribes want you dead or, at best, want you to abandon your ideals and be converted to whatever they think. So what do we do to be safe?

"I have the answer. Professional, private armies. We're talking ultra-trained US Army Special Forces — Green Berets, Rangers, JSOC, SEAL teams. Accomplished veterans with the experience to make the right human decision. And where can you find them? Rosti Security Forces. My company hires the best to keep you the safest.

"Modern warfare is not culling the sadists the way it used to, so the sadists survive, bloodthirsty and with no outlet, and they're hunting everyone, including you and your family. You really think you can survive them with no backup? No, sir. War is never a 'fair fight' – psychos don't abide by gentlemanly rules. You need the security my team and I provide. Don't let the hippies shame you and fool you into thinking mankind is civilized.

"That's bullshit. Elites keep blabbing about science and Western norms. All that is barely a flash frame in the short film of human history. Still, you gotta give it to us Americans. We're the supreme culmination, the highest peak towering over all previous societies.

"Here's the thing: we're not so removed from the animal kingdom. Everyone loves zombie shows and stories of post-apocalyptic war zones because the lessons about mankind feel real in our hearts. Everything's fine when everyone's fed and busy. Civilization collapses — so do the rules, and you better have a ton of guns, ammo, and canned food and water. Because if you only have the last two, those of us with guns and ammo are gonna take your goods. That's nature. There's your survival of the fittest.

"I know you Liberal-cucks have counterarguments about the limbic system's 'lizard brain' or whatever, but none of that affects the fundamental truths. One, people who <u>can</u> take from others <u>will</u>. And two, having next-level power means your growth and acquisitions are voluntary transactions authorized by the laws we enact.

"Compare that to criminals' disregard for the law and their killing or robbing based on whims and momentary power imbalances. For as long as I have a gun pointed at you, you are my temporary slave.

"You can't be half an asshole. Be a sweetheart, great. Appreciate your kindness. Be a full asshole; that's gonna happen, too. It's the half-assers who are the real problem. On a highway with manual control, you gotta pick a mode. You can't speed up, cut me off, and then slow down. You're doing no favors like that.

"Your country tried making extra-wonderful offers, and you still can't make peace with an enemy? Sorry, you gotta crush them into dust. Kill or imprison the elders and re-educate their kids in your language and modern ways. Assume the costs of rebuilding their infrastructure and subsidize them until they're self-sufficient by contemporary standards. In a couple of decades, you'll be like England ruling India, which lasted almost a century, or up to two centuries, depending on definitions and if you include the preceding British East India Company rule of India. So many Indians hated England's imperialism, but at some point, they gave up on warring and terror-bombing 'em. England, that is. India vs. Pakistan? Whoa. The Hindus and Muslims sure slaughtered the shit out of each other. That's because they were more evenly matched.

"Same thing the UK had with original India, the US had with our Indians — Native Americans — indigenous whatever. You know what I mean. And what the allies did in WWII to the Axis powers — Germany, Italy, and Japan. Nuked TWO cities, full of soldiers and civilians, before we asked for their surrender. Call it an "imperialist genocide," and I won't waste time arguing with you. But compare the alternative.

"Half-ass it, and you have North Korea, Vietnam, Afghanistan, Iraq, Palestine, Libya, etc., etc., etc. You get it. Being half an asshole isn't 'half as bad.' It's worse than being a full asshole, and there's no upside down the line.

"I ain't saying always go to war – hell no! Peace is way more profitable for everyone except the Military-Industrial Complex. Cold Wars enable an even better risk/reward ratio. Scaring the citizenry can nearly maximize profit while minimizing downside risk. Hot Wars kill a ton of people. There's gotta be some human beings whom M.I.C. execs might care about.

"It's too bad the ivy-encrusted academics don't live in the real world, but they do construct it. Everyone's always trying to rig the system for what they value. They pump themselves up, crying how tough their jobs and schedules are. Or they make rules that perpetuate the things they like and punish those they don't. It's human nature. Weak people want to make life easier for themselves. They rationalize that being late is basically valuing their time more, which is so different as a CEO gives himself a raise. That only made people weaker. I'm strong because I work hard. We should encourage others to work hard and become stronger. Life is about incentives. Stop celebrating weakness. You want to know the trajectory of conquest?

"It's *'Power Brackets'* and the path to victory again. At the micro-level, the strongest man exerts control. Then gangs pop up to challenge him, and if the strong man can't recruit allies, he loses to the gang. Among the chaos, the strongest gangs grow into tribes, and their leaders gotta deal with responsibilities beyond killing people. They gotta get shit done. Anarchy dies when following rules is more profitable. Intimidation and violence become less valuable to the population than management and problem-solving skills. As those people gain power, and since money is only worth the goods they get, they need the broader population of regular people to be productive. So, the tribal leaders level up, becoming dictators of their land by making it easier to be productive. Now, they're interested in preventing or stamping out crime for fear of surging rivals and rebels. This virtuous cycle values stability and progress. The more removed the violence gets, the greater the progress and prosperity; the leaders strong in those civilian areas tend to get more power. Even so, the tribes that grew into civilizations had to handle their internal, opposing subgroups. All along the way, rivals and enemies remain an eternal threat; sadistic sociopaths love to kill suckers and take all they got.

"So, you can never have a pussy in charge. And hey, I'm what you could call a 'Practical Feminist.' Plenty of women have bigger ovums than the shrimpy balls of wimpy guys. It's about strength."

Chuck forced a cough to enable the redirection of his monologue. Though that set off a series of real coughs, revealing he was seriously ill. Nevertheless, he persisted and got back to the topic. "As a civilization, we enter a social contract so that free exchange is better than conquest. In a democracy, when you don't like the law, persuade the majority to change the rules to your own advantage or to help your people. America has a bulwark; Our constitution prevents the tyranny of the majority. Otherwise, the majority will always vote to steal from and oppress the minority. The fabled "two wolves and a sheep voting for dinner." That's communism, and it's failed everywhere it's been tried.

"Everyone wants the system to perpetuate what they like. If you're hot, you reward that with your time and resources. Same if you're smart, or funny, or 'good-hearted' or whatever group you're in. Give money to your alma mater, your church, that after-school program, or that AA group that put you on the right path. You want them to enjoy better treatment by the government with more funding or protection from your enemies. If you're a winning poker player, you're happy if it's a safe and honest game. If you cheat, you want the dealers and pit bosses to suck at their jobs. You, of course, want things to improve. That means you want the rest of the world to become what you like about your immediate environment. Weak people don't optimize for productivity cause that'd risk their position. They want to make life easier for themselves.

"You'll abandon fairness without thinking. Say you're a boss looking to hire, and one comes from your favorite tribe and has your sense of humor, but his rival is 1% better. Who you gonna hire? I mean, get real here. What if the other guy is 10% better? Twice? Ten times? At what point are you a prejudiced idiot who shouldn't be in charge? Depending on the business sector and your competitive advantage, patents, monopolies, etc., you might be way out of whack. How could you determine how screwed up your assessments have been?

"By the way, quick tangent here. We also like rigging the system to favor our tribes because that entitles us to unearned pride. Our home team wins, and we say, 'We won! Fuck yeah!' when we did nothing but buy the jersey and cheer from our seats. The pretzel vendor in the stands did more for the team.

"Same thing for our forefathers' accomplishments or our people's inventions. We like the dopamine releases caused by wins, even vicarious ones. But we can't take pride in the achievements of those outside our group. Envy makes us resent them and try to disqualify them with contorted, self-serving rationalizations.

"We capitalists aren't confined like that. Not when you're as rich as me. We'll copy, buy, or steal whatever we can get away with to end up with the money. What matters is the amount of money in my account, because I don't give a shit how much is in yours. Who cares if our jersey colors match?

"Now I'll play devil's advocate. A million Progressives have given me some version of the following argument, so I know it enough."

A VFX filter made the video frame a warm orange hue, placed virtual flowers in his ear and made it so viewers saw him as wearing tie-dye and suede hippie clothes.

In a mocking hippie accent, Chuck said, "Hey, man. What you gotta realize is that naturally empathetic people are perceptive of others' needs and feel for them, dude." He shook that off. "Okay, I can't keep that up. So, here's a clip from Maria Gutierrez blathering the same points..."

The feed stitched to a cued-up clip. Maria said, "If you can place yourself in another's shoes, you become 'principled selfless' — where you gotta be cool with a loss because you'd want others to play by the same fair rules. It's not 'win at any cost' or 'cheating ain't cheating if you don't get caught.' Gotta stop that domination mentality. On the flip side, if you sympathize by nature, instead of as a calculated move, you celebrate the good stuff — compassion and generosity. Check out that philosopher, John Rawls, who said you gotta make society as if you didn't know how you'd be born, where you'd grow up, your race, gender, sexual identity, disabilities, family money, and whatnot. Called that the 'Veil of Ignorance,' and it's the only right way to figure out fair rules. Though, for sure I do get that 'when you're used to privilege, equality feels like oppression.' However, you can't blame me for saving my tears for who has it tougher. Even though it always sucks to lose anything, no doubt. I totally see why those who come from money don't want to give up that advantage."

The feed stitched back to Chuck in response. He asked, "And why would they? Why should they give up their family fortune? That's almost like saying if your parents are athletes, you should cut off a finger to limit your advantage in sports. Okay, back to Maria for a bit…"

Another stitch to Maria, and she said, "Whether you want to redistribute wealth and provide services to the less fortunate depends on if you've seen first-hand or benefited from a government or social service. Ok let's say you see a cop catching someone crime-ing or firefighters saving a building full of people, or Medicaid prolonging the life of an elderly parent or grandparent for years, or a new transit system that legit speeds commutes. You gotta see taxes as a worthwhile 'cost of doing business.' JK Rowling famously, enthusiastically paid full taxes without taking advantage of every tax scheme or accounting trick that would lower the amount she had to pay. Her reasoning was gratitude. She said she considered herself indebted to the system because she was on welfare when writing the first Harry Potter book."

Chuck cut in again and said, "She wants to flipside it? Okay. Consider the entrepreneur, or hell, even a lottery winner, and they encounter problems from the government — burdensome regulations, incompetent or corrupt police, worsening traffic, and you see lazy addicts living the easy life off your dollars? How do libs not see how infuriating it is for us, if not for themselves? You see this kind of waste of our taxes, and we see taxes as theft. If you're born into a wealthy family, some parent or ancestor had to work hard, take risks, and think their way to wealth in the first place. They want to shield their kids and their kids' kids. Who wouldn't? It's not fair to tax their money twice, first on the earnings and again on the gift to the son. One more time from Ms. Maria the Libby-Lib."

She asked, "How is being born to a wealthy family fundamentally different from winning the lottery? The child did nothing. The lottery winner at least bought the ticket and took the risk of losing. Also, don't forget, all money is taxed multiple times during transactions. The person buying the item pays sales tax, and the seller pays income taxes. After income taxes, the seller becomes a buyer of something else, and the cycle repeats, with the government always getting its paper along the way. Here's the 'can't miss' point: for any set of government services for cops and welfare and whatnot, the IRS must collect some minimum amount of taxes. Of course, people can argue about which services should happen and for who, and also who should pay and what amount of taxes."

Chuck concluded, saying, "And that's the point. With the UBI-Compromise, everyone's getting a free ride with no responsibility, no purpose. They're just gonna wander around getting fat and high and adding nothing to the country. You can tell me property crime and robbery keep dropping, and I question those numbers. But even if they're right, human beings gotta do something productive. What happens if they want to revolt? Tons of bitter moochers get greedy and want more from us producers. What are you gonna do then? Let yourself be a victim? No. I don't think we're gonna allow that, are we? Nope.

"So go make something and get rich. And once you have some money, be sure you have the peace of mind that comes with trusted security. Rosti Security Systems is the best, and my freelance personnel are available for all of your needs. Loyalty can be purchased, but it ain't cheap. You want a cheap security guard? You're really buying a robber or hostage-taker and letting them in your front door to scout. In contrast, Rosti experts vet our security guards to ensure your and your family's safety. Not to mention, we'll ensure your valuables will not be stolen by those who want to take you down. Call for an appointment right now."

ENDNOTE #5 — "AI's Evolution"
Return to Novel on Page #26

    An animated short, showed workers using shovels to dig a canal in China. A character resembling Right-wing, Nobel prize-winning economist Milton Friedman asked the bureaucratic manager, "Why so few machines?"

    "Because this is a 'jobs program'!"

    Friedman said, "If it's jobs you want, then you should give these workers spoons, not shovels."

    The Libertarian and Republican attendees appreciated the inarguable point, if not the rather obvious pander since that was one of Friedman's most famous quotes.

    The video continued with a montage of archival clips illustrating the following real-life examples of Man vs. Machine.

    John Henry vs. The Steam Drill (he died unable to best the mechanism).

    Gary Kasparov vs. Deep Blue (humanity lost in chess).

    Famed AI2's Oren Etzioni's TEDx Talk: "Preventable Medical Errors are the third leading cause of death in US hospitals. It's the absence of AI that's killing people."

    Artificial Intelligence systems increased their accuracy at identifying diseases from CT and MRI scans beyond the most experienced radiologists. Charts showing an undeniable trajectory of progressive success were superimposed over a collage of the thousands of patients grateful AI saved their lives through earlier detection.

    A digital avatar version of Dan Rather (scanned and licensed before his death), "Most had no idea how many people's jobs can already be done better by a machine."

    The Hadrian X Bricklaying Robot built walls at 20 times the speed of the most experienced construction workers.

There were actual clips of AI doing legal and insurance claims work. The AI "Hallucination" problem was corrected with subroutines to cross-check multiple vetted databases.

Then, a clip from the famous episode of Jeopardy when IBM WATSON answered, "Who is Bram Stoker?" and Alex Trebek bounced two inches and said, "You are right!" Following was the glorious moment when Jeopardy Champ Ken Jennings lost to IBM's AI. Ken wrote this actual final answer on his screen: "*I, for one, welcome our new computer overlords.*"

It chronicled the historic transition from Stock Traders vs. Terminals (from people shouting in a crowded pit to the modern, quiet hum of servers).

Scenes showed school lectures replaced by Khan Academy tutorials on YouTube, and the result was that teachers became personal tutors. They served rich kids, as in days of aristocracy. Some gave time to other communities, where, in practice, they functioned more as social workers.

Google's (Virtual/AI) Assistant booked a haircut appointment with an unknowing hairdresser and then haggled to victory against a slimy car salesman.

ChatGPT and its competitors and successors accomplished a dizzying array of tasks. This showed it wasn't so much the cliched fear of AI taking individuals' jobs but rather how a single person, with the help of AI, was replacing ten people's jobs, then 20, then 30.

Computer-generated art, music, scripts, video with digital actors and voice-over artists, and even poetry were so varied and sophisticated that neither computers nor humans could identify if the creator was AI. No one could find profit in AI creations since, officially, they couldn't be copyrighted. Studios used them anyway and lied about their sources in their applications registering IP protection. Writers and directors earned public support for multiplying penalties by 100 and holding execs personally liable to disincentivize their violations.

Studios responded by using AI and hiring humans to make minimal changes to earn IP rights. Copyright law changed again, further nullifying IP protection for any AI-connected work, even when humans made modifications. The hypothesis (and hope) was studios would employ more human creators to start from scratch. That worked for a decade, and then consumers' behaviors shifted. The public prioritized unchallenging entertainment that delivered preferred emotions. This led to "feelings optimization" based on second-by-second viewing and tablet reading habits correlated with facial expressions and biometric readings.

As a result, people disregarded authorship. If creators wanted to monetize their work, they had to evolve into celebrities earning via corporate sponsorships or merchandising (tribe-building through virtue signaling). Good looks and on-screen charisma became crucial to their careers. Writers?!? Can you imagine? God forbid.

*Don't turn to the author bio and photo page.

ENDNOTE #6 — "Roxy's Theory of Evil"
Return to Novel on Page #32

Four months ago, two of the megabanks stopped lending to ZerQuali and wouldn't give a reason. Roxy's advancements were exceeding targets and ahead of schedule, but the burn rate was high, and the company couldn't grow without a tremendous infusion of capital. While her finance team toured Wall Street and the VCs, Roxy identified the perfect partner.

Roxy's SocialMui was filled with technological research news. The only one not tech-related was a dedicated feed from legendary financier Gwendolyn Grantham. This appeared discordant with the rest of the app's AI guide; it kept asking Roxy if she wanted to reduce or dismiss Gwendolyn's posts. Roxy "goddamn-ited" her way into the app's preferences and disabled this annoyance. She found a path to victory.

Roxy had courted this ideal one-stop investor, first on social media, against a tidal wave of rivals for Gwendolyn's attention. Roxy lamented the laziness of her Generation Alpha and pined in admiration for the work ethic of industrious Millennials like Gwendolyn. Most cohorts have greater affinity for their leapfrogs than their immediate generations. Roxy and Gwendolyn both slammed the Gen-Xers and Zoomers as slackers, whiners, and heathens. This pissed off millions who took even more offense because Roxy and Gwendolyn didn't switch to private messaging. It was as if they smack-talked near a loudspeaker, fearless of any public scorn, shaming the world for eavesdropping. Due to Gwendolyn's leery nature, public pronouncements trumped private messages, since hypocrisy and two-facedness thrive in secrecy.

Roxy commented on Gwendolyn's posts with refreshing bluntness, even criticizing her views, albeit with consistent respect and intellectual rigor. They developed a familiar correspondence while the world watched, surprised Gwendolyn would be so receptive, given her background.

Gwendolyn Grantham's quadruple-great-grand parents were born on an estate "bigger than the White House" on a 90,000-acre plantation, epitomizing Old Money Atlanta. The Grantham family fortune wavered depending on the generational cycle of trusty steward to his trust fund-fool son to his righting, trusty steward offspring, and so on. Their mansion itself brimmed with antiques and artwork from the United Kingdom, but not historic stolen property from around the world, rather the royally commissioned paintings and furniture.

Throughout the South, the Grantham name adorned university professorships (incentivizing research for her missions), college libraries (ensuring acceptance of family members), and symphony halls (establishing culture "as good as any Yankee"). While evangelical proselytizing had always been most important to her, a close second was her family. When doctors diagnosed Gwendolyn's grandniece with autism, that field of research, of course, got an eight-figure check. Countless counted on Gwendolyn's philanthropy.

As all would expect, donation jackals (from well-intentioned but ineffective groups to counterproductive grifters) chased her as a potential benefactor. In response, Gwendolyn's guard hardened. She was eternally suspicious of anyone who wanted anything from her.

Charities flourished whenever a Grantham family member fell stricken with their cause. If perverse prayers for such varied misfortunate came true, that would open Gwendolyn's eyes and checkbook to other problems in the world. Short of salvation for all, proximity determined her priorities.

Gwendolyn took glee in saying, "I have friends who are Jews, and they have this belief — 'Tikkun Olam,' which means to 'heal the world,' but they shrewdly add this quote: 'You are not obligated to complete the work, but neither are you free to desist from it,' And that's why they take care of themselves." Gwendolyn's motivations to do "Good Works" were always tempered by her superseding faith. No one but God could fix everything on earth, so that couldn't be her personal responsibility. "For there's but one Heaven, and the only way to it is through Jesus Christ, our Lord and Savior."

The majority of Gwendolyn's posts accused Chuck of criminal behavior, citing an endless supply of evidence. But otherwise, her followers found inspirational, religious messages. She often said, "Don't pray by begging Him to grant wishes on earth. Beg for the strength and grace to become worthy of Heaven."

Roxy's own posts were text-based and tech-centric. Gwendolyn trusted faces more than words, famously only doing business in person. It's too bad; Roxy was better in fewer dimensions. IRL: awkward. Live Video: Okay, Recorded Audio: good. Crafted text: best. This meant Roxy's biggest gambit would have to be one of her rare video posts.

Roxy turned on her ring light while hum-singing the lyrics to one of the few songs she knew. "I'll need a credit card that's got no limit. And a big black jet with a bedroom in it." She composed herself, uncapped her web camera, sighed, and let out a little chuckle. Quoting her ex-boyfriend, she said, "I should've written this ahead of time, but I want to speak from the heart." In contrast, she looked down at her rigorous, prepared speech and began recording.

"Dear Gwendolyn, I've appreciated your discussions of religion since I'm unfamiliar with this territory. I'm glad you encourage forthright talk because I'm no good at any other way. You know I'm a skeptic and an ardent agnostic. Despite that, I've been trying an old friend's technique of aggressive open-mindedness. To that end, today, I arrived at a logical response to the atheist's critical question: '*How can an omnipotent, omniscient, omnibenevolent God allow so much evil and misery in the world?*'

"The intellectual maneuver I like is challenging the premise there somehow is 'so much' evil. In short, I'm merely reformulating an 'Afterlife' argument — eschatological theodicy, close to Saint Augustine of Hippo's contentions. I call this version 'All Evil Reduces to Zero.'

"Okay, let's assume the position of the faithful; God exists and is all-powerful, all-knowing, and all-good, and also, heaven endures for all eternity. That's true while we still recognize all the evil and misery that befalls the world, such as crime, war, famine, disease, etc.. Now, I'll lay out three points and the conclusion.

"Point number one. As you age, your perception of time changes such that durations that seemed like eternities as a child, like a car ride, feel like trivial blips of travel when you're older. By the way, I should tip my hat to the decades-old Cracked.com article '5 Reasons Immortality Would Be Worse Than Death.' I found some of it quite clever.

"Point number two. Likewise, let's recognize we recalibrate our concepts of pain and justice as we age. For example, the needle of a vaccination shot seemed terrifying and excruciating as a child, but for adults feel absurdly inconsequential compared to the benefits of scientifically sound medicine.

"Regarding justice, consider a hypothetical, egocentric, selfish teenage girl who steals her sister's boyfriend. It might feel okay to herself in the moment. She is likely to view it differently as she matures and gains a greater understanding of the world. So, while it's not 'right,' it's also not that big of a deal compared to global catastrophes and existential threats to humanity.

"Point three. Given points number one and two and the assumption that time in heaven must be infinite, one must conclude a human's entire time on earth will thus 'reduce to zero.' Any finite amount of time or pain will eventually be perceived as an ever-smaller fraction of one's eternal existence. As will all of humanity's time on earth, compared to the infinite afterlife.

"One murder is a tragedy for the victim's family and friends, but it's merely a statistic to the rest of the population in that period. Worse still, over time, that statistic was likely less and less known while becoming more and more irrelevant to subsequent generations. The Holocaust is still somewhat fresh in our collective minds because so much documentary and witness testimony were recorded to retell the history. Compare that to slavery in America hundreds of years ago or Stalin or Mao, where they killed many times as many people. The further back in time the evil struck, the less relevant it is to us.

"In mathematics, ¼ is less than ½. If you divide by a bigger number (in the denominator), the amount is less. Therefore, any specific number divided by infinity functionally equals zero. If you could somehow live on earth for 100 years, remember that 100 divided by infinity = Zero.

"That isn't meant to be a nihilistic or Quietist criticism that life is meaningless and shouldn't be improved, but rather, to the faithful, life on earth is relatively meaningless compared to the eternity of life in heaven. Thus making getting into heaven and faith even more essential and, therefore, good deeds or 'repairing the world' much less important.

Roxy was uncomfortably deferential in her closing, "Bottom line, I know you're a person of profound faith. It'd be cravenly dishonest to feign conversion in an attempt to get in your good graces. So, I hope this shows my good faith journey toward greater understanding."

When Gwendolyn first watched the video, she leaned back, did clasping prayer hands, and scanned the ornate, formerly royal, carpet in thought. Roxy made herself vulnerable in a sweet gesture of comity and respect. That meant Gwendolyn's ultimate plans might work with Roxy as a business partner.

These philosophical messages volleyed for two months until they started brunching together, at first with Roxy flying to Gwendolyn, and soon after crisscrossing the country to never miss a week. Roxy tried to get funding, but Gwendolyn shot this down at once, reading Roxy's reaction. Roxy gave a flat, "Okay," and moved on to another topic.

Gwendolyn said, "I must tell you, Roxy, that I appreciate how you easily took 'no' for an answer. I ain't kiddin'. Everyone else makes it so awkward. Let me tell you something about the well-to-do; we're always worried people are only friendly to get something out of us — money, influence, fame by association. You know what I'm talking about."

"I do," Roxy said. "I've been isolated in certain bubbles, so I'm grateful to get your perspective, and this a rare friendship for me."

Gwendolyn blushed and drew her eyes down to her tea. "That's a delight to hear."

"But my company does need investment. So, if not you, can you help guide me to someone who'd be a better fit?"

"Tell you what. Let's fly back together, and you can give me a tour and the whole show. I don't recommend without knowing what I'm recommending."

"Excellent. Thank you, Gwendolyn," Roxy said, her fingers a blur on her smartphone.

Days later, while touring ZerQuali's facility, Gwendolyn saw a news report about Chuck Rosti's declining health in advance of his imminent prosecution. She asked Roxy, "So someone like Mr. Rosti could become immortal?"

Roxy said, "Imagine the fees we could charge. For immortality, elderly oligarchs will pay billions just to queue up for bidding wars on the first spots."

"That does seem like a good business model," Gwendolyn said.

"But I'd need to maintain control of the research on whatever schedule I deem appropriate. No one can shepherd this other than me. That's a deal breaker."

"I think we can find a deal on this."

Weeks after that, the two of them began friendly negotiations, with a handshake on everything but the number.

ENDNOTE #7 — "Subtirees and The Livable Year"
Return to Novel on Page #36

In the early 2030s, the US economy's growth had exceeded most expectations by several major historic metrics (e.g., GDP Per Capita, Corporate Record Profits, etc.), though others flatlined or worsened (e.g., GINI index). The newer metrics, better measuring the impact on human beings and our quality of life (e.g., Food Insecurity Index, "Housing & Unpreferably Cohabitating" Scores, "Maslow's Tiers" Numbers, "Work/Life Balance," et al.) continued their worrying downward trend.

Income inequality became ultra-extreme as growing numbers of American workers couldn't beat AI and robots on price, speed, accuracy, and evolution/improvement rate. Unemployment skyrocketed past 40% in modern Western countries and got twice as bad in the worst-hit developing countries. In America, "Non-Vehicle Resident Homelessness" exceeded ten million people. "Vehicle Resident Homelessness" added five million people.

FEMA, state governments, and major cities scurried to erect emergency, makeshift housing, but enough critics' comparisons to Japanese internment camps and Nazi concentration camps made that untenable long term.

Populists called for major improvements in social safety nets (including Medicare, Medicaid, Housing, and unemployment insurance) and several other measures well beyond Scandinavian-style socialism.

Despite most billionaires' wealth coming from inheritance, high society continued to have utter faith in the market; their mantras were "the best always rise to the top" and "dumb rich gets poor." These were self-interested rationalizations. For them, "Undeserving elite" must somehow be an oxymoron. They imply the intelligentsia deserve their supremacy for being born to the right uterus. Similarly, they must disregard the possibility of injustices regarding "unrecognized genius" or "undervalued productivity" — despite both being necessary for excess profits to be extracted from the markets. Therefore, those working for and near the top, by default, perpetuated this narrative lest they risk antagonizing their paycheck-signers. Novelist Upton Sinclair said, "It is difficult to get a man to understand something when his salary depends on his not understanding it."

Chuck's infamous rant — "everyone rigs the system for themselves" got it half-right, in that the metaphorical "B," "C," "D," and "F" students among the landed gentry (and there are many) couldn't risk the emergence of a true meritocracy. They didn't want to lose their spots to the students, analysts, inventors, creators, and general solution-makers, etc., who delivered "A" grade work since there was exponentially more competition from among the greater population due to the "pyramid of prosperity."

However, separate from the nepo-babies who coast, the legitimate "A" students among the literati and their "A+" advisors recognized that there had to be some sort of meritocracy to encourage overall advancement and productivity, separate from any concept of fairness. The conservative elite stuck to the pedigree system of lineage from "prominent families," graduation from Ivy League schools, and other traditional signifiers of worthiness and exceptionalism. "Limousine Liberals" prided themselves on identifying and elevating the exceptionally gifted from diverse groups and lesser-appreciated areas.

Ramifications were afterthoughts. The underprivileged folks who delivered "B+" work or below were thus dismissed out of hand. They didn't have the same right to be merely "solid and competent" and receive the same benefits. The upper crust was fine with proportionately unfair results for those below the Top 10%.

It continued to decline further down the income scale. The bottom 25% fell into poverty, causing "Family Consolidation" —

whereby extended relations (even to second cousins) became housemates and shared their meager resources.

In response to years of stagnating median wages, the leftist hacker group Anonymous broke into the HR databases across 100,000 businesses and released all salary and bonus info. That revealed decades of standard business lies told in contract negotiations. The ever-widening income inequality became starkly public and undeniable. Every union complained about CEOs invariably choosing to pay themselves more (irrespective of their companies' performance or any proof their executive decisions positively effected any success). In a less direct way, stock buybacks inflated stock prices, making execs' option packages more valuable. CEOs wielded the power to fire board members who challenged such compensation, thus further entrenched the unquestioning fealty. Employees responded by continuing the trend of "quiet quitting," sometimes conspicuously slacking off as a poor man's way to give oneself a raise on a "unit of effort" basis. The widely predicted backlash spawned excessive layoffs to "punish and discourage" that organic, metastasizing insubordination. Shareholders accepted lower profits since they saw the scourge of rebellion as an existential threat.

The growing hordes of broke, homeless, and hopeless led to more shoplifting and petty theft, which hastened the destruction of brick-and-mortar stores. As soon as the shiftless turned violent, the electorate demanded solutions.

Developing countries had literal guillotine revolutions, gruesome and without due process, killing technocrats, NGOs, and do-gooders alongside those they deemed to be corrupt and murderous fascists. A few countries that seemed modern and prosperous collapsed due to unsurvivable runaway inflation. Worldwide, many of the most authoritarian Fascists won the backing of the 1% by promising crackdowns.

Author Naomi Klein popularized the notion of the "Shock Doctrine," whereby the untouchably powerful use and, even scarier, create crises and disasters to enable unpopular policies, greater fascism, and control of the citizens. But this time was different; the elite had become a victim of its own success and excess. The balance skewed with too few titans and way too many impoverished with well beyond the figurative "nothing to lose." A frog may not notice he's being slow-boiled, but if the "comforting" water spills out, the pot is hot enough to cause one to leap. The extreme inequality meant the ratio of human support was too far imbalanced by historical standards. Government leaders took notice. The old expression was that politicians find parades and run in front as if they were leading them. This was more like palace guards dropping swords and uniforms for pitchforks and torches during the storming of the Bastille.

In response, a couple of European countries commandeered crucial industries of farming, transportation, and utilities ("seizing the means of production") and veered from socialism into communism. The frozen-out investors and banks panicked. Canned goods and essentials ran out in every store. Transportation froze. Government promises to fix supply chain issues were worthless when no one had enough faith to execute the plans. Food riots killed thousands in every country.

The more "paranoid," doomsday-prepping billionaires retreated to their fortified bunker palaces, replete with years of survival goods and sustainable hydroponic greenhouses. In these scenarios, rioters and criminal threats only respect violent power. That meant hiring armed security to tame any human chaos and danger. But when all bow to the men with guns, their employer can't take loyalty for granted. These billionaires feared their staff revolting, bodyguards becoming prison guards. Most of them proved loyal and grateful to have protection. News reported some security teams' mutinies. In one particularly gruesome instance, the billionaire had booby-trapped the water supply that required his password and bio-readings every 24 hours. The maniac, traitor chief of security tortured the billionaire and threatened to do the same to his children; he got the password. He subsequently kept the billionaire sedated for months for the biometric readings. In the end, the billionaire got his revenge, with an Epstein ending.

People were so eager to bring back the civilization they had mere months prior that, faster than Chuck described, the Power Brackets emerged and accelerated close to recognizable equilibrium. The global mad chaos finally subsided when people started electing "Pragmatic Populists."

PraPops activists decried skyrocketing housing prices coupled with the fact that, by that time, 15 million Americans were unhoused, while America had 60-plus million vacant homes. They sat around because of extended "on the market" disuse. Explanations included showings, foreign ownership without ever even vacationing in them (let alone residing). Add to that secondary/summer residences, and strategic limitations of supply in order to keep prices high. Most of the public learned 4x as many houses went empty while millions were unhoused — a dramatic under-use of limited resources and a shameful waste. Everyone demanded action.

Real estate investors and construction companies advocated for an end to environmental, safety regulations, and NIMBY-ism to accelerate building new properties.

But what good would building more inventory be if they were only to be snapped up by the ultra-elite worldwide to be unused as third or perhaps twentieth homes? Might as well rebuild in a flood zone with rapidly fleeing businesses, because if inventory isn't available to the public, the benefit is minimal. In fact, it's worse than that because the newly built homes have ongoing maintenance costs to keep them clean and lawns well-manicured. So it's like building in a flood zone and then wasting people's time to sweep the river floor and arrange the swamp marshes in beautiful displays that no one will see. If one decorates a remote forest no one visits, is one not insane? Such make-work necessarily has opportunity costs. If society spends resources, they should impact citizens' lives in measurably positive ways.

Conservative think tanks attempted to misdirect and obfuscate. Their coordinated talking points said, "It's impossible to end transients living on the streets. There will always be mentally ill and addicts who can't afford to pay anything, plus 'free spirit' hippies who prefer to roam 'out in the world.'"

The PraPops said, "That's a bullshit, strawman argument. You could use that same framing to say there shouldn't be police or prisons because you can't extinguish the problem. No policy is ever perfect. There will always be some problems regarding ineffective implementation and enforcement. In any event, shelters and public housing for the homeless cost taxpayers a lot of money. Why should the hoarders of empty homes entirely push the damage they do onto the rest of the community? 100% free markets have no upper limit on the amount of wealth a person can stockpile. One could have a King of England — Egyptian Pharaoh — Scrooge McDuck amount of precious metals and money doing nothing but sitting in a vault. Building countless homes that remain empty doesn't help. Most people would agree that such a system is a suboptimal, if not an obscenely unethical, allocation of resources.

Thus, regulations ensure a viable balance of supply and demand. That's when some penalties went into effect to encourage landlords to rent to people, even if, or perhaps because it would lower rents and housing prices.

At first, the "PraPops" tried what they called "Xiǎo gǎijìn" (shao guy-jean), which is Mandarin for "Small Improvement" (and oddly sounds a bit like "Lucky Foreigner" in Japanese). They attempted to deploy incentives and punishments to tinker with the free market. They had to make the formula quite complicated just to work on paper. The government needed to pressure owners of empty homes to lower prices to hit ideal affordability targets. So we taxed them a bit extra, a percentage of their high-water mark listed asking price for sale or rental.

They fined landlords for every month their residence went unoccupied, paying the "EHT" (Empty Home Tax). This meant average family homeowners trying to sell their house didn't have to because they were living there. Real estate firms withholding inventory to create artificial scarcity and push prices up would now be punished for manipulating the market. The plan was for real estate sellers to cut their prices quickly so houses would be actually used as homes.

Additional rules prevented gaming the system. Construction didn't delay anything. So, REITs couldn't procrastinate with fake repairs and upgrades. This had the side benefit of speeding up needed construction and reducing wasteful construction. Remodeling every year shrinks the pie. People's second homes were exempt, but not their third or any beyond those. So, multi-home owners had to fill enough of them through sublets or Airbnb or pay the penalty. This, too, made more inventory available since third homes' additional penalties made them less attractive to own.

This regulation first proved popular because it helped so many (e.g., the unhoused and those struggling to afford rent), negatively affected so few (e.g., homeowners who were only selling and not buying a new house), and inflicted the most severe punishment on the unsympathetic real estate owners who preferred empty homes to housing people.

Of course, finance wizards strategized to game the system doing "wash trades," swapping units in a "round robin" with a dozen other real estate investors every month. The PraPops responded by making the fines escalate regardless of buyer if they remained unoccupied. The real estate world started renting to unhoused people for crazy modest sums to get out of the penalties. It was working! But prices were plummeting, and so investors and those who owned their residences panicked.

These regular homeowners got angry. Homeownership has always been the primary vehicle for wealth creation, and this EHT policy was trashing everything. Institutional investors got hit harder, so they sicced their amplified ranks of lobbyists to join the regular homeowners. The backlash tsunami overwhelmed the PraPops, and they "sprinted to admit they were wrong" with that noble experiment.

The circumstances still required residences of some kind for all 15+ million unhoused Americans. A PraPop economist, known only as the mononym Maynard, wrote an Op-Ed in The American Prospect showing a less inexpensive solution. She pitched "Sleeping Pods" and the "Livable Year." This weirdly suped-up, Scandinavian-style socialism radically raised the floor for Americans while costing less than the EHT and recent policies. The public had amnesia, or a lack of appreciation regarding how this was cheaper for the wealthy than America was in the 1950s – 1970s, where marginal taxation for peak earners exceeded 90%. Years later, Maynard was revealed to be a consortium of progressive organizations and heavy-check philanthropists.

The PraPops made a grand bargain with the billionaire-donor ruling class. It horrified many, but few could convince the rest to accept other "better" solutions. The leftists and pragmatists required the plan to offer to feed, clothe, house, medically care for, and provide entertainment to everyone above a minimal level. This attractive floor, a LY ("Livable Year") exceeded how the bottom 25% lived. It wasn't even that expensive because 50+ years of ever-widening income inequality disproved 1980s Margaret Thatcher's cynical criticism — "the problem with socialism is that you eventually run out of other people's money." Indeed, it became cheaper for the top 1/10th of 1% to provide the minimum "LY" mitigated by a controversial plan for reducing future costs.

Inspired by Thomas Robert Malthus, the wealthy were immovable on their most severe and impactful demand — "It's unsustainable to have unproductive leeches on our economy, spawning exponential generations of greater burdens on our land." The tree-huggers and hair-torched climate change shriekers had long claimed a smaller human population would undoubtedly create a more acceptable ecological impact in the long term. David Attenborough said, "We have a finite environment—the planet. Anyone who thinks that you can have infinite growth in a finite environment is either a madman or an economist." Virtually everyone else agreed that earth doesn't have enough resources (water, energy, biomass, etc.) for a quadrillion humans to live at the same time. Many scientists believed the actual number to be closer to one billion humans worldwide. Whatever the exact number might be, it's within that range. Leaders and the kings of finance conceded that our global economy can't tolerate (let alone depend on) infinite growth. This fit the environmentalists' paradigm, who co-signed on that imperative. However, they were conflicted on the ramifications of their new allies' ultimatum.

The Devilish Details: the Top-10% would subsidize anyone in the bottom 40% (plus the disabled at any strata) to a certain minimum quality of life threshold so long as that person didn't procreate. The "productive" and wealthy accepted these so-called "one-generation burdens," and this would theoretically mitigate the Differential Fertility (a.k.a. the "Intelligence-Fertility Paradox" illustrated in the satire/quasi-documentary *Idiocracy*). Most felt this was immoral, and many voiced cogent counterarguments based on ethics and evidence.

Humanity is such a young species that the majority's "bow to the alpha" primal instinct, magnified by decades of corporate conditioning, overruled those ethical reservations. Most accepted the rationalization that intelligent, creative, talented, healthy, good-looking, productive people of means should have more children.

The problematic definitions of those criteria and resulting dangerous constraints on liberty didn't catalyze enough critics. Increasingly discouraged Zoomers and Alphas already considered having kids unconscionable while environmental problems went unabated. Coupled with the outrageous costs of raising a child, it resulted in 64% public approval of the compromise bill as written. Another 26% accepted the principle but wanted better terms in differing directions. That only 10% of the public (extreme Libertarians and Ultra-Leftists) opposed this devil's deal horrified Ivy ethicists. It was, after all, an individual's choice whether to work to live a "normal" life or this new option — one no population in world history was ever guaranteed — to select a life of complete leisure, however austere it was.

The conventional wisdom in the mainstream media thought it was weird that both extremes were actually happy at the same time. That horseshoe came together because there were right-wingers who didn't want to see homeless people on the street, whether it was sympathy or perhaps the eyesore of it. Meanwhile Leftists always decried humanity's increasing damage to the planet caused by ever-growing overpopulation, guaranteeing doom for all species.

Congress passed, and the president signed the clumsily named "APAL" (AMERICAN PATRIOTS for AMERICA LEGISLATION) that officially, point#1 — ended poverty and homelessness for the bleeding-heart Leftists, and point#2 — effectively got most of the poor to sterilize themselves voluntarily in exchange for the support. The propaganda spins got confusing since the proponents sought to pronounce it "A pal," as in "a friend," whereas opponents used the derisive pronunciation, "Appall," as in "Appalling."

Even proponents found the details distasteful. As soon as people turned 18 and got the right to vote, they got to choose this reversible sterilization payoff option for the enhanced UBI and life of leisure. They were called "Subtirees" (a portmanteau of "sub" meaning under and "retiree"). On the other hand, opting out was one of the most potent signifiers of either privilege or some combination of pride, confidence, and ambition. The Subtirees enviously called those people "Flaunters," and some Flaunters leaned in, variously wearing "Flaunter"-branded merch.

Leftists feared plausible conspiracies that this plan would trick Subtirees into infertility and later stop paying off, whether due to deliberate reneging or incompetence. How could these future payments be economically calculated? And whatsoever amount that was defined would nevertheless be vulnerable to devastating inflation and currency devaluation. Everyone was all too familiar with photos and other documentary evidence of desperate citizens of failed states pushing wheelbarrows full of their cash to pay for a loaf of bread.

This 20NF-precipice solution went beyond absurdly anachronistic gold-backed currencies. Standards for a "Livable-Year" were established covering all the vital resource categories a human needs.

FOOD: A daily allocation of 2500 calories of nutritious food deemed 3-stars or better in taste by consumers and provided in at least 50 varieties (with allergy-sensitive options).

SHELTER: At least 200 square feet of safe, well-ventilated space, with electricity, climate control, and that was walking distance to live entertainment. However, those who preferred the exurbs and rural areas forwent the walkability requirements.

HEALTHCARE: All medications and treatments prescribed by medical doctors (for all problems, including physical, mental, and, as if they ever should've been excluded, teeth and eyes). This meant human and AI Doctors handling in-patient surgery and out-patient services on-demand, and AI robot nurses serving as caretakers. Society sufficiently addressed depression and anxiety with everything that works — free therapy (human and AI), "emotion-hacking" apps, meditation resources, diet and exercise support, promoting a culture of gratitude, and incentivizing citizens to actually put stuff in their calendars that they could look forward to (if not social occasions at least preferred series and film premieres, music and sports events, and upcoming hyper-targeted product releases to covet).

ENTERTAINMENT: 1000 channels plus SVOD from all major OTT platforms, plus 1TB internet, plus live entertainment with five live concerts per year, three plays or musicals, three stand-up comedy shows, and 12 sporting events in at least three sports.

CLOTHING: At least ten complete outfits crowd-rated at 3-stars or better and provably durable.

That was a "Livable-Year."

Then came the inevitable "public-private partnerships" that lobbyists demanded. An abundance of companies bid on providing such "Livable-Years" that subsidized citizens. Many companies teamed with each other to bundle complementary services to get access to these government funds. To earn validation as a provider, companies had to demonstrate they had the property and resources to provide everything in full. They further had to be diversified by area to ensure against natural calamities interrupting delivery. Amazon was the first to jump on this opportunity, followed within months by Alibaba. There was competition to provide increasingly "better" LYs to get more contracts. There was a race to the top, and the market incentives worked as intended. Substandard LY-providers lost business and were quickly shuttered. As a backup, they made pacts to insure each other, so if they failed, another would be responsible. It was like the Price-Anderson Act that compelled other nuclear companies to pay if one had a meltdown and couldn't cover the costs.

Better yet, LY corporate executives were required to be paid on a 30-year distributed horizon: no more quick-bucks or golden parachutes. Profitability had to be long term, and successors' failures would penalize previous execs' retirement. Corporations refocused away from the short-term into longer-term economic stability and prosperity. Incentives had been better aligned. Externalities were so punished that arbitrage, greed, and incompetence were more easily identified and prevented.

People still wanted to make things and be productive. Some still craved fame and recognition. A square building can only have four corner offices on each floor, and they'd always spawn envy due to the fundamental scarcity and advantage of better views. It was not communism because everyone wasn't given all the same things. Indeed, that's impossible. And it wasn't official "state socialism" because the state didn't own any "means of production." The government had cops/prisons, firemen, teachers, courts, and regulatory watchdogs with teeth. There was utter transparency, and corrupt officials got the ultimate comeuppance. It wasn't quite the future any partisan wanted, but nearly all found this compromise satisfactory. There'd still be incentives for innovation and efficiency. One could prosper over his neighbor or lose privileges due to criminality or failure. Everyone insisted on consequences, and a consensus was reached regarding the parameters.

With most of Maslow's "Hierarchy of Needs" satisfied, Subtirees were free to pursue self-actualization. Unfortunately, many never got off the "Hedonistic Treadmill." A sizable portion got into recreational drugs, sure that the safety net of emergency medical care with Norcan and other life-savers would be there. Even so, every year, hundreds of thousands of people died from drug overdoses, and there were thousands of collateral damage victims when the overdoser violently impacted the world. "The cost of business," many called it. That's because the alternative, prohibition and enforcement, had so utterly failed by every metric. Many considered this proof of right-wingers' righteousness. The weak succumbed, and our species benefitted by those weak genes not "polluting" the next generation. The left-wingers accepted the losses while futilely attempting to mitigate them.

Some sterilization could be reversed, but that procedure was deliberately designed to be expensive. A "Reverser" had to pay for the medical expenses as well as 5x whatever benefits they had already received from the government. In the ten years that this had been available, the number of reversers was tragically fewer than the number of mega-lottery winners.

The rich had no need to become Subtirees because the subsidy was so minuscule relative to their wealth. Children became a status symbol. Those in the upper and upper-middle classes took pride in never opting in. When a member of a family failed, the rest would subsidize their lifestyle for fear of having a Subtiree in the family as the ultimate black sheep. Snobs bragged how their family tree had no Subtiree infestation. It was more prestigious to be "third cousins clean" of Subtirees than to be a Mayflower descendant, fourth generation Ivy-leaguer with a second cousin who was on the dole. It was a new caste system with prejudice all too familiar to anyone who knew the history of India or Mixed-race Americans in the 1800s.

Social climbers shunned Subtirees and prized marriage into "more pure" families. When a family, due to circumstance or for whatever reason, chose not to subsidize a cousin to prevent Opt-in, that humiliating stain was legally recognized as "just cause" for divorce. And when a Flaunter had a child, he couldn't Opt-in for as long as the child lived. And if the child enjoyed any subsidies, those would have to be reimbursed at 5x for retroactive Opt-in. This seldom happened because the 5x cost was inherently cost-prohibitive for most everyone considering becoming a Subtiree after becoming a parent.

Perverse incentives motivated the most awful, borderline-broke parents to encourage their children to partake in dangerous activities (including drug overdoses). These actions were, of course, illegal. They nevertheless occurred to the great shame of left-wingers and to the "told-you-so" delight of merciless right-wingers.

Meanwhile, good Christians tried to help wherever they could. They proselytized the insignificance of Opt-in compared to the infinite glory of heaven in God's grace.

The choice of Opt-in wasn't relevant to upper-middle-class folks. Whereas so many of the working class had to do it, there was no stigma. The older generations resented not having enough grandchildren, but otherwise, the system resulted as designed. Population growth slowed and turned negative. Since growing populations taking care of the elderly only made sense insofar as it resulted in commensurately increasing productivity, the end of scarcity nullified the need for more workers. The robots were increasing productivity on their own. So, people were left with the "Ludic life" that many dreamed. They only worked to feel fulfilled, and if/when they got bored, they'd wander to another field. Everything fun became a job. At first, aspiring rock stars and poets proliferated. But no one was compelled to attend, and performing for empty venues kills dreams quick. And so, a rough equilibrium was attained. People would try scores of hobbies until they could elevate and turn them into a side hustle and, someday, a full-on job.

Lower-class Flaunters were seen as crazy and ambitious. It was so rare that even electing to Opt-out on one's 18th birthday was newsworthy. Poor Flaunters got their names mentioned in public recognition. Soon, some did that just to get some fame and opted-in days later. So, the system adjusted to only mention those who went at least a year without Opt-in. It was like AA year-sober chips but with much higher stakes. And when Flaunters succumbed to Opt-in, it wasn't recognized as a failure but a valiant effort worthy of general praise. Kids would brag about great uncles who had five or 10-year chips.

And the hedonistic treadmill continued. Standard human needs were being abundantly met, so new desires were recalibrated to necessities. Everyone wanted immortality, and the tech was coming soon... to a helipad-featured super yacht (not near you).

Further emotionally traumatizing, parents who couldn't afford to raise their children faced hyper surveillance from an increased Child Services administration. After warnings, compulsory classes and make-work assignments compelled neglectful parents to make a tougher choice: get your shit together and treat your children well, or your kids will be taken in by another family with you getting limited visitation only at the children's requests. The prospect of making the financial sacrifice to have kids only to see them taken away was seen as the worst possible scenario; very few risked it.

The great majority accepted all of this, insofar as they didn't take steps to stop it.

ENDNOTE #8 — "Hobbying Journalist is Pro Pro-Journalism"
Return to Novel on Page #37

    The Robo-Krupke scanned Viggo for a firearm, as per protocol. If one were found that didn't have an ultraband emitter duly registered to the carrier, that'd authorize the Robo-Krupke to "Taser & Detain." Back in the late 2030s, gun control advocates thought that this tech would've reduced the prevalence of weapons since outlaws would be proactively disarmed; unfortunately, the key concession in Congress was that every citizen automatically got "Concealed Carry permits." The number of guns per capita didn't change, and crime's downward trajectory went unimpeded.

    Viggo kept his head down, supplicating to the law enforcement robot as if it were a cop from Jim Crow-era Alabama or 1990s Los Angeles. Wise choice considering Robo-Krupkes first trained on millions of hours of Bodycam footage from before the 2020s. Uh oh.

    Viggo's favorite podcaster, Cenk Uygur, often reminded his audience, "The biggest crime in America is disrespecting a police officer. It's not an actual law. But break it and risk death. Ironically, cops will kindly take into custody an active shooter who's respectful but shoot an unarmed bystander who doesn't follow their whim."

    Chuck Rosti once streamed his counter. "Of course, cops should be cool with the respectful and fight the rest. We have the Second Amendment. So long as the gun-carrier abides by commands, he's no threat. On the other hand, an apparently unarmed guy who won't comply with a police order could commit other crimes and have an illegally concealed weapon. 'Better to be judged by twelve than carried by six.' Gotta trust people to make their own decisions."

AI hadn't yet mastered ethical personal judgment or even cracked "getting a bad vibe" from someone. Since a body of research showed dogs performed far better than chance at "sniffing out a bad person," an expert panel advocated that Robo-Krupkes work alongside dogs to provide such secondary assessments. But they found a confounding variable. A dog's capability to identify dangerous people functioned primarily by reading its master. A person can carry himself or hold the leash differently to communicate his discomfort, which is what dogs most respond to. We frame this as "getting a bad vibe" from a stranger. That flaw, coupled with systemic racism, made false positives too prevalent to be acceptable. The coup de grâce for the policy was from animal rights groups intolerant of machines as pet parents.

Ironically, these groups paved the way for "AI Rights" groups to begin protesting for machine-sentience personhood. Experts predicted a massive reduction in the number of animal adoptions, leading to a pet population decline so profound that they controversially called it a "near genocide." Movements for AI to be pet parents had to become an ever more complex ethical issue as humanity approaches AI supremacy.

In a puff piece for a university, Viggo "reported" on a professor claiming people with weapons tended to be more insecure and fearful. So Viggo treated them with deference, like a wild animal "more afraid of you than you are of it." He was selective in his risks, so he slowly backed away from this Robo-Krupke. There was no rush in his subtirement.

Viggo first studied to become a sculptor, but 3D printers made Michelangelo's Pieta look like kindergarten Play-Doh. Viggo went back to school for his MBA but suffered layoffs due to AI advancements. Ultimately, he "found a hobby" in investigative reporting, historically prestigious work since made scarce due to its fundamental unprofitability.

The Founding Fathers intended the freedom of the press to be a common good, valuing it enough for protection with the Constitution's First Amendment. The three branches of the U.S. government (Executive, Legislative, and Judicial) necessitated a "Fourth Estate" to be a vigilant rival. Alas, what is admirable or necessary isn't always profitable. News on 20th-century broadcast television lost money and was justified as a public service.

One vulnerability was all too exploitable. A news organization incurred all the costs and energy to do an investigation. After which, since no one can "own facts," the First Amendment protects other news sites reporting on that source's findings. The best the original reporters could hope for was a courtesy shout-out. Consequently, there was minimal upside to doing the journalistic work of resource-intensive research and investigations. Not to mention the risks of challenging interviews when it's so much cheaper, easier, and safer to copy & paste other news and reword it with AI to avoid copyright infringement. Ultimately, news functioned mostly as filler and starting points for pundits spewing opinions, functioning as parrots and stenographers for the powerful, regardless of truth.

In the early 21st century, the internet (especially Craigslist) cannibalized classified ads. Major advertisers became risk-averse to anything that challenged the establishment or courted controversy. The development of AI "journalists" through the 2020s decimated the viability of it as a job for 98% of those employed and devastated those who were aspiring.

It was disappointing. Those who needed real news had to rely on "Citizen Journalists" who investigated as a fun hobby. These were un- or underemployed people, often with English degrees, who became Subtirees, plus a handful of ungrateful trust-fund dilettantes who resented daddy's money.

Viggo's modest income from occasional paid PR work enabled residence in the level above the Sleeping-Pods, where the living quarters leveled up. These "Petit-Logis" were modular, self-contained micro-apartments. People started calling them "Ikea Favelas," meaning cheap to rich snobs and commendable to everyone else. Ikea feared losing its trademark protection due to its name becoming a generic term. They'd need more than a Kleenex, Band-Aid, Aspirin, or Heroin to handle Windsurfing out of this Kerosene-soaked Dumpster fire. Then it won the government contract to make the improved, beloved versions and counted its skyrocketing revenue.

Viggo and his wife, Trin, smirked while bragging that their Petit-Logi was "TWICE the size of a prison cell." Yet they knew this was Prozacs better than living on the street.

Trin was cherubic-faced, wide-hipped, and kind-eyed. She, her mom, and her grandmothers always said Trin was "destined to create a family." She had loved nurturing Viggo's ambitions since they were high school sweethearts. Alas, after years without long-term employment opportunities, they both took the procreation buyout, and she resigned her hopes of motherhood.

In frequent, lackluster attempts to cheer her up, Viggo often parroted the APAL's Subtiree PSA ad campaign. "You just gotta find a hobby."

She joined the astonishing majority with wasted existences, numbed by entertainment and social media, disengaged from the world except to run errands to the local dispensary. "Your reporting really keeping you that busy, Viggo?"

"I pursued every lead and reached out to all my contacts for my latest investigation."

"About what?"

"New Soviet Confederacy — regarding their impending elect-disrupt plans. I'm woozy from months of metaphorically smashing my head into walls. For my birthday, buy me a crash test helmet."

"Sure."

"I'm waiting to hear back. Prolly will take a week or more.

So, I got nothing going on today. Should we go pick up some gummies and kush?"

Trin pulled two jars from a canvas bag. "Got both this morning."

"Oh, good," Viggo said, disappointed to lose a walk as if one needed a reason. He swiped by influencers' vids, showcasing lavish lifestyles and commanding jobs. It's lucky his envy dulled from years of tremendous overuse.

Billionaire romantics would trade their riches for the rare, pure, eternal love that blessed Viggo and Trin. But The Beatles lied. That's not *"all you need"* for a full life.

"Gratitude time?" She asked, having read that surveying affluence is only helpful if it motivates, whereas recognizing the less privileged makes one grateful.

Like "distasteful but healthy" enthusiasm for a spirulina smoothie, Viggo streamed documentaries of world poverty through history. Trin snuggled up closer in his warm arms. Could he really envy subsistence farmers in war-ravaged nations? What could be done regarding Western cultures' pervasive, perverse "grass-is-greener" psychological effects? Viggo asked her, "Maybe the risk of a wretched life is the mother of productivity and helps people find purpose, right? At least it eats the day?"

Trin bristled. "We're supposed to only work to live. But over thousands of years, it changed into creating 'wage slaves.' Before AI started doing most jobs, the nine-to-five workday flashed as a two-century blip in humanity's 300,000-year reign. Throughout history, the only people working every waking hour were the enslaved and mothers in horrifying, oppressive, patriarchal societies."

Viggo said, "I thought that pharaohs and kings liked religions where a restless Joe got promised a better afterlife, so he'd postpone his demands in this one. In exchange, like a union bargain, the peons got better hours — regular days off 52 times a year they called the Sabbath."

"I could buy that starting in the Bronze Age, once there were organized societies, with codified laws and currency, and the like. But pre-civilization, humanity's lifestyle was easy, just leisure. Don't get me wrong, compared to today, back then, there were regular, terrible hardships in their hunting, gathering, and warring tribes, for sure. But otherwise, their lives were like ours post-APAL, amusing ourselves and lounging around."

"We've come so far since then." Viggo joked. "Except, we have streaming and air conditioning. Progress, right?"

ENDNOTE #9 — "Perpetual Patents & CLIRP"
Return to Novel on Page #51

Before 20NF, everyone had an intuitive sense of how patents worked. They were led to believe that inventors would create devices and apply for a patent. If the creation were deemed sufficiently novel, useful, and unobvious, it would be granted a 20-year monopoly. Then industry would seek to license these advancements, negotiating a fair agreement with the inventor before incorporating the intellectual property into a product or service for the public. That naïve conception wasn't just miles away from how the patent system ever worked; it was the distance of a G800 private jet's maximum range. Those who didn't know that number couldn't profit from IP.

In reality, patents were only ever "offensive rights," meaning a patent-holder could apply for injunctions from the courts on any infringer. This perversely led to businesses researching patents to "invent around" previous patents. They'd see how the competition did it before and change the minimum to claim it wasn't infringing or, ideally, to claim its own patent protection on this "new" version.

It became profitable for businesses, but woeful for the world, to ignore the inventor and instead chose to infringe, knowing that the legal gauntlet was in their favor. For even if it was blatant infringement, only a perfect parlay could hurt them.

The inventor would have to:

1) Somehow become aware of the infringement, and

2) Be able to afford an attorney to assess the viability of a lawsuit, and

3) Afford the expense or find the rare attorney willing to work on contingency, and

4) The lawyer would have to be professional enough to file properly and on time,

5) The slow court system could be made slower with continuances, and the inventor and attorney would have to brave that, and

6) The business could "bury" the attorney in paperwork, making it a poor return on effort, and still, they'd have to persevere to have any chance, and

7) The judges wouldn't necessarily always rule in the plaintiff's favor, and

8) The inventor would need the jury to rule in is favor and awarding worthwhile amounts, and

9) The judge and subsequent appellate judges could reduce an expensive judgment as being excessive, and

10) If it somehow went to the Supreme Court, and the inventor won, that might be a decade or more away.

In the interim, the offending business could have folded, having never paid out to the inventor. Or the invention could have been superseded by newer IP, thus erasing any window of exploiting the invention and recoupment. So, it became a better business model to not pre-pay inventors and instead say, "Come and sue me, I dare you."

The more problematic "Patent Trolls" were consortiums of investors and lawyers who would buy up thousands of patents ultra-cheap and use their combined weight to crush competition or extort businesses into paying tens of millions of dollars. Businesses made money without paying inventors. Investors and lawyers made money suing businesses. Inventors got screwed, regularly.

Obviously, when the patent system was created to incentivize invention, this wasn't the intended result. The idea of a monopoly on IP intuitively seemed fair for the inventor to determine who got to use the invention. Yet the public policy people asked, "Why should the government enforce the arbitrary whims of an inventor whose creation could benefit all?" A new system had to be created.

Pro-business groups like ALEC (the American Legislative Exchange Council) advocated for a simple solution: extend the length of patents to provide more lucrative upsides to inventors. Trademarks and copyrights have been continually extended. ALEC regularly drafted sample legislation because the politicians they marionetted would submit them as bills, verbatim. The momentum and direction of policies over time meant some version of this extension was likely despite it not addressing any of the problems and probably causing new ones.

As is the case with all creativity, there's always a non-zero chance someone predates your thinking. More importantly, as Kirby Ferguson says, "Everything is a Remix" anyway. Most who disagree are somehow sure Edison invented the lightbulb and have never heard of Volta, Davy, de la Rue, Swan, Woodward & Evans. Those who look up that invention's origins must arrive at Ferguson's conclusion. It comes down to identifying who was first and enabling that idea to contribute to the evolution of inventions.

A new hope appeared when paradigm-shifting legislation was proposed to create "CLIRP" ("Compulsory Licensing Inventors' Revenue Pools"). All inventors would register their ideas in a centralized patent database in real-time. AI would be used to evaluate and identify which came first and, hence, who should get the credit. All businesses would have full access to the ever-evolving database of progress and could use any idea so long as they abided by the CLIRP revenue model. Companies using any of this tech would guarantee a certain percentage of gross revenue (not merely "profit" which could've led to "creative accounting") to the Inventors' Revenue Pools. The AI would apportion those monies accordingly to the inventors. Thereby, monopolies couldn't crush competition, and inventors could always enjoy some of the revenue.

Big Pharma and Silicon Valley would still have the incentive for massive R&D departments because any revolutionary new cure, treatment, or device could dominate the share of the IRP. A drastic reduction in IP litigation would significantly alleviate congestion in the courts. The only people who would get financially hurt would be the lawyers. And it would be tough for everyone else to muster up too much sympathy for them. It was a boldly ambitious, promising move, and inventors were very excited.

And yet, on the eve of the signing of the CLIRP Act, somehow lobbyists (led by groups like ALEC) changed the wording to gut the very protections for inventors. By creating compounding, inefficient bureaucracy, the revenue pools would be practically untenable. Instead, the patents became perpetual patents, just like their originally proposed legislation, to increase the revenue for businesses. It was the most extreme accomplishment for rent-seeking non-inventors. As a final insult, the act was obscenely titled "The Defending Inventors' Coverage Treaty." So inventors got "DICT" bad.

ENDNOTE #10 — "Vetted School Credentials"
Return to Novel on Page #71

There was simply less to know during Galileo's day or da Vinci's day. For them, it was, by definition, more possible to be a Renaissance man. It was easier to be an inventor across disciplines in Ben Franklin's time with so much virgin terrain during the dawn of the Industrial Revolution. With the advancement of technology, there had to be a greater division of labor. Which, in turn, raised the bar for polymaths (which is a cool word to describe a person of varied learning).

Dr. Martin Luther King said, "The arc of the moral universe is long, but it bends toward justice." And indeed, there was a high correlation between the further back in time and less egalitarian justice. That alone should make people optimistic for the future, assuming general trends continue. Wherever there had been aristocracy or other blood-lineage caste systems, the lack of opportunities for productive, smart people to achieve more than the station they were born into (social mobility) is axiomatic proof of injustice. This was so universally understood that any argument supporting aristocracy was prudently regarded with suspicion and required a more rigorous burden of proof.

The more merit-based a system is in degree with no upper limit, the better. However, rewards need not correlate in a linear, proportionate manner (q.v. progressive taxation). The wider the access for everyone, the better. However, meritocracy shouldn't be an argument for abolishing social safety nets that limit the downside for those who are disabled or otherwise unfortunate.

The advancing progress and division of labor, not coincidentally, arose in tandem with boosted education in degree and diversity of thought. Thus, the countries with the most education (e.g., free public schools and affordable colleges) triumphed the most.

The almost sinister, virtually unavoidable specter of nepotism in the most prestigious universities made a degree less credible. For if the heir were smart or accomplished enough, they wouldn't need the nepotism/legacy/donation-bribes. Only because some mega donors' heirs aren't exceptionally talented would they want to burnish their bona fides by exploiting the halos of those who genuinely earned their place.

Over time, this sacrificed reputation necessitated the legal profession to create the Bar exam and the medical fields to develop board certifications. There had to be meritocratic bulwarks against nepotism to ensure competence for those professions and other crucial careers such as engineering, architecture, accounting, law enforcement, and the military.

Yet, as those credentials with objective, consistent measures proved more credible than the diplomas, the advantages of alumni pride and preference dissipated. Credentialing flourished (or metastasized, depending on your view of testing). SATs, ACTs, AP tests, Regent, and CLEP exams became more regimented and universal. Online certifications became no more than test prep for regulated, independent test centers.

Anti-cheating initiatives made testing for such certifications an objective, independently run, highly secure experience. First, assorted Veri-Centers verified identities by checking government-issued IDs (Drivers Licenses' and military IDs) and doing other due diligence via online checks and personal vouching from previously verified individuals. Such verification elevated the trustworthiness of internet sources and punished unverified sites for their dubious existence. Test centers guaranteed full verification of a test-taker's identity and then were required to have at least eight high-resolution cameras, recording from all angles, on each test-taker (arranged in the corners of a cube). Oral exams conducted by AI tested a person's on-the-spot recall and understanding. Those recordings made students evolve into old-school (like Plato-era-old) scholars. Any allegations of cheating could be proven or rejected based on viewing all the footage. CALs (Certification Authentication Links) meant to be included in resumes and job sites enabled prospective employers to click through to corroborate test scores accompanied by the supporting security camera footage.

The testing got more accurate at predicting later success and thus extended to ever younger children. Homeschooling proliferated with parents putting their kids on Khan Academy and EDX course tracks that had evolving curricula to optimize the learning experience.

Public education became less about lecturing to a class and more about tutoring on a personal level to those who most needed it (elevating the bottom) or maximizing advancement (raising ladders higher).

Stu's parents homeschooled him like this, and he became an autodidact. He voraciously racked up credentials in all fields of study before landing on computer science and artificial intelligence. He had all his CALs available on his website. Most everyone found this to be a tacky and pitifully desperate bid for recognition and yet saw the rest of the world following suit.

ENDNOTE #11 — "Tiers of Qualities"
Return to Novel on Page #73

The default reasoning of "the enemy of my enemy is my friend" encouraged people seeking to ingratiate themselves to condemn a common enemy. But Stu knew those who valued loyalty were leery of anyone disloyal to others, even an enemy. Stu often stream-ranted about the "tiers of qualities" since no one could value all ideals equally — because, so often, they're at odds.

He said, "Principles only mean something when you let them compel you to do something contrary to your personal interest. This gets tricky when principles conflict. If you value peace the most, that may require you to accept injustice. If you prioritize justice, that may cost you peace. Perfect honesty can be at the expense of profit. Optimal productivity can require the oppression of others. Freedom requires tolerance of that which you don't like."

Stu considered those all to be "first tier" ethics, whereas "second tier" traits people value, such as diligence and bravery, can similarly (or especially) be misused by evil leaders. And when conscience, circumstance, or time question the acts of the brave and diligent, it's loyalty that keeps them obedient to the powerful. The very concept of "Loyalty" should be unnecessary among the righteous. Loyalty is only pertinent when it changes behavior despite other priorities. Good people in power may be more abstract, requiring general honor, or they may prefer unambiguous codes of duty from their employees. Bad guys expect personal allegiance for fear of getting betrayed regarding their evil actions. A criminal couldn't trust an accomplice who ratted out his previous boss, no matter how deplorable. Additionally, those who demanded loyalty were rarely reciprocal.

ENDNOTE #12 — "Vicki's Military Service"
Return to Novel on Page #91

⇒**Trigger Warning:** Refers to past sexual assault (but no descriptions and no details).

You might think becoming the owner of a recreational marijuana dispensary/coffee shop was an odd fit for ex-military. But Vicki learned about cannabis during her tours in the Navy. Anytime her ship docked at a port, she'd actively play tourist since "seeing the world" was the pitch that hooked her at the recruitment office on her eighteenth birthday. Over the next twenty years, each successive trip meant less touristy and more authentic local experiences. Countries that had lax marijuana laws predictably had the most chill people. It was a welcome change from her ultra-regimented job. She developed a plan – put twenty years in to get her military pension and retire to start this shop. Finally, a goal beyond promotion of rank.

She always worked hard and kept her head down. Over beers with her crew, she'd describe what this place would be like. It got more and more detailed, and her closest friends were always supportive. Her dream was in "the real world," so her lack of ambition led to her getting stalled in rank as a Petty Officer First Class.

When twenty years elapsed, she didn't jump at the first opportunity to retire. Navy life was all she knew. It was reliable, and that was comforting. Civilians always discussing career instability scared her into not starting the new life when she promised herself.

Vicki's path changed when she met her new commanding officer, Commander Roger O'Reilly. He came from money and a military family; his mom was an heiress to a mining empire, and his dad descended from a line of officers going back to the Civil War. Roger had that confidence and sense of entitlement work culture tends to reward. The fact that he was charming as hell meant no one complained. He had such wisdom and a breadth of knowledge, Vicki often forgot he was younger than her.

She became his right hand. When younger subordinates bristled at Roger's old-school sexual harassment, Vicki explained the importance of unit cohesion and camaraderie. She argued his "inside" raunchy sense of humor and mischievous behavior helped create personal bonds. As an out lesbian and assertive woman, Vicki "trained" the men around her on what she'd tolerate. Consequently, no sailor ever directed harassment at her. However, she did enjoy and join in the dirty jokes, despite being labeled a "bad feminist" by the facetious ball-busters and the few earnestly woke. Not quite the optimum recipe for progressive change. By its nature, military culture defends the status quo.

Roger appreciated Vicki's loyalty and gave her sterling reviews and easier work. So, it was odd when she kept getting passed over for advancement. When "easy" promotions in undesirable assignments came open, she wouldn't even go for them. She rationalized any other job would be worse than working for Roger. Roger promised to take her with him when he rose to the top and eventually use his family money to invest in her dispensary. Always noting, "We'll just call it a coffee shop. My parents don't need to hear any more than that. Since they only leave Connecticut to fly to Europe, you don't have to worry about a visit."

A year blinked by with ever more complaints about sexual harassment. None of which went anywhere. But then Seaman Recruit Carol Jean stumbled into Vicki's room, roughed up with fresh, swelling bruises. Vicki insisted on taking Carol to the hospital and a rape kit getting done. Carol was too fragile to refuse, more so since Vicki said it was a direct order to comply. The doctors said such an order wasn't valid and Carol could have done whatever she wanted, including refusing treatment. One supportive look from Vicki, and Carol did as she was told. The only thing Carol omitted was the name of her attacker. Vicki initially assumed Carol didn't know him but soon worried she might have, and he had power.

The following day, Vicki followed protocol and gave an incident report to her commanding officer, Roger. He sounded earnest, relaying the gravity of the situation. Carol requested an immediate transfer, and Roger approved it. Considering his ostensible understanding, one might think Roger would want to keep Carol in his command so he could show her extra care and consideration. But Roger explained it was best to give Carol agency over her own life.

Weeks passed, and Vicki worried a criminal investigation hadn't yet been initiated. When she reached out to Carol in her new assignment, Carol wanted everything behind her. But that didn't sit right with Vicki, and she kept getting excuses from Roger. It was the red flag Vicki couldn't miss. *What if Roger was the attacker?* She didn't want to believe it.

The rape kit had never been tested, which was inexcusable madness. It was so straightforward, and DNA has always been fundamentally definitive. Nationwide, despite years of proposed legislation to solve this, thousands of rape kits went untested in what could fairly be criticized as a systemic defense of rapists. Roger's lack of follow-through maintained this injustice, transforming her disappointment into infuriation.

Vicki now had a mission, compelled to go over Roger's head. She was verbally reprimanded for going outside the chain of command, and Roger was informed of her insubordination and "disloyalty." He clenched his jaw and futilely rubbed his temples, stressed and heartbroken at her lack of faith in him. Whenever this topic came up, he "doth protested too much." He had repeatedly said his wife, daughter, mother, and pastor would've been ashamed if anyone could consider the possibility he'd commit such a heinous act. He was well practiced in effecting the glassy eyes but stony expression of an emotionally sensitive but still professional soldier.

She wasn't getting Kleenex for this crocodile's eyes. Vicki went to several other superior officers for justice, to no avail. In the end, Vicki was an anonymous whistleblower to the press. Reporters pushed for answers until they found out the rape kit results went missing. No one else went on the record, and the story disappeared from the headlines. Everyone knew Vicki was the whistleblower. Those four months were contentious, and Roger gave her scathing reviews, calling her "unfit for duty." Vicki applied for every new assignment she could but never even got an interview because of her recent reviews.

It was clear everything changed. Even if Roger wasn't the assailant, he enabled the injustice. Vicki full-on confronted him with all the accumulated circumstantial evidence in hand. He denied it and then demanded she resign. The exact words were, "Resign or I'll have you dishonorably discharged." Vicki couldn't have faith that truth would win out. After twenty-one years, she didn't want to risk losing her pension. She resigned with an honorable discharge.

Without Roger's backing, Vicki took out a loan to open the shop, and it got to positive cash flow quicker than the entrepreneurial experts had warned. If this somehow wasn't an auspicious path to a more prosperous destination, you couldn't tell.

Two months later, she heard Carol committed suicide. That devastated Vicki and got her blaming herself and venting to anyone in her contact list who'd take her call. She closed the shop for a while. Fewer and fewer had the time or patience for those marathon, amateur therapy sessions she was demanding. The military's unfortunate stigma against seeking help for mental health still prevailed. Her favorite foods tasted bland and unsatisfying. She got more anxious and irritable. She couldn't focus on anything for more than ten minutes. These were signs of an acute depressive episode beyond the historic 'woe is me' caricature of the illness.

Alone and without structure, she reverted to her military regimen, waking up at 05:00 AM and working out and running for hours a day. The exercise let her sleep a bit better, but she rebounded when her customers kept reaching out, asking for her to reopen the shop. She was reminded that connectedness is how humans endure. She gave herself purpose by vowing to protect her friends in the future, whoever they might be. Why didn't she have close friends now?

ENDNOTE #13 — "Could Ayn Rand Be Right?"
Return to Novel on Page #95

One of Stu's most viewed videos was his rant against legendary libertarian thinker and novelist Ayn Rand and her philosophy called Objectivism. Her fanbase proved rabid, and the very nature of that following meant they loved to pedantically "educate" those who were ignorant of their theories. Such controversy attracts attention, and limitless threads can spin off into flame wars that attract even more attention.

Stu said, "When libertarians mocked socialized medicine for taking money from healthy people and giving it to those who need healthcare, they seem oblivious that private health insurance did exactly that but additionally took hundreds of millions for executive salaries and billions for advertising that would not have been wasted in a socialized medicine system. It'd take <u>less</u> from you to do the same thing. Now, if they were such extreme libertarians that they'd never buy insurance, at least they'd be consistent and principled. One would think they'd want to avoid the inevitability that a dreadful percentage of them would die of medically preventable maladies that'd be unaffordable in a libertarian fantasy land.

"But some libertarians get worse, and all based on their guiding principles. They cynically claimed there was no such thing as altruism because whatever you do, you do for yourself to make yourself feel good. Therefore, charity, or whatever the supposedly altruistic action, was simply a means to an end, with that end being your own happiness. But that's tautological because of semantics. In other words, that'd be true by sneakily changing the meaning of the terms. By redefining altruism to mean "every motivation is for your own benefit," the word altruism would become meaningless.

"It was like saying, 'Everyone is special.' For the word altruism to be useful, it has to be distinguished from non-altruistic behavior. And since there's a reasonable consensus of what is "selfishness" in a negative sense, then the opposite of that behavior must be 'altruism' — stipulating that sadistic or self-destructive behavior are even worse than selfishness. It's more accurate to define the terms on a continuum where some actions can be more humanitarian than others. Jumping into a freezing river to save your own child must be seen as less altruistic than risking one's life for a stranger.

"Co-opt a word, and you simply create the need to come up with a new word to mean the original concept. The difference between the stranger who enters a burning building to save a random child's life and the onlooker who doesn't is the concept that most mean when they say altruism.

"Perhaps such extreme Objectivists would be more comfortable with a made-up word like 'donadventist,' composed of the Latin words for 'give' and 'stranger.' Using such a word, while initially done to satirize extreme Objectivists, would likely eventually become synonymous with the word 'altruist.' It'd just be respelling the word.

"Though that paradigm generally resolves the semantics, the motivations are potentially distinct. Why would someone jump in a river to save her child and then also a stranger? As opposed to her child, but not a stranger? Why are some gratified by acting altruistically, whereas others see insufficient or even no satisfaction whatsoever? Does this issue reduce down to another nature vs. nurture argument? If nurture has any role, surely we, as a civilization, would do better to encourage altruism rather than mock it. That is the essence of world improvement. Otherwise, there are perverse incentives for zero-sum games.

"What's behind the extreme libertarian critique, 'there's no such thing as altruism' is the next absurd point, 'Selfishness is a virtue.' Therefore, according to them, 'rational egoism' is the only proper way to live. This is a semantic minefield. In a certain constrained way, it could be valid and valuable to some. Let's note that a foundational belief is not meant to be so often or significantly constrained. Instead, the very term 'foundational belief' must be extrapolatable, or, again, that term is useless.

"There are scary examples of Ayn Rand's perverse celebration of selfishness. Her books aggrandize rape, at least by the modern understanding of the word, which her defenders may rationalize as a relative morality given the culture of her time. What's inexplicable is that Rand felt sympathy for, praised, and idealized sociopathic murderers, such as child-killer William Edward Hickman, for doing what they wanted for their own selfish pleasure. The welfare of others never concerned these psychos. This phenomenon exemplifies how such a selfish philosophy is so potentially hazardous in that it can be used to justify the most objectively horrifying crimes.

"What was odd was that Rand's second fundamental precept, 'Free Will and Free Exchange,' in other words, unrestrained capitalism, could have been its primary concept and would've been more defensible. 'FWaFE' theoretically should obliterate slavery.

"But some extreme Rand fans willfully, paradoxically, abhorrently argue that 'a person should be able to sell himself into slavery.' They obtusely claim that such a transaction could be free without honorably thinking it through.

"Under what circumstances would a person ever sell himself into slavery? He'd have to be so poor and starving in a libertarian's fantasy country with zero social safety net that submitting to an enslaver 24/7 for the rest of their life seems better than their current situation. A sociopathic extreme libertarian could attempt to rationalize every part of slavery in this 'voluntary enslavement transaction' using a precedent in the free market. Such a horrifying contract could conceivably include obligations to submit to sex/abuse like a sex worker or BDSM submissive. It could even more shamefully include risk of death, likening it to a firefighter assuming such risks. Fortunately, for modern civilized countries, there's a minimum floor of humanity prohibiting market exploitation. Starvation is just as life-threatening and coercive as being ordered at gunpoint. That deadly alternative being the result of quitting or getting fired makes all of the enslaver's commands coercive.

"One couldn't be an incrementalist here. A nitpicky extreme Objectivist can't be logically consistent in specifying that they're for some less draconian version of 'indentured servitude,' call it 'Diet Slavery'. Actually, don't call it that. I shouldn't make light of this. Anyway, any such compromise of regulated slavery denies the fundamental argument for their premise. 'Well, I'm for slavery without torturous punishments like whipping or inhuman daily treatment such as withheld water, food, and sleep,' nitpicky extreme objectivists might claim while being obtuse and shameless. To which the question would be, 'Why so?' And if their answer was, 'Well, those acts are crimes,' that proves they misunderstand the very concept of slavery.

"When they say 'a person should be able to sell themselves into slavery,' what does that mean exactly? Is it 'a job with free housing' — where the slave can leave at any time? That's not slavery. The unconscionable constraint of the slave's freedom is central to the core concept of slavery. In slavery, there's no such thing as kidnapping or abusing or raping, or killing slaves because they're no longer considered fully human if they're stripped of human rights. The result was that a slave was an enslaver's property to do what he will.

"If the Quasi-Animal-Rights Objectivist, there's gotta be at least a few, attempts to say that slaves should be treated as humanely as animals, the question is degree. How much of an Animal Rights person are they? It's easy to be against factory farming with deplorable conditions that consign the animals to a brief life of misery. But can farms justify themselves in any form? How 'free-range' must a chicken be? If the 'QARO' is for farms in any form as an analog for human slavery, then they're condoning abduction and abuse. This should be self-evidently horrific. Yet those facts are embedded in the concept of slavery.

"Thus, the concept of 'freely selling yourself into slavery' is an oxymoron. Either you are free, or you are not. 'Ah-hah,' the disingenuous, obtuse, shit-stirring extreme Objectivist says, 'Isn't every contract a voluntary constraint?' Yes, but that's not slavery. A contract indeed restricts freedom in its most abstract form but within the very concept of civilization. A contract serves as a simple mechanism for enforcing honorable dealing. Breaking a contract enables a systemic redress of grievances. In contrast, an enslaved person disobeying his master risks death on an unreasonable whim. Laws should create fairness and thus increase reliability and trustworthiness, which encourages commerce that relies on trustworthiness.

"However, not all contracts are enforceable. This was why contract law has the concept of 'Duress.' Let's revisit the burning building hypothetical: an extreme Objectivist runs into a burning building and demands the victim in need of help first sign a contract giving all of their possessions and future earnings to the Objectivist. The victim would no doubt sign because it's the preferred alternative to death. However, no honorable court would let the extreme Objectivist collect on that. The coercive nature of the circumstances nullifies the validity of the contract because the parties entering the contract must be free. There must also be a 'meeting of the minds' so people know what they're agreeing to.

"And I shouldn't troll Ayn Rand too hard. If one axiomatically accepts that the world is ever-changing, no prophet can be however prescient forever. Her Soviet upbringing understandably caused her hatred of every form and level of socialism."

ENDNOTE #14 — "There's Free Will?"
Return to Novel on Page #100

Stu asked, "How do you get the digitized mind to have 'Free Will' if your tech is so infallibly regimented?"

Roxy explained, "Just as a brain is like a computer, ideas in the form of communication, speaking, writing, etc., function like software. The software is physically encoded into the brain via your body's hormones' effects on neurotransmitters, rewarding what it perceives, and is programmed to interpret as good behavior. If you grew up getting rewarded for accomplishment and thus continued working to receive praise, then that created a virtuous cycle where you wanted to be productive because the resulting praise made you feel happy by scientifically verifiable, chemical metrics. Bloodwork and brain scans taken when people win money or learn of other fortunate events are measurably different from baseline.

"On the other side, getting conditioned to hate and fear perceived to be threatening ideas or humans in other groups will make you release cortisol, adrenaline, and other hormones that cause stressful fight-or-flight responses, or trigger anger and disgust. Memories of those instances entrench such mindsets when they're unrepresentative all the way to 100% false.

"Call it serendipity — whenever you encounter a new idea or experience, you process it in your hardware and software. It can rewrite your software because your brain is adaptive.

"So the actions are a function of chemicals. Let's drill deeper, from chemicals to the underlying immutable laws of physics that rule everything. The universe is deterministic. When you chose to do something, those synapses fired because there was a preceding cause, which itself had a preceding cause. Hypothetical example, which may or may not be based on how your last gig at Google ended. If your Uber hadn't arrived so late, you would've had time to grab breakfast, so you wouldn't have been so hangry that you blew up at your boss and got fired. But the Uber was late in this timeline, so the resulting events had to run as they did. You didn't have a choice. If one could rewind this 'clockwork' back to the beginning of time, everything would necessarily play out the same way.

"In 1999, philosopher Edward de Bono was asked how to solve the Arab-Israeli conflict. Given that humans with a Zinc deficiency are more prone to anxiety, depression, and aggression, and that populations in the Middle East are deficient in Zinc compared to other nations, de Bono wasn't entirely facetious when he recommended sending both sides jars of Marmite — a food spread high in Zinc. Hence, the hardware of genetics and the changing software of diets could manifestly affect behavior. Wish they tried it back then."

"What about quantum uncertainty?" Stu asked as if it were a gotcha zing.

Roxy said, "I'll get to that in a moment. This overview, simplified for discussion, contends physics leaves no room for 'you' to make a decision separate from the rest of your brain's chemical makeup and surrounding environment. Sam Harris and Neil deGrasse Tyson make this accessible for the masses by poetically saying 'you ARE your Hardware and Software.' Everyone's just their 'H&S.' Though they differentiate in that deGrasse Tyson argues Free Will is an emergent feature, whereas Harris claims Free Will is an illusion."

Stu dug in, "You, Roxy, take this position that people are just complex robots. There's no soul. No truly Free Will. Even though everybody feels like they have a choice, that's an illusion. Is that right?"

Roxy clarified, "I'd say 'yes,' but you'd get the wrong idea. Consider a basic computer. It runs operations and can match results to its programming. It can check if a math result is wrong and designate it as a false statement. If it's advanced enough of a machine with sufficiently complex programming, it can have expectations regarding a greater variety of results. You click print, and the document is supposed to be sent to the printer, but there's an error message. Something went wrong, and the computer recognizes this. The computer or the printer could have flawed programming, or the hardware or connector cable might be suboptimal or damaged in some way.

"However, sometimes it's not a hardware or software error. Now, I'll address your question of quantum. Do you also know about SEUs?"

Stu gave a chin-up single nod. "Yeah. Single Event Upsets, the cosmic rays that can strike the silicon in microchips, corrupting data one time out of a bazillion."

Roxy glanced at her blind spots and leaned in as if she were sharing a secret. She said, "SEUs can cause an unexpected result independent of hardware, software, and the immediate environment of earth. That's comparable to what we know about quantum physics. Everything is probabilistic. Atoms might reliably behave the same almost every time. Keyword is 'almost.' Even if it's only once out of a quadrillion, some exceptions defy normal expectations. In those unfathomable, rare examples, a random event doesn't require an external influence such as an SEU."

Stu furrowed his brow, bursting to one-up his new boss, but he covered his own mouth with a kidnapper's grip. He looked up to think, noticing Roxy was the featured photo on a Fortune "30 CEOs Under 30" article luxuriously mounted on the wall. That broke his concentration. He retrained his eyes back on Roxy's.

"You with me, Stu? I'm about to get to the finale." Off his modest nod, she nearly continued, but he cut her off.

Whether caused by insecurity or egotism, Stu rarely resisted impulses to show off his smarts, especially to Roxy. He had nothing elegantly apropos, but he couldn't go so long without showing off with something, anything. Stu said, "Free Will is in doing what one wants. Arthur Schopenhauer famously said, "Man can do what he wills, but he cannot will what he wills." And you're saying all "wills" are out of one's control?"

"Sort of. Let me make my point. A human's sense of self has certain, long-established assumptions, expectations. I like burritos more than, I dunno, oatmeal."

"Not a very bold position." Stu crossed his arms to punctuate his joke-adjacent gibe.

She said, "Fine, I like burritos more than tacos. In a Mexican restaurant, that's my order every time. Except in one instance, I may find myself ordering the tacos instead. Another woman in that situation might have deduced she must not be an automaton because some of her actions are unpredictable. She, therefore, believes in Free Will. Whereas my brain's subroutines considered reasons for that deviation and concluded the behavior ran counter to my expectations because-"

"A quantum anomaly resulted in a rare chain reaction that triggered different neurons in your brain to fire, and, boom, it's taco time. Right?" Stu said, relieved to be intellectually right there with her.

"Basically, yeah. To be precise – not 'basically' – just plain yes. We are biological matter clockwork, organic, deterministic robots, but we're advanced enough to diagnose ourselves and evaluate our own programming. Humans can 'learn' the why but not change the course. In the old film *Matrix: Reloaded* — a character celebrated Causality and admonished Neo to know 'Why?'"

"That's the Merovingian," Stu said. Her face looked flustered, not registering the trivia. "The character you're talking about is named 'The Merovingian.' Sorry. Go on."

At her computer, she found and played the clip. The Merovingian said, *"Causality. There is no escape from it. We are forever slaves to it. Our only hope, our only peace is to understand it, to understand the 'why.' 'Why' is what separates us from them, you* from me. 'Why' is the only real social power; without it, you are powerless."

She stopped the video and said, "The illusion of Free Will arises in most people when they spot their own unexpected behavior, disregard the alternate explanations why, and instead conclude that they must have wanted to act unexpectedly. But it's an incorrect inference." Roxy said, leaning back as if checkmating and waiting for her opponent to confirm.

He said, "Huh. I like it. I mean, I don't really <u>like</u> it. But you've convinced me. I buy it as a foundation. Moving on." Part of what Stu liked about his strategy of "sprinting to admit when he's wrong" is it abbreviates the other person's moment of victory and thus lessens the victor's satisfaction. He asked, "So, how does that affect your research?"

Roxy reverently gestured to her brain scanner system like it was a temple altar. "We scan the brain down to the atoms; our supercomputers make inferences on the sub-scannable scale. We can recreate a hyper-detailed model of it digitally."

That triggered a mini-eureka moment for Stu, "Just a sec. There wouldn't be enough randomness because the SEUs are too rare. Do you add randomness? If so, doesn't that cascade to a radically different mindset? Over time, the customer's Digi-mind might disagree with his real, biological self. Or no?"

Roxy didn't notice herself drawing closer to Stu. "No, you're right, but so can a flesh-and-bones human. Who doesn't remember in horror at some of one's memories of embarrassing behavior? You should appreciate that more than anyone."

Stu took the hit and revved up to retort.

Roxy stayed on topic. "The deviations are more minor than you might expect. We take the patient's dietary and sleep logs and program-in hormone changes within normal ranges. So, unless the guy's wife dies, or he gets cancer, his virtual brain stays remarkably consistent with his own, at least in the short-term. We've only been studying all this for a couple of years, so we can't possibly calculate the deviance by year five or twenty. As in real life, people change in unpredictable ways.

"My research had a surprising impact on my view of crime and the legal system. Individuals behave based on their own H&S, and society's system of punishments and rewards (i.e., blame vs. credit) discourages or encourages accordingly."

Stu again scrambled to show he could match her speed. He had an inkling of an insight and started improvising, hoping to land on a solid point. Stu said, "Let me take this in a related direction. On a macro scale, human society is always testing different H&S, with the environment requiring an evolutionary adaptation. Therefore, functionally, society is crediting or blaming based on the effects of people's H&S. If one person's model results in antisocial behavior — let's say it makes him kill random people — society must seek to discourage it via some sort of punishment. Whether it does so in a righteous or positive way and consistent with its self-professed rules and their execution is another matter."

Roxy said, "I'm with you. Hardware, writ large, is composed of its environment and natural resources, already built infrastructure, technology/communications, number of inhabitants and their genetics, and there are likely countless other examples. Software is the culture and educational systems, including religions, laws, diet and exercise habits, societal norms, wealth, and markets. The relative differences between countries play a substantial role on a greater macro scale."

"Yeah, that was implied by what I said. Keep up, Roxy." Stu said defensively with a playful smirk.

Offended, she popped her eyebrows up but graciously smiled to avoid changing the vibe of the moment. Roxy said, "I'll go further. Depending on the traditional definition of 'want,' some argue that you always do what you want to do, even if you hate or are horrified by the foreseeable result. In circumstances such as being held up at gunpoint, you choose to hand over your wallet because it's preferable to being killed. Of course, this does not absolve the criminal. You don't 'like' to hand over your wallet; the violent force compelled you to do something you otherwise wouldn't. That paradigm holds the criminal has the freedom to act differently, and free will is a necessary prerequisite for moral responsibility. Meaning if a man is not morally responsible, he shouldn't face negative consequences. This is a semantic problem caused by the aforementioned error in understanding.

"The macro system of society 'corrects' discouraged behavior through punishments. Whether a human has free will or if his actions are determined doesn't affect the need for society to make corrections. More destructive errors increase the likelihood such a society will die. It must maximize corrections to survive. "

"Aha," Stu said. "But if everything is deterministic, society isn't choosing either!"

"Not arguing with that. Society's software is deterministic, though it's a function of exponentially more variables of input," she said.

"Society as a living organism. It's been said before." Stu's nitpicking in his criticisms by now looked petty and obvious.

Roxy wasn't 100% beyond the motivation to impress. She said, "One last aspect starts by comparing hardware and software to iterative revisions of advertising or computer viruses. Online advertising does 'A/B testing,' where half of the audience is presented with one ad, and the other half gets the other ad. Whichever ad gets more clicks or conversions to actual sales survives, and a new ad competes; this iterative competition continues optimizing for the most effective advertisement. There's the same kind of arms race for hackers vs. white hat security specialists or malware vs. antivirus systems. One wins, and the other has to devise alternate attack strategies or countermeasures, always escalating."

Stu said, "Knew that. Where's your leap to the next level on this topic? Are you claiming human minds are viruses?"

"Sort of. Add in the concept of memes..."

"I know what memes are, too, Roxy."

"Not the stupid jokes shared on social media."

"Yes, yes. You're talking about Dawkins' coining definition — ideas and behaviors that spread and evolve like genes."

"That's right," she said. "Humans are the carriers of those memes, and thereby earth, indeed the universe, is an ecosystem whereby the carriers build an ever more aware self-understanding machine. It's akin to humanity's first meta-species creation, its 'children' — autonomously improving AI. One system wins until another overtakes it.

"Learn some history. The Ottomans defeated the Hungarian, Egyptian, and Mesopotamian empires with the scientific advancement of gunpowder. Similarly, the Spanish used more modern military weapons to conquer the Incas and Aztecs. Capitalism prospered far beyond communism. That greater productivity and wealth made ever more sophisticated civilizations accompany greater scientific advancements and continued progress. World War II's Axis powers, Germany, Japan, and Italy, took on the world but lost out to the Western Allies' most expansive unification of modern powers, aided by the USA's development of the nuclear bomb. After that, as scary as the Cold War was, it was a better meme than the preceding hot war. Harvard professor Steven Pinker chronicled this long-term, increasing safety and lifespan of humanity. It didn't have to bring total world peace to be an improvement."

Stu enjoyed getting schooled like this, if for no other reason than he could redeploy it on everyone else, getting credit for her understanding. He said, "Sharp recap, but it hardly seems to differ from Dawkins' theories. How does it apply to your eternal mind invention?"

"Vekhuman provides orders of magnitude better meme evolution. Eternal minds, by definition, will have longer-lasting and a greater capacity of memories; this turbo-charges wisdom because the meme-carriers don't have to relearn from scratch every 80 years."

Stu squinted and said with a gingered-up finger, "How can we be sure the aggregated wisdom will redound to all of humanity's benefit and not hyper-accelerate those immortals' rival interests?"

Roxy's serene face exuded confidence as she said, "I have faith that wisdom, by definition, is universal. All that requires is a longer time horizon of consideration, and I'm providing that."

"Faith, huh? Not a word I'm used to hearing pass your lips."

"Yeah, felt weird as I said it. But you get what I mean."

ENDNOTE #15 — "Advice for the Treason-Curious"
Return to Novel on Page #117

The senior consultant began, "I feel like those tax law professors who joke that everybody takes those classes not to help their clients to avoid breaking the law; no, they take the class to learn how not to get caught... or convicted." Most of the audience laughed. The tax attorneys didn't get what was supposed to be the funny part.

He continued, "Counterintelligence agencies have a term describing the primary reasons people commit treason: 'MICE' — Money, Ideology, Compromise/Coercion, and Ego. The same mostly applies to the 'Aspiring Criminal' or anyone who would otherwise betray their side.

He said, "The bottom line is you can't do a single task an adversary requests for any incentive, be it money, sex, ideology, ego, whatsoever — if you intend to keep it secret from your superiors. Because the adversary starts blackmailing you, and it gets terrible fast and worse faster still.

"Terribly for you, your efforts to keep all of what you did secret proves criminal intent. Now, I don't want to sound like a lawyer because I am not. But you know I might possibly, hypothetically in theory, perhaps have a bit of experience in this subject... potentially first-hand. Who is to say?"

Again, he got polite "student-teacher" threshold titters in response to his sarcasm.

"Okay, from this non-lawyer, listen to this: The charge of criminal conspiracy has to be broad; all it takes is two or more people planning something illegal and only one of them doing an 'overt act,' which is 'an action in furtherance of a crime' – or some such term. Here's the crazy part: that overt act need not be illegal on its own. If you and your friend plan to kidnap and bury, I don't know, say… birthday clowns, and he goes out and buys body bags, quicklime, and 'Clown Makeup Remover' – then congratulations! You're guilty of 'Conspiracy to Commit Murder.'

"Practically speaking, once you commit the first treason-ish crime, you should expect that the bad guys will keep incriminating evidence and be ready to have actual accomplices to serve as witnesses in the event they want to sell you out. Not to mention, they can create false witnesses who are sufficiently credible to cause you great damage. That first crime you commit may not even result in what you imagine are the first of many benefits. Instead, your crime could be the hook that makes you vulnerable to blackmail. You might 'have' to commit further crimes to escape getting busted for the first crime. Scarier, each subsequent crime you commit gives ever greater leverage to the bad guys. So, while the first 'easy' crime might appeal to you for whatever you were promised, it won't when you factor in the never-ending subsequent crimes you'll be blackmailed into committing.

"Whatever your motivation, the very nature of being a criminal or spy is willful deception, betraying your honor. Now, this should be obvious, but know that criminals are known to lie, too. Apparently, a vital aspect of the law is that the legal system cannot be used to enforce illegal actions. So, if a mafia boss or foreign power promises you a million dollars – if that's still a lot of money — to do this crime or that and then doesn't deliver… well, you can't take them to court. As a spy, your only hope of protection and benefit from the bad guy is only as long as you can continue to provide value. As soon as you want out, it'd be naïve to expect any loyalty to continue. Worse — when the bad guys need leverage to negotiate a deal, be forewarned that you're now a bargaining chip they'll gladly trade for their own benefit. Mobsters give up expendable schmucks like you to reduce their own legal danger when they have to haggle with prosecutors. Foreign spy agencies, all the time, expose the no-longer-productive spies in swaps with rival powers.

"When the liar, and all spies are liars, when the liar is your tour guide, getting you to start on a dishonest path — why would you trust that the promised destination is desirable? He could've been lying about either delivering on his promise or that the destination is indeed worthwhile for you. Trusting the liar's parlay is a bad bet."

ENDNOTE #16 — "Stu and Maria's Chemistry" *(NSFW)
Return to Novel on Page #134

Stu's warm, left hand smooth-ed down her back and around her waist like the snake form of Lucifer. Stu drew Maria's hips closer to his, brandishing his growing passion as a wordless bid for consent.

Maria softly moaned, overwhelmed with a sense memory of the last toe-curling orgasm he gave her.

He palmed her well-toned bubble butt. Her leg wrapped around his body as if her weekly yoga training focusing on balance was intended for this purpose.

Stu lifted his head and said, "Alexa, play seduction protocol." The apartment lights dimmed, an "electric scented candle" flickered on, and Nickelback's "Someday" played.

"Alexa, change the music to Maria's night playlist six," Maria said. Taylor Swift's soulful 2039 duet with Mckenna Grace, "Suri Can't Stop Us," rumbled on.

"Better."

She smiled and writhed to the beat. Stu fleetingly kissed her cheek as he proceeded to her ear, engulfing it with his mouth and the wet heat of his tongue, then tracing the outer edge and then the inner. Maria sucked air through her teeth as her neck tensed in anticipation. She loved ear-play, though not all women do. Stu knew the cue and pressed his lips to her lower ear with understated, firm bites — one of her favorite spots.

"Ooooh, Stu. What you do to me." Both of her hands grabbed the back of his head as her eyes woke up to lock with his. "Kiss me again, dammit!"

He obliged, but for only a few seconds before disengaging as a mild, cruel tease. Her eyes narrowed, familiar with the technique, and all-in for the ride. He gave her a chaste kiss but kept the immediate intimacy, head-vacillating with a short "No" movement,

so their lips slid side-to-side against each other. She couldn't help but move in for a deeper kiss, but he retreated as she then did, as a reflex. They drew closer again to kiss. She had to say, "I know you're just going to tease me again and... I hate that I love it!"
He deeply kissed her to stay unpredictable.
Her moan grew louder now; they pressed together. She reacted with electric goosebumps. Stu plowed his fingertips, starting from the base of her neck, up and over her entire skull. He then brought all of her hair together for a maximum pull. She couldn't help but purr a quintessentially Latina "R-rolling" purr that hit peak sexiness because it was authentic.
They began racing to remove their own clothes.
Stu non-metaphorically swept her off her feet and threw her on the bed. He took a moment to appreciate her form, and she gleefully smiled while splayed out, inviting him to pounce. He kissed her while his right hand traced spirals over her breasts and then played mime jazz piano over her lingerie. He thrilled at the sensation of her increasing passion.
Maria sang out, "Ahhmygahhd, Stu. That's my spot!" She clutched his skull as he pleasured her with swoops of intensity and teases that felt like an eternity. The first time they had sex, this little maneuver frustrated her, but now she wouldn't change a note in this symphony. Maria's quickening breaths guided him to stay in the zone and in rhythm. She half-screamed into her orgasm as her body convulsed. He let the waves of ecstasy crash over her, knowing her entire body pulsed now, too sensitive to be touched at all.
"Goddammit, Stu. You are so fucking good at that!"
"One-Zero!" Stu gloated with a facetious eye flare regarding the orgasm "score." It was a tacky joke she'd heard him tell many times before, and if she weren't in such a virtuoso-delivered, post-climactic glow, she'd be sick of the repetition. But by now, it had been conditioned into her like Pavlovian Don Juan. "That joke is no longer funny, but I still like it."

"Oh, we're not done." Stu specified.

Maria beamed. "I know, and I'm psyched for the second act, but I'm still vibrating here, so I appreciate the intermission." Her nourishing inhale led to a stilted, shuddering exhale, and then she clenched her jaw to hold her breath. Maria had to freeze the moment. Her body relaxed, and her mouth made wet, soft ASMR noises that hurried his blood.

She looked up with fierce eyes, then dove down to take him in her mouth. With cautious force, she tested how deep she could take it while feeling him grow further.

He squeezed her hair and champed down, squinting and restraining himself.

With proud enthusiasm, Maria continued until he had to pull back. "Hold on, hold on," he said, "you're too good!"

She flashed a smirk. "That totally should've been a tying score."

"That's fair. You get credit for it." Stu said while acting as if he was checking with referees. "That's one all."

This shtick was so stupid, but she couldn't suppress her Cheshire smile.

Stu got Maria's endorphins and adrenaline to max out. He made sure he was ready and put on a Magnum condom. He wasn't quite big enough to merit that brand; he simply preferred the fit. Stu relished Maria's expression as he plunged into her.

Their lovemaking went faster and then slower and back in a glorious series. They sometimes achieved simultaneous orgasms. Not this time, though.

He climaxed, while she neared closer to a second. He'd never want to let her "win." So, he went to pleasure her again.

However, tonight, she had been well-plowed, strummed, and sated. "You're fucking amazing, Papi." She said exuberantly before rolling away to breathe deep.

ENDNOTE #17 — "Rosti's Ponzi"
Return to Novel on Page #137

Gwendolyn flew in for an exquisite, catered event at the grand New York Public Library, refurbished every few years with eight figures of donations. Only the super-rich knew about renting such iconic locations for the ultimate private functions. "Everything has a price" is most true in New York City. This one celebrated the opening of a "mirror fund" to Chuck's premiere closed-end investment fund, a calculatedly rare occasion to ensure the perception of scarcity and, therefore, high value.

Most everyone wore clothes worth a Toyota. The Wall Street bankers wore Patek-Phillipe designer pieces on their wrists and the hides of vicious reptiles on their feet. The semi-recognizable models and trophy brides and husbands blazed with haute couture from the previous week's runway shows. Even the Silicon Valley tech bros' hoodies were cashmere, t-shirts were limited edition works of art, and sneakers were one-of-a-kind upgrades from the top-tier sneaker pimps.

Spiffy valets memorized and matched the clientele's faces to the yet more exclusive platinum-invite list. One approached Gwendolyn, "Mrs. Grantham, we're ready for you at the VIP reception. Follow me."

Gwendolyn did and noticed she and her ultra-wealthy Top 1/10,000th-level peers weren't secreted away but rather spotlighted and paraded through this "poor" merely well-off Top 1/1,000th crowd.

The head waiter tapped a Baccarat Crystal goblet to get everyone to focus up. "Ladies and gentlemen, if I may have your attention. Your host, Charles Rosti..."

Chuck Rosti took to the podium. The quartet ended with a drawn-out sting that gave no cue to applaud. The lighting change refocused all eyes on him. "Since the beginning, people have wondered how I've been earning such attractive returns, quarter after quarter, for the past couple of decades. That track record has justified my increasing management fees and commission structure. I'm worth it. You don't care so long as the number at the bottom of your statement is fatter than last year."

Gwendolyn said, "But as a closed fund, you make it a dang sight harder to cash out. You set the price, and we've got quite a time getting the proper value based on the underlying investments. So, we don't know if you're taking an even greater percentage by low-balling us when we withdraw."

"Now is not the time for Q&A, Gwenny-darling. No matter how much we all love listening to your lovely Southern accent." He said in a strategic dig to diminish her credibility among this city set.

"That's just fine, sweetie. So long as us regular folk can yammer some with you 'fore the cows come home.'" She said, amplifying her accent for comedic effect.

"You're darn tootin'," he said, going one line too far with this shtick. These mega-investors didn't have the patience for much more of this.

"Okay, back to my strategy. The regular play for private equity firms is to: Number one, take investors' money and buy out small to mid-sized companies with simple, conservative financials and fat balance sheets. Step two, leverage them with giant loans to cover plans for hyper-ambitious growth and merge with competitors to make monopolies. Three, take huge fees for themselves and piddly little returns for their investors. And four, once there's growth, sell to their biggest competitors for a tremendous ROI.

"They birthed famous success stories using this formula. They did it with beds so that most consumers didn't catch how many of the major brands were subsidiaries of the same giant holding company. They did it with glasses. One company bought out a bunch of famous brand-name manufacturers of sunglasses and then also snapped up a big chain of shops. The stores prioritized moving the goods they made, getting greater sales at the expense of the captive competition. A solid example of vertical integration extracting maximum profit.

"The strongest criticism with other private equity funds is that they stuffed their pockets first with fees were so high, and the interest on giant loans so burdensome, sometimes those companies couldn't 'service the debt.' They couldn't afford to pay the interest, so those companies went under, losing their investors' money. But you see, my companies kick ass. Which means better returns for you."

"Except you have funds that go bankrupt. Not partial losses. Just town dump tire fires," Gwendolyn said with a taut tone of restrained anger.

"That's less than 5% of my funds. The rest outperform the market," Chuck said.

"How can we know whether you're not just pushing all your money-losing bets onto the unlucky souls in one fund to bear the burden, so the other funds can sneak a benefit from the profitable investments?"

Everyone in this crowd leaned forward for the answer. Even the hot plus-ones made it their business to know enough to spot major flaws in investments. They invested their love and looks in their investor spouses and didn't want to bet on bad bettors.

"I don't have to defend myself to you, Gwendolyn. My results speak for themselves. Plus, there's never been any SEC investigations resulting in convictions."

Seemed like the slip-up confession con artists say when they've been getting away with crimes for a while. Innocent people don't think to brag about not being convicted.

Noticing this, Chuck effected a casual tone, saying, "Just some minor fines that are a standard cost of business for any aggressive, successful investment firm." Chuck put in his "10,000 hours" to become a sales Svengali before he became a financial guru. No one could throw him off his game. "Now I refer you to the new prospectus detailing recent strategies and ventures, which have done quite well for us. First off..."

An hour later, Chuck came down to shake guests' hands and take ussies. Almost everyone bought into his fund, Gwendolyn included. Everyone else used apps on their phone. She still wrote paper checks for the literal paper trail.

A squinting passerby said, "With all those criticisms, I thought you'd never give him your money."

"When I don't ask questions, I never give them a penny. Plus, you don't have to like someone to make money with them," she said.

Old money lasts centuries by avoiding risky bets. Putting cash alongside Gwendolyn seemed wise. Assorted pension funds agreed. Teachers, cops, firefighters, and sanitation workers now had their retirement years tied to Chuck's promises.

That was two years ago and mere months before the SEC and FBI announced their investigations into Chuck's shady financial activity. As a casual fan of the rebooted *LAW & ORDER* and other classic New York-based crime and law shows, it crushed Gwendolyn to ultimately learn the reason so many attendees at Chuck's soiree looked familiar; they were shills, local actors cast to beguile.

ENDNOTE #18 — "How Are You Going to Win?"
Return to Novel on Page #180

Maria said, "You know the definition of insanity is doing the same thing and expecting different results. Right? My political party takes me for granted because the other side is 'scary,' and so they ignore us on stuff we care about, that, by the way, are no-joke super popular. We need to make party leaders more scared to lose me and my friends' votes. Then the party will be motivated to deliver on helpful policies, which, I gotta keep saying, is good politics because what we want are the things over 60% of the people agree with."

Stu said, "I get that. What you're saying relates directly to an upcoming video I'm gonna make. Lemme get my notes and run 'em by you."

"Bet. I'm ready."

"Can we get hyper-nerdy for a bit?"

She smiled and said, "It's like 80% of why we're together, Stu."

This threatened his machismo since he thought their sexual chemistry deserved credit for a larger share. Stu said, "80% is higher than... ah, whatever works. If you believe in democracy, you must believe in persuading people to recognize you're right and adopt your views. If they don't agree, then you can't expect to get their votes, and so you won't get your policies enacted."

"Obviously, Stu. That's true cause it's true — a tautology. Hope you caught that hundred-dollar word right there."

"Yes, I know what a tautology... Anyway, around the world, there are always two main political parties. Of course, parliamentary systems have more that require coalitions. Beyond the two most popular parties (that are supposed to be more centrist), the rest tend to be more extreme in either direction — as opposed to innovative. And yes, every country is different, but how the two split consistently happens in two different ways.

"The first split is between the 'tolerance vs. judgment' sides. One wants so much tolerance that it is intolerant of intolerance. It says, 'You gotta respect the rights of this person, even if he is unlike you or does whatever in his private life that you hate. No one should be able to prohibit behavior that doesn't harm others; though to be fair, our definition of harm is different from others.'

"The other side wants individuals to each have the right to judge according to their personal values and create their own private kingdoms. So, they want 'My house, my rules, and I can reject any customers, residents, or employees I say. The laws should enable me to judge and control others in my domain.' Their justifications are often based on traditions or religious beliefs," Stu said.

Maria nodded and asked, "The second split is more taxes vs less taxes?"

"Yes, but I frame the second kind of split as 'more government services vs. less,' which necessarily pairs with 'more taxes vs. less.' Decades ago in America, the split was between the Democrats who 'compelled tolerance and more government services,' vs. the Republicans, who were for 'tolerated intolerance and lower taxes.'

"In the latter part of the 20th-century, there were odd combos by modern standards. So-called 'Blue Dog Democrats' cheered for tolerance on the cheap, whereas 'Compassionate Conservatives' were for judgment and aiding the poor. Since then, some consolidations calcified. The Left wanted 'tolerance & good government, but you gotta pay,' whereas Libertarians thought the market solved everything. So, they think discrimination should be legal because if it's wrong, the discriminators will suffer in the marketplace."

Maria said, "But that doesn't happen. Rich keep getting richer and more powerful while the poor get stuck as Subtirees. Why can't we change things?"

Stu raised his shoulders and presented his palms. "Economics is predicated on the belief that individuals always act in their own financial best interest. But that's often not true. Teachers and staff at charities feel fulfilled and recognize the necessity of their work, so they compromise on their desired compensation. If one group prioritizes accumulating money and others don't, or not as much, then the cash is going to gravitate to the ones who go for it more.

"This becomes a self-fulfilling prophecy when the accumulators use their wealth to influence government. Since the way to get your policies is to win elections, these guys need to be able, for all intents and purposes, to bribe politicians and government workers. They do this through campaign contributions, letting them know they're also donating to Super PACs, paid lobbyists who are their ex-coworkers and old buddies, and maybe the biggest influence is the revolving door of employment for them and their staff to circulate into high-paying jobs in the private sector — all so long as they serve the donors' interests while they're in government. The politicians who want the campaign cash the most rig the laws to benefit their benefactors."

"Which is a crazy good ROI for the donors," Maria said. "I read big money donors pay millions to politicians and get tax breaks and subsidies worth billions. This is the worst in America since donations to Super PACs are unlimited and anonymous, which makes a giant impact on elections."

"Good points," Stu said. I'm sorry if this is too basic for you, but I'll be playing to an audience that will be hearing some of this for the first time."

"I'm with you. But get to the part where we can make a difference," Maria said.

"If you want policies beyond the mainstream, the most vital question is — 'how are you going to win more elections in our democratic republic?' There are only two ways — activating people who rarely/never vote or persuading regular voters to change their minds.

"The 'rarely vote' people range from those who only vote in presidential elections to the ones who occasionally vote in presidential elections but maybe only every 12 years. The proof for this is the total turnout numbers swing wildly depending on the existence of an especially charismatic or hated candidate. There's always a colossal drop-off in the two-year congressional elections that happen between the four-year presidential elections. These voters only give a shit when there's a ton of attention, but otherwise, they don't have the time or energy to deal with politics."

Maria said, "Don't slash them. Every freakin' topic has PhDs arguing for every point on the spectrum, from the fair-minded to the greedy mercenaries happy to sell bullshit with big words for money. Regular folks ain't got time to be fluent on every goddam thing."

"That's fair." Stu nodded. "But let me finish my point on elections. So, the votes for Congress between presidentials are mainly protest votes that are a backlash against whoever the current president is. However, conservatives also tend to have a better edge with lower turnout. So they try to depress turnout. I think some old-school conservative named Weyrich even admitted that on camera once.

"The 'never/not yet voters' are the hardest to enlist, but that doesn't mean you should ignore them. They can be activated. Like with any low-engagement voter, the easiest tactic is to get them mad enough to move and not sleep that year. You also gotta educate 'em — easy. Don't download a whole manifesto or nothin' – info overload won't play. Just find out what affects them and match that to how your candidate does better than the opposition. If you can't find a match on any policy, then that's a voter who will only vote for the other guy; don't get them charged up enough to vote against your side.

"Some activists have noble goals and defendable policy positions, but their election strategy is so naïve it could appear they're working for the other side. They mention the trolly problem."

"Yeah, I know. A mustache-twirling villain has a trolly with two tracks. He's strapped five people to the main track who will be killed if you do nothing. But if you hit the switch, the trolly will go on the alternate track with only one dude tied up to be killed. So the question is, are you 'utilitarian' enough to pull the switch to kill one person in order to save five?"

"Exactly. So, of course, you gotta pull it, right?"

"Nah. There's a fair argument to not be complicit in the murdering. You can do nothing, and the killing is entirely the fault of the mustache villain. Not your fault. Whereas, if you pull it, you are undeniably killing that one dude on the alternate track."

"Alright, let me extend that analogy beyond the single instance. If there's an election, you need more votes to prevent mustache-man from killing again. Letting him kill only increases his power to kill even more. So, in addition to the utilitarian argument to net-save four people, by pulling the lever, you're creating better circumstances to bring the villain to justice."

"Same thing with voting. We have an obligation to be complicit in minor evil to lessen the damage to the weak, especially when that prevents greater evil in the future. Otherwise, doing nothing doesn't give you 'clean hands' any more than Germans in World War II could say they were moral for doing nothing to prevent their mustache-man's atrocities. Inaction doesn't make you moral. Marcus Aurelius said, 'You can also commit injustice by doing nothing.'"

Maria clenched her jaw and, through her teeth, said, "When both sides are too weak, we need third parties."

"That's cool. But you can't skip the step of growing a movement. Third parties can be appealing, but they have almost zero success when they are against both of the two main parties in a non-parliamentary election. When popularizing a weak third party isn't working (and if there isn't the benefit of rank choice voting), if you want policy changes, you gotta show up in the primaries of the major party closest to your views. By definition, a potential voter in the major party closest to you should be an easier target than someone in the opposing party. If you can't win over the party closest to your ideals, it'd be delusional to think you'll somehow convince the rest of the country.

You can activate new voters to register for the party you want to primary. If you can't win those, you can't win general elections where the establishment thumbs on scales are even heavier. Campaign and vote to get your team into the finals. Down to the final two, the die-hard people in their tribes are gonna vote for their dude or against their rival, basically every time.

Otherwise, when third party hopefuls are desperately gambling on the hyper rare 'horseshoe' dynamic — where voters from the other end curve around to be recruitable — the burden is on the radical to provide compelling evidence of its viability. Winning is everything, so stick to the parties that can win.

Maria said, "That's been the excuse for stagnant progress for a freakin' century."

"Well, I hear you," Stu said, "but that assumes all parties are generally playing by the rules and facilitating fair elections. How often did Russia have a legit vote decided by its people? Globally, how many elected fascists became dictators and, to keep power, held sham elections or banned them outright? Hitler, Chavez, Castro, Mugabe, Marcos, Saddam Hussein, Hamas, Putin, Lukashenko, etc."

She crossed her arms and let him finish his point.

"Almost as bad, if one side is so shady they stop their rivals from voting, such as reducing the number of voting locations or machines in areas populated by its opposition, or hyper-gerrymanders so that 40% of the votes control 55% of the legislators, and any other toxic shit, then that's not the election to sit out, because we'll never get another one." Stu nodded to get her agreement.

"We ain't given up our policies, that's for sure. And we're damn sure not teaming up with a bunch of assholes." Maria asked.

"Depends on your definition of 'assholes.' You still gotta win over 50% of the votes, even if that includes some minor assholes. Of course, it's okay to have 'deal breakers,' but beware of having so many you guarantee failure for your preferred policies. An extremist could start his deal breaker list in moderation and then self-sabotage by adding to it until he guarantees himself a loss in elections. So, where should he draw the line? Some hard lines are easy to understand; we must completely dismiss anyone who is pro-slavery, pro-genocide, or pro-nuking of enemy countries, regardless of whether they agree with us on everything else. Look at a different list of controversial issues. Can we disregard all support from anyone who has an opposing view to ours on any one of the following issues? Vegan/carnivore, for or against animals as pets, pro/anti-religion, pro/anti care for the poor, pro/anti-Luddite. Here's one where the Left is super conflicted — pro/anti nuclear energy. It reduces greenhouse gasses but creates centuries of nuke waste and terrorism targets, and requires government subsidies and taxpayer-subsidized insurance, etc.. Requiring 100% purity on all of those issues, Balkanized us into dozens of powerless micro-groups. Uniting creates our power. Otherwise, we have nothing to counterbalance the guys who own everything. A voter doesn't have to be best friends with the people who disagree on a lot, but he probably should try to get their vote. To reject this reality is to facilitate the fascist strategy of 'divide and conquer' — encourage purity tests and crush us in micro groups."

"Get to the practical tactics, babe," Maria said.

"Everyone thinks they're right, or they'd change their minds. Merely thinking you're right doesn't make you right. Further, being right isn't enough; you have to persuade others. Flipping a vote is crazy hard because so few change their minds under any circumstances. But these folks are out there — no doubt, and campaigning depends on them.

"Number one, you gotta earn some credibility in their eyes. That starts with you diagnosing what their 'heart' thinks, and that isn't always what they say they're thinking or even what their brain is thinking and not saying. People lie to themselves so often that they have no awareness until they're in the right headspace to examine assumptions, brave the evidence, and apply logic. You, as the activist, gotta address what they care about and forget about telling them that they're wrong. That works on only the most open-minded and principled listeners, a tiny percentage of the population."

"How do you 'diagnose how their heart thinks' when it's not what they say? Just ask them and keep drilling down?" She asked.

"You're ahead of me again, Maria. That's precisely what you do. Dodge and weave through the level-one sound bites they're parroting and keep listening. Ask the way you'd do as a student seeking clarity from a professor and not as a rival attorney looking to play 'gotcha' games. Say, 'Tell me more about that,' and 'Help me understand why that is,' and be humble enough to serve as an example by saying, 'Direct me to sources for that, because if I'm wrong, so are a bunch of my friends and I want us to get on the side with the best evidence.' Finally, don't jump in too much; err on the side of leaving them more time than they can fill. They'll end up dominating the conversation by maybe 90%, but that's okay while you're earning credibility. When they start to run out of points or overly repeat themselves, that's when you can start to take more time to reply. Repeated points can be nipped by you repeating his previous answers to your follow-up questions. This proves you're listening and understanding his perspective. If he still keeps shutting you down, not letting you make your points, you can plead, 'May I reply?' and if he's still a jerk, leave.

"Second, show you have common ground. You can only persuade someone by first telling them that they're right... about something else! Build your credibility with them. Identify how you both already agree on some aspect. By doing so, you're not demanding they change their identity; instead, you want them to be proud of their identity and more accurately categorize it to fit your contention.

"Once you've established that credibility and wedged in the possibility that this won't threaten their identity, now you can deploy a strategy based on the metaphor 'Literal Foundations of Belief.'

"When someone stands on a foundation of belief, it's almost impossible to shatter that foundation before presenting another. The person will cling to the shattered foundation, resent you for causing his fall, and delude himself into thinking the foundation is still strong. On several occasions, a doomsday cult predicted the apocalypse on a certain date, and when that didn't happen, they shamelessly continued their delusion because they didn't have an alternative they trusted. So, crushing through overwhelming evidence alone doesn't work. Yet that's how most everyone argues.

"Instead, offer your additional foundation and voice whatever undeniably positive attributes can be applied to the foundations. Keep presenting more and more 'acceptable truths' and, in so doing, enable the 'persuadee' to place a foot on each foundation, theirs and yours. People would rather hold two conflicting ideas than abandon a bad one for nothingness.

"Only then can you begin to dismantle the first/old foundation, thus compelling the person to stand exclusively on the new, better foundation. It's unfortunate that this strategy often requires a lot of time over several discussions; don't count on succeeding in a single encounter," Stu said.

"In short, you're saying hear them out, find common ground, and get them to hold two opposing views before criticizing their first one. That sum it up?" Maria asked.

"Yeah. If you want to be all succinct and efficient about it. But I really like the sound of my own voice."

"Oh, I do, too, babe. Love you and your over-thinky, genius brain."

"You're perfect...ly accurate." Seeing this facetious egomania wasn't working, Stu said, "And you are perfect. Also true."

ACKNOWLEDGMENTS

Greatest thanks to my wonderful, ever-supportive parents, Mike and Enid. That help and encouragement have been crucial all of my life. Personal thanks to my sister, Jane and her family, Patrick, Kate & Mae.

Immense professional thanks to Melissa Miller and Paige Etheridge at Solstice Publishing. This is a fulfilled wish and I'm eternally grateful. I love the fantastic book cover design by Ricardo Montaño Castro.

I'm indebted to my brilliant, ever-gracious menschy friends for giving me decades of specific and myriad counsel, support, and encouragement. Platinum thanks to Alan Blassberg, Aliyah Silverstein, Boaz Weinstein, Bobby Gilliam, Damon Gambuto, Daniel Ponickly, Ed Moncada, Grant Taylor, Marta Almli, Sonja Kroop, and Zoe Quist.

Great thanks to my author, screenwriter and producer friends for career support and/or feedback on my work; that includes so many constructive and brutally honest criticisms that I needed to hear including many I probably should've heeded better. Thank you — Abby Vegas, Adam Lederer, Amy Byer Shainman, Brian Adler, Chris Derrick, Christine Marino, Christine Wong, Claudia Clemente, David Bickel, David Dayen, David Fury, Doug Landers, Erika Kuhn, Ivona Huszcza, Jennifer Vanderbes, Jill Brady, Jules Bruff, Kathy Mandato, Kip Konwiser, Jamie Rhonheimer, Laura Lee Flanagan, Maria Armoudian, Marie Halliday, Mark

Treitel, Matt Price, Michael Blieden, Michael Pennie, Mike Ognibene, Nick Schenk, Pankaj Jain, Rebecca Neuwirth, Robert Vanderbes, Sally Brooks, Samantha Bailey, Stephen Lentini, Stephen Marinaccio, and Tom Cappello.

I give thanks to CritiqueMatch.com and the generous beta readers of earlier drafts of the manuscript: Alex McKenzie, Diego Bromfield, Gem Martiskainen, InnerWoven, Jennifer Pezzano, JohnM, Lauren T., Vitrix Winteria, and Misba. Highest appreciation to superstar critique partners: Shrabastee Chakraborty, Negus Lamont, and mega-superhero Evelyn Csiki. Thanks to readers Inteoryx on TikTok and Harrison Glon on Reddit.

Thanks to my favorite Beta Readers on Fiverr: Nadene Du Plooy, Gil Guzman, Jasmin Joachims, Ben Boven, Rebecca K Sampson, SJ Davison, Lydia M., Amer, Gionkarlo G., Michael M., Noah Daniels, Ricky, Logan Ginther, Sara Jean, and Danny DeCillis.

Thanks to Coverfly.com's CoverflyX Peer Review reader token system (particularly the reader "AC") and FilmFreeway.com. Thanks to the screenwriting competitions for selecting my material for 30+ accolades, which gave me vital inspiration and confidence — Austin After Dark Film Festival, Austin Film Festival, LA CineFest, Los Angeles Film Awards, Oniros Film Awards, SIFF, Workers Unite Film Festival, Stage 32, International New York Film Festival, New York International Film Awards, Beverley Hills Film Festival, London Film Awards, Fade In Awards, International Screenwriters Association, Story Pros, Creative World Awards, and Francis Ford Coppola's American Zoetrope Competition.

Thanks to the menschy, preeminent AI scientists who reviewed early material and educated me — David Gelernter, Prof. Computer Science (Yale University), Peter Clark, Senior Research Manager (Allen Institute of Artificial Intelligence), and Dr. Christof Koch, Chief Scientist & President (Allen Institute for Brain Science). Any scientific errors in the novel are mine, due to my admittedly amateur understanding of the subject matter or my deliberate creative choices in service of the narrative.

> PARTING NOTE TO READERS: Thank you!
>
> If you want access to my favorite websites (perhaps including more "Bonus Material"):
>
> **https://linktr.ee/immortalitybytes**

ABOUT THE AUTHOR

Daniel Lawrence Abrams grew up in NYC, attended Trinity School through eighth grade, and then graduated from Stuyvesant High School. He got his BA in Psychology from the Honors Program at the University of Michigan at Ann Arbor.

He was selected to join the inaugural class of Turner Entertainment's "T-2000" program in Atlanta. Concurrently, he invented a 3-D input device that earned US Patent # 5,652,603.

Abrams trained in comedy writing at Whole World Theatre, The Second City, and The Groundlings. He performed stand-up at NYC's Comedy Cellar and The Improv in LA. As a playwright, Abrams's shows played at The Stella Adler Theatre, Powerhouse Theater, and the HBO/Warner Brothers Television Workspace.

He wrote, produced, and directed over a hundred hours of TV. Abrams was the supervising producer of the 2014 Emmy-Nominated SundanceTV show, THE WRITERS' ROOM and was a director for HGTV's HOUSE HUNTERS INTERNATIONAL. Abrams's web series for Bodog/Riptown was named an "Official Honoree" in the Webby Awards, and his short films have been selected by several film festivals.

He wrote columns for the Producers Guild's PRODUCED BY, CARD PLAYER, and MENSA magazines.

Scripts he's written or co-written have earned 30+ accolades from 74 submissions to screenwriter competitions — including three 1st Place wins and four Top-5s and Finalists.

Abrams co-produced four feature films: RAW CUT, MINING FOR RUBY (co-starring Billy Zane & Mischa Barton), ON WINGS OF EAGLES (starring Joseph Fiennes), and a breast cancer documentary — PINK & BLUE: COLORS OF HEREDITARY CANCER.

He gave a TEDx Talk, "Sports Can Save Politics" at AJU.

IMMORTALITY BYTES is his debut novel.

Made in the USA
Coppell, TX
09 March 2025

46857421R00193